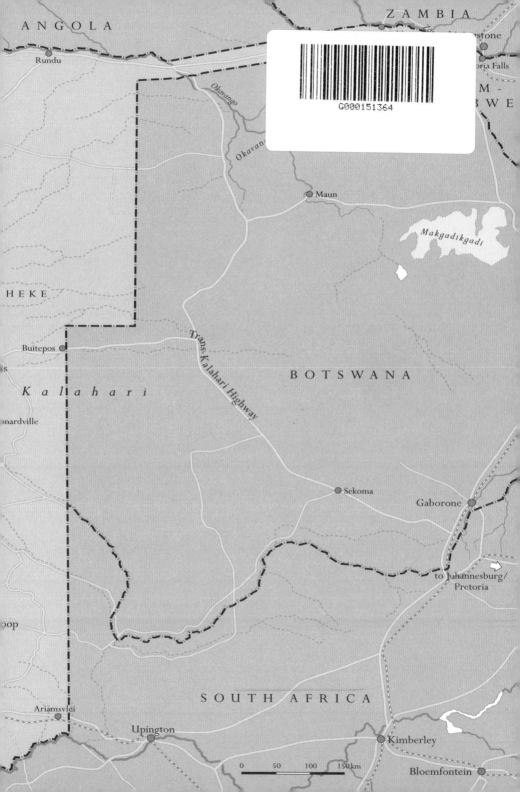

Bernhard Jaumann

THE HOUR
OF THE JACKAL

Translated by John Brownjohn

JOHN BEAUFOY PUBLISHING

First published in the United Kingdom in 2011 by John Beaufoy Publishing,
11 Blenheim Court, 316 Woodstock Road, Oxford OX2 7NS, England.
www.johnbeaufoy.com

10   9   8   7   6   5   4   3   2   1

Originally published under the title *Die Stunde des Schakals*.
Copyright © 2010 by Rowohlt Verlag GmbH, Reinbek bei Hamburg.
English language translation © 2011 John Brownjohn.
Endpaper map © Peter Palm, Berlin/Germany.

The translation of this work was supported by a grant from the Goethe-Institut,
which is funded by the German Ministry of Foreign Affairs.

Hardback ISBN 978-1-906780-42-5
Trade Paperback ISBN 978-1-906780-43-2

Designed and typeset in Bembo by Bookcraft Ltd, Stroud, Gloucestershire, UK
Printed in India by Replika Press Pvt Ltd.

1

GUNSHOTS

No more lies, no tall stories! Only the truth counted, and the truth was death. Life too, perhaps, but death even more so. Not everyone could call a life his own, whereas death came knocking on everyone's door. Sooner or later.

He thrust the AK-47's curved magazine into the receiver and checked that it was firmly engaged. Thirty rounds, 7.62 mm. He could feel the sweat-sodden shirt clinging to his back as he bent sideways. The blood was boiling in his veins, but only because of the heat that had accumulated in the car although the windows were wound right down. He deposited the Kalashnikov on the passenger seat beside him and sat back. A DJ announced *Summer in the City* over the car radio. It was an Afrikaans station, Radio Kosmos, 94.1 megahertz.

The sun was still two hand's-breadths above the chain of hills on the other side of the Klein Windhoek River, but it wouldn't become much cooler even after sundown. All Windhoek – all Namibia – was groaning in the January heat and yearning for the dark clouds that would bring rain from the north-east. Not that there was any sign of them at present. The north-eastern sky was radiantly, preternaturally blue.

He wiped his palms on his thighs. The AK-47's selector switch was in the central position. Automatic fire. All he had to do was keep the trigger fully depressed. Truth or falsehood didn't come into it. He had a job to do.

The palm trees in front of No. 15 were casting long shadows across the asphalt. There wasn't a soul to be seen between him and the crossroads, and not only because it was swelteringly hot or because Ursulastrasse was a cul-de-sac. The residents of Windhoek's Ludwigsdorf district didn't walk the streets; they remained inside their own little versions of paradise, behind high walls topped with barbed wire. If they had to leave their houses they did so by car and made sure the electric gates shut behind them before driving off. Any pedestrians were either beggars or criminals. Even a strange car parked in the cul-de-sac's turning circle would probably arouse suspicion.

But he was well prepared. He had stolen a white Toyota Corolla, made himself some stencils and sprayed the bodywork with the 'Group 4 Securicor' logo. He'd even had some duplicate licence plates made, just in case some suspicious neighbour called head office, only to receive confirmation that it really was one of the firm's cars. Doubtless a thoroughly exaggerated precaution. After all, G4S vehicles were often to be seen standing around inside the city limits.

On the valley side, the turning circle gave way to a narrow strip of parched grass. A few aloes with spiny reddish leaves were growing in front of the low, waist-high wall guarding the slope. All that could be seen of the house further downhill was its gable end and satellite dish, but he knew that from the wall itself he would be able to overlook the terrace and most of the garden. The sun was now behind the water tower on the hillside opposite. It had started to turn orange, but was still too dazzling. He would wait until it went down.

The radio was now playing *Johnny is nie dood nie,* a song by Koos Kombuis. Uninterested in Johnny's death or survival, he turned it off. Through the open car window he heard children's voices shrieking beyond the wall of No. 15, then a loud splash as if someone had jumped into the swimming pool – or been pushed in. Water sloshed around and some indignant, spluttered words he couldn't understand rose above the din. Perhaps there was nothing *to* understand. Perhaps everything was simply the way it was – the children's voices, the AK–47 on the passenger seat, his sweaty back, the truth, the stories, the gable end and satellite dish, and the sun, which had now turned red and was seeping into the range of hills opposite.

It was nearly time. He picked up the gun and opened the driver's door. The street was still deserted. He got out. He thought he could feel the asphalt burning through the soles of his shoes as if hellfire itself were blazing just beneath them, but that was pure imagination. Hell didn't exist, or there would also have to be a heaven. It was all just lies, just stories. A dog started yapping inside the gates of No. 11. Another joined in, its low, raucous barking reciprocated by more dogs in the neighbouring properties. That was normal. Most of the people who lived in this district kept two animals, a small, nervous one to act as sentry and a vicious attack dog.

'No problem,' he muttered. Slowly he made his way down to the low wall and rested the AK–47 on it. The barking was gradually subsiding. A child's voice inside the wall of No. 15 shouted, 'Give it here! Go on, give it here!'

In the garden below him an expanse of improbably green lawn gleamed beyond two acacia trees. The sprinkler system was on. A girl of around fourteen was seated on the terrace, punching away at a mobile phone. That had to be the man's daughter. Over to the left were three fruit trees – lemons, *naartjies*, or some other citrus trees to judge by their shape and leaves. The soil around the trunks had been raked into circular ridges about a metre in diameter, so that water from a garden hose could collect in the resulting depressions. The man who was casually holding the hose in his hand wore faded shorts and a white T-shirt stretched taut over his paunch. His neck and face were red and bloated. His eyes could not be seen beneath the peak of his baseball cap, which was pulled down low, but there was no doubt about it: he was the right man. His target.

He wiped his sweaty palms again and gripped the Kalashnikov. As he took aim he felt an urge to call to call out – to tell the man

5

down there that everyone had to pay his debts sooner or later. That there was more truth in death than in life. And that, at the very least, that damned girl should go inside the house.

He didn't call out, of course, just gave a little cough. The sun had set, leaving a dull orange glow above the hillside opposite. He felt a strange kind of anger well up inside him. At himself, at life, and at the fat man down there. Why must he be wearing a white T-shirt, of all things? Why not a dark red or black one? Anyone who wore a white T-shirt had only himself to blame if …

Firmly gripping the butt of the AK-47, he squeezed the trigger and kept it depressed. Automatic fire. Even before he released it, his victim collapsed without a sound. The garden hose escaped from his hand, writhing and rearing like a spitting cobra on the defensive. The water spurted in the direction of the terrace. The girl had jumped up and plastered herself against the brick wall. Her face was averted.

That was the last thing he saw. He went back to the car, replaced the gun on the passenger seat, got in and started the engine. At the crossroads he turned left. He was feeling neither better nor worse than usual. Even his heart was not beating particularly fast. His anger had gone, but nothing else had taken its place. He had fired at people in the old days, but then he had been a soldier. Nobody called it murder when a soldier killed someone. He had become a killer only now. It left him unmoved. He'd thought he would feel different; how different he couldn't tell. He coughed a couple of times, then turned on the Toyota's headlights.

※◎※

It was 10.27 p.m. when Detective Inspector Clemencia Garises learned of the murder via her mobile.

The call reached her at home in Katutura township. 'Send a car for me right away,' she bellowed into the phone because the television was on full blast. The grumpy constable on duty pointed out that it was Sunday night, but he would see what he could do.

That meant he would do precisely nothing, and she shouldn't take herself so seriously. In any case, she had probably been informed only because her superiors didn't feel like collecting a white man's body from somewhere on a Sunday night. Unlike them, Clemencia was quite happy to get away from home. After supper, her family plus half the neighbourhood had settled down in front of the TV to watch the highlights of the third round of *Big Brother Africa*. The Namibian representative, a girl who had qualified for three months' claustrophobia in Johannesburg, had been eliminated in the second round. She hadn't done her country justice, they all agreed. She was far too shy and boring and had always looked as if she wasn't herself.

'Clemencia would have done a far better job,' Miki Matilda had declared.

'Me?' said Clemencia.

'You're miles prettier than her. Why don't you put in for it sometime?'

Clemencia merely brushed this aside, but Miki Selma had protested fiercely. 'You really want Clemencia to shmooze with some total stranger with the whole of Africa watching?'

'The whole of Africa, exactly!' Miki Matilda had said triumphantly. 'It'd be ridiculous if a few men didn't take a serious interest in her. Perhaps she'd find the right one at last.'

'Mikis ... ' Clemencia tried to protest, but she hadn't been able to get a word in.

'It's your business, I know, but surely I'm allowed to give an opinion.'

'No woman ever found happiness on television,' said Miki Selma. 'Clemencia would do better to look around for someone in the neighbourhood. One who doesn't drink or smoke or — '

'A girl must grab any chance she can get,' Miki Matilda broke in.

'Fire burns the person who lights it,' Miki Selma countered, citing one of her favourite proverbs, but Miki Matilda wouldn't be put off.

'How old are you now, Clemencia?' she demanded. 'Twenty-nine? Thirty?' Miki Matilda knew precisely how old Clemencia was, but there wouldn't have been much point in getting worked up over it.

'Thirty-one,' said Clemencia.

'Thir-ty-*one*!' Miki Matilda emphasized the enormity of that fact by lingering on each syllable. 'I was almost a grandmother at thirty-one!'

'When you were thirty-one the South Africans still ruled this country,' Clemencia replied. 'Times have changed. Namibia's independent now, and I'm a detective inspector.' But she might as well have said nothing at all, because Matilda and Selma continued to debate what befitted thirty-one-year-old women in general and Clemencia in particular, so she'd been glad when her mobile phone rang.

She clambered over her family's legs and went outside. The brickwork was radiating the heat stored during the day. The air resembled soft, lukewarm water, and the sky above Clemencia's head was a cloudless, starlit vault. Darkly silhouetted against it was the spire of the Holy Redeemer parish church. From somewhere in the gloom between the one-storeyed houses and the corrugated-iron huts erected around them came an unintelligible babble of voices that culminated in peals of laughter. The muffled, rhythmical bass notes of kwaito music were issuing from the other end of the street. Their source was the Mshasho Bar, where Clemencia's younger brother Melvin was probably getting drunk on tombo beer. She would sometime have to make another attempt to talk some sense into him.

The neighbour from the house across the street drove up in his rattletrap Ford, which he had upgraded into a taxi by buying an appropriate sign. Illegally, of course, not that Clemencia worried about that right now. The man was far from pleased, having just finished a twelve-hour stint, but he declared himself willing, in view of her policewoman's status, to drive her to the other side of town. In Katutura there were still pedestrians to look out for, but the white districts of Windhoek were deserted at this hour. You could make good time if you ignored the traffic lights. On Nelson Mandela Avenue Clemencia told the driver to put his foot down. Less than ten minutes later the Ford was toiling up Ludwigsdorf Hill, and then they were there. Two City Police patrol cars were parked outside some closed gates. The street had not been cordoned off and there were no policemen in sight.

Clemencia got out and located the bell on the right of the gateway. There was no nameplate. She pressed the button. The air was still warm and soft, but it seemed to smell of death. That may only have been because of the unnatural silence that never prevailed in Katutura, even in the depths of night. She rang again.

A uniformed constable appeared at last. She identified herself and was ushered into the living room, which was at least twice the size of her family's entire house. Although the windows and the door to the terrace were open except for the fly screens, it was as hot as if the sun had set inside there. Despite the heat, a teenaged girl had buried herself in the sofa with her knees drawn up. She was hugging a leather cushion and giggling softly to herself. Or was she whimpering in despair?

'The doctor gave her a sedative injection,' the constable told Clemencia in a whisper, 'but she won't calm down – doesn't respond to questions and screams if anyone touches her. Not even her own mother can get near her.'

A man and four women were seated at the dining table. All white. The mother was unmistakable. Pale and stony-faced, she stared fixedly at the ashtray in front of her. That her hands were shaking was noticeable only when she put the cigarette to her lips and sucked at it greedily. She barely raised her eyes when Clemencia introduced herself.

'Are *you* heading the investigation?' the man beside her asked in Afrikaans, looking Clemencia up and down.

'Nice of you to turn up as well – three-and-a-half hours after the event,' one of the other women said sourly.

Clemencia asked for a brief account of what had happened.

'Look, said the man, 'Mevrou van Zyl didn't see a thing, so don't go asking her the same fucking questions as these patrolmen. She's already spent hours answering them.' Clemencia watched Mevrou von Zyl stub out her cigarette with a nervous gesture and promptly light another. It wasn't her fault she'd turned up so late. It wasn't an easy situation for the dead man's friends and family, she realized that, but couldn't she expect a little cooperation all the same? She asked the patrolman where the body was. He led her out onto the terrace, where two of his colleagues were waiting like sentries. As soon as they were out of earshot, Clemencia gave the trio an earful. Why hadn't she been notified sooner? she demanded. They merely shrugged.

'Over there,' said the patrolman, pointing into the darkness. Clemencia made her way over to some low trees. One of the constables who were following her turned on a torch. A garden hose was snaking across the lawn. The big, dark patch visible in the beam of the torch could have been coagulated blood. There were no scene-of-crime tapes to be seen, let alone a body.

'You can't leave a dead man lying around for hours,' the patrolman said apologetically.

'Really?' said Clemencia.

'It brings bad luck,' he explained.

'Because evil spirits will haunt the spot?' she asked. The patrolman pursed his lips.

Oh yes, if it would bring bad luck, of course you had to refrain from securing a crime scene properly. Far better to send for an ambulance and have the victim carted off, even before the inspector in charge was informed.

'The killer shot him from up there.' The patrolman shone his torch up the slope beyond the garden wall. The beam petered out in grey scrub.

'Probably with an automatic weapon,' said another of the uniformed constables. He fished a plastic bag full of cartridge cases out of his trouser pocket. At least he hadn't stuck them in there loose, but Clemencia preferred not to know how he'd picked them up. She asked if there were any eye-witnesses.

'His daughter was present at the time, but she isn't talking,' said one of the policemen.

'We were going to leave it to you to question the neighbours,' said his colleague.

The neighbouring houses were in darkness, as far as one could tell. Whites went to bed early. They had reasons for getting up early too. In Clemencia's district, Katutura township, an estimated fifty per cent of the residents were unemployed. Nobody knew for certain.

Clemencia gauged the height of the garden wall by eye. Around two-and-a-half metres. In the light of the torch she could see the electrified wires running along the top. They had provided the man with as little protection as the alarm system.

All that broke the silence was the warm breeze rustling the leaves of the lemon trees. Clemencia went back into the house. The murder victim's daughter stared at her wide-eyed. When asked what her name was, she started whimpering softly again. Clemencia turned to her mother. 'If you need help, I have the phone number of a psychologist who — '

'I'm a doctor myself,' the man at the table broke in.

' — who specializes in traumatic cases like this,' said Clemencia.

'The girl just needs rest!' snapped the doctor. It sounded like 'Just get lost!'

Clemencia sat down facing Mevrou van Zyl. 'I'm sorry, but I have to ask you a few questions.'

The woman dragged at her cigarette.

'Alone,' Clemencia added. She waited until the doctor and the other women had retired to the kitchen. Then she asked, 'Had anyone been threatening your husband?'

11

Mevrou van Zyl shook her head curtly and stubbed out her cigarette in the ashtray two or three times. She stared at the butt, from which a thin skein of smoke was rising. Some twenty centimetres above the ashtray it curled, writhed as if in pain, and dissolved into slowly fading streaks.

Clemencia proceeded to question her, but it was a laborious task. Mevrou van Zyl had to be badgered into uttering a single word, and even then she said little of use. Her husband had led a perfectly normal life. Born in Pretoria, school, military service, professional training. He had moved to Windhoek because she hadn't wanted to leave the place, which was her home. They'd raised a family and he'd worked his way up to a senior position. He tended the garden after work and went to the NG Kerk on Sundays.

Any personal interests, predilections, enthusiasms?

Mevrou van Zyl shrugged her shoulders. He'd been fond of shooting, and he regularly watched the Springboks playing rugby on TV.

Anything else?

No, that was all.

Political involvements, financial speculation, gambling, criminal record?

No, no, no, and no again. It was as if she were hoping to bring her husband back to life by categorically precluding any conceivable motive for murder.

'Still, someone thought they had a reason to shoot him,' Clemencia said quietly.

Mevrou van Zyl lit another cigarette. Benson & Hedges. She put the packet on the table and looked Clemencia in the eye for the first time. It was only a brief glance, but it told Clemencia quite enough: the woman was lying, or at least concealing something of importance. What was more, she would persist in concealing it because she had weighed Clemencia in the balance and found her wanting: an overly young and inexperienced member of an

12

untrustworthy police force and the wrong race. That was a pretty damning indictment. Clemencia knew she was no match for it.

As gently as she could, she said, 'I promise you, Mevrou van Zyl, that we shall do all in our power to catch the murderer.'

'Shoot him!' Mevrou van Zyl said quietly.

'We shall — '

'I don't care who he is and why he did it.' The widow sprang to her feet. 'Find the man and shoot him out of hand!' she yelled, her voice breaking. 'Why are you wasting your time here? Go on, get out! Gun the bastard down!'

Still on the sofa, her daughter whimpered more loudly, then burst into hysterical screams that seemed to cut off her air supply and ended in a gurgle. The doctor who had been abrupt with Clemencia flung the kitchen door open and hurried over to the sofa. The women followed him in and tried to calm the widow down.

Even though Clemencia knew it was unfair, it all seemed so wrong. The whites complained, day after day, that constitutional procedures were being insufficiently observed, but as soon as they themselves became the victims of crime, all was forgotten. Then they wanted vengeance, wanted to see blood flow. Yet the danger of being killed was still ten times greater for a black. No one gave a damn if a sixteen-year-old Katutura girl was raped and murdered on her way to the outside privy, or if an old woman was knifed for being too slow to hand over the thirty Namibian dollars she'd hoped would see her through the coming week, whereas the murder of Meneer van Zyl would make headlines.

'What now?' one of the constables asked in a low voice.

Clemencia knew how to conduct an investigation. She had not only completed her course at Iyambo Police College with flying colours but was the only member of the force to boast a master's degree in forensic science. Her studies in South Africa had been facilitated by a full bursary, and she had recently returned from

13

a six-months stay in Helsinki financed by a Finnish government programme designed to professionalize public servants in Third World countries. She had passed through the various departments of the Finnish CID, attended lectures on criminological technique and forensic medicine, been taken out on operations in the field, and studied the work of homicide squads. But her knowledge availed her nothing. She wasn't in Finland any more, she was in Windhoek. In southern Africa, another world.

'Our shift is nearly over,' the constable whispered. 'We can't do anything more here anyway.'

Clemencia dialled the number of the Scenes of Crime Unit, which was responsible for securing evidence. In view of the time that had already been lost, they would probably say they might as well wait until morning. But they didn't; they didn't even answer the phone. Clemencia wondered which she hated more, her colleagues' lack of professionalism or the ill-disguised racism of the whites.

✳✳✳

He was sitting in the departure lounge of Hosea Kutako Airport on one of the seats that had been bolted together into a longish row. He had chosen one of the seats in the middle because they seemed to be the least popular. If had been worth his while, he would have debated why people who liked to hog the limelight in everyday life preferred to sit on the sidelines in airport departure lounges. And why they turned a critical gaze on anyone who deprived them of such seats.

He had no wish to be looked at. That apart, he didn't care where he sat. To call a seat 'yours', as if thousands of other individuals wouldn't occupy it after you, was presumptuous in any case. People were always on the move, blindly groping this way or that. Only their final destination was certain: no one evaded death.

He coughed. He hadn't sat down because he felt tired or weak. He'd sat down only because he would have been more conspicuous

14

standing up, and because from here he had a good view of the glass doors that opened automatically whenever a passenger emerged from customs and immigration. A rope some five metres from the doors kept those who were waiting at a distance. A few of them were equipped with signs reading 'SWA Safaris' or 'Karivo Lodge' or 'Beyer Family'. The young men who held them up whenever one of the new arrivals peered round enquiringly all looked the same: bush hat, khaki shirt, shorts, kudu hide boots. None of them was wearing Group 4 Securicor uniform.

He, too, had written a name on a big sheet of paper. It was lying face down on his lap. The long blue sports bag reposed between his feet.

'Ideal for tennis,' the salesman at the Sports Warehouse had told him. 'Holds up to three rackets, and there's still enough room for anything else you need.'

'Perfect,' he'd replied.

He waited. He saw a few red-faced game tourists come through the doors and purposefully head for the counter where their guns would be handed out. An overtired mother carrying one child in her arms and towing another behind her followed in the wake of her husband, who was wheeling a heavily-laden baggage wagon over to the Avis desk. The safari sheep were gradually assembling behind the 'SWA Safaris' sign and eyeing one another as if they wondered who would be slaughtered first.

And then came the man whose name he had written on the sheet of paper. He was pulling a trolley case behind him and carrying a small aluminium suitcase in his other hand. Tall and muscular, he looked in good shape although he must have been pushing fifty. You could tell he took regular exercise. He probably spent two hours in the gym each evening after work, always at the same time, always going through the self-same programme: cycling, weights, twenty lengths in the pool. A man of principle, or at least of habit.

15

He himself was different. He set no store by habits. They merely fooled you into believing that you could impose laws on life. In his view they were a vain attempt to render the future predictable by clinging to the unchanging habits of the past. It was all a lie, all self-delusion. He was interested in the truth, and the truth could not be coerced. It remained as bitter and unique as it pleased. He coughed a little, then stood up, slung the sports bag over his shoulder, and went over to the man with the sheet of paper held in front of his chest.

The man looked at what was written on it, looked him in the eye, and said, 'What do you want?'

'Meneer van Zyl sent me to — '

'Where is he?'

'He's sorry, he couldn't make it himself. I'm to take you to him.'

The man let go of his trolley case and looked him up and down. 'Private security firm?' he asked.

'Windhoek is a dangerous place these days.'

The man grinned. 'Then it's a good thing I've got you with me. Let's go.'

He gripped the handle of the trolley case and, without looking round, made for the exit.

Let's go … As if you yourself could always decide when something was to happen. He experienced a resurgence of the sensation he'd had yesterday evening. The anger he'd felt when he saw that the corpulent Boer was wearing a white T-shirt. This man was wirier, had habits and was carrying an aluminium suitcase, but in other respects they were similar: men who didn't know how wrong they were about everything that mattered.

Out in the car park he opened the Corolla's boot and stowed the man's luggage in it. His own bag he tossed onto the rear seat. When he had paid the parking attendant and passed the barrier, the man asked him how long he'd worked for van Zyl.

'It's just a one-time job,' he said.

16

What was van Zyl doing that was so important? He didn't know. Yes, the heat was really trying. Yes, it would get even hotter in the afternoon. No, he had no idea how hot. Yes, he could turn on the aircon.

'Not keen on talking, eh?' said the man.

'One moment, please,' he replied, pulling over onto the strip of sand beside the road. Then he got out and opened the sports bag on the back seat. He took out the Kalashnikov, held it to the head of the man in the passenger seat, and said, 'Perhaps you'd like to drive for a bit, Meneer Maree?'

❊

Blood was dripping from a garden hose. The lawn was black. Lemon trees rustled in the wind, their branches laden with cartridge cases instead of fruit. A white girl was hugging a leather cushion and screaming. A man was coming nearer and nearer, grinning derisively. He bent down so low that his face went blurred and dissolved. In its place, darkness suddenly fell, alive with flitting shadows, and from somewhere came the muffled beat of goatskin drums. Rhythmical, monotonous and incessant, they sounded as if they were accompanying magic rites in which people danced for dark, new-moon hours until dawn, when they would collapse, utterly exhausted, and fall asleep beside the ashes of a long-extinguished fire.

Clemencia Garises opened her eyes. She was lying naked on a bed. It took her a moment or two to regain her bearings. She wasn't in the wastes of the Kalahari or beside a kraal fire in the Kaokoveld. She was in her room at home, where she had grown up. In Katutura, the seething, vibrant home of 170,000 people, where death was omnipresent. A lot of things existed there – almost anything, in fact – but no bush drums beating like something out of a Hollywood film about safaris through darkest Africa. Clemencia sat up. The drumming was coming from the door.

'Open up!' Miki Matilda called from outside, rattling the handle. Clemencia always locked her door. Less because she was afraid of burglars than because she defended her little domain with tooth and claw against her family's attempts to invade it. The modest house had only two rooms, admittedly, and it might have seemed presumptuous for her to claim one of them for herself when her eight or a dozen relatives shared the other room and the corrugated-iron shacks that had been erected in the garden and the front yard over the years, but Clemencia simply needed something of her own.

There are two possibilities, she'd said when she landed her job in the police: either I rent a little flat in the centre of town and fork out two thirds of my pay for it, or I inject the money into the household, but then I'll want a room to myself. The family council had voted for the second alternative, not that they had genuinely accepted Clemencia's condition. On the contrary, she had to wage a daily battle for her smidgen of privacy. She often tired of this and came close to moving out, but she couldn't do that without letting her family go to the dogs. The little vegetable stall Miki Selma ran outside the house brought in almost nothing. Clemencia's sister Constancia did two days' cleaning a week in Klein Windhoek, but no one else had a regular income. The outlook would have been bleak indeed without Clemencia's contributions. Her brother would definitely have gone off the rails, if he hadn't done so already.

'Come on, open the door!' Miki Matilda called.

Clemencia put something on and opened it. 'What is it?'

Miki Matilda congratulated her on sleeping so soundly, then remarked, in the same breath, that the morning hours were the best time of all at this season of the year – or rather, the only bearable ones. Instead of wasting them, people should briskly embark on their day's work, especially if they were as healthy and favoured by fortune as Clemencia and herself – not, alas, that this applied to all their fellow creatures.

'What do you want?' Clemencia asked.

'It's Joseph Tjironda. You don't know him. A good friend of Petrus's. He and his family live on the outskirts of Wanaheda.'

'What's the matter with him?'

Miki Matilda didn't know exactly. Something serious, it seemed, because Joseph's son had sounded worried on the phone. He hadn't been able to explain, unfortunately, because his mobile had run out of credit, but he'd asked Miki Matilda to call him back right away and – bang – hung up.

'So why haven't you called him back?' asked Clemencia.

'I'm out of airtime too,' Miki Matilda confessed.

Clemencia went back inside her room and fetched her mobile. She made sure Miki Matilda didn't register the access code she keyed in – she might leave the phone lying around unattended sometime – and asked her to make it snappy.

Surprisingly enough, Miki Matilda refrained from any long-winded chitchat and spent nearly all the call listening. In view of this, the explanation she gave when it was over sounded very terse: 'Joseph Tjironda is sick.'

'What's wrong with him?'

'Pains.'

'Head, chest, stomach, left upper thigh, right toe?'

'I'll have to see him first.'

Miki Matilda enjoyed quite a good reputation among those of her acquaintances who believed in traditional healers, but when new patients entrusted themselves to her they normally wanted to test her abilities first. The most important test consisted in her telling them where it hurt – a complete reversal of the normal doctor-patient role. You could afford to make one mistake, but no healer who failed to locate the seat of the problem at the second attempt could be trusted to cure it.

Clemencia had once asked Miki Matilda how she could tell whether someone had a headache or a stomach ache. Miki Matilda smiled. You could simply tell when you had a bit of experience, she said. For all that, Clemencia preferred to go to a qualified physician when she was ill.

'I must go right away,' said Miki Matilda, handing back the phone.

'Best of luck,' said Clemencia, and slammed the door. She had to get going too. When she opened the door after getting dressed, Miki Matilda was still standing outside.

'Can you lend me the taxi fare?' she asked. 'The man could well be dead by the time I got there on foot.'

That was something of an exaggeration, no doubt, but Clemencia had no wish to be branded a heartless murderess for weeks on end, so she forked out the seven dollars fifty for an inner-city taxi fare. Then she herself took a taxi to police headquarters in Bahnhofstrasse. None of her colleagues in the Serious Crime Unit had turned up yet, but she managed to get hold of a serviceable police car with a full tank and drive it out to Ludwigsdorf.

She waited for forensics near the spot from which the murderer had opened fire. It would be outrageously lucky if there was anything to be found, given that her colleagues of last night had trampled around on any potential evidence. She looked down into the van Zyls' garden. By day it resembled a miniature paradise: a big, shady terrace and a lush green lawn. The dead man had been lying beneath the lemon trees.

Suddenly, from behind her, a male voice demanded to know who she was and what she was doing there. Clemencia turned round. An elderly white man was standing in the gateway with the palm trees in front of it, rifle at the ready and levelled at her. Raising her hands a trifle, she managed to convince him, after some argument, that she could identify herself as a detective inspector provided he didn't shoot her on the spot for reaching into her pocket. While the man was studying her ID, she made a mental note to have the area patrolled. A couple of uniformed policemen would have to show their faces in the district for at least a week to come. Their presence wouldn't help to solve the case, admittedly, but it might prevent the neighbours from believing that the state couldn't and wouldn't protect them. It wouldn't be the first time someone shot one of the poor devils who rummaged in the dustbins at night.

When the forensics team turned up, Clemencia proceeded to question the neighbours. Although they couldn't have failed to hear the shots fired at van Zyl, it was understandable that none of them had ventured out into the road straight away. However, one man watching from his veranda had seen a Group 4 Securicor car drive off at speed. He'd been too far away to read the number plate or see its occupant or occupants. This was a start, at least.

Clemencia knew that the security firm's employees earned just five Namibian dollars and sixty-six cents an hour, or roughly the price of a can of cola. Although no one dauntlessly ventured into a murderer's line of fire for that money, one might have expected the patrolman to have at least alerted headquarters by radio. Clemencia discovered after phoning the security firm that no such alert had been received. The only alarm call had come from Mevrou van Zyl, who had dashed into the bedroom on hearing gunfire and pressed the alarm button. The first G4S car had reached the scene of the crime seven minutes later, long before the police but too late to catch the killer. The possibility that one of the firm's cars had been in the immediate vicinity could be ruled out. Headquarters maintained constant radio contact, and patrol cars had to notify their every change of location.

A driver could, of course, have disregarded this rule for more or less innocuous reasons. This would need checking, likewise the question of whether any G4S operative had fallen out with Meneer van Zyl in the past. Clemencia thought it more likely that the car had only served as camouflage, which meant that the killer's preparations had been elaborate. The gun also suggested that a professional had been at work. Not everyone kept an automatic weapon in his gun cabinet.

21

No, this was no case of a burglar who had been taken unawares and lost his nerve, nor had he acted in the heat of the moment. Someone deliberately intending to eliminate Abraham van Zyl had coolly planned his execution and carried it out. There had to have been an important reason for this. Had van Zyl presented a threat to someone, and if so, why?

Police headquarters possessed no file on Abraham van Zyl, or, if there was one, it could not be found. The same applied to his corpse. When the pathologist went to perform an autopsy to officially ascertain what was obvious in any case, namely, that the man had died of gunshot wounds, he found the morgue empty. The staff on duty the previous night explained that a defect in the refrigeration system had compelled them to transfer the bodies already on the premises to temporary accommodation, or there would have been hell to pay. They had been so fully engaged in this task that they refused to accept the new arrival. No one knew where the body bag had been taken, and hours elapsed before it was discovered in a distant corner of the police garage.

'At least it wasn't in direct sunlight,' Clemencia said drily when reporting to her boss. Ndangi Oshivelo listened calmly to her litany of disasters, merely making an occasional note. Clemencia agreed with him that operational procedures needed organizing far more effectively. At his suggestion she had outlined her ideas for a programme that addressed the most urgent measures to be taken in the spheres of communication, organization and professional qualifications. Of course, nothing could be done without extra funding and basic political consent, but Oshivelo had promised to back the plan. He could do this not only because he was Deputy Commissioner and head of the Serious Crime Unit, which dealt with cases of homicide. Having been a prominent SWAPO activist in the 1970s and 1980s, he maintained excellent personal contacts with many Party members who now occupied key positions in the government and civil service.

While moving on to the procedure to be adopted in the present murder case, she looked at the two portrait photographs on the wall behind her boss. One was of President Hifikepunye Pohamba, the other of Sam Nujoma, the father of the nation.

'I think we should concentrate on motive. If we know why Abraham van Zyl was shot — '

'Who?' asked Oshivelo.

'Abraham van Zyl. The victim.'

Oshivelo nodded, plucking at his grey beard. When he sat back in his chair like that, he bore a faint resemblance to ex-President Nujoma.

'Does the name mean anything to you?' asked Clemencia.

'No.' Oshivelo shook his head. 'Go on.'

There wasn't much more to say. Clemencia needed some men to examine the dead man's social milieu – friends, relations, colleagues – and check his financial transactions. The usual, in other words. In addition, soundings were to be taken in the relevant quarters to discover whether anyone had recently purchased an automatic weapon. Oshivelo assigned her four men – the best he could do, he said.

Clemencia assembled her team an hour later. At least it included Angula. The other three men made it clear that they resented taking orders from a woman. One of them was a white man, Bill Robinson, who had intimated on a previous occasion that he had no objection to the Affirmative Action Law under which formerly racially disadvantaged personnel were to be promoted to senior posts. On the contrary, he said: he merely insisted that the letter of the law be observed, in other words, that *qualified* blacks be given priority. In his opinion, however, an inspector's qualifications entailed several years' practical experience in the field – 'at the sharp end,' as he put it – and not just a degree and good examination grades. Clemencia could stomach the envy latent in those remarks. What infuriated her was that Robinson would probably have extracted more information from Mevrou van Zyl than she had, and not because he was the better detective.

Oshivelo was present when Clemencia briefed her team. Although she realized he wanted to check her leadership qualities, she behaved no differently than she would have in his absence. She began by stating what she expected: no going-it-alone, the sharing of all information, meticulous record-keeping, and the availability of every team member at all times. Finally, she alone, in consultation with the Deputy Commissioner, would decide what information was given to the press. Sensing that her tone had been harsher than she intended, she hurriedly moved on to the present murder case. It wasn't until she proceeded to assign individual tasks that Angula, the most senior member of her team, spoke up.

'The victim isn't by any chance Abraham "Slang" van Zyl?'

Slang, the Snake?

'He used to work for the Civil Cooperation Bureau of the South African secret service. He's supposed to have been involved in the murder of Anton Lubowski.'

'So we ought to have a file on him,' said Clemencia.

'We couldn't even question him at the time – he'd decamped to South Africa.'

Clemencia had been twelve years old when Anton Lubowski was shot. Although she hadn't grasped the underlying circumstances, she could well remember his memorial service. Everyone in Katutura had gone, and the graveyard of the Ephesians Lutheran Church overflowed with mourners. SWAPO flags flew everywhere and the air was fraught with a muffled hum of anger rather than grief. Clemencia herself held a little paper flag in her left hand, loudly joined in the African anthem, *Nkosi Sikelel'i Africa,* stuck her right fist in the air in imitation of the grown-ups, and felt that some great and unprecedented event was about to occur at any moment. The obituary address was delivered by Theo-Ben Gurirab, who had later become Foreign Minister, and every other Party bigwig

24

had attended. Clemencia still had a vivid memory of the murdered man's children: his son in a SWAPO T-shirt, but, more especially, his little daughter, who wore a pretty red, blue and green striped dress such as she herself would have liked to own.

'Why should van Zyl have come back to Windhoek?' Robinson queried.

Angula wiped the sweat from his brow and shrugged. 'Maybe South Africa became too hot for him in 1994, when Mandela and the ANC came to power. Van Zyl was bound to have done any number of things, in South Africa as well, that could have cost him his life. The circumstances of Lubowski's murder were no secret after five years or more.'

'And we gave him a resident's permit?' Robinson shook his head although he, too, must have been aware that Immigration were even more inefficient than the police.

'So the murder victim hailed from South Africa and his wife is Namibian?' Clemencia sensed that they were on the right track.

'If I remember rightly,' said Angula, 'Lubowski was also shot with an AK-47.'

'Nearly everyone had access to an AK-47 in those days,' Robinson pointed out. 'SWAPO fighters, Koevoet paramilitaries, and anyone who knew someone on one side or the other.'

'But not now,' said Angula, 'and if someone is resurrecting the old days … '

'New team orders,' Clemencia said decisively. 'Angula and van Wyk, dig up all the information you can find about the Lubowski case, with special reference to Slang van Zyl. Robinson, you go and see the widow and make sure her husband was the same Abraham van Zyl.'

'Can't I simply phone her and ask for his date of birth?' Robinson grumbled.

No, not good enough, Clemencia told him. Mevrou van Zyl needed questioning thoroughly. Then they would have a potential motive, or at least something that differentiated the dead man from all his neighbours. It was improbable that any of them had been involved in the most sensational political murder in Namibian history.

'Take it easy,' said Oshivelo. 'Even if he was Slang van Zyl, that far from means his murder has some connection with the Lubowski case. After all, twenty years have gone by since then.'

That was undeniably true. Clemencia looked up at the ceiling. The fan was vainly stirring the heat. Only her boss's office was air-conditioned.

'Twenty years is a long time,' Oshivelo went on. 'We're living in a different country now. The old wounds may not have healed completely, but at least the scabs have formed.'

'Maybe,' said Clemencia. She wondered why Oshivelo was sticking his oar in; it was unlike him. 'Still, it's a lead we ought to follow up.'

'Of course,' said Oshivelo, 'but you should bear in mind that murders can be committed for a variety of reasons. Why shouldn't an ex-racist get killed purely by chance?'

Perhaps because Mevrou van Zyl had been so uncommunicative on the subject of her husband's past? Perhaps because the past wasn't as past as all that? Perhaps because the van Zyls and their circle of friends – and, presumably, the whole world in which they moved – were still as fundamentally racist as they had been in the apartheid era? Clemencia remained silent.

Bill Robinson stood up and said he'd get going. Even before he reached the door, someone from the switchboard came in with an urgent message for the Deputy Commissioner. The Group 4 Securicor people had rung. Information had reached them that a burnt-out car of theirs had been spotted in the bush near Heja Lodge. The patrolmen they'd sent to investigate had discovered a charred corpse in the driver's seat. The odd thing was, none of their cars was missing. Nor was anyone on their payroll.

26

'Damn it!' said Oshivelo. 'Has the body been identified?'

The man shook his head.

It was oppressively hot in Room 214. A corpse in a bogus G4S car ... In all probability, just the sort of vehicle in which van Zyl's murderer had driven away from the crime scene. Although Clemencia registered this, she wasn't a hundred per cent with it. Was it really possible that Oshivelo had never heard the name Abraham van Zyl? A man like him, who had been in the very forefront of the political campaign at the time of Lubowski's assassination? He had occupied a responsible position in the Namibian CID since independence and must have had an intimate knowledge of investigations into the Lubowski case. Could anyone have simply forgotten a thing like that?

✖✕✖

Ndangi Oshivelo, Deputy Commissioner of the Namibian Police:

I first met Anton Lubowski in 1983, at Osire internment camp. Having charged me with setting off a bomb in Klein Windhoek, the South Africans had carted me off to Osire to beat a confession out of me at their leisure. I had not been permitted to inform a lawyer, of course, but my comrades had seen to that. I don't know how Lubowski managed to get to see me. It probably had to do with the South Africans' desire to see me swiftly tried and convicted, and they could hardly open the proceedings without a defence counsel if they wanted to preserve at least the semblance of a constitutional façade.

I was naturally glad to see Lubowski when he came in, but I also felt there was no a chance that such a man could help me. It was clear that he came from another world, with his perfectly tailored grey suit, tasteful tie, signet ring and briefcase. Worn somewhat too long, his curly hair didn't really go with his respectable get-up. It was as if he meant to convey that he wasn't just a lawyer. A young man of thirty-one at that time, he looked as if everything came easily to him by right – as if his main task was to enjoy life to the full.

It later transpired that he also had a quite different side. If need be, he willingly underwent what others of his kind did their utmost to avoid. The South Africans arrested him a total of six times. In 1987 he himself was detained in Osire Camp and spent over three weeks in solitary confinement in a rusty corrugated-iron hut — no picnic, as I can confirm from personal experience. A little window near the roof let in just enough light for you to tell day from night. The walls became unendurably hot by day, but the nights were bitterly cold. You were given only one blanket and deprived of all your clothes except your underpants. You sat there day after day, night after night, staring into space and feeling your body tremble. You would happily have gone mad if that wasn't precisely what your tormentors intended.

Anyway, Lubowski walked up to me that time in Osire and came to a halt. Even before saying hello, he pointed to the bruises on my face and turned to the warder who was supervising our conversation. 'I suppose he bumped into a door, eh?' he said.

The warder hesitated, then shrugged his shoulders.

'I'd like the name, rank and number of the door,' said Lubowski.

The warder said nothing, but Lubowski somehow succeeded in identifying two of my assailants and subpoenaing them. He gave them a hard time at my trial and proved that I'd been tortured. The confession I'd signed was thus invalidated. Together with the alibi I possessed for the time of the bombing, that did the trick. They had to acquit me.

Lubowski and I were friends from then on, even though his world continued to be alien to me. The snappy suits, the silk shirts, the snow-white bathrobe he would often still be wearing when I rang his doorbell in the morning ... Lubowski was not the sort of man to be content with a pool in his garden. Shortly before his death, when we were all, himself included, working twenty hours a day for the Party, he had a sauna installed as well. It was with him that I rode in a Mercedes for the first time, and with him that I first sampled oysters. They came from Lüderitz Bay, his birthplace, and were, he told me, the very best of all. In 1984 he officially joined SWAPO. Since he was the first white man to take that step, public interest was immense.

28

The Party leaders, too, licked their lips. As living proof that we weren't pursuing racial vested interests, and as a bridge-builder to white groups of liberal persuasion, Lubowski was invaluable. Accordingly, he rose high in the Party hierarchy, flew off into exile in Luanda, attended international conferences, and was probably second only to Sam Nujoma as the SWAPO representative most often invited to give interviews. In his own circles he was accused of being a traitor, socially ostracized and professionally boycotted. He told me a few weeks before his death that he had given up counting after the thirtieth anonymous threat to murder him.

Every political assassination is reprehensible, but what was done to Anton Lubowski on 12 September 1989 was also quite pointless. Everything had long been settled. The South Africans had finally accepted UN Resolution 435, the route to Namibia's independence had been mapped out, the timetable was agreed on, and elections for the constitutional assembly were impending. Did anyone seriously believe that the wheel of history could be reversed?

His bag lay in front of him. It contained the AK-47. He had dismantled the weapon and wrapped the parts in blankets and dirty garments. The money he carried on his person, Seventy thousand South African rand. He had never in his life seen so much money, still less possessed it. He wondered how much of a future 70,000 rand signified. For an ordinary person, probably quite a lot, but he wasn't an ordinary person. He was something else.

He was in the car park overlooking Windhoek's Independence Avenue with his back leaning against a Land Rover that shielded him from the sun, waiting for the Intercape Mainliner to Upington in South Africa. The bus had been due to leave at 6 p.m. It was now 6.45. but he didn't mind waiting. An hour or two didn't really matter. The truth, death and he himself had one thing in common: they could afford to be patient because they knew they would prevail in the end.

Above the car park, the segmented portal of the Supreme Court seemed to glow in the evening heat. The building resembled a mausoleum for some prince of the underworld, a place of fire and death. He nodded to himself. True justice knew no mercy. The sky above the court building was cloudlessly, implacably blue. Perhaps it would rain when he returned, three or four days from now.

A female employee of the bus company came over to him with a notepad in her hand. The Mainliner would be here at any moment, she said. Would he care to check his bag in? He shook his head. He would need his bag on board, he told her. All it contained was a blanket, some water and his medication. The woman asked if he was ill.

'Just a cold,' he said, and coughed.

'There's something going around,' she said. 'A virus.'

'I'll be all right,' he said.

'Cholera has broken out up north,' said the woman.

'It's just a cold,' he repeated, trying to smile. He felt the sweat trickling down his forehead. Only because of the heat, he thought, nothing else. Apart from a bit of a cough, he was fine. He was feeling strong. He had time enough to be patient.

When the sun had disappeared behind the Kalahari Sands Hotel, the bus drove into the car park. It was a double-decker with a trailer for baggage. He watched the employees carry away the mountain of bags and suitcases they'd stacked on the asphalt beforehand. Most of the passengers were already pushing past the conductor and up the stairs, where the most popular seats seemed to be. There was a lot of room left on the lower deck. He stuffed his bag under the seat nearest the door and sat beside the window. A young Nama woman and her little girl installed themselves on the other side of the aisle. When she looked over at him he averted his gaze and concentrated on the cars driving past down Independence Avenue. Some two thirds of them had already turned on their headlights.

The daylight was fading fast – evanescing among the build-ings, dissolving into the air, disappearing. Night was the primeval state, it suddenly struck him, because nothing was needed to create it. Daylight required the sun, but as soon as it ceased to intervene, darkness prevailed.

The bus drove off, gliding slowly through Windhoek's sparsely populated streets. Once they had passed the police post at the summit of Heroes' Acre and were toiling uphill into the Auas Mountains, they left the urban glow in the sky behind. Ahead, a stretch of road could be seen in the beam of the headlights; to the side, the light was swallowed up by impenetrable darkness after only a few metres.

'I'm going to Keetmanshoop to visit some relations,' said the Nama woman across the aisle. The little girl had rested her head on her lap and was staring at him wide-eyed.

He grunted.

'And you?' asked the woman.

'South Africa,' he said.

'To work?'

He grunted again although there was no reason not to speak to her. She'd done him no harm, after all, nor had her daughter. He could for instance have asked her if she was going to see the little girl's father, or if there was a father at all and not just some man who had got her pregnant. But he shut his eyes and rested his head against the window pane. It vibrated gently. The woman didn't speak again.

At some stage he dozed off. The cold draught from the air-conditioning made him shiver when he awoke. He coughed. He could have done with the blanket from his bag. The woman and the little girl across the aisle were tightly cocooned and fast asleep. The window pane was trembling. Darkness reigned outside. The stars were far away. So far away they mightn't have existed at all.

❊❂❊

It was just as hot next morning as it had been the day before. The sun blazed down on Windhoek as if it meant to extinguish every spark of life. However, the enquiries conducted by Clemencia and her team had made some progress. It was ninety-nine per cent certain that the man found in the burnt-out Corolla was one Leon André Maree. Although his next of kin wouldn't have recognized him, his body was so badly charred, an aluminium suitcase in the boot of the car had withstood the flames. Among other things, it contained a South African passport and an air ticket in the name of Maree.

Clemencia's Aunt Selma would have pointed out that the murderer could have left the suitcase behind deliberately, in order to mislead investigators or even fake his own death, but that sort of thing happened only in the tattered Agatha Christies Miki Selma borrowed from the municipal library. To eliminate all doubt, Clemencia had sent a tissue sample to South Africa and asked her opposite numbers in Bloemfontein to obtain some samples for comparison from the address on the passport. It would, however, be at least ten days before the DNA results became available.

She felt sure the dead man's identity would be confirmed, because there was another clue that weighed more heavily with her than the aluminium suitcase. Now that they knew where to look, they had quickly discovered that Leon André Maree, like Abraham von Zyl, had been a member of the CCB outfit presumed to be responsible for Anton Lubowski's murder. Maree's nickname was 'Chappies', after a then popular brand of South African chewing gum, which he apparently couldn't live without.

The air ticket proved even more of a lucky find than the passport. Maree had left Frankfurt the previous night on board Air Namibia flight SW 286 and must have gone through passport control at Hosea Kutako Airport at around 9 a.m. Heja Lodge, in whose grounds the body had been found, was situated halfway between the airport and Windhoek, just short of the roadblock at which cars heading for the city were checked. This and the fact that his baggage was in the burnt-out Corolla suggested that the murderer had picked up his victim at the airport and driven him straight to the crime scene. If Chappies Maree had got into someone's car at a busy place like the International Airport, it meant that he harboured no suspicions and might even have known the someone in question.

The CCTV at Hosea Kutako airport conformed to international standards and was, according to the management, in perfect working order. Unfortunately, however, the tapes from the previous day had already been wiped. When questioned, the security staff were equally uninformative. They had probably been too busy watching female European tourists peeling off their winter woollies. At all events, no one could remember seeing Maree, let alone any person who had met him. It was pointed out to Clemencia that new arrivals had to fill in a form stating the purpose of their visit, and that this might be of interest. The immigration officials found the said piece of paper after about an hour, but Maree had been unimaginative enough to tick the 'Tourism' box. Purely by chance, Clemencia's eye lighted on the destination address, which also had to be specified on the immigration form. It was only too familiar to her. She had visited it two days earlier and would go back there without delay.

On the way she received a call from the forensic pathologist. Not only had this body not gone lost; it had already been autopsied. Chappies Maree was dead when the car was torched. Shot, five rounds in the chest. The projectiles had still to be examined, but they were at least of the same calibre as the ones that had killed van Zyl.

They came from the same gun, of course. Clemencia ran over the times in her mind. The flight from Frankfurt to Windhoek had taken ten hours. Maree was bound to have checked in and might even have been on board the plane by the time van Zyl was shot. His mobile would have been switched off. The killer had wanted to ensure that no one could warn his second victim.

33

Clemencia drove the last few metres through Ludwigsdorf and parked outside the gates. Mevrou van Zyl greeted her with the enthusiasm of someone with a mosquito whining around her head at night. Clemencia even believed her assertion that it hadn't occurred to her to warn anyone. With her husband dead and her daughter on the verge of a nervous breakdown, she'd had other things on her mind. Clemencia asked about Chappies Maree. He was an old friend of her husband's, said the widow, and had arranged to pay him a brief visit.

'To reminisce about their old days in the Civil Cooperation Bureau?' asked Clemencia.

Mevrou van Zyl now admitted what could no longer be denied. Yes, Maree had served in the CCB like her husband, but neither had ever been brought to trial over the Lubowski affair, so both must be accounted innocent. She couldn't contribute any details, never having questioned her husband about professional matters.

'Professional matters?' said Clemencia.

Her husband had been no murderer, Mevrou van Zyl said firmly. During the 1980s he had, on government orders, defended his country, which was under threat from more than just internal terrorism. Fidel Castro's Cubans were installed in Angola, the Communists were also in power in Mozambique, and almost all the neighbouring states south of the equator considered themselves members of the front against the Republic of South Africa. There had been a war on, the widow declared, as if Clemencia had grown up in a different universe. 'We may have lost that war,' she added defiantly, 'but that far from means we were in the wrong.'

'The preceding decades are sufficient proof of that,' Clemencia couldn't resist saying. Unprofessional of you, she would have been told by Matti Jurmela, her Finnish mentor, but the Finns had never had to suffer under apartheid. Mevrou van Zyl said nothing, and Clemencia stared at the photos on the wall above the sofa. Abraham van Zyl in uniform, grinning broadly. Abraham van Zyl, rifle on shoulder, standing over a dead gemsbock. Abraham van Zyl with a gang of boozy companions. Abraham van Zyl. Abraham van Zyl. No sign of his wife anywhere, not even a wedding picture.

The wedding photos of Clemencia's parents were the only ones in which her mother appeared. Although he couldn't afford it, her father had employed a photographer to take some black-and-white snaps outside the church and beneath the jacaranda trees in Parliament Garden. Clemencia could never decide whether she genuinely had a personal recollection of her mother's face or was only breathing life into those photographs. She had been only four when her mother was killed by a ricochet for which no one could be held responsible. It had been a warning shot. The South African unit combing Katutura for SWAPO terrorists had been under considerable nervous strain, her aunt was told. Clemencia's father couldn't bring himself to go to the police. He'd sat on the bench outside the house for days, stony-faced, silent and motionless. He had never really got over it, even today.

Clemencia briefly wondered whether to tell Mevrou van Zyl this. Then she said, 'What's past is past. We want to find a double murderer.'

'Really?' Mevrou van Zyl gave an incredulous smile.

'Yes, really,' said Clemencia. Some hours later, when she was viewing the Internet's store of information about the Civil Cooperation Bureau, she wasn't so sure. The CCB had been an unscrupulous gang of murderers whose main aim was the elimination of anti-apartheid activists. They had also destroyed ANC facilities and undermined the UN arms embargo against South Africa. In its bare five years of existence the Bureau had carried out an estimated ninety or a hundred criminal operations ranging from bomb attacks on ANC kindergartens to perverted attempts at intimidation like the one practised on Archbishop Desmond Tutu, who in 1989 had found a baboon foetus hanging up in the garden of his house in Cape Town.

Summoned into being in 1986 by Magnus Malan, the then defence minister, the CCB worked in secret and was largely independent. Cover firms were established and units operated in civilian clothes. It seems that some CCB recruits didn't even know that they were working for South African Special Forces. Accordingly, they murdered either for money or from racist conviction, which rendered their activities even more unsavoury. It also made it more understandable that someone had decided to play the avenging angel.

Although Clemencia held no brief for vigilantism, its targets in this case were certainly no innocents. The killer was getting rid of baddies. They weren't just any old criminals, either. Colonial troops or Nazis, Idi Amin or Pol Pot might have been still worse, but to Clemencia the apartheid system remained the epitome of inhumanity. It was the hell into which she had been born. Her family had been at its mercy, and her mother wasn't its only victim.

The assassination of Anton Lubowski was attributed to CCB Regional Group 6. In addition to Slang van Zyl, Chappies Maree and several others, its members included an Irish mercenary named Donald Acheson, who was said to have carried out the killing. Arrested not long afterwards, he had evidently been released. Clemencia hoped to learn more from police and court records, but what her team had assembled was definitely an embarrassment of riches. Stood up on end, the folders formed a rampart some two-and-a-half metres long.

'1989, 1990, 1994, 1998, 2001 – that's everything there is on the Lubowski case,' said Angula. 'We were in luck. The director of public prosecutions is considering whether to reopen the proceedings, so all the files had been collated.'

On opening the first file, Clemencia came straight to the autopsy report. Anton Lubowski had been hit by seven rounds from an AK-47. Notwithstanding that, someone had also shot him in the head at close range, using another weapon of smaller calibre. This argued against a lone killer. Why should anyone have laid the

Kalashnikov aside, drawn a pistol, removed the safety catch and fired again? Why, if he had wanted to make sure, hadn't he simply taken a few steps nearer with the gun already in his hand?

Clemencia leafed through another file. In a document dated 1990, a judge had devoted twenty-four pages of typescript to justifying Donald Acheson's release from custody on bail. Reading between the lines, one gathered that the evidence against him was slim, and that further progress would be impossible without additional witness statements. There had previously been a dispute between the prosecution and the accused's counsel as to whether the members of CCB Regional Group 6, who had fled to South Africa, could realistically be persuaded to volunteer evidence to the Namibian authorities. The problem was that Namibia had since become independent, and that the enforced subpoenaing of foreign nationals from their native land was not legally feasible. In default of their evidence, the prosecution of Acheson seemed to hold out little prospect of success. Thus, despite considerable public interest in solving the murder, the judge could not accept responsibility for keeping Acheson on remand indefinitely.

'Needless to say, Acheson fled to South Africa as soon as he could,' Angula said when Clemencia had finished reading. She put the file back. To read the whole lot, even superficially, would have taken her days. She plonked the first five files on her desk and shared out the rest among the others. Angula suggested they might get to the heart of the matter sooner if she personally questioned the judge in question. Since retired, he was now living on his farm, Lewensvrede, half an hour's drive from Windhoek.

Clemencia nodded. 'Perhaps you could get me the number of this — '

'Fourie. Hendrik Fourie,' said Angula. He handed her a slip of paper with the phone number on it and added, almost apologetically, that he had taken the liberty of obtaining it from the Supreme Court.

Clemencia knew that Angula's attitude to SWAPO was on the cool side, but that alone did not explain why he had never risen beyond the rank of plain constable. He might not possess any outstanding intellectual ability, but that was something equally lacking in many who had gone places in the force. Angula was at least dependable. He had a memory like an elephant and a sense of what was relevant. Clemencia could consider herself lucky to have him on her team.

She called ex-judge Fourie.

'It's about Lubowski, isn't it?' Fourie asked.

'How did you know?'

'I heard on the radio that Slang van Zyl has been shot.'

'Since then, so has Chappies Maree.'

There was a momentary silence at the other end of the line. Then Fourie said, 'Come and see me.'

Clemencia headed south down the B1. The air-conditioning wasn't working, but as long as she drove fast along the asphalt road with the windows open, the airflow cooled her down a little. Just as she turned left on to the sandy farm track, her mobile signalled a text message from Miki Matilda. 'Call me!' it read.

Clemencia dialled Matilda's number, driving slowly along a dried-up river bed. Her aunt reported that the condition of her patient Joseph Tjironda was more serious than she had feared. She still didn't know who was behind it, but an evil spell had been cast over Tjironda's entire house. Although she had already initiated the appropriate countermeasures, Tjironda couldn't remain there until they took effect. He was very weak and needed rest, so she, Matilda, was wondering whether Clemencia, who spent so much time away from home in any case, might be willing, just for once and for such a good cause, to give up her room to him.

'No!' said Clemencia, and hung up. An evil spell? Good God! She shook her head.

The Auas Mountains were sharply silhouetted against the sky

ahead of her. The blue above them looked even deeper and more intense through the tinted lenses of her sunglasses. A game fence ran for kilometres beside the track, but she eventually came to a gateway. She drove through it and replaced the chain. There wasn't a soul to be seen anywhere. The track became perceptibly steeper and stonier. The sparse, dry grass had lost all its colour, the squat grey bushes beside the track looked as if dust had been their only nourishment for weeks on end. Here and there, camel thorn shrubs jutted defiantly from among the rocky outcrops.

The sound of the engine startled a flock of guinea fowl. Instead of escaping into the bushes, the panic-stricken birds ran along in front of the car, fluttering aside only when its wheels were about to run them over. A bird of prey, possibly a snake eagle, deserted its treetop and flew off with ponderous wingbeats. If it had stayed put, Clemencia wouldn't have noticed it.

On reaching the summit, she looked down from afar on a gently sloping plain with two cypress trees jutting from it. Beneath them was a dense expanse of paler green through which, in one or two places, could be glimpsed the whitewashed walls of the farmhouse or its outbuildings. Immediately above ground level this oasis seemed to dissolve into a thin strip of shimmering air, as if it were hovering in a void or were just a mirage conjured into being by the heat.

The outlines solidified as Clemencia drew nearer. Shortly before she reached the first trees, her route was barred by another gate. Two barefoot children opened it and followed the car up to the main building. An elderly white man rose to his feet on the canopied veranda. He was slim, with a tanned face, and his sun-bleached hair had a yellowish tinge.

'Judge Hendrik Fourie?' Clemencia extended her hand.

'Ex-judge,' said Fourie. He shook hands and turned to the two children, who had lingered beside the police car. 'Go on, ask her!'

The little girl might have been five, the boy was somewhat older. He hung his head and stared at his bare feet.

39

'Well, go on, the policewoman won't eat you.'

Clemencia tried smiling. The girl gazed at her steadily, the boy dug his toes into the sand. Both children were very dark-skinned. Clemencia said, 'Anything I can … ?'

Fourie made a dismissive gesture. No, he said, they must ask themselves. They had to learn that few things in life came easily. He hadn't many workers on his farm despite its 15,000 hectares, because he didn't run it as a commercial concern. Cattle breeding didn't pay these days. Anyway, Taleni and Nangolo were the only children here, and he took a certain interest in their education. They were far from stupid. He was even toying with the idea of sending them to a good school in Windhoek.

Clemencia asked about their parents. The mother worked as Fourie's housekeeper and lived with them in one of the three cottages behind the main building. Nobody knew where the father was or even if he was still alive. He had often disappeared for brief periods in the past, but it was a long time since he'd shown his face there.

'All to the good, perhaps,' said the children's mother, who had brought two glasses of iced tea out on to the veranda.

The boy was still standing beside the police car. The girl had lost interest in Clemencia and was tugging at a big Weimaraner that lay in the shade of some fruit trees with all four paws extended. Its tail gave a couple of weary thumps. The iced tea was refreshing, and it was relatively cool beneath the canopy over the veranda. A bird was twittering in the rose bushes. Further away, peacocks and turkeys were strutting around a small pond. Clemencia could almost have believed that all was well with the world.

She said, 'I know the evidence was insufficient, but I'm asking your opinion as a private individual, Meneer Fourie: Were van Zyl and Maree really responsible for Anton Lubowski's death?'

Fourie put his iced tea on the balustrade of the veranda. 'Van Zyl and Maree, yes,' he said, looking Clemencia in the eye, 'but others were involved too: Donald Acheson, Staal Burger, Ferdi Barnard, and at least one other man whose real name I don't know. They did the dirty work here in Windhoek. Then, of course, there were also the instigators in Pretoria, where Regional Group 6 of the CCB was based. Believe me, if it had come to a trial I'd have convicted the entire bunch.'

Fourie was absolutely sure of his ground, and he was just the man Clemencia needed. The Lubowski killing had probably been the most important case he'd ever handled in the course of his professional career. He hadn't forgotten the smallest detail. Clemencia had only to ask the right questions. First about the members of the murder squad. If two of them had been killed, the others' lives were also in danger.

Fourie shrugged his shoulders. 'Staal Burger, perhaps. He's living somewhere in South Africa and poses as an innocent farmer. Still, how your killer proposes to get at the others is a mystery to me.'

Clemencia continued to ask questions. Ferdi Barnard's whereabouts were known, but that would avail a potential murderer little unless he could scale the walls of Pretoria's maximum security prison. In 1988 Barnard had been sentenced to life for murdering an anti-apartheid activist named David Webster. The South Africans had shunted Acheson off to London in 1991, since when nothing had been heard of him. All Fourie knew of the sinister sixth man was his nickname, Donkerkop, and the fact that he had probably been resident in Windhoek at the time.

'What makes you say that?' asked Clemencia.

'There also existed a CCB Regional Group 8, which was responsible for former South West Africa. Its members were clearly not trusted to carry out such a major operation as the Lubowski murder, so the killers were flown in from Pretoria. However, it's extremely unlikely that the latter could have dispensed entirely with local assistance. The South Africans had to get hold of weapons and a getaway car. They also needed someone who knew the area

41

and could house them inconspicuously. Donald Acheson was even found a job on the *Windhoek Observer*.'

Donald Acheson. And Donkerkop, or 'Blackhead' in Afrikaans. Perhaps he still lived in Windhoek.

'You'll laugh,' said Fourie, mopping the sweat from his brow, 'but for years I wondered if every passer-by with pitch-black hair was him.'

Clemencia did't laugh. She asked if Fourie had a theory as to who could be intent on bloodthirsty revenge.

'Not Lubowski's family, anyway,' said Fourie. 'I got to know them all, his parents, his sisters, his ex-wife, his children. They've fought tirelessly ever since to get the case cleared up. They want justice, not revenge. They not only want to learn the truth, they demand that the truth be officially confirmed by a trial. They aren't going to kill the suspects, not now of all times, when the Namibian and South African legal authorities are reviewing the case. There can't be a trial without an accused, and without a trial uncertainty will prevail for ever.'

'Who, then?' asked Clemencia. 'Who could be so embittered?'

'No idea.' Fourie looked over at the little girl, who had hauled the dog to its feet and was now trying to sit on its back. 'After all, twenty years have gone by. Perhaps it wasn't revenge at all.'

'If not, what?' said Clemencia. Her mobile phone beeped. The text was from Miki Matilda, urgently requesting her to call back. Not now, Mikis, not now!

'You'll find out,' Fourie replied. 'I'll gladly tell you all I know.'

'Good. Then let's begin by … '

Clemencia's mobile beeped again. *It's really important!!!*, the message read. Clemencia excused herself and withdrew to telephone. She went down the veranda's three steps and turned left. Euphorbias were growing in a rockery there. The nearer part was dominated by succulents that looked like sticky pastry cases, except that they were green and prickly. When Miki Matilda answered,

Clemencia said, 'Look, you're not getting my room if you ask a hundred times! We made an agreement, and — '

'It's your brother.'

'What about him?'

'The police have locked him up.'

Damnation! Clemencia had seen it coming. Melvin had been drifting away little by little, and she'd done nothing about it.

'What's he been up to?'

Grievous bodily harm, the policemen had said. Apparently, Melvin had beaten someone up in the bar. That was all Miki Matilda knew.

'You'll get him out, Clemencia, won't you?'

It was clear that Miki Matilda expected Clemencia to be sensible and take advantage of her job in the police at long last, but her tone also conveyed a hint, if not of reproach, of incomprehension that she could choose to work with people capable of arresting her very own brother.

Clemencia didn't know what to say. She looked down at the euphorbias. Growing among the pastry-case plants were others that resembled pigs' ears. Beyond them was a small quiver tree whose bark was peeling off in several places.

'Melvin's in a holding cell,' said Miki Matilda. 'Here at Katutura police station.'

'Okay,' said Clemencia. She told the retired judge she had to leave at once, regrettably, but would like to resume their conversation as soon as possible. Fourie was coming to Windhoek next day, so they arranged to meet at a pavement café at the mouth of Post Street Mall.

The barefoot boy was standing in front of the driver's door when Clemencia returned to her car. 'Could I ride with you a little way, ma'am?' he asked. 'With the blue light and the siren on?'

43

Donkerkop:

The night Lubowski died changed everything. I wanted nothing more to do with politics and avoided the people I'd consorted with before. It was as if I had to blot out the whole of my previous life because I couldn't forget my mental images of that night. For nearly two decades I would wake up bathed in sweat again and again, hearing the echoes of those shots in the darkness of my room. Although I instantly grasped that it was a nightmare, and that it was all in the distant past, I couldn't refrain from turning on the light and checking to see if there was blood clinging to my hands. Despite this, I never seriously considered turning myself in. Who would have benefited? It wouldn't have brought Lubowski back to life and I couldn't undo what I'd done.

Jesus, I was only twenty-two at the time. My head was full of fast cars and little else, just a few half-baked ideas and any amount of brooding anger. That was all I knew. My friends, their parents and their parents' friends – all of them said there was only one thing worse than the kaffirs who were ruining the country, and that was the whites who were helping them to do so. They should have known better, that was why. What had been here before the first whites rolled up their sleeves? No schools, no hospitals, no railways, no roads, no electricity, not even a brick building. Just goats and cattle and a few native tribes which – if half of them didn't die whenever there was a drought – liked to bash each other's heads in. No one could seriously want to revert to that state of affairs, least of all a white man.

'Only the stupidest calves go looking for their own butcher.' That was the kind of saying that went the rounds with us. But no one could fail to see that Lubowski wasn't stupid, and that made the matter even worse. He wasn't just a cowardly, pants-wetting fouler of his own nest. He knew what he was doing. He was a traitor, a renegade. That really spelled his doom. No army in the world can allow its men to go over to the enemy.

What infuriated me most about him was his arrogant way of talking – as if he knew it all. The way he postured in his smart suits and poked fun at dumb Boers who couldn't summon up the courage to accept essential changes.

44

On one occasion, I forget where, he spoke of a future in which blacks and whites would enjoy equal rights in a free, independent Namibia.

'South West!' I yelled from the back, meaning South West Africa.

'South-west is a compass reading, not a name for a country,' Lubowski said quietly into the microphone. That was the only time we exchanged a few words. I saw him only two or three times apart from that, but I naturally knew all about him. Not only because he was always in the newspapers and because all whites born in the country knew each other anyway. My father had been a neighbour of the Lubowskis' in Lüderitz. He had lived only a few houses away from them before he moved to Windhoek.

Anyway, I threw myself into the anti-Lubowski campaign and soon got sick of the everlasting 'something-must-be-done' hogwash. I joined forces with a few like-minded individuals who were prepared to write anonymous letters or even beat up the odd SWAPO sympathizer when he crossed their path on his own. Two or three such operations, and the CCB came to regard me as a kind of free-lance associate long before I knew that any such outfit existed.

I got to know Ferdi Barnard and Slang van Zyl in August 1989. It was a cold winter's night, and I and a couple of friends had gone to play darts at the Alter Wirt. I don't recall who introduced us, but we drank so much Windhoek Lager and Jägermeister that we only hit the dart board by accident. That, shouted someone, was because the stupid board wasn't well-defined enough. We needed a target that would motivate us better – a photo of Lubowski, for instance. Then we'd see him plant a dart right between the bastard's eyes.

Everyone applauded loudly except me. 'It's easy to talk,' I drawled.

'And you're a guy who does more than just talk?' Ferdi Barnard said sarcastically.

'I am.'

'Oh yeah?' Barnard made some mouthing movements with his hand.

'I happen to know that Lubowski recently received a photographic enlargement of himself in the post,' I said. 'He may even have recognized himself in spite of the fact that someone had riddled it with shotgun pellets.'

45

'And you happen to know that, do you?' said Slang van Zyl.

'You bet your life I do,' I said.

'Good man.' Van Zyl slapped me on the back and called for Jägermeisters all round. That was as far as it went that night, and Barnard and van Zyl remained wary the next few times we met as well. They tested me politically, letting me talk and listening with a smile as I and my friends drew up blacklists of those in most urgent need of elimination. Or rather, black and white lists, because they always featured Lubowski and one or two other white traitors.

I made the acquaintance of Donald Acheson, then Chappies Maree and Staal Burger. It was the latter who asked me if I was really as good a driver as he'd heard.

'Man,' I told him, 'I've just got a feeling for cars. As soon as I turn the ignition key, I know what kind of engine's under the bonnet. Whether it's got any minor defects and what it can do and how I can get the most out of it. I only have to drive a couple of metres and the car and I are one. So much so, I often wonder why I don't drink petrol.'

'Good,' said Burger. 'The thing is, we need a driver.'

That was two days before the assassination. They didn't tell me they planned to kill Lubowski until the night it happened.

'Kill him?' I said.

'That made you tuck your tail in, eh, boy?' said Ferdi Barnard. Staal Burger laughed.

'Bloody hell,' I said. 'It's all the bastard deserves.'

The police station in Mungunda Street looked somewhat friendlier in brilliant morning sunlight than it did at night. The brickwork was neatly rendered to somewhere above head height, the paintwork and ornamentation looked as if they had been refurbished not long ago. The sliding grilles over the two entrances were open. Clemencia paused outside the one on the right, above which hung a lilac lantern inscribed 'Police'. By night its dim light was anything but a guarantee of safety and protection. A footprint was clearly visible on the wall beside the door – one metre fifty from the ground. Clemencia had no wish to know how it had got there.

She waited. Von Fleckenstein had promised to be there at nine. She didn't know if he was any use as a defence counsel, but he was the best when it came to getting people out on bail. He had asked her on the phone last night if Melvin had any previous convictions and whether his opponent was still alive. In that case, he said, there shouldn't be any major problem, but her brother would have to be patient for a night. They were lucky that some additional hearings had been arranged during the summer holidays, on account of the road safety campaign, or the cells would have been overflowing with drunk drivers. The reason for the magistrates' extra shifts was probably that Clemencia's colleagues in the traffic police, in their enthusiasm for the fray, sometimes arrested a few local VIPs, and the latter couldn't be left to under lock and key for too long. In her experience, no one ever minded cramming twenty or thirty people into the tiny holding cells.

She hadn't managed to get in to see Melvin the night before. Visits had to be personally approved by the station commander, and he, of course, was no longer available. Clemencia could have brought pressure to bear, as most of her colleagues would have done, but unlike her they didn't always insist that regulations were there to be observed. She had asked the desk sergeant at least to see that Melvin got the flea powder she'd brought with her. This he had solemnly promised to do.

Three girls in miniskirts came mincing out of the police station. Twenty at most, they looked as if they already had several years' experience on the streets behind them.

Just as Clemencia was getting out her mobile to phone the lawyer, von Fleckenstein drove up in an ancient Mercedes 200 with red leather upholstery and a veneered dashboard. He pulled into one of the parking bays outside the entrance and heaved his bulky frame

47

out of the driver's seat. Then, with surprising alacrity, he strode past Clemencia and into the police station. She followed him in, only to meet him coming back with a probationer constable in tow. Having adjured the youngster to keep a watchful eye on his treasured gem of a car, he turned to her and said, 'Right, let's get on with it!'

A quarter of an hour later, Melvin was seated facing them in one of the offices. His left eye was swollen shut and his lip split. Other than that, he was displaying precisely the same defiant expression he'd worn when feeling unfairly treated as a child. God Almighty, little brother! thought Clemencia. Life was hard enough without asking for trouble all the time.

'Everything okay?' asked von Fleckenstein.

'In this lousy dump?' Melvin retorted, scratching his elbow. Inflamed bites were visible below the sleeve of his football strip.

'Didn't they give you the powder?' asked Clemencia.

'What powder?'

'At least the fleas find you tasty,' von Fleckenstein said cheerfully. 'Your opponent has two fractured ribs.'

'Is that all?' said Melvin.

'It's enough for a technical KO.'

'I'd have killed the bastard if they hadn't hauled me off him,' Melvin said.

'Listen, youngster!' Von Fleckenstein crossed his fleshy arms on his paunch. 'If you like it so much in the pokey, keep talking that way!'

Melvin stared at the water cooler in the corner of the office. Plastic mugs were stacked on the shelf beside it. Further to the left stood a uniformed constable.

'All right, fire away,' said von Fleckenstein. 'Take it from the beginning.'

'Can I have some water?'

'No.'

Melvin started hesitantly. He'd been hanging around in the

48

Mshasho Bar since eleven that morning. Drinking, chewing the fat, drinking. At some point a guy joined him at the bar and asked if he needed any money. Melvin had guffawed at this. Anyone could see he was a millionaire, he said. The man didn't laugh. He took two hundreds from his pocket, flapped them in Melvin's face, and pocketed them again.

What was it about? Melvin had asked.

The man ordered two beers and asked after his family. How were his father and his sisters?

'They're okay,' Melvin said.

One of his sisters had two children, didn't she?

'Jessica and Timothy,' Melvin agreed.

Did Jessica have a boyfriend?

Melvin laughed. Jessica had only just turned eleven.

Really? The man nodded, then asked if Melvin, being the children's uncle, looked after them now and then.

'Why?' said Melvin.

Well, did he sometimes take them for walks or go and watch a football match when 'Black Africa' were playing?

'No,' Melvin told him.

The man took a long pull at his bottle. Then he said he wouldn't at all mind looking after Jessica for an hour or two. As if in passing, he added, 'Two hundred dollars!'

That was when Melvin hit him. The first punch didn't connect properly, so he'd taken a couple himself, but at some stage the other man went down and Melvin started kicking him. If the others hadn't pulled him away, he would have gone on kicking the swine until …

'Yes, we know,' said von Fleckenstein.

Melvin scratched his arm. His shirt was yellow with green sleeves, rather like the strip of the Brazilian national team, and bore the name 'Kaká' on the back. Melvin had cut the letters himself out of some scraps of green material. Constancia, Jessica's mother, had sewn them on for him.

49

'Can the boy have some water?' von Fleckenstein asked. The constable took a mug and filled it.

'In the bar they say you can get rid of the HIV virus by fucking a virgin,' Melvin said. 'It isn't true, though, is it?'

'No,' said Clemencia, 'it's utter nonsense.'

'Even if it was,' Melvin said, 'not Jessica!'

'Nothing will happen to her,' said Clemencia, although she was well aware she was no more able to guarantee this than anyone else. The inhabitants of Katutura couldn't keep their children locked up all day long, there wasn't room. They had to go out into the streets, went here and there with their friends, messed around in the dry river bed, roamed as far as the UN Plaza. For all that, Jessica must be warned to take care of strange men. They must keep an eye on her. Someone else in the family would have to take over Constancia's two days' cleaning.

'Do I look like someone who would sell his little niece?' Melvin demanded. His lips were trembling with rage.

'No,' said Clemencia. Melvin looked every inch the shabby, flea-bitten youngster who had left school without a certificate and hung around aimlessly since then. Who occasionally earned a few dollars by doing shady jobs he refused to talk about. Who promptly took the money to his favourite haunt and came staggering home next morning, drunk. Who, as soon as he was sober, sat down and made his young nephew a toy car out of wire. Who had once confessed to Clemencia that he had no idea what the word 'future' really meant. Whose greatest dream it was to watch Brazil playing in the World Cup in South Africa. But who also realized that this would remain a dream for ever. Melvin was Clemencia's little brother. Nothing would ever change that.

'The hearing is at twelve,' said von Fleckenstein. 'The judge will set bail at three to five hundred dollars. You'll be out by twelve-thirty if you — '

'I don't have three hundred dollars,' said Melvin.

50

' — if you promise not to touch that man again. He knows the score now, anyway.'

Maybe he does, thought Clemencia, but what about the thousands of other men who couldn't get any retroviral medication? Who vainly dosed themselves with beetroot juice or other miraculous cures? Who clung to any hope, however idiotic, because they had nothing to lose?

'I don't have even ten dollars,' said Melvin.

'I'll lend you the money if necessary,' von Fleckenstein told him, rising to his feet with an effortful groan. At the door he turned round. 'By the way, lending money means you get it back.'

Melvin didn't speak as he was conducted back to the holding cell, but he looked so forlorn that Clemencia promised to attend the hearing. She would simply have to postpone her talk with Fourie. She failed to reach the ex-judge on the phone but left a message on his voicemail.

She looked in on the family on her way to headquarters. Tomatoes, onions and pawpaws were neatly arrayed on the trestle table outside the house. Behind them reposed some little packets of potato crisps, the remains of a whole carton Melvin had brought home a few weeks ago. It had fallen off the back of a lorry, he claimed. Miki Selma was just moving her stool into the meagre shade cast over the table by a tarpaulin. Constancia was at work in Klein Windhoek and her children were out somewhere, but Selma volunteered to go and look for them at once. She would also launch a whip-round for Melvin's bail from the neighbours. Meantime, Clemencia's father would have to sit and look after the vegetable stall.

Clemencia drove off. The township looked the same as ever. Nothing indicated that little girls were worth 200 dollars here, that policemen stole flea powder and a stall displaying a few tomatoes couldn't be left unattended for an instant. Children were playing in the streets as if it were the most normal thing in the world. Jessica and Timothy were nowhere to be seen, but that didn't mean anything, Clemencia told herself – not a thing. You mustn't drive yourself mad with worry. At the red lights before Independence Avenue she shut her eyes for a moment and vainly tried to clear her head.

It wasn't until she entered the offices of the Serious Crime Unit that the wider world in which people murdered each other with Kalashnikovs caught up with her. On her desk she found today's edition of *The Namibian*, which was headlined 'Belated Revenge for Lubowski?' Beside it lay the Scenes of Crime Unit's report. It confirmed that van Zyl and Maree had been shot with the same weapon. The perpetrator had torched the Corolla with the aid of petrol. No fingerprints or other clues had been discovered. That only left the route they had followed hitherto: the one that led via the victim. Who had known that Chappies Maree would fly to Windhoek? What had the former agent been doing in Germany, and why had he wanted to meet up with van Zyl? Had the other members of the group, insofar as they weren't in jail, intended to join them? Staal Burger must be located in South Africa as a matter of urgency. Perhaps he would talk if it were made clear to him that his life was at stake.

At the staff conference Oshivelo declared that Clemencia's approach was absolutely correct and proposed that all available personnel be put to work on solving the above questions and their corollaries. Examination of the old Lubowski files could be deferred. In his experience, a twenty-year-old murder provided no useful motive. Instead, they should concentrate on the victims' more recent past. He, Oshivelo, found it hard to conceive that men with such a criminal background had suddenly mutated into law-abiding citizens just because the political situation had changed. They must check to see if the gang of ex-agents had subsequently engaged in shady dealings on their own account.

'Gun-running, diamonds, drugs,' Robinson hazarded. 'Their former connections would have come in handy.'

52

What if it involved a lot of money which one of them hadn't wanted to share with the others?

'Staal Burger? Donald Acheson? Or this guy Donkerkop?' Robinson queried.

'Or a business partner who felt he'd been cheated,' said Oshivelo.

Clemencia said nothing, just listened as Robinson piled hypothesis on hypothesis and Oshivelo firmly mapped out the course their investigations should take. Her original point of departure, the political background, dissipated with every word they uttered. Every sentence made it seem less likely that revenge for an assassination long consigned to the history books could be a serious motive. Even Anton Lubowski's photograph, which Clemencia had removed from the file, now looked more faded than was justified by the two decades since it was taken.

Had this really been no more than a bitter dispute between criminals? There was something to be said for this theory, she couldn't deny. Perhaps she remained sceptical only because it irked her to be nudged in one particular direction. True, the double murder had caused a stir. The public were expecting results and Oshivelo himself was under pressure, but he had entrusted *her* with the case. He ought to let her handle it as she thought right.

Clemencia glanced at Angula. He was sitting there like a graven image, but his face was one big negative. She forced herself to smile. Don't take umbrage, she told herself. Show no weakness, remain self-assured! 'Gentlemen,' she said, 'thank you for your valuable suggestions. From now on, and with immediate effect, we'll look for evidence of serious criminal activity. I'm sure we'll soon produce positive results, so let's get to work.'

Oshivelo nodded and they all rose. Clemencia waited until the others were almost at the door.

'For safety's sake, Angula and I will stay with the Lubowski files,' she said, tapping *The Namibian*'s headline. 'The press have tasted blood. We don't want to be accused of pursuing only one line of inquiry.'

She looked Oshivelo straight in the eye as she uttered the last words. If he stabbed her in the back now, in front of the others, he could take her off the case. Either he let her get on with it, or he dropped her. He would have to decide how much he valued her work.

Oshivelo hesitated for a moment. Then he said, 'Keep me informed, inspector.'

Clemencia's mobile said 11.43 a.m. by the time they had all left the office. She would have to leave herself if she wanted to be in time for Melvin's bail hearing. She quickly called Fourie and let his mobile ring until the message cut in. Nothing, no one. A knock at the door, and Angula came in again. He said he'd found something that might be important. He hadn't uttered a word during the conference, so it seemed to be something for Clemencia's ears alone.

'Well?' she said.

'Magnus Malan, the former South African defence minister, stated in parliament in 1990 that Anton Lubowski had worked for the apartheid secret service. Allegedly, he supplied information about SWAPO – information of great military and political importance. Those accusations were later repeated by two different parties: a former member of the South West African police force and a well-known South African reporter with excellent police contacts.'

'Lubowski an informer?' Clemencia said incredulously.

'There are plenty of statements to the contrary, of course.'

'But the South Africans kept locking him up.'

Angula nodded. 'Six times.'

'But?' said Clemencia.

'Six times up to 1987. Not after that.'

'Meaning what, Angula? What are you trying to say?'

'Nothing. Only that we shouldn't rule out any possibility. If people have been vainly trying to pin the Lubowski murder on the

Civil Cooperation Bureau for two decades, it may mean, theoretically, that there's nothing to prove.'

'In that case, who ... ?' Clemencia left the sentence unfinished.

Angula's pale palms came into view as he raised his hands defensively. 'I'm only a humble constable,' he said.

His implication was pure nonsense. It was obvious that Malan had been trying, in parliament, to whitewash himself and the murderous gang he'd recruited. If he portrayed Lubowski as a South African agent, the CCB could have had no interest in eliminating him. On the contrary. It would then seem logical that the enemy, or SWAPO, had liquidated the traitor in its own ranks. Malan's statement was merely a political dirty trick, a nasty little gambit in the destabilization campaign against the SWAPO government that had just come to power.

'Should we pursue the diamond-smuggling theory instead?' Angula asked – casually, it seemed.

SWAPO had fought for independence. It had resorted to violence and conspiracy, but not to anything more than was absolutely necessary in that war against an inhuman ideology. Clemencia was firmly convinced of that. All that worried her was the extent to which Oshivelo was playing down the Lubowski connection. He had fulfilled an important role in the struggle for independence and was one of the Party members who could see what went on behind the scenes. Lubowski's murder had been a really big thing. Oshivelo must know what had happened. He couldn't simply behave as if he'd only just heard the names of the CCB agents for the first time. If he did, there had to be a reason.

'Stay with it, Angula,' Clemencia said, 'and if you find anything, not a word to anyone but me.'

'It could become a hot potato, boss,' said Angula.

A snappy riposte would have been appropriate. That it was hot enough already in this damned office. That the rainy season was imminent, thank God. That you only burnt your fingers if you were over-hasty. That ... All she said was, 'More than possible, Angula.'

By the time she finally got going she was, of course, far too late for the bail hearing. There wasn't a sign of Melvin in the court-room. Von Fleckenstein was there, but he was busy getting another delinquent off the hook. When he'd finished he handed Clemencia his card and said, 'You owe me 250 dollars.'

Clemencia drove back to Katutura. Her father was sitting on the bench outside the house. Jessica and Timothy were vainly pestering him to tell them a story about the old days. Miki Selma proudly announced that she had collected forty-three dollars and twenty-five cents towards the bail money.

'Where's Melvin?' asked Clemencia.

Miki Selma jerked her thumb in the direction of the Mshasho Bar, from which loud kwaito music was irradiating the whole neighbourhood.

'He's celebrating his release,' said Miki Selma.

✹✹✹

Judge Hendrik Fourie (ret.):

Releasing Donald Acheson on bail in 1990 was probably the biggest mistake I ever made in the course of my professional career. Given the facts avail-able to me, however, I scarcely had a choice. I was unaware that our own authorities – public prosecutor's office and police – were handling the case in so slipshod a manner that it verged on sabotage. At first I thought it was just indolence that prompted the public prosecutor to keep requesting a postpone-ment of Acheson's trial. I approved this once, then twice, but the third time I lost patience and set a date by which the indictment had to be made out.

I was absolutely staggered when the public prosecutor withdrew the charges against Acheson on the grounds of insufficient evidence. I did not, however, grasp the full extent of the disaster until years later, when allega-tions appeared in the press to the effect that senior police officers had been involved in Lubowski's murder. I conducted the requisite preliminary examination. On closely studying the files, I realized that the evidence against Acheson, but also against the rest of the CCG group, would have sufficed not only for an indictment, but, in my opinion, for a conviction as well. The fact that I spoke of 'the height of incompetence' in relation to the public prosecutor's office was held against me in various quarters, but my choice of words was extremely mild under the circumstances.

At all events, I made everything public. My final report named names, made it unmistakably clear that no one other than Acheson had done the shooting, that van Zyl, Maree, Burger and company had been actively complicit in the crime, and that their employers had been based at CCB headquarters in Pretoria. I appended my remarks on the murder's political objective and exposed the lies Malan had told in his notorious parliamentary speech, as well as a few other diversionary tactics staged by various parties. I also demonstrated that one of our police officers had suppressed important clues to Lubowski's murder.

In short, I rubbed the authorities' noses in the case so hard, they had no choice but to reopen it. Or so I thought, but I was much mistaken. Once the initial sensation had subsided, the public prosecutor piped up. He wasn't convinced by my arguments, he said. On the contrary, he considered that Donald Acheson — whose nickname, 'The Cleaner', was public knowledge by then — was innocent, and that the evidence against him suggested he'd been framed. Supposedly, certain unidentified persons wanted to pin the murder on him.

Incredibly enough, the public prosecutor flatly refused to prefer charges, at least while some of the accused were in South Africa and had not been extradited. The deputy minister of justice promised to see to this, but the matter soon came to nothing. The Namibian government never lodged an official extradition request.

The rest is quickly told. In 1998 another judicial enquiry was undertaken by the Supreme Court, but it brought to light no more and no less than my own. The Lubowski family eventually brought the case before South Africa's Truth and Reconciliation Commission. Years later, its National

Prosecuting Authority examined the Commission's findings with a view to a judicial review, and the files are now being studied by the Namibian prosecutor-general's office. No trial was ever held, either here or in South Africa.

How can this be? Well, purely in theory, I could have been mistaken. Perhaps the evidence genuinely wasn't sufficient. Either that, or there were too many people who had too much to lose if the whole truth came out.

2

VOICES

He had eaten next to nothing for twenty-four hours. In Upington, before boarding the connecting bus to Johannesburg, he had ordered a couple of chicken wings but abandoned them after the first morsel. Thereafter he had only drunk water. Tap water from a bottle he filled himself, because carbonic acid burned his guts. Still water was all right. What more did one need? He wasn't hungry, anyway. No, he was feeling fine, alert – light as a feather in the wind.

At the central bus station in Jo'burg he borrowed a phone book from a souvenir shop but failed, predictably enough, to find her listed. He knew nothing about her apart from the fact that her name was Mandisa Khawuta, that she lived in Soweto, and that her husband had made a habit of shooting the cashiers of the petrol stations he held up. Despite this, he took a train to Soweto and got out near the brightly painted cooling towers. At the station he accosted a group of loitering youths and offered them a thousand rand if they could take him to Mandisa Khawuta.

'This is Soweto, man,' said the one wearing a black woollen beanie. 'A million people live here.'

'Two thousand rand,' he replied.

It took them three hours. He checked that she was the right Mandisa Khawuta, then sent her four children out of the shack and said what he had to say. She barely looked up from the fire beneath her saucepan of maize mush.

'How do I know this isn't a joke?'

He coughed. Jokes weren't his thing. Jokes were for people who clung to life, who wanted to forget that death was waiting for them around the next corner. Death didn't laugh at jokes, but at what seriously mattered to people who clung to life. It was a savage, scornful, merciless laugh that would bury them all.

He took the Kalashnikov from his blue sports bag, went to the door of the corrugated-iron hut, and asked, 'Shall I shoot that old man over there?'

She looked at him closely for the first time, then shook her head.

'Nothing doing without a down payment.'

He counted out three thousand rand, letting the notes fall to the mud floor. The rest of the money he put away. He cocked the AK-47 and said, 'I've found you once, Mandisa Khawuta, and I'll find you again.'

She nodded. Apparently, she'd grasped that he wasn't joking. He impressed on her that she mustn't lose any time. He would deduct two thousand rand for every twelve hours that went by.

'Okay?'

'Okay.'

Outside he patted one of her little boys on the head. He had no need to turn round to know that she was watching him. Then he returned to the centre of Jo'burg and caught the next bus south. Although the temperature was considerably lower than in Windhoek, he was sweating. At one bus stop a man got in and started preaching on the theme of Cain and Abel, *Genesis* iv. God told Cain: '*Vervloek is jy dan nou* … ' He was now accursed and driven from the face of the earth, which had opened its mouth to receive his brother's blood. The soil he tilled would bear no fruit, and he was fated to become a fugitive and a vagabond. Cain, the weakling, was afraid that anyone might kill him, but the Lord said no: 'Whosoever slayeth Cain, vengeance shall be taken upon him sevenfold.'

He would have laughed out loud if it hadn't hurt his chest so much. God, the Lord, also did things by halves. He hadn't grasped, any more than his creatures had, that you must finish what you'd

60

begun – pursue it to the bitter end. Everyone would die, he himself and God and a few more beforehand.

They got to KwaZulu-Natal. He had never been to the province before, but the bus driver seemed to be a frustrated tourist guide and jabbered incessantly into the microphone. He learnt that all manner of peoples had slaughtered each other here in the old days. That was why the area had towns named Vryheid and rivers named Blood River. Somehow that struck him as quite logical.

※❖※

Fourie had gone away. To South Africa. His housekeeper didn't know exactly when he would be back, but he didn't appear to have taken much luggage with him. Clemencia asked after the woman's children.

'The boy wants to be a policeman now.'

'It happens,' said Clemencia, and asked her to call as soon as Fourie returned. Then she sat down at her desk to prepare for the press conference. She and Oshivelo had already discussed the general direction it should take: they were following up a number of leads, but it was too soon to speculate. They intended to allay the newshounds' predictable dissatisfaction by requesting their assistance. Someone might have seen the person who met Chappies Maree at the airport.

Robinson came in to submit his report. He was grinning so broadly, one might have thought the killer had surrendered to him personally. However, what he and the others had found out was really less than spectacular. Van Zyl had asked his firm for a week's leave starting on the day of Chappies Maree's arrival in Windhoek. A female colleague had stated that van Zyl and a friend intended to go hunting somewhere in the Kalahari. Van Zyl's widow largely confirmed this but said that the destination of their planned excursion had been a game farm in the Erongo Mountains, or in quite a different direction.

61

'And?' said Clemencia.

Robinson sat back and crossed his legs. In the first place, he said, it was close season for most types of game; secondly, he had checked with Hosea Kutako Airport that Maree had not imported a hunting rifle; and, thirdly, no van Zyl or Maree had made a booking with the game farm in question.

'A hunting trip,' Robinson said contentedly. 'That's the kind of pretext I'd employ if I wanted to leave my wife and kids at home and no one was to know I had some criminal business to transact.'

The rest was wild speculation. Robinson genuinely favoured the illegal diamond trade theory. He had already begun to check hotel reservations in Lüderitz, Klein-Aus and the environs of the restricted area, albeit so far without success. He now proposed to contact the Protected Resources Unit, which was responsible for the security of the diamond mines. If a few handfuls of rocks had gone missing recently, it might be possible to tackle the case from another direction. Clemencia considered this a waste of time, but since Oshivelo had apparently given his approval she merely nodded. When Robinson started musing aloud about the necessity of flying to the restricted area, she shooed him outside.

The press conference was attended by the usual suspects: *NBC Radio, The Namibian, The Sun, Die Republikein.* They had to be on their guard against the lady from the *Windhoek Observer,* who had mastered the art of taking quotations out of context. The young reporter from the German-language *Allgemeine Zeitung,* who was also there, was the only one to address Clemencia as 'Miss Garises' instead of 'Detective Inspector' or 'Ma'am'. He seemed favourably disposed towards Clemencia for some reason. At all events, he had on previous occasions questioned her more courteously that was usual in one of his kind. Clemencia had almost got the feeling that he tried throw her a lifeline, particularly in awkward situations.

Oshivelo said a few words of welcome and handed over to Clemencia. She kept it brief and businesslike. Two murders, one

62

gun, one perpetrator. A few details about the circumstances of the killings. Confirmation that both victims had once belonged to the CCB. Other leads were being pursued but could not be disclosed for tactical, investigative reasons. Then the sweetener for the press: a request for assistance. Civic responsibility, cooperation between the citizen and the state, et cetera. Clemencia distributed some specially prepared photographs of Chappies Maree. The few questions relating to failings on the part of the police or underlying political factors she parried with ease. It was all over in less than half an hour. Oshivelo gave her an approving nod.

The reporter from the *Allgemeine Zeitung* was waiting for her outside. Might he have a word with her? A head taller than Clemencia, he was slim and so white-skinned, he probably needed to wear sunscreen after dark. Having introduced himself as Claus Tiedtke, he ran his fingers through his fair hair and came straight to the point.

'An elderly German-speaker came to see me in the newsroom a few months ago. He claimed to have spotted Donald Acheson in the middle of Windhoek.'

'Acheson, the Cleaner?' Clemencia said incredulously. Acheson had disappeared in 1991, after the South Africans deported him to London. Since then he could have been in Australia, South America, or some other distant part of the world. Always assuming he was still alive.

'I advised the man to go to the police, but he'd already done that. Your colleagues kept him waiting for a while, then told him that no charges were pending against Donald Acheson. He started to argue – tried to tell them that Acheson was one of the CCB's most notorious killers – but they sent him packing. Seething with rage, he came to our newsroom and kicked up a fuss – insisted that we publish a report on this scandalous state of affairs. I think he was less concerned about Acheson than eager to expose the inefficiency of the Namibian police.'

'Which you naturally declined to do,' said Clemencia. She didn't read the German-language newspaper, but she could well imagine its opinion of local police efficiency.

'Quite so, Miss Garises.' Claus Tiedtke smiled. 'There are plenty of other and better grounds for doing that. Anyway, I considered the matter too questionable – and, to be honest, not newsworthy enough – to merit space in the paper. Besides, the man didn't want his name quoted. I told him I could do nothing without confirmation from another source and soon forgot all about it.'

'Until van Zyl and Maree were murdered,' said Clemencia. She wondered why it hadn't occurred to any of the policemen who had sent the witness away to inform her.

'It may not be important at all,' Tiedtke said.

'No, no, many thanks. I suppose you don't recall the man's name?'

He shook his head. 'Only that he had seen Acheson buying ammunition at a gunsmith's. Rosenthal Guns.'

A vanished killer spotted at a gunsmith's, of all places. It fitted too well to be true. The whole thing was probably nonsense and the putative witness was just a know-all with nothing better to do all day but air his obsessions. Besides, he must have known Acheson pretty well for a chance encounter to enable him to recognize the man at once after nineteen years. On the other hand, busybodies of that type usually came forward after a case had made headlines, not before. If he had turned up yesterday or today, Clemencia wouldn't have wasted another thought on him, but several months ago? No one had then been talking about Lubowski, the CCB or Acheson.

'I'll take care of it,' Clemencia promised. She nodded to Claus Tiedtke and walked off. Then she looked in on her team. Angula, seated amid stacks of files, was doggedly ploughing through them. When asked if he was making any progress, he somewhat cryptically replied that the problem was cross-referencing. That was all he could say for the moment. Robinson was heatedly asking van Wyk why in hell the diamond mine guys thought they were a cut above everyone else. Tjikundu was on the phone. His demeanour was so determinedly official, Clemencia felt ninety-nine per cent sure it was a private call.

'Just hang up,' she whispered to him before she left headquarters. She decided to walk although the midday sun was beating down. She would have got there by the time she completed the paperwork for a vehicle. At least she could think in peace. If Acheson really was back in the country, he had to be found – preferably before he fell prey to another burst from an AK-47. The killer had shown himself to be well-informed, at least in the case of the second murder. Did he also know where Acheson was hiding?

Acheson, the onetime mercenary in colonial Rhodesia, the policeman in the service of South Africa's apartheid regime, and later – doubtless because that wasn't sanguinary enough for him – a CCB killer. A man who had regularly sided with historical losers, who had fallen over again and again, but had always regained his feet in the end. A man devoid of scruples.

And what if he wasn't a potential victim at all? Perhaps van Zyl and Maree had decided to talk after all, for some reason. If they had been only indirectly involved in Lubowski's assassination, their crimes would by now be subject to the statute of limitations. But not the act of the man who had pulled the trigger. Acheson might have been blackmailed by his accomplices! Had Maree flown to Windhoek to discuss the final details of the hush-money handover with van Zyl and then collect his share? Perhaps it really wasn't about revenge. Perhaps the chief perpetrator had wanted to get rid of accessories who could be dangerous to him. Once a killer, always a killer?

Clemencia crossed the intersection and walked past the Kudu Monument. She hugged the walls of the buildings in Independence Avenue although, even there, only a few covered shop entrances offered protection from the sun. Mobile phone shops, photographers, jewellers, travel bureaux. Outside Kentucky Fried Chicken a lottery seller proffered a bunch of tickets. The newspaper boys had already gone, but seated as usual outside the Telecom building was the Rastafari with his animal figures fashioned out of wire and cheap beads. The pedestrian lights to Post Street Mall were on red, but a Herero mother towed her child across regardless. A parking attendant in a faded protective vest fed a coin into an expired meter although there wasn't a traffic warden in sight. He would doubtless point out to the brand-new Isuzu's owner that slipping him ten dollars would still be a bargain because it saved him from copping a thirty-dollar parking ticket.

Clemencia dived into the shade of the huge gum tree in front of the Zoopark Café. In the adjoining park old folk were seated on the benches, reading. A little child was crawling across the grass. Office workers from the neighbourhood were dozing beneath the trees during their lunch break. The park looked idyllic, but there was something wrong with it: not the plastic bags bobbing on the surface of the little pond, but the lush, fresh green of the grass, which existed only because it was watered every day. It had no right to be there in this heat, so it was a painful reminder that something lovelier, softer and livelier was possible – elsewhere, at least: in a country where it rained regularly. Where you didn't, after months of drought, yearn for the first thunderstorm …

Clemencia shook her head. At the Fidel Castro Street intersection she crossed over and walked down the arcade. Tourists in bush shirts were queueing up at the Nedbank cash dispenser. A Group 4 Securicor car was parked a few metres further along. At Venning Street Clemencia turned right. The Rosenthal Guns building came into view after thirty metres. The blank façade facing Talstrasse was reminiscent of an air-raid bunker. Around the corner, a security guard was seated on the kerb with his gun propped upright between his knees. A Citi Golf was parked a few metres away. Claus Tiedtke was leaning against the driver's door, sweating.

'I could have driven you here if you'd said something, Miss Garises,' he remarked.

'Testing me, were you?' Clemencia asked.

'I've had experience of the authorities,' he said, 'but I guessed you were made of different stuff.'

'If you're going stand around here much longer, you'd better put on some sun cream.'

'Black is beautiful,' he said.

'But you'll only go as red as a lobster,' said Clemencia. She climbed the steps to Rosenthal Guns, rang the bell, and opened the grille when the buzzer sounded. Without a word, she showed her ID to the assistant behind the counter. The man said, 'Let me guess, ma'am. You want to practise on our indoor range because the police have run out of ammunition.'

'I'd like a word with the manager,' Clemencia told him.

'Only joking,' said the assistant, but he took her to see his boss. Rosenthal not only computerized the records they had to keep by law, but – the manager assured her – maintained them more meticulously than anything in Namibia bar the Met Office's rainfall measurements. No one named Donald Acheson had shopped there in recent years, not that that necessarily meant anything. People who dropped out of sight tended to acquire a false identity and the papers to go with it.

'Can you ascertain who bought 7.62 millimetre cartridges in the last few months?' Clemencia asked. The manager could, though the ammunition was widely available and certainly not exclusive to the AK-47, so the list of purchasers was correspondingly long. Clemencia had it emailed to headquarters, then called Tjikundu and told him to contact all the customers with English names. An Irishman by birth like Acheson would be unlikely to adopt an Afrikander or German identity. It was worth a try, at least.

'How am I to tell on the phone whether any of them is our man?' asked Tjikundu. His English was poor. He would be unlikely to spot an Irish accent.

'Speak Afrikaans,' Clemencia told him. 'Anyone who doesn't speak the language has never worked for the South African secret service. Start by asking for their personal particulars and rule out anyone under sixty. Acheson must now be sixty-nine, and he won't have made himself look that much younger. Those with firearms licences dated before 1991 can also be excluded. And ask them where they were at the time of the murders.'

'Is that all?' Tjikundu grumbled.

Clemencia refrained from pointing out that he liked telephoning and merely said she would look in again that afternoon. Claus Tiedtke was still standing outside when she left the gunsmith's, though he had retreated into the scant shade of a street sign. He looked at her expectantly.

'If you've nothing else on, you can drive me home,' she said. He tried to pump her on the way to Katutura, but she answered monosyllabically, telling him only that the story needed checking. When they got to Frans Hoesenab Straat, Tiedtke killed the engine and got out too.

The vegetable stall in front of the house had been cleared and abandoned. Music was blaring from the Mshasho Bar. The neighbour across the way was tinkering with his cab. Miki Matilda was excitedly complaining over the garden fence that the doctor at Katutura Hospital had simply dosed her patient Joseph Tjironda with antibiotics without wondering – or, better still, without asking Miki Matilda herself – why such a usually healthy man should suddenly have developed pneumonia. Clemencia asked Tiedtke if he would like to come inside. A glass of water surely wouldn't hurt him. He locked his car and followed her.

Melvin was not only at home but had sobered up sufficiently to be teaching Jessica and Timothy some kung fu techniques of his own devising. The children were in high delight. Miki Selma's sole proviso was that they must be careful not to yank the clean laundry off the line, and Constancia had no objection to her children being trained in hand-to-hand combat. It was no solution, admittedly, but it couldn't do any harm for youngsters in Katutura to learn how to defend themselves.

Tiedtke hung around in the front yard, looking rather forlorn, until Clemencia told him to sit down on the bench beside her father. By the time she returned with a glass of water, the rest of the family were arrayed with their backs to the wall, staring at the perspiring white man. Tiedtke winked at Timothy and asked him what his name was. The boy nestled against Miki Matilda and didn't react even when she cuffed him on the back the head and said, 'Go on, tell the meneer your name!'

Clemencia handed Tiedtke his glass of water. Her relations watched him drink as if none of them had ever suspected that white people needed fluid. Tiedtke put the glass down on the bench beside him. 'That was good,' he said.

'Because it's hot today,' said Miki Matilda.

'Unbearably,' said Tiedtke.

'That's the summer for you,' said Miki Selma.

'Let's hope it rains soon,' said Tiedtke.

'Let's hope so,' said Miki Matilda. Conversation petered out.

'Don't you have anything to do, all of you?' asked Clemencia.

'Yes,' said Miki Selma.

'Any amount of things,' said Miki Matilda. She remained rooted to the spot like the others.

'Yes, well … ' said Tiedtke, getting up. Clemencia went out to the car with him. The others lined up along the fence.

'Nice family,' said Tiedtke. He didn't sound the least bit sarcastic. Clemencia was still debating what to reply when her mobile rang. It was headquarters. Staal Burger had been located in South Africa. He was now a sugar-cane farmer in the province of KwaZulu-Natal. Did Clemencia want to phone him herself?

Tiedtke was already sitting in his Citi Golf. Clemencia put her head through the window and asked, 'Could you possibly drop me at headquarters?'

The house was situated outside Hluhluwe. He had to walk for over an hour, first along an asphalt road, then on a farm track, but he didn't mind. On the contrary, he had spent long enough sitting in the bus. He had filled his water bottle, so he took a swig whenever the pain transfixed his gut. Then he could go on. His sporadic bouts of shivering actually felt quite pleasant under the scorching sun. His cough sounded different now, that was all. Hollower, deeper? A doctor would probably pronounce him sick, but he knew better. He wasn't sick and never would be. He would remain healthy to the end. Then he would die, just like that.

He had passed a pineapple plantation; now he was passing fields of sugar cane. Taller than a man, the plants grew in serried rows to left and right of him. Their stems were bending in the warm wind, rustling like the sound of a distant sea.

He had been in hospital, so he knew what it was like. People slowly died around you in those rickety beds, in that stench of sweat, despair and disinfectant. Everyone had to die, but not like that! He had simply walked out, promising himself never again to set foot in a hospital. Why should he? He wouldn't get sick, he would simply die. He coughed.

When the house came in sight at the end of the lane, he paused and drank a little water, then slung the blue sports bag over his shoulder and struck off sideways into the plantation. He cautiously forged a path through the jungle of canes but put his feet down firmly. Where sugar cane grew there were mice, and where mice lived, snakes were never far away. He respected snakes. Once, in Ovamboland, he had seen a black mamba strike. Three or four times. His companion had died of shock, not of its venom, of that he'd been convinced. Now he was the one who inspired fear. And brought death. He wondered if snakes respected him too.

Hearing laughter, he came to a halt and peered through the sugar cane. Ahead of him lay a transverse path, a low hedge, and beyond it a stretch of green lawn extending almost as far as the old country house. Running the full width of the building was a covered veranda with a refectory table on it. Some two dozen people – men, women and children – were seated round the table, and a man standing at its head was giving a speech. He scrutinized the man's features. Yes, there was no doubt about it. He put the blue bag down and squatted on his heels. Forty metres, not more. One burst, and well before the guests had grasped they were still alive he would have disappeared into the dense sugar cane. It would be so simple. But he mustn't rush things.

The veranda door was wide open. The windows were open too. Perhaps the same applied to the windows on the other side of the house. He worked his way through the plantation and to the right, doing his best not to make the foliage rustle and taking care not to bend the canes upwind. Where the garden hedge made a ninety-degree turn to the west he broke cover, crossed the track at a crouch and dived into the shelter of the hedge. He crawled forwards on all fours until he could still just see the veranda at an angle. Running along the side of the house were some fruit trees whose shade he would make use of. He selected the window he would climb through, then shut his eyes and rehearsed each of the requisite movements in his head. It could have been darkest night, and he would still have made it with the unerring certainty of a sleepwalker. He deftly assembled the Kalashnikov. Then he awaited his opportunity. An opportunity always presented itself if you were patient. You had to be ready to seize it, that was all.

The man at the table concluded his speech. Everyone clapped. 'We won't be as young the next time we meet!' someone called out. He ran his hand over the barrel of the Kalashnikov. A babble of voices, a hum of conversation. Someone who didn't interest him was telling a story that didn't interest him about someone that meant

71

nothing to him. No more lies, he had promised himself. Death was the only truth. That being so, no story was worth listening to.

He didn't know how much time had gone by when the telephone rang inside the house, but he knew that his opportunity had come because the sound came from the open window he'd decided to climb through. Someone on the veranda called out, 'Telephone!' When the man who had given the speech stood up and made for the door, he sprang to life too. He darted along the hedge until the corner of the house was between him and the party at the table, then vaulted over the hedge and sprinted to the window, crouching low. When the ringing stopped and a deep voice inside said, 'Yes?', he peered over the window sill. The man inside the room had his back to him and was looking through the open door in the direction of the veranda. The telephone stood on a waist-high chest near the door. It was an old-fashioned black phone with a receiver connected to the set by a thick, spiral cord.

'Yes, Daniel du Toit Burger speaking,' said the man. 'Who's calling?'

He had to deposit the Kalashnikov on the window sill for a moment. Hoisting himself over the sill with both hands, he slipped into the room without a sound.

'Serious Crime Unit Windhoek?' the man asked. He grasped the door handle with his left hand and shut the door.

❊⊙❊

Daniel du Toit Burger. Formerly better known as 'Staal' Burger. There had once been a South African radio series called that, but it was probable that the nickname derived from the fact that he had carried out his assignments for the criminal apartheid regime like a man of steel. Hard as nails, and so devoid of scruples he might not have been made of flesh and blood.

'You knew Chappies Maree and Slang van Zyl?' Clemencia asked.

72

The man at the other end of the line seemed to think for a moment. Then he said, 'That was a long time ago.'

Clemencia had put the phone on loudspeaker so that Robinson and van Wyk could listen in. Robinson pointed to her and silently mouthed the word 'diamonds'. She said, 'Your two former CCB colleagues have been shot and killed in Windhoek, Meneer Burger.'

'Impossible,' he said.

'Impossible?'

'I recently spoke to Maree, at least. At about ten o'clock on Monday morning. And he was in South Africa. In Upington.'

Upington was 800 kilometres from Windhoek. And a few more kilometres than that from Heja Lodge, where Maree had been murdered on Monday morning. Clemencia said, 'I thought you hadn't been in touch for a long time.'

'Maree called me. I hadn't heard from him for years and was far from unhappy about it. I've started a new life – I don't have the least wish to rake up the past.'

'Are you sure you spoke to Maree himself?'

'Of course.' A brief silence. Then Burger added, 'For a while I had quite a lot to do with him.'

The condition of Maree's body had made it impossible to determine the exact time of death. Clemencia had assumed that the killer didn't spend hours conversing with his victim. Maree had certainly been in his power at around 10 a.m. It was improbable that he himself had decided to call his old secret service buddy.

'Maree wanted to meet you in Upington, correct?'

'How do you know that?'

'It wasn't Maree's own idea, he had an AK-47 rammed into his chest. The man who killed him shortly afterwards wanted to lure you into a trap as well.'

If Burger had gone, he wouldn't have been so easy to get hold of. He would have gone to meet his murderer and would probably be dead by now. Clemencia surmised that he now realized the

73

danger he was in. Perhaps there was a chance of extracting some information he wouldn't be willing to divulge later on. 'What did Maree want from you?' she asked. 'If he suggested you spend a whole day driving to a rendezvous in Upington, it certainly wasn't for a chat about old times over a cup of coffee.'

Burger said nothing for a moment or two. Then he said, 'It was about a deal, apparently.'

'What sort of deal?'

'I've no idea. I told him I wasn't interested in anything he had to suggest.'

Robinson scribbled the word 'Diamonds' in caps on a slip of paper and added three exclamation marks.

'And Maree left it at that?' asked Clemencia. 'Wouldn't you try a bit harder if someone was holding a Kalashnikov under your nose? Maree's life depended on whether he managed to talk you into meeting him.'

'I can't help you,' said Burger.

'Is it possible that he mentioned the name Anton Lubowski?' Clemencia asked. Robinson picked up the slip of paper with 'DIAMONDS!!!' on it. He seemed to be debating whether to crumple it up, but merely flattened it with his palm.

'What the hell … ?' Burger's voice tailed off.

'You ought to come clean,' said Clemencia. 'In your own interests. After that call from Maree, it's highly probable the killer will try — '

All Burger said was, 'He's here.'

'What?' said Clemencia. 'Who's there? Meneer Burger?'

✺❂✺

The room looked like something from another age. The framed paintings between the windows depicted ox-wagon scenes and mission stations. The bookshelves on the end wall were laden with pewter mugs and leather-bound volumes. A paperknife and an inkwell plus pen reposed on a desk of polished, reddish wood. The rocking chair in the corner would probably creak if he sat down on it, but that didn't matter. The man on the phone was welcome to notice that he had a visitor whom it would be wise not to keep waiting.

The rocking chair really did creak as he sat back. The man on the phone spun round and froze. 'What the hell ... ?' he said.

'We need to talk, Staal Burger,' he replied. The Kalashnikov, too, rocked up and down. If he fired a burst now, the bullets would riddle Burger from throat to belly.

'He's here,' Burger muttered.

Of course he was there. 'Hang up,' he said in a low voice.

'The man with the Kalashnikov,' Burger stammered, white as a sheet. He clamped the receiver to his ear as if that could protect him – as if he wouldn't be killed as long as he was speaking to a third party. As long as he could hear a voice that came from who knew where and could do nothing, absolutely nothing, to save him.

'Hang up, Staal Burger,' he repeated. He felt another upsurge of anger. Were they all as stupid? Why didn't they grasp that their lives hung by his forefinger?

'It's the police,' said Burger. 'A woman inspector – she's after you.'

Why did they all try tricks and evasions? Why couldn't they, even in the face of death, do justice to the truth? But no, they wriggled and lied and cheated.

'Yes,' Burger mumbled into the mouthpiece, 'yes.'

Why couldn't they simply do as they were told? 'For the last time,' he said, 'hang up!'

'The inspector wants a word with you.' Burger held out the receiver.

That was enough! He used the rocking chair's momentum to jump to his feet. He still wasn't standing four-square when a shaft of agony pierced his gut. He bent over the Kalashnikov, feeling the pain transfix his body. His muscles went limp, his knees buckled, his fingers opened, the gun hit the floorboards with a dull thud. As if in slow motion, he saw the receiver slip from Burger's hand and the telephone cable describe a leisurely, elegant arc as it fell. Burger started yelling, but not for help or the police. He simply yelled and turned towards the door while groping for the butt of the Kalashnikov.

The pain was already subsiding, his fingers could grip once more. It had only been a momentary weakness so brief that it mightn't have happened at all. If it had, it was already over. Things always happened faster than you thought.

Still yelling, Burger wrenched the door open. Sunlight flooded in from the veranda. He had a firm hold of the Kalashnikov. The barrel was steady.

✖◈✖

'Meneer Burger!' cried Clemencia. She heard the receiver hit the floor in spite of his yells. 'Meneer Burger?'

'What is it? What is it?' Robinson whispered excitedly.

Good God, he could hear precisely what she could! How was she to know exactly what was happening 1500 kilometres away? Apart from the fact that everything seemed to be going haywire. Forcing herself to remain calm, she said, 'Hello! Can you hear me?'

Why didn't the killer come to the phone? What risk would he be running? He was far away in another country. They couldn't have intervened there even if they'd been on the spot.

'We realize the Lubowski case was a flagrant injustice,' Clemencia said. 'Believe me, I ... '

It was absurd. The killer would never let the police hear his voice, not voluntarily. Why should he say anything when it was clear that they would use any clue against him? What would he gain by speaking to her?

'You can trust me. My mother was shot too, just like Lubowski.

Maybe not by the same individuals, but by members of the same criminal gang, and none of them was ever brought to — '

At that moment shots rang out. A burst so clearly audible through the phone's loudspeaker that they all instinctively ducked.

'Jesus!' Robinson hissed.

'Don't do it!' Clemencia whispered into the receiver, although she knew it was far too late.

'An AK-47,' said van Wyk. 'Fifteen rounds at least.'

'The bastard!' said Robinson.

'Hello?' Clemencia said. 'Can you hear me?'

�֎

Burger's body was lying in the passage. He stepped over it and made for the door to the veranda. A second burst was unnecessary, the guests had precipitately fled. Several chairs had been overturned, others still had men's jackets hanging from them. He searched one and found a car key. When he pressed the unlocking button the lights flashed on a white BMW. That would suffice him for a quick getaway. He would steal another car as soon as he got the chance.

He went back into the house, avoiding the pool of blood in the passage, and returned to the room with the rocking chair. As he stowed the Kalashnikov in the blue sports bag, which he had left there, he was shaken by a brief fit of coughing. The receiver was lying on the floorboards, the mouthpiece end slightly raised by the elastic cable. He bent down and picked it up.

✖️

Someone had coughed! A hollow, murderous bark. The killer was still there. Clemencia said, 'Listen to me!'

'Hang up!' Robinson hissed. 'Our South African colleagues … '

They must be alerted urgently. They had to cordon off the crime scene, set up roadblocks at once, right away! Clemencia listened. She couldn't hear any more coughing or faint breathing.

77

She couldn't hear a thing, but she knew he was there. He was down there down in KwaZulu-Natal, standing beside Staal Burger's dead body with the receiver to his ear. She said, 'I'm Detective Inspector Clemencia Garises of Windhoek. I suppose you wouldn't care to introduce yourself, would you?'

Robinson was keying a number into his mobile.

'You've no need to tell me your name,' she went on. 'We'll find it out anyway. But I'd like to know one thing … '

'Enquiries?' Robinson whispered. 'The number of the police in Hluhluwe, South Africa, quick as you can!'

'Why?' asked Clemencia. 'Why this bloodbath?'

'Hluhluwe, H–L–U–H–L–U–W–E, South Africa,' Robinson said urgently.

'Why now?' asked Clemencia. 'Twenty years after Lubowski's death?'

The killer was there. She could sense his presence, sense the sweat on the hand that was holding the receiver. She had somehow to coax the man out of his shell – provoke him sufficiently to elicit a reaction, be it only a sarcastic laugh. She wanted to know what someone sounded like when they'd just shot someone.

'Why ask me to spell it if you … ' Robinson's voice rose. 'Then kindly connect me with International Directory Enquiries!'

Should she try to fool the killer? She could claim that van Zyl had survived the attack. She could ask, derisively, if he wouldn't like to come back and finish the job. Maybe he should get hold of a field gun if he wasn't capable of nailing someone with a Kalashnikov at twenty metres …

She said, 'I can't imagine murdering three people, myself, but I know you had a reason. A better reason than revenge. Or was it something that left you no choice?'

'I'm in a queue!' Robinson said grimly. 'It's enough to … Ah, at last!'

'Maybe we'll never catch you,' said Clemencia. 'But maybe our

78

South African colleagues will shoot you in the next ten minutes. Maybe I'm the last person you'll ever speak to. Your last chance to tell someone the truth.'

She heard her voice die away, waited for some response, some reaction – anything at all. Then came a faint click.

'Can you hear me?' she asked. The silence sounded different now. She'd been cut off. The killer had replaced the receiver on the cradle. Slowly, carefully. She felt she could see the phone with his eyes. She debated, with him, whether he should wipe off his finger-prints. No, he didn't care about that. It was unimportant.

'H–L–U–H–L–U–W–E,' Robinson recited with barely suppressed indignation.

'He'd have been a fool to answer in any case, boss,' said van Wyk. Clemencia nodded although she didn't altogether agree. The killer *had* reacted. She didn't think it purely fortuitous that he had hung up when she asked him for the truth. He wasn't a contract killer who did other people's dirty work for money. No, he had a motive of importance to him personally – one he considered to be no one else's business, least of all that of the police. Perhaps because it weighed on him so heavily that he didn't want to be confronted with it?

This was all speculation, of course. And, even if it was, it was totally unproductive now. Robinson was right to urge the Hluhluwe police to lose no time. Of course they must examine the crime scene. They should not only examine every last inch of it for clues but set up roadblocks first. Seal the place off, secure every farm track. The murder was only ten minutes old. The killer had been in the house two minutes ago, so he couldn't have gone far. They didn't have any men to spare? In that case, they should call out the fire brigade, the local rugby team – even, as far as he, Robinson, was concerned, the church choir! It was immensely important …

'They hung up.' Robinson couldn't believe it. 'They simply hung up!'

79

'If we're lucky,' said van Wyk, 'they'll send one miserable patrol car to Burger's house.'

'If they possess one,' Robinson growled. He pressed the redial key. Clemencia spoke to their South African colleagues this time, but all she could elicit was a vague assurance that they would take the requisite steps. An hour-and-a-half later came the confirmation that Staal Burger was dead. At least ten rounds in the chest and stomach region. They knew which car the perpetrator had used for his getaway and were in the process of setting up roadblocks. There was still no news three hours later. The killer had escaped.

Clemencia took a taxi to Katutura. When she opened the garden gate, half the family came out to meet her. That was unusual.

'Has something happened?' she demanded. She had been expecting more bad news ever since Melvin's punch-up.

Miki Matilda peered up and down the street. 'Didn't he bring you home again?' she asked.

'Who?'

'Why, the fair-haired German boy.' Miki Matilda winked at her and giggled delightedly.

'*Must* you go with a white?' asked Miki Selma.

'Why not?' Miki Matilda protested loudly. 'Whites are human too. There are as many decent types and scoundrels among them as there are with us.'

'Did you go to the cinema together?' asked Jessica.

'You, go inside! You're far too young for this sort of thing.' Miki Selma readdressed herself to Clemencia. 'Just because he's fair-haired and tall and worships you, that doesn't mean you should — '

'I could fancy him myself!' screeched Miki Matilda.

'Hands off the fresh meat, you old witch!' called their female neighbour from across the way.

Jessica plucked at Clemencia's sleeve. 'Did you kiss each other when it got dark?'

'Jessica!' Miki Selma swiped at her and missed.

'You're crazy, the lot of you,' said Clemencia. 'As if I hadn't got enough problems … '

Jessica tittered.

Miki Matilda burst out laughing.

Miki Selma opined that a little self-restraint wouldn't come amiss. The beginning was one thing and the end another, as the proverb so aptly put it.

Their neighbour across the street warbled a song in the Oshiwambo dialect, its lyric consisting mainly of words like 'love-sick' and 'bliss'.

✳✳✳

Donkerkop:

It was the night of 12 September 1989. I was behind the wheel with Acheson and his AK-47 beside me. Chappies Maree and Ferdi Barnard were in the back armed with automatics. Van Zyl and Staal Burger weren't there. Their job was to phone us as soon as Lubowski left his office. Until then we waited in the entrance to a vacant lot a few hundred metres from Lubowski's house on the luxury residential hill facing south. The sun had already gone down in the west, behind Khomas Highland.

Acheson had rented the red Toyota Conquest from a car hire firm. Hardly a James Bond motor, I remarked, and Ferdi Barnard gave me an irritating lecture on the importance of being inconspicuous. We weren't in a goddamned action movie, he said, but in sleepy old Windhoek, where a Jaguar or a Porsche would stand out like a —

'I get you,' I told him. 'I was only joking.'

'But it wasn't funny,' said Barnard. 'This is no time for jokes, man. It's deadly serious!'

I shut up. Maree was chewing gum and staring out of the window, Acheson constantly fiddling with his Kalashnikov. He was a madman on ten times more intimate terms with guns than with any human being. Ferdi Barnard was the only one who spoke. He kept blathering at me from the

81

back seat. You couldn't afford to make any mistakes in a business like this. Total concentration was essential. You shouldn't think of anything but the job, in fact you shouldn't think at all. You and the job must be one – so close you couldn't get a cigarette paper between them.

'You are *the job,' Barnard told me. 'Right, Chappies?'*

'Uh-huh,' Maree grunted.

'I get it,' I said.

'I get it, says the youngster!' Barnard laughed. 'What d'you mean, you get it? How often have you done anything like this, eh?' He appealed to the others. 'The boy acts as if he'd won at least two world wars single-handed. We have to be able to rely on you.'

'You can,' I said. My job was to drive the car, and drive it I would. Barnard was getting on my nerves.

'Rely on you at all times,' he persisted. 'Now and tomorrow and in ten years' time. You realize what'll happen if you start blubbing after the event? If you go running to a priest or confide in anyone else?'

'I'm no traitor, man,' I said.

'I'll tell you what you are, boy,' said Barnard. 'You're wet. The kind that shoots his mouth off first and then tucks his tail in. Know why someone turns traitor? Do you? Tell him, Chappies!'

'You tell him,' said Maree.

'Either because he gets a shedload of money for it, or because he's a crybaby. And you're a crybaby!'

'Get stuffed,' I said, but Barnard kept bad-mouthing me, trying to make me look ridiculous, drag me in the dirt. Coward, loudmouth, greenhorn, mummy's boy, weakling, et cetera. He went on and on at me. I didn't know why he was acting like that, nor did I wonder at the time, or I'd probably have thought it was his way of dealing with tension.

I realized only later that every word was carefully calculated to soften me up for what they had in mind for me. And it worked a treat. I wasn't to get a chance to think clearly, and I didn't. I was so strung up, I shouted at Barnard over my shoulder – told him they could do their own dirty work without me if he didn't put a sock in it.

82

'What did I tell you, Chappies?' Barnard's voice dripped with scorn. 'The boy wants to bail out before it even starts. What d'you think he'll do when the blood starts flowing? He'll shit himself. If he can manage to put the car into first gear, he'll drive straight to the police and moan that he didn't want any part of this.'

'He won't bail out,' said Maree. 'He won't bail out, you'll see.'

'I've seen better men than him throw up,' said Barnard.

'Shut your trap!' I yelled at him over my shoulder.

Acheson cocked the AK-47 and told the others to pipe down. He was a madman, as I say, and capable of anything. Even Barnard had a healthy respect for him. All he did after that was mutter unintelligibly to himself or utter sudden giggles between times. When I looked in the rear-view mirror he would be grinning stupidly. That infuriated me even more. Then came the call from Burger and van Zyl. It could be only minutes before Lubowski arrived home. I started the engine and was about to take off, tyres squealing, when Chappies Maree said, 'Hang on!'

He wound the window down, spat out his wad of gum and promptly replaced it with another. Then he dumped an automatic on my lap. 'The safety catch is off,' he said.

'What am I to do with it?' I asked.

'You never know,' said Maree.

'Mind you don't shoot your balls off, man,' Barnard said from behind me. 'If you've got any, that is!'

✵✿✵

Robinson was in a state of high excitement. His face was even redder than usual, and he kept saying he'd caught the killer. He was a hundred per cent certain – he had a gut feeling about it. It was almost weird, the way everything fitted so perfectly.

The man had been arrested while trying to enter Namibia by way of Ariamsvlei. A Kalashnikov had been found in his luggage.

He had guessed that the killer would return at once after murdering Burger, Robinson boasted. That was why he had alerted

the southern frontier posts, and they had notified him immediately. He had moved heaven and earth to get the suspect flown to
Windhoek the same night in Namibia's only police helicopter.

'But how did the man get to the frontier from KwaZulu-Natal
so quickly?' Clemencia asked.

'We'll find that out in due course,' Robinson told her. He
had already ascertained that the suspect had worked as a guard
for Proforce, the predecessor of Group 4 Securicor, seven years
earlier. The firm had fired him after he'd been accused, though not
convicted, of diamond smuggling. He also had no alibi worthy of
the name for any of the killings. It hadn't yet been established that
his Kalashnikov was the murder weapon. The ballistics report was
still awaited.

'Any connection with the CCB agents?' asked Clemencia.

'We'll find that out too,' said Robinson. 'I guarantee it.'

She followed him into the interview room. The suspect was a
weedy little man in ragged clothing. An Angolan. He was sitting
slumped on his chair and looked exhausted. You couldn't tell a
murderer from his face, but Clemencia doubted if this man was
capable of the ice-cold determination required to execute three
people. He looked more like someone who tried to muddle along
through life and knew from experience that he would always fall flat
on his face. She wondered if, twenty years from now, her brother
Melvin would be confronting some police inspector in the same
down-at-heel condition.

'How are you doing?' she asked.

'I just don't know what you want with me,' the little man said.
He spoke English with a Portuguese accent.

'Have you contacted a lawyer?'

'A lawyer?'

Robinson grinned. 'He hasn't asked for one. Anyway, talking
one-to-one is better. More productive, too.'

Talking would be useless. The man not only knew nothing

but had probably done nothing of interest to the Serious Crime Unit, even a blind man could see that. 'As far as I'm concerned,' Clemencia whispered to Robinson, 'you can carry on until the ballistics report comes in, but I'll tell you one thing: If you try to beat something out of him – if you so much as lay a finger on him – I'll put you behind bars till you turn black.'

'Not me!' Robinson said indignantly. It wasn't entirely clear whether he was referring to her ban on the third degree or the prospect of turning black.

In the room next door Tjikundu was running through the list of purchasers of 7.62 mm cartridges. There remained a handful of men who couldn't be definitely excluded from suspicion, but none of them smelt like a winner. Van Wyk was seated beside Tjikundu, typing a report on the murders of van Zyl and Maree, which the police in Hluhluwe had requested. He proposed to relieve Robinson after that. He'd fled the office he shared with Angula. Self-defence, he explained.

Clemencia saw what he meant when she went to investigate. Angula was squatting on his heels with his back to the wall. Not only were both desks piled high with files, but the whole floor was strewn with countless documents. A couple of beaten tracks were all that enabled him to get to the furthest mounds of paper. The room was sweltering, but the window had to remain shut. If someone were thoughtless enough to open the door – Angula looked up at Clemencia disapprovingly – the draught would blow his files all over the place and disrupt their careful arrangement.

Clemencia surveyed the chaotic scene. 'These files aren't your personal property, Angula.'

'There's some interesting stuff in them,' said Angula, 'but what's almost more interesting is the stuff that *isn't* in them.'

'For instance?'

'For instance, how Donald Acheson came to be arrested the very day after the murder. The police must have got the idea that

85

he might have shot Lubowski. Apparently, Acheson's landlady informed them that he'd left the house on the night of the murder carrying a heavy object in a plastic bag. She'd thought it was a car jack, but she couldn't, looking back, exclude the possibility that it was a Kalashnikov. That's the only thing remotely resembling a piece of evidence. But no one can tell me that *that* was how they got on to Acheson. Why did they promptly report his arrest to the press on the strength of such slender evidence? The fact that he worked for the CCB wasn't public knowledge at the time. No one even knew of the CCB's existence.'

'And what do you infer from that?'

'The police had been tipped off by someone. However, I can't believe that the CCB cronies he hung around with all the time would have tried to get rid of him that way. It was obvious that they themselves would immediately become a police target. Which they did. But if ... '

Angula picked up a stack of documents, aligned the pages carefully, and replaced them neatly on the floor.

'Well, go on.'

'If someone quite different shot Lubowski, the whole thing suddenly makes sense. Even before the police have gained the least idea of what is really going on, someone presents them with a murderer on a plate, a former Rhodesian mercenary who can readily be credited with the killing. The world and his wife are horrified by a murder that could severely compromise the peaceful transition to independence, and now comes this swift and successful manhunt! Nobody thinks twice about it. No, the police gratefully accept their gift and work hard to get Acheson and Co. convicted. Nobody thinks of looking in any other directions and the real killers rub their hands.'

Clemencia crouched down until they were at eye-level. Angula's face was as expressionless as ever.

'Angula, what case are we working on at present?'

86

'What?' said Angula.

'Our current case,' she said. 'Three murders. January 2009!'

'January 2009.' Angula nodded. 'And the real killers are still rubbing their hands.'

This was a total digression on his part. They'd assumed that the CCB people had been murdered for having killed Lubowski. If they weren't guilty there was no motive for their murder and, thus, no good reason to delve into events that occurred in the last century. Not now, at any rate. Not while a killer was at large with a Kalashnikov. Later on, they could always …

Angula started to hum the opening bars of *Land of the Brave,* the Namibian national anthem.

'Angula?' said Clemencia.

Angula stopped humming. 'The tune originated at Anton Lubowski's funeral.'

'What do you mean?'

' … "whose blood waters our freedom … "', said Angula, quoting a line from the anthem. 'Nations are born in blood, just like babies. The difference is, a nation's blood isn't so easily washed off. It clings and clings and — '

'I want the murderer of van Zyl, Maree and Staal Burger, nothing else!' said Clemencia.

Angula looked at her dispassionately.

'Is that understood?'

'Yes, boss,' he said, and readdressed himself to his mountains of files.

She would have to keep an eye on Angula, Clemencia told herself. Not only on him but on Robinson's interrogation methods, and Oshivelo's tendency to control the direction of their enquiries, and the switchboard's habit of neglecting to pass on emergency calls for several hours, and Melvin's brushes with the law, and the safety of her nephew Timothy and her niece Jessica. And, and, and … It was all a bit much. Her office was swelteringly hot although she flung the door and windows open. The air streaming in might have been issuing from a hair-dryer.

To plunge into cold water, to submerge, to swim a length or two – that would be just the job right now! She had meant to go to the municipal baths two weeks ago, but in vain. The superintendent hadn't turned up for duty, so the gates had remained locked for safety reasons. Clemencia thought of Finland, of indoor swimming pools whose superintendents were always on the premises, of ice-bound lakes, of endless, snowy expanses and of having to scrape the frost off your windscreen in the mornings. She would grant herself just a moment, just five minutes in which to return, at least in spirit, to the cold, far-off land where people took as long to thaw out as the countryside after the interminable winter.

Not that she would have wanted to live there. Home is where your dead lie buried, her father had told her once. Her mother lay buried in Katutura cemetery. In the baking, sandy soil, in the parched, sun-scorched 'land of the brave'. Although she had rebuffed him, she couldn't get Angula's remark out of her head. Nations are born in blood like babies. But Namibia was already grown up and would celebrate its nineteenth birthday on March 23rd. Wasn't it time to forget its labour pains, its sacrifices?

Or was Angula right after all? Was the country still haunted by the shades of the past? Wasn't it intolerable that those who had stained their hands with blood should be rubbing those same hands with satisfaction? Home was where your dead lay buried. Anton Lubowski also lay buried in Katutura cemetery, probably not far from her mother. No one had ever investigated *her* death. Her mother had just been an ordinary woman hit by a random bullet. No shelves of files existed on the subject, no enquiries had ever been conducted. A company of South African soldiers whose names no one knew, an unlucky ricochet, a shrug of the shoulders, and that was that.

The phone might have been ringing for a while before Clemencia heard it. Lawyer von Fleckenstein reminded her that he had put up 250 dollars' bail. Then Miki Selma called, having probably spent the money she'd collected for Melvin on recharging her mobile. She only wanted to ask how Clemencia was. And that tall, fair-haired white man – what was his name again? When she proceeded to add that she'd just seen a TV appeal to use condoms, Clemencia hung up.

The phone rang again at once. It was wellnigh miraculous that the South African policeman had got through to her at all. He said he'd already called three times, only to be informed by the switchboard operator that Clemencia was out, but that his request for a return call would naturally be passed on to her as soon as she returned. It had evidently been too much trouble to fob him off a fourth time, so he'd finally been put through.

Clemencia naturally assumed he was calling about Staal Burger's murder, but the detective knew nothing about that. He was based in Pretoria, Gauteng Province, not in KwaZulu-Natal.

'So how did you come to get in touch with me?' she asked.

It transpired that he played for the same rugby club as a colleague from Bloemfontein, who was working on Clemencia's request for a DNA comparison with Chappies Maree. That was how he had learned of the two murders in Namibia.

'And now that Ferdi Barnard, the third of the former CCB agents, has been found dead in Pretoria Prison, I thought it would be a good idea to make enquiries. Fortunately, because the Burger business fits like a — '

'What?! Ferdi Barnard has been murdered in jail?'

'It looks like suicide, at least at first sight,' said the South African policeman. 'His sheet was torn into strips and knotted together. If anyone helped Barnard to hang himself with it, the only person who qualifies under the circumstances is his cellmate. A certain Thomas Khawuta, a man with multiple convictions for robbery and murder. Ever come across the name?'

Clemencia replied in the negative. However, she said, whether murder or suicide, it was more than strange that Barnard's death had coincided with her own two cases and Burger's execution.

'Yes indeed,' said the South African. 'And there's something stranger still. The last visitor Barnard saw before he died came from Namibia. His name was ... just a minute.' Clemencia heard a rustle of paper, then his deep voice came over the line again. ' ... Hendrik Fourie.'

'What?!' Clemencia couldn't believe her ears.

'Fourie, a judge. He visited Barnard on official business.'

'He isn't a judge any more, he's been retired for some time,' said Clemencia. What business could Fourie have had with Barnard?

'Retired, eh? Anyway, you know the man. All the better. We'd like to ask him some questions. The thing is, Barnard buttonholed a warder after Fourie's visit – said the judge had threatened him with a violent death. No one took it seriously, of course. Not until he really did die a few hours later. Don't get me wrong, we're not making any imputations against this judge of yours ... '

'Ex-judge,' said Clemencia.

' ... we'd merely be interested in knowing what really went on between him and Barnard.'

So would she, thought Clemencia. Keenly interested.

'Unfortunately, Meneer Fourie was in something of a hurry to leave our delightful country. If I'd got through to you a little sooner, you might have been able to catch him at Windhoek Airport.'

'I'll keep you informed,' Clemencia promised. She made a note of the South African's phone number, hung up, and immediately called Fourie's farm. The housekeeper told her that the judge had got home a quarter of an hour ago. He was having a shower at present. Was it very urgent?

'No, no,' said Clemencia. 'I'll call again later.'

She tried to enlist Angula, but he asked her to take someone else. There were a few documents he simply had to look through, and ... Clemencia stormed out. Robinson was still questioning the

Angolan, van Wyk was nowhere to be found. That left Tjikundu.

'Take your gun and come with me,' she said. Although Hendrik Fourie had seemed anything but dangerous on her first visit, she would now have felt uneasy about confronting him on her own.

✖❖✖

The table was a discarded camping table whose defective hinges had been splinted with two lengths of battening. There were some plastic plates lying on it. He swept them on to the floor with his forearm and put his blue sports bag on the scratched Formica table top. Then he counted out the money in batches of ten 100-rand notes. He coughed, averting his head.

Mandisa Khawuta was standing two metres away, watching in silence. She had her arms around her children and was hugging them to her, two on the left, two on the right, as if to protect them from something. Or as if to convey that they all belonged together for ever more, come what might. That was nonsense, of course, but he wasn't here to explain the way of the world to a Xhosa family: a woman and four children whose fate interested him neither more nor less than that of some stupid Boers. He had a business transaction to complete, that was all.

He had heard the report of Barnard's death on television at the bus station. The accompanying pictures had included Pretoria Central Prison's frontage seen through its two security fences. The open spaces between them provided a field of fire for the guards stationed in the concrete towers above the façade. The flat roof was enclosed by a high, latticework fence. The windows were also barred, of course.

The inmates were guarded more closely than any head of state. Not a chance of breaking out or in. Still, anyone could die anywhere. One place was as good as another. Death took whomever it chose wherever it chose.

'Brother ... ' the woman said hesitantly.

He put a finger to his lips. Whatever she was trying to say, he didn't want to hear it. He quickly counted the piles on the table. Twenty-six, twenty-seven, twenty-eight. Another two thousand rand to go. He was just a messenger.

'Thomas, my husband – he always was a bastard,' the woman said. 'Never troubled to get a job, lounged around, drank, beat me and the children whenever he felt like it.'

He coughed as he counted out ten more hundreds. He was the messenger of death. It was no business of his what other people liked or disliked about their lives. He was the angel who looked in briefly from the hereafter, like a dark shadow. And sometimes, inexplicably, he brought light into wretched corrugated-iron shacks. The idea pleased him.

'I'd never have thought Thomas would do this for us,' said the woman. He felt sorry for her suddenly.

'Listen,' he said. 'They'll come. They'll ask you how you got rich so suddenly. They'll put two and two together, take the money away from you and confiscate it as evidence.'

He put the last thousand rand on the table and eyed the squalor around him. The tattered mattresses on the mud floor, the bag of maize flour beside the plastic can full of murky water, the upturned plywood crates that served as chairs. Taking two paces forwards, he kicked down a sheet of corrugated iron sandwiched between two posts driven into the ground. The light of the setting sun flooded in. He said, 'Perhaps you ought to take the money and your children and push off before they get here.'

❊❂❊

To hear the farmers talk, it was high time the rains came at last. Decent rain, too, not just a few measly drops that would be sucked up into the parched air before they even had a chance to soak into the soil. Thick grey clouds were needed, the floodgates of heaven had to open and send down a regular deluge. It would have to rain for a week or two, so the grass began to sprout and the yellow morgensterns flowered and the cattle and game had something to eat.

Desperation and superstition proliferated with every day that passed without a downpour. Farmers put their reliance on allegedly infallible portents of the end of the drought. Wasn't that the call of Diederich's cuckoo, the rain bird par excellence? Or was it more significant that toads were croaking everywhere? Many people thought it quite certain that the first full moon of the new year would bring a turning point, especially since it had displayed a clearly visible halo in the last few nights. If all else failed, you could still pin your hopes on the Kaiser's birthday, January 27th, always provided you were an old-established 'South-Wester' of German stock who secretly dreamed in black, white and red.

But even when it did rain at last, nothing had been gained. That was because – as any farmer would readily confirm – the rain always fell on neighbouring farms while a curse seemed to lie over your own. Logically speaking, therefore, it rained nowhere when it rained. One could only wonder that farms existed at all, and that kudu, oryx and springbok hadn't become extinct ages ago.

'Talking of springbok ... ' Judge Fourie asked his housekeeper to bring their visitors from the police a little of her home-smoked dried venison, then prattled gaily on. About the lateness of the rains. About the lamentations of his neighbours, who had been farming their land for generations but still hadn't come to terms with the fact that it was semi-desert, not the lush meadows of Ostfriesland or the foothills of the Bavarian Alps.

Tjikundu was seated a little to one side, nursing his glass of iced tea in both hands. The barefooted boy had perched on the balustrade of the veranda and was watching him intently. His sister was nowhere to be seen, but he'd opened the gate for Clemencia as before, eyes shining as if he knew for sure that she'd come for his sake alone. Once he'd noticed that Tjikundu was wearing a holster with a genuine pistol in it, however, Clemencia had become secondary. Initially at a loss to cope with the boy's undisguised admiration, Tjikundu had adopted a studiously cool and nonchalant manner worthy of John Wayne. This accorded with his function, because Clemencia had impressed on him that he must remain in the background and leave things to her.

So far, however, she had done nothing, just listened calmly to Fourie's monologue. The time had come, though. Fourie had had long enough to straighten out a few things in his mind. She'd given him enough rope. After all, he knew what enquiries she was engaged in and couldn't behave as if it were of no interest to her that he'd visited Ferdi Barnard. When he drew breath, she asked, 'How was South Africa?'

'Too many people, too much traffic, too noisy. Still, at least it rained there, and — '

'Did you go to KwaZulu-Natal as well?'

'Pretoria was quite enough for me.'

'Were you visiting friends?'

'Friends? More of an acquaintance, but — '

'Meneer Fourie,' she said, 'I want to know every word you exchanged with Ferdi Barnard.'

The old judge looked taken aback for a moment. Then he smiled. He put out his right hand and picked up the kitchen knife the housekeeper had brought with the smoked game. Tjikundu put his iced tea down on the balustrade. His gun was still in its holster. The barefooted boy was staring at it spellbound, probably itching to ask him if he could fire it sometime. Fourie proceeded to carve the almost black meat across the grain, producing slices so thin they were almost transparent. His hand was quite steady.

'Well,' he said, 'when I learned that Maree and van Zyl had been murdered, and when we spoke of Lubowski, those old stories suddenly came back to life in my mind. The unresolved case, my frustration, my decisions and omissions – all those things went round and round in my head again. Just as I had years ago, I wondered if it was my fault that the investigation had come to nothing, and it suddenly occurred to me that searching for the truth sometimes requires persistence. It may sound odd, but the death of those two former agents has rekindled the flames. The Lubowski murder is back on the agenda, and not from my point of view alone. If two of those involved have been killed, the third might possibly — '

'Meneer Fourie,' Clemencia broke in, 'you're retired! Why on earth — '

'Quite so,' said Fourie. 'I simply don't know what to do with my time, and a brief trip to South Africa wouldn't break the bank. I called a former colleague in Pretoria. He assured me that obtaining a visitor's permit would present no problem. He arranged it at once – told me simply to turn up at the prison. So I promptly packed my bag.'

Fourie deposited the knife on the table and made a gesture of invitation. Tjikundu helped himself to some smoked venison. The boy did likewise, imitating his every movement. Clemencia shook her head. 'What did Barnard say?' she asked.

'Nothing, he laughed in my face. Said he'd never heard of Lubowski, or Chappies Maree, or Slang van Zyl – said he didn't even know any Ferdi Barnard, not any more.' Fourie seemed quite calm. Tjikundu took another two slices of meat and handed one to the boy beside him.

'And then?' said Clemencia.

'And then? He asked to be taken back to his cell and I left.'

Clemencia nodded. 'And now, joking apart, what really happened?'

'What do you mean?'

'What have you to do with Barnard's death?'

'Eh?'

'Oh, you didn't know that he was found hanged on the night of your visit?'

Fourie didn't reply. Strange for such a voluble talker – at least where farmers and the rainy season were concerned. Clemencia said quietly, 'Before he died, Barnard complained to the prison staff that you'd made death threats against him.'

Fourie leant forwards as if about to spring to his feet. The knife was lying beside the wooden board with the meat on it. Tjikundu stopped chewing. His hand went to his holster. Fourie sat back again. 'This is quite absurd,' he said.

'How do you account for Barnard's accusation?' Clemencia demanded.

'Under these circumstances,' Fourie said stiffly, 'I see no point in continuing this conversation,'

He was no different from the rest of Clemencia's customers. The truth was fine as long as it didn't affect you too closely. When someone started sniffing your own stench, you got on your high horse and didn't think, circumstances being what they were, that there was any point in uttering another word.

'We were going anyway.' Clemencia rose. Tjikundu looked regretfully at the remaining slices of smoked venison but didn't venture to help himself to another. Clemencia said, 'I'm afraid I must ask you to come with us, Meneer Fourie.'

Fourie laughed aloud. 'You mean to arrest me?'

Yes, she did. Why not? Just because he had a white skin, had been a judge, and could doubtless mobilize a lot of influential friends? 'Yes,' she said, 'on suspicion of instigating Ferdi Barnard's murder.'

'You can't be serious,' said Fourie.

'Deadly serious.'

'You'll have problems.'

'Possibly.'

'No, not possibly. Assuredly!'

'All right, assuredly,' said Clemencia. 'Would you like to pack a few things before we leave?'

Fourie said it wasn't worth it, he would be released at once in any case. He wanted to make a short phone call. Clemencia signed to Tjikundu to escort him into the house. The barefooted boy remained on the veranda with her. She smiled at him, but he shook his head and said, 'Meneer Fourie is the *baas*!'

He didn't even sound reproachful, just surprised that Clemencia didn't realize this. If she did, she would never have taken it into her head to arrest him: the *baas*, who fed everyone on the farm, who decided what happened, whose word was law, and on whom everyone and everything depended!

Clemencia crouched down, gripped the boy by his shoulders, and explained that everyone was equal before the law: he himself, his mother, Meneer Fourie. They were all human beings and citizens with the same rights and obligations. This was extremely important. Many people had spent decades fighting for it, and quite a few had even died for it. He must never forget that.

The boy pursed his lips. She only hoped he had understood. Fourie was standing beside her when she straightened up. She indicated the car beneath the cypress tree. Tjikundu went on ahead and opened the passenger door. Before following him, Fourie stroked the boy's head and said, 'Do your maths homework. I'll be back soon.'

Lawyer von Fleckenstein was already waiting for them when they got to police headquarters in Windhoek. Leaning against his old Mercedes, he informed Fourie that, in view of the special circumstances, the magistrate had agreed to look in that evening. He, Fleckenstein, would stay there until the detective inspector had made out her charge sheet. He would then call the magistrate, and the matter would be settled in fifteen minutes flat. He turned to Clemencia. 'If it isn't one thing, it's another. You really take the biscuit.'

'I don't know if we'll manage to make out the charge sheet today,' Clemencia told him. 'To the best of my knowledge, we have twenty-four hours in which to do that.'

Von Fleckenstein tittered. The whole thing seemed to tickle him immensely. Tjikundu conducted Fourie to the Serious Crime Unit's offices on the second floor, where he would take him to the interview room and keep him waiting for a while. Clemencia realized that she didn't have much firm evidence against the former judge. She would have to release him no later than tomorrow, but at least he would have to stew overnight like any other detainee.

Matti Jurmela in far-off Helsinki would have condemned this as unprofessional, adding, after a short pause, that what mattered was doing your job to the best of your ability, not your principles. That was undoubtedly right, except that Namibia wasn't Finland but a young country where little barefoot boys still believed that their *baas* could never be arrested simply because he was their *baas*.

Clemencia said hello to some colleagues from the Commercial Crime Unit, who were just knocking off for the day. They crossed Bahnhofstrasse and congregated around the hot food stall in the car park. Beer cans reposed in a plastic tub of water that had probably once been ice, and morsels of meat were sizzling on the grill. The chili sauce in which you dipped them was a luminous red, but that might have been the effect of the evening sunlight. The sky was cloudless.

✵⊛✵

Judge Hendrik Fourie (ret.):

Although I wasn't expecting to be arrested by the police, I would not, even if I had been able to see into the future, have behaved at all differently. The question is not whether you're prepared to take a risk, but whether your own intention makes it worth accepting its worst possible outcome. If your answer is yes – and mine was – your only choice is to intervene.

That actions have consequences which are laid down in accordance with a certain scope for discretion, and are thus foreseeable, is a principle of criminal justice. Those who murder people know what they're in for. There must be no exceptions. Not only for the sake of the victims and their dependants, not only because of some ideal of justice, but because it would invalidate a rule which, although quite simple, is essential to human coexistence: those who say A must also say B. If they don't say it themselves, it must be said to them – unmistakably. Otherwise, everything goes to pot.

Of course, neither police nor public prosecutors are gods. They often grope in the dark, and sometimes, for all their efforts, they fail to root out a guilty party. That is bad enough, but it doesn't cast doubt on the foundations of the law. Which is precisely what happens when, as in the case of Lubowski's murder, the perpetrators are known by name and their motives and actions can be reconstructed – all acts of sabotage notwithstanding – yet no consequences of any kind ensue.

Yes, I said acts of sabotage. Did you know that a kind of operational log was found in which the activities of CCB Regional Group 6 were meticulously recorded? In 1994, when this piece of evidence came into my hands, precisely two pages were missing. What the first referred to is unclear, but the second was that of 12 September 1989, the day on which Anton Lubowski was shot. Attempts were made to persuade me that the CCB itself had removed incriminating material. But why just two selected pages? Why not the whole lot, which testified to plenty of other abominable crimes on the unit's part? No, someone had deliberately sought to prevent the solution of the Lubowski case, and that someone was definitely not a member of the South African secret service.

Although I didn't sweep this or any other matters under the carpet at the time, I may not have been explicit enough. I certainly didn't proceed with sufficient vigour, either because I failed to realize the fundamental importance of the case, or because I feared the possible consequences for me personally. But that is fifteen years ago. I'm an old man now, and what one has to lose counts less and less with every passing year.

What does all this have to do with my visit to the prison in Pretoria? Well, I had decided to step in. I wanted to make up for what I'd neglected to do while still a practising judge. My concern was the truth, the whole truth and nothing but the truth, so I showed Ferdi Barnard some newspaper

99

cuttings about the murder of his two former cronies. I told him he was next on the death list and said his only chance of escaping with his life was to make a full and immediate confession – one in which every minute and every detail of 12 September 1989 was truthfully recorded, every accomplice and accessory identified by name, and all the underlying factors clarified.

'*Will I be killed if I tell you nothing?*' *Barnard asked.*

'*Yes,*' *I said.*

'*Does that mean you're responsible for the death of Maree and van Zyl, Your Honour?*' *he asked.*

'*Of course,*' *I told him, but he didn't believe me. I hadn't sounded credible enough.*

'*This man Lubowski, who exactly was he?*' *Barnard asked, and he laughed.*

✖

Clemencia would have liked just to sit down in front of the television. She would have tolerated the long-winded NBC news and watched patiently as some fuzzily photographed civil servant stated, in equally fuzzy language, that the aims of Vision 2030 must somehow be achieved. She would even have put up with Miki Matilda's inappropriate comments as long as no one addressed her directly. She wouldn't have cared when Constancia sent her children to bed, or if thudding kwaito music came drifting down the street from the Mshasho Bar, or if Melvin was getting drunk there. She yearned for a little normality, that was all, but the evening developed into one big disaster.

Even before she got back to Katutura, Claus Tiedtke called her on her mobile and asked if she knew someone named Selma. It seemed that this Selma had bearded him in the newsroom, allegedly at Clemencia's behest, and asked if he was a Catholic. No, he'd told her, he was a Lutheran. Although he had nothing whatsoever against other denominations, the question had struck him as rather odd.

It wasn't odd, it was a downright liberty.

Taking Miki Selma to task – indeed, even finding her – had proved quite difficult. Clemencia could hear uproarious laughter as she approached the house, and on opening the gate she found half the Holy Redeemer Parish's gospel choir crowded into the little front yard. Its members had evidently assembled there after a performance, because the women were still wearing their ankle-length burgundy surplices with the gold piping. The few men, who wore matching shirts, were sitting a little apart on the bench against the wall. The women were just discussing whether a bride had the sole right to determine her bridesmaids' outfits, especially if the latter had to bear the cost of them themselves. Conversation gradually died away when Clemencia was sighted.

'Hello, my dear,' called one of the older women, whose name she couldn't remember, perhaps because Miki Selma never called her anything but 'the Crow'. The two of them had quarrelled bitterly, at least until last week, over who should lead the choir. The Crow couldn't sing to save her life, according to Selma, which was why she should never be allowed to cross their doorstep. The vegetables would rot as soon as she opened her mouth.

'Back already, Clemencia?' asked another woman.

It was 9.30! Why shouldn't someone come home from work at that hour?

'Where's Selma?' she asked. The Crow pointed to the dark alleyway between the house and its outbuildings. Clemencia ducked under the awning that provided shade during the day. Embers were glowing in the sheltered barbecue near the second door. Beside it stood the big cast-iron *potjie,* which was empty save for a few smears of mealie porridge. The door on the left was open.

The television set was on inside, but no one was watching it. Miki Selma was presiding on one of the beds in her choral robe, surrounded by the rest of the family and the remaining half of the choir. She had a pencil in her hand and was scribbling in the margin of an advertising brochure. 'If we have six bridesmaids,' she was saying, 'we'll naturally need six ushers as well.'

'What's going on here?' Clemencia asked from the doorway.

'Nothing, nothing.' Miki Selma carefully folded up the brochure. It appeared to be advertising special offers from Woermann Brock.

'Well, I'm off,' said Melvin, trying to squeeze past Clemencia.

'For a drink?' she asked. It was a miracle he was still there.

'To work,' he said.

'At this hour?'

'Beggars can't be choosers these days.'

'What sort of work?' Clemencia demanded.

Her brother eyed the door frame. He thought for a moment, then grinned and said, 'Unloading stuff.'

'Melvin, I didn't get you out of a cell so you could ... ' Clemencia broke off. Some dozen female members of the Holy Redeemer gospel choir stared at her expectantly. She took her purse from her pocket, fished out a twenty-dollar note, and put it in Melvin's hand. 'All right, go and have a drink, but don't do anything stupid.'

Melvin withdrew. The female choristers remained silent until Miki Selma said she had a few more matters to discuss. Would Clemencia care to go and stretch her legs outside somewhere?

'Did you tell that reporter you'd come to see him at my sugges-tion ?' Clemencia demanded sharply.

'At your suggestion?' Miki Selma retorted indignantly. 'I never said any such thing.'

'It's about Clemencia, you said,' one of the other women put in.

'And it *was* about Clemencia. Someone has to look out for her.'

'Nobody has to look out for me, you least of all!' Clemencia hissed.

Miki Selma drew herself up to her full but inconsiderable height, folded her arms on her bosom, and said, 'Every lion has a right to roar in its lair, and this is still mine! Have a little more respect, girl!'

The gaggle of female choristers murmured approvingly.

Clemencia drew several deep breaths. Miki Selma was her aunt, her father's younger sister. She was a member of the family, a human being and consequently endowed with common sense. You could at least try to reason with her. Very calmly, Clemencia said, 'You can't just buttonhole a total stranger and ask him what his religion is!'

'You're making a fuss about nothing,' said Miki Selma.

'We asked the priest,' said someone else.

'You can only marry a Catholic,' a third woman chimed in.

'And promise to have your children baptized Catholics,' Miki Selma amplified contentedly.

Enough was more than enough! Clemencia turned on her heel, unlocked her door, went in and locked it from the inside. The room was like an oven. She tore off her clothes and flopped down on the bed. The window pane was vibrating in time to the bass notes from the Mshasho Bar. The choristers' giggles were clearly audible through the wall. Clemencia wondered whether to go back and announce that she was converting to Islam.

No, sarcasm was useless. She had to find a solution, a clear-cut, definite solution. She must look for a place of her own. Tomorrow, and preferably on the other side of town, in Avis or Kleine Kuppe. Family or not, she simply couldn't take it any more. Miki Selma was screeching with laughter. Clemencia clamped the pillow over her ears, but she heard her mobile ringing. It was Claus Tiedtke. He wanted to know if everything was all right, and whether she felt like going to the Blitzkrieg with him. 'Submission' were playing there, and it was bound to be a gas. She declined with thanks.

Nonetheless, the next morning found her feeling as if she'd spent the entire night in front of a heavy metal band's loudspeakers. She brewed herself a mug of rooibos tea and put a spoonful of sugar in it, then added another. Miki Selma, who had fried some eggs, brought her two unasked. After humming and hawing for a bit, she declared that everyone only had Clemencia's best interests at heart.

Clemencia refused to accept this peace offering. She picked up the plate, went back to her room, and looked up the number of an estate agent in the telephone directory. He merely laughed when he heard how much she could pay for a nice, quiet little flat a long way from Katutura. Never mind, she told herself. She would manage it sometime, even if she had to become some fat cat's kept woman!

My God, Miki Selma and her choristers had been seriously planning her wedding to a man she'd only set eyes on a couple of times. A man of whom all she knew was that his name was Claus, that he worked for the German-language newspaper and had skin the colour of fresh goat's cheese. But you *like* goat's cheese, Miki Matilda would have been bound to put in, cackling, and Clemencia would have said, yes, but only on a plate, not at the altar, and Miki Selma would have protested that the Sacraments were no joking matter, and then ...

Miki Selma put her head round the door and asked, very sweetly, if Clemencia would like some toast as well. Outside, Timothy was grumbling because he was being made to put a pair of shoes on and go shopping with his mother for some writing materials for the new school year. He wanted to watch Miki Matilda slaughter the chicken whose liver she needed to counteract the spell on her patient's house. Melvin was loudly asking to be left in peace. After all, he hadn't been arrested for burglary last night. Clemencia left the house as soon as she'd finished her fried eggs.

The neighbour across the street was singing as she hung up some washing. Her husband was just replacing the battery in the engine compartment of his old taxi. He'd been careful ever since one of the only two other cars within a wide radius was stolen. Being unable to afford an immobilizer, he removed the battery every night. Clemencia waited until he'd finished, then got him to drive her into town.

At headquarters, Robinson was still questioning the Angolan. Although ballistics had stated that his AK-47 was not the murder weapon, Robinson didn't trust their findings and had persuaded Oshivelo to order a fresh examination. Currently in a good cop phase, he steadfastly insisted on calling the suspect 'my friend' and offered him one cigarette after another. The Angolan was sitting on a plastic chair in the interview room, resigned to his fate.

But the retired judge had gone. Only persistent questioning enabled Clemencia discover that he had been released shortly after she left the night before. Tjikundu had had no choice. After two phone calls from von Fleckenstein, he had been instructed, pretty forcefully and by higher authority, to make out the charge sheet at once.

'Oshivelo?' Clemencia asked.

Tjikundu shook his head. 'Right from the top.'

The magistrate had skimmed the charge sheet and asked Fourie for his response to it. Fourie regretted threatening Barnard with murder, but stated that his perhaps somewhat drastic language had been motivated only by a wish to get to the bottom of the Lubowski case. The magistrate nodded, expressed no doubts, asked no questions. Crows didn't peck each other's eyes out, even when one was black and the other white.

Under those circumstances, it was only to be expected that Clemencia should receive a summons to report to her boss. Surprisingly, however, Oshivelo didn't haul her over the coals. He paced up and down his agreeably cool, air-conditioned office, invited her to take a seat, and glanced at her with paternal solicitude. She had rubbed higher authority up the wrong way, he said, but he was naturally behind her. However, he could have argued her case more easily if she'd informed him of the facts in good time. That a shot had been fired across Fourie's bows was – just between the two of them – perfectly in order. Where would they be if every old age pensioner thought it incumbent on himself to play the policeman? Still, enough was enough. Or did Clemencia propose to go on hounding Fourie?

'He knows all about the Lubowski case,' said Clemencia.

'So you still think our murders are connected to it?'

'More than ever. First van Zyl and Maree here, then Burger and Barnard in South Africa. Barnard had been in prison for the last ten years. That doesn't suggest he was involved in diamond smuggling or similar criminal activities.'

It didn't suggest, either, that he and his accomplices had been blackmailing the chief culprit. As long as Clemencia was groping in the dark for a confounded motive, it was all speculation.

'To the best of my knowledge,' said Oshivelo, 'Barnard killed himself, and not with a Kalashnikov. Besides, his death occurred in Pretoria, twelve hundred kilometres from Windhoek. We aren't responsible.'

'No. After all, we have enough murders of our own.'

'Exactly,' said Oshivelo. The sarcasm in Clemencia's tone seemed to have escaped him. For the past few days he had only seen things he wanted to see, and the Lubowski trail definitely wasn't one of them.

Clemencia rose. 'Do you believe in coincidences, chief?'

Oshivelo stroked his grey beard. Then he went over to the window and looked out, his bulky figure silhouetted against the dazzling glare. Without turning round, he said, 'Coincidences look bad when you're reconstructing an affair at a later point in time. That's because you know the beginning and the end and would like to proceed straight from one to the other. When you're in the middle of an affair, the end is still in doubt and many outcomes are possible. In such a situation, coincidences differ little from the causal connections that seem so logical in retrospect. Then, there are only events that lead us one step further into the darkness of the future – towards a conclusion of which we don't have the faintest idea.'

It struck Clemencia that Oshivelo had switched from the impersonal 'you' to 'we'. She would have liked to know exactly who he meant.

�֎

Ndangi Oshivelo, Deputy Commissioner of the Namibian police.

I think I knew Anton Lubowski pretty well, but I find it hard to say what he really was. At times he gave the impression of being a spoilt rich boy who courted death purely to combat his own boredom. On a few occasions I suspected him of gambling in a coolly calculating way. Any perceptive person could see that we would win in the end. Had Lubowski simply decided to back the right horse in good time?

Most days, however, he seemed to be suffused with positively unbridled idealism. Utterly consumed by words like freedom, justice and human dignity, he didn't care a jot that they came cheap in the airless confines of space. What mattered was to implement them in a world that already existed and reposed on quite different foundations. This necessitated not only lazy compromises but dirty tricks and ruthless action. That the means should match the end can be maintained only by someone who has no notion of politics, let alone of a nation's fight for independence.

We knew what we were doing when we sent guerrilla units across the Angolan frontier and into northern Namibia to attack South African positions there. Militarily, this was unimportant. We were sending our people to almost certain death just to show that we existed, that we were a power to be reckoned with. Ultimately, our men died so that SWAPO got another mention in the international press. Many people would call that cynical, but it was absolutely essential.

Although Lubowski thoroughly justified the armed struggle whenever he was interviewed — and he was forever being interviewed in his latter years — one sensed that he found the subject disagreeable and was simply unwilling to stab his comrades in the back. He was very much a fighter, but after his own fashion. I remember him telling me about a German stage play one night. It was about someone who wanted to translate the Bible and couldn't decide how to formulate the opening sentence. In the beginning was the word, the meaning, the strength, the act? I don't recall which variant Lubowski favoured — probably the word — but it's characteristic that what came at the beginning mattered to him at all. We were only interested in what emerged at the end.

Once, after a skirmish on the banks of the Kunene, we doctored the casualty figures in our press release. We had reports that one or two South Africans had been hit and turned them into four enemy dead and eleven wounded. Correspondingly, we adjusted our own casualties downwards. Lubowski asked if this was really necessary.

I think he genuinely believed that you could stick to the truth as long as you were on the right side. And by the truth he meant facts and figures, circumstances and causal connections. We didn't argue about it at the time, but I realized that this kind of truth could only be material. You had to sound it out to see if it served the higher truth that had to be fulfilled. But history isn't the same as all that has happened. If it can be recounted at all, it's always dependent on selection, interpretation and evaluation. What can't be recounted isn't history; it never happened.

Be that as it may, Lubowski dabbled in politics without being a politician. That is why he would have come to grief sooner or later — and sooner rather than later, I believe. Far be it from me to belittle his services to the cause. He got a considerable number of comrades out of jail, me included. He could sway people, he could organize, he raised any amount of money for us as deputy election campaign manager, he gained us attention and sympathy far beyond the borders of Namibia. He served our cause even by dying. I freely admit this, and I'm not ashamed to say so. And although it's unforgivable to deprive someone of his life by violent means, I sometimes think that Anton Lubowski died at the right time. Perhaps it was his destiny to be the last prominent martyr to shed his blood for independence.

3

FRONTIERS

Robinson yelled that he had plenty of time. More than enough, in fact. In the time at his disposal, the interviewee could theoretically crawl to Angola and back on all fours. But only theoretically, because if he failed to come clean at last, he wouldn't be going or crawling anywhere. Was that clear?

The suspect had doubtless heard all this, because Robinson shouted it loudly enough for every word to be clearly audible outside in the passage. Clemencia opened the door to the interview room. Robinson was leaning over the table, propped on his knuckles. The Angolan, who was cowering even lower on his plastic chair, looked as if he might sooner or later disappear into it.

Clemencia gave Robinson a warning glance. Robinson removed his fists from the table and displayed his upturned palms in a gesture expressive of innocence. He grinned, resumed his seat, crossed his legs and said, at normal volume, 'I've plenty of time.'

Clemencia shut the door and walked down the passage to her office. Claus Tiedtke was leaning against the wall outside. Smiling rather sheepishly, he explained that he'd tried to call her but her mobile had been turned off.

'How was the concert at the Blitzkrieg?' she asked.

He shrugged. 'I didn't feel like going on my own.'

Miki Selma would have welcomed that information, Clemencia felt sure. Men who hung around bars on their own needed watching. It was very gratifying that Claus Tiedtke was different, even though he needn't have been quite *that* different. There were some decent types even among the Damara menfolk. But hey,

Clemencia's choice had fallen on him and her wishes must naturally be respected. Stupidly, poor Claus Tiedtke still hadn't grasped that he was her future intended and that Miki Selma and her fellow choristers were probably busy choosing him a suitable best man at this very moment.

Clemencia must have smiled at the thought, or so she inferred from his own satisfied smile. So that he didn't imagine her smile was meant for him, she kicked open the door to her office and asked, over her shoulder, if he didn't have anything to do in his newsroom.

'Exceptional matters take priority,' he said. There would simply be one or two fewer news items and the pages would be filled with large-format rain pictures, which readers sent in by the hundred. Bonding with their readers was very important. If it wasn't raining, like now, a few nice holiday snaps from Swakopmund would also fill the bill. Tomorrow, for example, Clemencia would be able to admire two glorious sunsets, one looking over the jetty, the other with some children cavorting along the beach, and …

'What exceptional matter brings you here?' Clemencia asked.

'First and foremost, of course, the indelible impression you made on me — '

'Which naturally takes precedence over keeping the public informed.'

'Naturally.' Tiedtke grinned. 'Seriously, though, it's about Donald Acheson.'

'We've resolved that,' said Clemencia. She had no idea what had come of Tjikundu's investigation. Too much had happened in the meantime.

'I've found the witness who claims to have seen Acheson,' Tiedtke said.

'Really?' She gestured to him to enter the office. He put his hand on her back and gave her a little shove. Miki Matilda would have approved of this. A man was a man, not a dish rag, and had to assert himself sometimes. On the other hand, Miki Matilda would probably have said that the proof of whether a man could assert himself the way a woman liked did not take place purely in passing, but somewhere quite else. Clemencia grinned to herself.

She stopped grinning when Claus Tiedtke came out with his story. He had questioned the witness at great length. The man had shared a cell with Acheson for several weeks early in 1990. Although this didn't necessarily enhance his credibility, it did explain why he thought he'd recognized Acheson after nearly twenty years.

'Why?' asked Clemencia.

'The man was so scared of Acheson, he never took his eyes off him day or night. Acheson's movements, his walk, his gestures had etched themselves into his memory.'

'Go on.'

The witness had remembered the exact date of his recent encounter with Acheson, and Tiedtke had gone to Rosenthal Guns. He had persuaded the junior manager, a former classmate of his at the German private secondary school, to let him look at the books and noted down who had bought ammunition on the day in question. These names he had compared with the gun licences listed in central police records.

'How did you get to see them?'

'A journalist has connections. I made the young lady's acquaintance when I was researching an article and bumped into her few times after that.'

Probably because she had made such an indelible impression on him. Clemencia said, 'Anyway … '

'Anyway, there was only one person on my list to whom no gun licence had been issued. A man named James P. Doyle.'

Clemencia got the picture. In order to buy ammunition in Namibia, you had to show your gun licence. Anyone who applied for one had to have his fingerprints taken. All ten of them. Since Acheson's fingerprints had been on record since his arrest in 1989, he would have had to count on his second identity going up in smoke. So he had forged his licence, and that was why it wasn't registered.

Clemencia could also have arrived at that conclusion herself. She looked at Tiedtke. 'I'd be grateful,' she said, 'if this didn't appear in tomorrow's *Allgemeine Zeitung*.'

'Nothing but sunsets!' Tiedtke replied fervently. 'I won't write a word without your say-so.'

'Good. And the name was James P. Doyle?'

Tiedtke nodded silently, but Clemencia gathered that he wasn't quite through yet. His cheeks were flushed – not solely, she suspected, because of her presence. The thrill of the chase? She asked, 'Do you know where Acheson is hiding out?'

'On Rooisand Farm in the Kalahari. Between Gobabis and Leonardville. Less than three hours from here.'

Hadn't Maree planned to take his crony van Zyl on a hunting trip to the Kalahari?

'At least,' Tiedtke amended, 'James P. Doyle is living there. We won't know if he's Acheson until we get his fingerprints.'

'We?' said Clemencia.

'I never promised not to investigate this. I'd sooner you were there too, but I'll go and see him on my own if necessary.'

'Out of the question,' said Clemencia. 'You're staying here.' Acheson, the Cleaner! The most notorious killer in the apartheid secret service. The man who had very probably shot Anton Lubowski, even if they'd never been able to convict him. Someone who had disappeared without trace eighteen years ago. Who had known Maree, van Zyl, Burger and Barnard well. Who, if he hadn't killed all four of them himself, might well be next on the killer's list. And who, at the very least, must have some idea of what was really going on.

'But this could be the scoop of a lifetime,' said Tiedtke.

'It's too dangerous. Quite apart from being against regulations.'

112

'But Miss Garises … '

'Don't you dare take off on your own!'

'If it weren't for me, Miss Garises, Acheson might celebrate his hundredth birthday out there in the Kalahari before you caught up with him.'

Clemencia had to concede that she was indebted to Tiedtke, but that didn't mean he was entitled to get under her feet in an operation like this.

'We could go to the Blitzkrieg together sometime,' she said.

From his expression, this wasn't the response Tiedtke wanted to hear.

'It really isn't on,' she said, shoving him out of the office. She stood beside the window for a moment and forced herself to think calmly. She couldn't afford to make any mistakes, not now! She must mobilize her team and, above all, inform Oshivelo. The thing was too big to warrant going it on her own. If they had a chance to lay hands on Acheson, the chief could hardly oppose it. Or could he? Where anything even remotely connected with the Lubowski case was concerned, she no longer trusted him at all.

What if he doubted it really was Acheson? What if he simply permitted her to send a couple of clueless village constables from Gobabis to the farm. They would almost certainly botch the thing, fail to recognize that James P. Doyle's papers were forged, and ask the wrong questions. And, even if they insisted on taking his fingerprints, they would happily drive off with them. Even before they'd got back to their station in Gobabis, Acheson would be over the frontier and into Botswana.

No, she would have to detain the man herself and bring him back to Windhoek. She wouldn't let her team in on it either, or she might as well notify Oshivelo right away. The only person she considered discreet enough was Angula. She made her way out into the passage and down it to the second door along. Angula had moved some of the Lubowski files out into the passage itself.

They weren't unimportant, he said, just temporarily less important. Anyway, he needed more room in order to see things in perspective.

That really did appear to present a problem. The quantities of paper inside had not diminished at all. On the contrary, the desks were piled high with dozens of books and additional files whose covers betrayed that they came from the National Archives. The chaos on the floor was just as impressive, but Angula seemed to have found it necessary to add another dimension: he had hammered some nails into the walls and suspended a washing line from them. Clipped to this in serried rows were individual sheets, some extracted from the files, others covered with Angula's spidery handwriting. The motes of dust shimmering between them, coupled with the hot, dry air, provoked an almost irresistible urge to cough. Although the whole scene didn't look as if it would ever produce results, Angula claimed he was making excellent progress. Or would be, if only people wouldn't keep interrupting him …

Clemencia reminded him which of them was the boss. Besides, she needed him urgently. Angula listened calmly to her quick briefing on Donald Acheson. Then he nodded and came with her, though not before clamping a few selected files beneath his arm. Down below in the vehicle park Clemencia signed the requisite form and was issued with a decrepit Citi Golf whose chances of making it to Gobabis were fifty-fifty.

To prevent Angula from perusing his files for the next three hours, Clemencia made him drive. He didn't argue but spent the first hour sulking. He didn't break his silence until they had almost got to Witvlei and Clemencia wondered out loud what possible motive Acheson could have had for killing his former accomplices. That, he said, was a total misconception. Acheson had had nothing to do with Lubowski's murder, he'd simply been earmarked as the scapegoat, and if the public prosecutor hadn't opposed the idea — surprisingly so — it would have worked.

'Stop talking nonsense,' said Clemencia.

'It's as clear as daylight, boss. All I'm missing is few more pieces of the puzzle.'

'You don't seriously believe Lubowski was liquidated by SWAPO itself?'

'I still can't prove it beyond doubt.'

'And you never will,' said Clemencia. Perhaps she should have dispensed with Angula's company. She had no use for a man so obsessed with abstruse theories that he hadn't room in his head for anything else.

'Why not?' Angula demanded.

'Because Lubowski was loyal. Because he fought for independence. Because SWAPO and the fight for independence were one and the same thing. And because Lubowski was killed by the CCB.'

Angula's hands tightened on the wheel. Clemencia could see out of the corner of her eye how hard he was wrestling with himself. And then, suddenly, out it came: 'I'll get them! This time I'll get them, Oshivelo first and foremost!'

'Oshivelo?'

There was no holding him now. Angula blurted out the words as if they'd been pent up inside him for ages, and none of them had anything to do with the Kalashnikov killer. Angula seemed to have spent the last few days concentrating exclusively on quite irrelevant events in the past. He could recite the political developments of the late 1980s by the day and hour, he had reconstructed SWAPO's internal organization from various sources and drawn up a detailed list of its personnel.

Oshivelo, for instance, was far from being a fighter who had faced the enemy in the field, said Angula. From 1986 onwards, if not before, he had worked for SWAPO's internal intelligence section, which meant in practice that he had spied on his comrades. He wasn't the only one, of course. The party leaders had been dominated by a positively manic fear of traitors. As soon as he, Angula, could find the time, he would tot up how many of their own comrades had disappeared without trace in SWAPO intern-ment camps. It wouldn't surprise him if they numbered almost as many as those who had died in action. The process had been so quick! One word of criticism and you were suspect. If you were suspect you represented a threat, and if you represented a threat you had to be eliminated.

If that went for your own people, whom you had seen grow up in some village in Ovamboland, whose families had been oppressed by the South Africans, and who almost automatically became SWAPO members at birth, how much more did it apply to someone like Anton Lubowski, who hailed from another world and had virtually defected from the enemy? It was only natural that such a man should be doubly and trebly checked. Had no one discovered the suspicious payments into Lubowski's bank account? Three instalments between February and August 1989, which amounted to 100,000 rand and came from a South African secret service front man? The Harms Commission had unearthed those payments with ease later on. Without casting aspersions on government fact-finding committees, the SWAPO comrades had quite different resources at their disposal. There was firm evidence that certain SWAPO bigwigs knew of the payments. It was not for nothing that Lubowski had spent the afternoon of the day he was murdered going over his financial affairs. His accountant had confirmed that.

Angula said that many people had been killed for far less, as he had already pointed out, but Lubowski was a prominent figure. He couldn't have been simply buried in a hole in the ground in Angola. Something better had to be devised, and the best idea of all, of course, was to get rid of him without exposing him as a traitor. That would have unsettled the Party and damaged its international reputation. No one wanted to do that a mere two months before the crucial elections, so they needed someone to pin the murder on. And Acheson was the ideal person.

Angola still hadn't finished. He drew a deep breath. 'But to revert to Mr Ndangi Oshivelo,' he said. 'He'd been represented by Lubowski, had made friends with him and was a frequent visitor to his home. What could be more natural than to let Oshivelo loose on him? But, more than that, to whom would the SWAPO leadership have entrusted a contract killing if it wanted to minimize the number of those privy to Lubowski's treachery? Someone who knew of it already. Someone familiar with the victim's habits. Someone who could get close to him without arousing suspicion. Someone like Oshivelo!'

Accusing the head of the Serious Crime Unit of murder was a bit much. No, it was monstrous. Clemencia controlled herself with an effort. 'Have you any proof of this, Angula?'

'If I got hold of SWAPO's top secret documents, I'm sure I'd — '

'So you haven't?'

'Why was Oshivelo earmarked for such a senior post as soon as SWAPO was in the driving seat? Because he'd earned himself a reward. Because someone with something to lose keeps secrets better.'

'That's not enough, Angula – not by a long chalk.'

'And why, boss, is he doing everything he can to prevent us from following the Lubowski trail?'

Clemencia had wondered that herself, more than once, but that didn't justify accusing Oshivelo of such a crime. The whole idea made no sense in other respects as well. 'Know your trouble, Angula? You've forgotten what we're really dealing with, namely, four former agents of the Civil Cooperation Bureau. According to your theory, they're innocent, but someone executed them in the last few days.'

Angula nodded. 'A professional killer who was extremely well-informed. As if he'd been briefed by someone who had been watching van Zyl and company for a long time.'

'Okay, Angula,' said Clemencia. 'Get it all off your chest. Spit it out. Then we'll have a good laugh together and forget the matter.'

'About two years ago, a lot of confiscated firearms disappeared from our armoury. Allegedly a break-in, but it was never solved, of course. I've checked the list. It included a Kalashnikov.'

'Are you suggesting that Oshivelo — '

'I don't say he did the shooting himself, not this time.'

No, this was more than an obsession, it was plain ridiculous! Clemencia refused to listen to any more of it.

'Maree flew in specially to meet van Zyl, and it seems they planned to visit Acheson together. They had something in mind. Perhaps they had at last found out who had pinned Lubowski's murder on them and intended to — '

'That's enough!' Clemencia snapped. 'I like you, Angula, you know that, but if you make one more such insinuation I'll report you to Oshivelo, I swear.'

Angula didn't answer, just stared ahead through the windscreen. The B6 stretched away across the plain, straight as an arrow. Leafless bushes cowered in the sand to left and right of them. There was nothing else to be seen far and wide.

'You've got a bee in your bonnet,' Clemencia said in a more conciliatory tone. 'These things happen, but I won't let you go on digging a hole for yourself.'

Angula changed down, grimly floored the gas pedal, and overtook a lorry from Botswana.

'Angula?'

'I'm just a humble constable,' he said. He didn't speak again until they got to Gobabis. At the local police station Clemencia showed her ID, warned of potential danger ahead, and requested assistance. She said she'd been obliged to refrain from asking in advance because the matter was top secret. The station commander looked impressed and assigned her an escort of eight armed men in two cars.

Keeping far enough apart to avoid being shrouded in dust, they drove south along the course of the Schwarzer Nossob. For forty kilometres the road overlooked the valley from the edge of a highland plateau almost bare of vegetation. Scattered farmhouses hid beneath closely planted cypresses and palm trees like tropical islands in a sea of sand and rock. Far away in the east, a few white clouds were hovering so low, they seemed to be almost resting on the horizon. One could more readily imagine that they would expire of thirst on their way across the Kalahari than that they would bring rain. For all that, they were the first clouds for months. More would appear in due course, greyer, denser and heavier clouds that would sometime release their first raindrops – isolated raindrops that exploded in the dust until the floodgates of heaven suddenly opened and the rain teemed down as if it meant to drown the whole world. A few days later the Nossob might also begin to flow. The river bed was dry now, of course, and recognizable only by the rows of trees that fringed its winding course.

Beyond Hoaseb the track ran along beneath the banks of the river bed, which were now markedly steeper. The valley narrowed, the vegetation became denser. Evidence of the drought was still clearly visible, but the very fact that substantial trees had managed to survive here for decades made the river valley look almost idyllic.

'Prosopis trees, all of them,' Angula muttered. 'An imported plague.' Clemencia hadn't known he was an expert on trees. She said nothing, just stared out of the window. Emaciated cattle were lying in the shade here and there. A warthog trotted across the dusty road with its tail erect, and once the sound of the engine startled a small herd of springbok. They bounded off, then halted with their erect heads all turned in the direction of the cars. What if the real danger lay in quite another quarter?

The turn-off to Rooisand was marked by a timber gateway with a signboard suspended between the uprights. It bore the inscription 'Game Farm and Trophy Service' and, in smaller lettering, the name of the proprietor, James P. Doyle. The tall game fence was pierced by a barred gate secured by a chain but not padlocked. The long, curving driveway led uphill. Already in sight, the farm buildings stood on a slightly projecting rocky outcrop overlooking the river bed. It afforded a good view of the Nossob Valley and the road in both directions.

The shade trees were comparatively sparse and not as tall as the water tank situated a short distance from them. The long, low farmhouse appeared to have been enlarged several times without regard to creating a unified design. The L-shaped outbuildings formed an open courtyard. All the barn doors were shut, so it was impossible to tell if they were garages, workshops, cold stores or storerooms. Angula pulled up just short of the yard.

Clemencia couldn't imagine that three approaching police cars had gone unnoticed. It looked as if they had been deliberately ignored. There was no white man to be seen, but a dozen or more black labourers were busy erecting a barbed-wire fence around the buildings. More precisely, two teams were working on two fences running parallel a few metres apart. The double fence already enclosed some two-thirds of the farmhouse. The only stretch still missing faced the river bed. Big rolls of barbed wire were lying in the back of a pick-up, waiting to adorn the front of this defensive barrier.

'Just like the 'eighties,' Angula muttered.

Clemencia had never been outside Katutura as a child, but she gathered what Angula meant from the stories told by her late grandfather, who had then been working on a farm near Tsumeb. At the height of the war of independence, white farmers fearful of SWAPO guerrillas or bandits had transformed their houses into fortresses. Double anti-terrorist fences had been nothing out of the ordinary in those days. At night, dogs were turned loose in the narrow gap between the fences. Raiders could shoot the animals with relative ease, of course, but at least they prevented the farmers from being caught unawares in their sleep.

Clemencia had only once seen part of such an installation, but it had been converted into an enclosure for free-range chickens. The rest of the anti-terrorist fences were swiftly dismantled. No one liked living in a high security prison or relished being reminded of a dirty war. Only a certain James P. Doyle seemed to think it necessary to revive those memories, but his underlying motive wasn't nostalgia.

Clemencia got out of the car. How revealing a fence like this could be! It might almost have been addressing her – making a series of short, categorical statements that left no room for doubt. They were:

Donald Acheson lives here.

He isn't the killer.

He's mortally afraid.

He knows the killer is coming.

✵✹✵

Returning to Namibia by way of Botswana was risky. It entailed crossing two frontiers instead of one, and doing so with a dismantled AK-47 in his sports bag. On the other hand, the alternative route via Gobabis was twice as long. That would also have presented a risk. The longer he took, the greater the danger that things could go wrong. Besides, he had no objection to getting the business over quickly, even though he knew that nothing would happen thereafter. He was feeling a trifle tired, and the bouts of coughing were getting on his nerves. They simply wouldn't stop and were so violent, he fancied he could taste his own lungs. It must have been the confounded South African climate.

He had decided on the Botswana route in a *Hungry Lion* snack bar near the bus station in Jo'burg. It was all he could do to swallow half the breadcrumbed legs of chicken, but it was a good thing he'd forced himself to eat them, or he wouldn't have overheard the lorry

121

drivers at the next table. One of them, who had been talking about a trip to Windhoek, mentioned that the Botswana police penalized you mercilessly for exceeding the speed limit by so much as a whisker. It later transpired that he had to deliver some furniture to *House & Home* branches in Namibia.

A padlocked lorry, no one he would have to talk to or beware of, and maybe even a leather sofa to sleep on in the back! He might almost have believed it was a lucky coincidence, except that neither luck nor coincidence applied in his case. Destiny, more like, and destiny simply fulfilled itself. There was nothing coincidental about it. It needed no explaining, and there was no point in speculating whether something should be regarded as lucky or unlucky. What had to happen happened, period, and what had happened was that he'd overheard this lorry driver talking at the next table.

He had followed him out and accosted him, offered him 2000 rand for the trip, another 1000 to ask no questions, and yet another 2000 to forget he'd smuggled someone across two borders. The man had nodded and put out his hand. His name was Morgan, he said. Like Tsvangirai, Zimbabwe's new prime minister.

'Nice name,' he'd replied, and shook hands. Having bought himself a torch and a jerry can of water, he got in as soon as the driver left the depot. They pulled up in the next lay-by and opened the rear doors. The freight was stacked to within half a metre of the roof. Garden furniture, sun umbrellas, swing hammocks, fans. He climbed up and crawled over the top. He didn't find any leather sofa, but right at the back was a pile of plastic-covered mattresses on which he could stretch out in relative comfort. Then Morgan shut the doors and darkness fell.

At first he turned on the torch in order to reassemble the Kalashnikov, then only when he had to have a drink. This was difficult, because he could barely sit up straight without hitting his head on the metal roof. But he had to drink if he didn't want to shrivel up in the heat.

He felt all right in other respects. He liked being shut up in the dark. It made everything look the same. There was hardly any difference between opening your eyes or shutting them, lying there awake or asleep, being dead or alive. He wondered why people were so afraid of death, and even more so of being buried alive. The answer eluded him. He couldn't even recall if he himself had suffered from that phobia earlier on.

When not compelled to cough he slept or dozed in the limbo between wakefulness and slumber. It slowed his thoughts until they congealed into strange, inconsequential shapes that meant nothing to him. Totally unaware of crossing the frontier between South Africa and Botswana, he didn't sit up with a start until someone hammered on the side of the lorry and Morgan's voice asked if he'd like to stretch his legs. They were beyond Sekoma, he said, and there was nothing far and wide but desert and salt pans. It was quite safe.

'No,' he said, 'I'm okay.'

Wouldn't he like a beer? Didn't he need a pee?

He didn't answer, and a few minutes later they drove on. He slept, he coughed, he drank tepid water. At some stage the lorry halted again. Morgan killed the engine, then opened the rear doors and said he had to grab a few hours' sleep. Besides, the Namibian frontier didn't open until seven a.m.

There was nothing to be done. He abandoned the Kalashnikov and climbed out over the cartons. The night was bright compared to the lorry's dark interior. Morgan, drinking beer from the can, complained that he seldom landed any trips to Zimbabwe these days because the country was bust and no one was buying any furniture. It was a crying shame, because a handful of foreign exchange would buy you the dishiest girls. You wouldn't believe the good times he'd had there. Once, for instance, in Bulawayo …

'I'm not interested,' he cut in.

'Okay, okay, man,' said Morgan.

'I'm not interested in talking,' he said. When Morgan had finally, after another beer, gone off to doss down in the cab, he walked a few hundred metres into the desert. The sky was filled with stars from zenith to horizon. It was silent as the grave. Not even a nocturnal animal could be heard. He sat down on the ground and waited to see if a Kalahari lion came past. He might exchange a few words with that.

'How's business?' he would ask.

'So-so. How's business with you?' the lion would reply.

'In the red.'

'Well, good hunting.'

'Same to you.'

He bent over, racked by a long fit of coughing. He felt better after that. Feeling cold at some stage, he stretched out on his back and shovelled sand over his legs and chest. No lion had come past by the time the eastern sky turned grey and the stars were paling. He returned to the lorry and woke Morgan.

'Time to go,' he said, and got the man to shut him in again. They drove on for a couple of hours. It was gradually getting hot. Then the lorry came to a stop for twenty minutes, crawled another hundred metres and stopped once more. This had to be Buitepos, the Namibian frontier post.

Dazzling daylight flooded in as the rear doors swung open. He flattened himself on the mattresses and reached for the Kalashnikov. Morgan's voice said, 'It's all furniture for Windhoek, sir.'

Another voice said, 'It'll have to be checked.'

'If you say so,' said Morgan.

'That carton there, unload it!'

'I can't,' said Morgan, 'I've got a bad back.'

Footsteps, a scrape of cardboard, paper rustled.

'Okay,' said the strange voice, 'furniture for Windhoek.'

The doors were bolted again and they drove on soon afterwards. Another hour-and-a-half to Gobabis. They had agreed that

124

Morgan would let him out just short of the town. He would go in on foot and see if he could snaffle a car somewhere. There was plenty of time. He couldn't do anything before nightfall in any case.

The lorry stopped again. Had they already reached Gobabis? He hadn't even dismantled the Kalashnikov. He turned on the torch and wedged it between two cartons to keep his hands free. He had only just started to unscrew the barrel when he heard a voice outside:

'Driver's licence!'

A traffic cop. He screwed the barrel up again. The policeman must be standing right beside the cab. Morgan was still behind the wheel, it seemed, because his voice sounded definitely fainter. 'Have I done something wrong, sir?'

'Do you know what the speed limit is here?'

'I was only doing — '

'A hundred and seventeen k.p.h., that's what you were doing. The limit is eighty.'

'I didn't see any sign,' said Morgan.

'It's beside the road, like all road signs. You drove past it exactly three kilometres back, and my colleague checked your speed one kilometre further on.'

'But the road was clear and — '

'Your papers, please!'

He turned off the torch, just in case the policeman wanted to inspect the load. Why should he, though? Even if he did, he would no more discover him than the customs officer at the border had. He must keep calm, that was all. He drew a deep breath and heard it rattle very faintly in his windpipe. As if the airflow had caused something lodged there to vibrate. An obstructive, irritating foreign body. Not now, he thought as he felt the urge to cough mount up inside him.

'You know how it is, sir,' he heard Morgan say. 'I'll be in big trouble if I'm late getting to Windhoek, just because speed limits have suddenly been imposed all over the place.'

An urge to cough could be suppressed. He didn't have to cough if he forbade himself to. Not right now, at least. Not, at least, until that bloody fool Morgan had paid his measly fine.

'There are hundreds of people queueing up for a job like mine. If you get there so late the stuff can't be unloaded, the boss simply finds himself someone else. Someone who isn't so particular.'

It was pure imagination that his lungs were tying themselves in knots. It was imagination that his bronchial tubes were on the verge of exploding, nor was it true that the mucus in his windpipe was steadily congealing and depriving him of air. It was all just imagination. He clamped his mouth against his forearm and drove his teeth into the flesh. No way would he cough, not now.

'I'm a responsible driver, sir, believe me. I obey the rules, but you can sometimes fail to see a sign, especially on an open road where no one would expect it. I mean, if there'd been a village I could understand ... '

'There were road works.'

'But no one was working there!'

What if he quickly breathed out? Without a sound, quite inaudibly. No more than a quick, decisive exhalation through his mouth. Just to clear his throat. Just so he didn't choke and the convulsion in his chest didn't kill him.

'Look, sir,' said Morgan, 'couldn't you turn a blind eye for once?'

He wouldn't cough. He fought the urge with all his might, even when he felt the pain in his lungs gather strength and turn into a wild beast that clambered up inside his chest, biting and scratching. He should simply take a sip of water! He felt for the jerry can and feverishly twisted the cap but felt he wouldn't manage it because the prickly monster was irresistibly eating its way up his throat. He knew it would tear his gullet apart if he didn't give up, but he didn't. He fought on, even when it was too late. Even when the beast had already broken through and a preliminary, hoarse bark emerged from his lips.

He had lost. He sat up with a jerk and cracked his head on the lorry's sheet metal roof, but all he could feel was that he was coughing, that every fibre of him was coughing, that his innards were turning themselves inside out. He coughed as if he had to spew up his very soul, the air roaring and rattling and whistling in his throat. And he just couldn't stop. Not a trace of release or relief. More and more violently, the coughing expelled itself from his body with such force, he thought he would suffocate because it gave him no chance to draw breath.

As though through cotton wool, he heard the policeman outside ask what was going on. He tasted blood on his tongue, gasped for breath and went on coughing, ever harder and more agonizingly. Morgan was ordered to get out at once. The driver's door opened and shut. The paroxysm still wasn't entirely over, even though he scarcely had the strength to cough any more. His gums tasted of sulphur, his throat was smarting, red-hot needles pierced his lungs. He drew the back of his hand across his lips. They were dry and raw.

'I've no idea,' said Morgan as the rear doors swung open. Light flooded in. The Kalashnikov was lying beside him. He uttered a feeble cough.

'Come out of there!' The policeman probably thought he'd caught an illegal immigrant.

'Okay,' he replied. Grasping the gun, he crawled over the cartons and made for the daylight. He almost hoped the policeman had drawn his pistol, but he hadn't. He was standing there, two metres below him, staring incredulously at the muzzle of the Kalashnikov. Everything might have turned out differently if the weather in South Africa had been less unhealthy. Or if Morgan had kept to the speed limit. But it was idle to ask whose fault it was. Many things simply happened.

His forefinger curled around the AK-47's trigger.

The two bull terriers were chained up, but with enough play to enable them to bar access to the front door. They stood there stiff-legged, baring teeth that could have severed a throat with one bite. *Varkhonde,* 'pig dogs', as the Boers called them because of their appearance. Except that they didn't carry a gramme of fat. Everything beneath their dirty white fur was muscle. It was a hundred per cent certain that they had been trained as attack dogs, and Clemencia wouldn't have been surprised to learn that they had been schooled to go for blacks – for 'kaffir smell', as someone like Acheson would probably have said. 'Anyone at home?' she called loudly. The bull terriers growled.

The double fence behind the house was already complete, so no one could easily make off that way, but Clemencia had stationed two of the policemen from Gobabis at the rear. Two more had remained with the cars and the rest were standing guard behind her and Angula.

'Police!' she called. 'Open up!'

No response, although the workmen had assured them that the *baas* was at home. Angula stooped, picked up a stone and flung it at the door. Without a sound, one of the bull terriers sprang at him, only to be brought up short by its chain after two bounds. The other dog tensed, then promptly froze again, its little eyes twinkling angrily. They heard a key turn in the lock. The door opened and a man with a shotgun over his shoulder emerged.

So that was what he looked like! He must have been nearly seventy but looked younger. His grey hair was crew-cut, his tanned face deeply furrowed. His eyes were alert and faintly suspicious, his features not unattractive. He appeared to be in good physical shape and he moved in the deliberate, self-assured manner peculiar to men who feel comfortable in their own skin. There was nothing to distinguish him from other white farmers who had spent a lifetime maintaining and ruling their miniature kingdoms. Apart from the fact that he'd been a racist killer.

'Mr Donald Acheson?' asked Clemencia.

If he was surprised he didn't show it. 'There's no one here by that name. My name is Doyle. What do you want?'

Clemencia jerked her head at the fences. 'You're barricading yourself in?'.

'Tsotsis, black thugs,' he said. 'There have been a lot of incidents in the district recently.'

'May we see your gun licence?' Angula asked.

No reaction.

'What we'd like most of all is a chat with you,' said Clemencia. 'May we come in, Mr Acheson?'

'I'm James Doyle, how many more times must I tell you?'

'You're only wasting time,' said Clemencia. 'We have your fingerprints from 1990.'

'We're arresting you first for illegal possession of a firearm and forging documents,' said Angula. 'Then we'll see what else we can think of.'

'You'll be safer in a cell in Windhoek than you are here,' said Clemencia.

'Like Ferdi Barnard, you mean?' The man laughed. He had clearly decided to stop playing hide-and-seek. He patted the butt of his shotgun. 'I take care of my own security.'

'Can we talk now, Mr Acheson?'

'I've no objection,' said Acheson. He turned and shouted, 'Sit!'

The bull terriers promptly sat down on their haunches but kept their heads poised, ready to fly at the throat of anyone within reach at the first sign from their master. Clemencia and Angula remained close behind Acheson as they followed him into the house. The light was on in the living room, which it needed to be because the only window was boarded up. There was an open brick fireplace in one wall. Above it, staring glassy-eyed into space, were such of

129

Africa's animal kingdom as possessed horns: the stock in trade of James P. Doyle's trophy service. The gun cabinet beside the door was the biggest Clemencia had ever seen. On the table were a radio, a crushed can of Windhoek Lager, a brimming ashtray, and a lone plate smeared with gravy. Clemencia sat down on an unoccupied chair.

'Well?' she said.

Acheson spoke as if he were addressing a bunch of clueless tourists. He had returned to southern Africa in 1997 because he'd had enough of Europe. Too many fools, no room to breathe, no freedom. Namibia hadn't been his first choice, but things had gone even further down the tubes in Zimbabwe, Angola and South Africa. So when some friends informed him that this farm was available to rent for his lifetime, he'd taken the plunge. He was his own master here, the blacks still treated you with respect, and he made a reasonable living from the game hunters he pulled in.

He lived under a false name purely to avoid unnecessary trouble. He'd had nothing, absolutely nothing, to do with the Lubowski affair. They knew how the police and the press operated. You didn't have a chance once they got you in their sights. The slanderous campaign against himself and his former colleagues had borne fruit at last, but he wasn't shitting himself. Let the goddamned killer come. Then they'd see who killed whom.

'You were framed?' said Angula.

Acheson hesitated. 'You can say that again!'

'By SWAPO?' Angula couldn't leave his obsession alone. Clemencia gave him a warning glance.

'Nice try.' Acheson laughed. 'If I'd known that I'd have said so at the time. But how *would* I know, if I had absolutely nothing to do with the Lubowski affair?'

'SWAPO,' Angula began, but Clemencia cut him short. 'We've discovered that Chappies Maree and Slang van Zyl intended to visit you here.'

'Then you know more than I do.' Acheson propped his shotgun against the table and went into the kitchen, where he fetched himself another beer without asking whether he could offer them anything. Briskly, he lit a cigarette. They were anxious to capture a killer, Clemencia said quietly, so it would be helpful to know his identity. Without a few pointers to his motive, however, they would never track him down. Even if Acheson was tired of life, he ought at least to bear in mind that others could also be in danger. Acheson merely shrugged.

Clemencia realized he would never talk. He was convinced he would survive, just as he had survived everything else. Being the next potential murder victim scared him as little as the prospect of being grilled by the Windhoek police. He had played the innocent for seven long months in 1990 without caving in, without making the smallest mistake. They would never be able to hold him for as long as that − it wouldn't even take a lawyer of von Fleckenstein's calibre to get him out. She would arrest him all the same. What else could she do?

'Detective inspector?' called one of the policemen outside. Angula went to the front door.

Acheson dragged at his cigarette and knocked the ash off. He and his colleagues in the South African secret service had never hesitated to beat information out of their prisoners in the old days. Whenever they interrogated someone, pools of blood had had to be mopped up afterwards. Victim after victim had suffered at their hands, yet their strong-arm tactics had ultimately proved to no avail. They had lost notwithstanding, because human dignity, truth and justice were more powerful weapons and must remain so. However noble and important the end, it didn't justify the use of every possible means. Clemencia felt vaguely incensed even so − incensed that someone like Acheson still believed he could do as he pleased regardless of casualties, and that he cared as little for the truth as he did for human life.

Angula, calling from the front door, asked if he should shoot the bloody dogs. Acheson grinned, stubbed out his cigarette in the ashtray and left the room. The policeman he returned with said they had to leave at once. Every man was needed because a colleague had been shot. Clemencia asked for details. A burst from an automatic weapon, possibly a Kalashnikov! An abandoned lorry from South Africa!

'You've no need to go anywhere,' said Clemencia. 'The murderer is on his way here.'

The uniformed constable shook his head. His orders were quite clear: back to Gobabis with the whole squad. If they were to take this man with them – he pointed to Acheson – they would have to do so right away.

'Give me another ten minutes,' Clemencia told him. She turned to Acheson. 'He's here. Somewhere out there.'

Acheson smiled and sat down again. Mechanically, he tapped another cigarette out of the packet. Nothing had changed at first sight. His expression and his movements were no different, yet he suddenly looked twenty years younger. The energy he radiated was palpable, the air around him seemed to crackle with electricity.

It was the changed situation, the danger. What would have induced fear and paralysis in another man, Acheson merely found challenging. He couldn't wait to confront the killer gun in hand. Him or me, that was the question that counted, the only thing in life he relished. Kill or be killed, that was what everything boiled down to. It was as simple as that, and to him as a mercenary, a torturer, a killer, it always had been. The greater the risk, the greater the satisfaction.

Politics had probably never interested him. He had fought for the apartheid regime only because it employed him to do what he liked best: murder people. But that was an eternity ago. For many years he'd had to content himself with shooting kudu and springbok. That, too, enabled you to watch as a living creature tremulously breathed its last, but it wasn't quite the same. And now, after all this time, an adversary was on the doorstep. Him or me!

Clemencia had known that such a thing as bloodlust existed, but this predator on two legs was drunk with it even before the killing started. It suddenly dawned on her that she was holding a trump card in her hand. All she had to do was up the ante a little before she played it. She said, 'I don't know which I'd rather, that the killer killed you or you the killer. Both, probably.'

'Let me worry about that.'

'I can picture the two of you going for each other. You fire, you're hit but you go on firing. You don't feel the pain, the onset of death, because you're both obsessed with the thought of pumping one more bullet into each other's body. You go down, firing again and again until — '

'Do you believe in God, lady?' Acheson demanded. He was still grinning, but his face had hardened. 'If so, be grateful to him that you didn't cross my path in the old days.'

He was ready now. 'Oh yes,' said Clemencia, 'the good old days! But these days the state thinks its task is to clear up murders and prevent them. It's my duty to confiscate your arsenal of weapons and take you to Windhoek, where a comfortable cell is waiting for you. And I'll do that, too, unless … '

Acheson swigged at his can of beer. He wiped his lips and said, 'Unless what?'

'Unless it would be more conducive to our enquiries not to.'

Acheson looked at his shotgun, which was still leaning against the table. It was a Browning New Elite, calibre 9.3 × 62. He said, 'I have a theory. I also have a name. That's all I can offer you, and you'll only get them if you don't arrest me.'

Clemencia agreed, but Acheson wanted insurance. She was to return to Windhoek, where he would call her and communicate the promised information. Clemencia wouldn't have trusted him to do that, but she didn't commit herself. She was now in the stronger

133

position. Either he talked, or he could wait for the killer to catch up with him in a cell.

They must leave now, the policeman outside called. Clemencia rose.

'Wait,' said Acheson. 'I had nothing to do with the Lubowski affair, as I said. I only heard that Maree, Barnard, Burger and van Zyl were involved. Plus one other man nicknamed Donkerkop. He seems to have had some reason for feeling annoyed with the others.'

Annoyed was hardly the word. And Acheson was lying, at least where his own role was concerned. Even if the rest of his statement were true, he had, of course, been present at Lubowski's murder. He wouldn't be number five on the killer's death list just because he'd heard a few rumours.

'You promised us a name,' said Clemencia, 'not a nickname.'

'Martinus Cloete,' said Acheson. 'Of Windhoek.'

'What reason did he have to feel annoyed?'

Acheson shrugged his shoulders. 'Ask him yourself.'

'Good work, boss,' Angula said. He drew his pistol and levelled it at Acheson. 'Right, you're under arrest on suspicion of — '

'No, Angula,' said Clemencia.

'Boss?'

She turned to Acheson. 'If you'd see us safely past your dogs, Mr Acheson.'

Once outside, they saw a cloud of dust hovering above the farm track. The policemen from Gobabis had left in something of a hurry. Before she got in behind the wheel of her car, she said to Acheson, 'I'd be lying if I wished you luck.'

He didn't answer. For as long as she could see him in the rear-view mirror, he continued to stand in the gap in his anti-terrorist fence, Browning on shoulder, watching her car recede. When they got down into the Nossob Valley and were finally out of sight around the first bend, Clemencia pulled up. She told Angula to drive on to Windhoek and find out all he could about Martinus

Cloete, aka Donkerkop. No one could tell if Acheson had been telling the truth, but it was the hottest tip they had.

'What about you, boss?' Angula asked.

'I'm staying.'

Acheson might be an unreliable witness, but he was an invaluable decoy, at least if he wasn't in a cell in Windhoek but holed up at his farm, apparently not under police surveillance. The killer was nearby and would try to complete his self-appointed task, of that Clemencia felt sure. She had never been so close to him, never had a better chance of catching him.

'He's already shot one policeman,' said Angula.

Clemencia could imagine what Matti Jurmela would say now: We're paid to do our job, not play the hero. The last heroes have been long dead. Their profession died with them, and a good thing too!

But that applied to Finland, not Africa. People died quicker in Namibia, admittedly, but not so permanently. You could never be sure the dead were really dead, and even if they were, the ghosts of dead heroes meddled in the affairs of the living every day. Clemencia took out her automatic and checked the magazine. Her hands were trembling.

Angula tipped his seat back. He said, 'You should also get a little rest, boss. We could be in for a sleepless night.'

❈❖❈

He was sitting in the passenger seat of the police car with the Kalashnikov across his thighs. Morgan was driving. They had hefted the dead traffic cop on to the cartons and locked the lorry's rear doors. This would have gained them a little time, but not much.

The policeman with the radar gun would have heard the shots if a couple of lorries hadn't chanced to roar past at the vital moment. Having unsuccessfully tried to reach his colleague on the phone, he would set off on foot after the second or third attempt. Two

135

kilometres would take him twenty minutes at most, probably less. Circling the abandoned lorry with his gun drawn, he would spot the traces of blood on the asphalt and summon reinforcements from Gobabis. The rear doors wouldn't be forced until they got there. A red alert wouldn't be issued for at least two hours.

An hour-and-a-half had gone by. They had jolted along a farm track until they reached the D1707, then followed it in a westerly direction and later turned south. They were now driving along the D1715 and had just passed the entrance to Marie Noord Farm. He would try to get within a few kilometres of his destination by car. The police had no idea where he was. They would only be blocking off the main roads. He could wait for nightfall somewhere in the veldt. He coughed.

'What's done is done,' Morgan said suddenly. That was so self-evident, it didn't need saying. Thankfully, Morgan had remained silent until now, carrying out all his instructions silently and at once, but the shock seemed to be wearing off. As long as he didn't revert to the brothels of Bulawayo!

'It's no business of mine what happened,' Morgan said, glancing sideways at him. 'I didn't see or hear a thing.'

'Keep your eyes on the road,' he said.

Morgan stared ahead but went on talking. Hurriedly, a voice that was far too high, as if he knew perfectly well that talking was useless. 'Why don't you just dump me beside the road and drive on by yourself? If they question me, I'll say I've lost my memory. I can't remember a thing. I don't even know who I am.'

Who *did* know who he was? You cobbled an idea of yourself together until something happened that smashed your self-image to pieces. Instead of learning from this, you promptly began to stick the bits together again a little differently but no less wrongly. And so it went on until …

'I don't want to die!' Morgan wailed suddenly. 'I've got a family, I've got children. They need me!'

136

They all had families. Death didn't care, it took whomever it wanted. Sooner or later it took everyone – the traffic cop, Morgan, himself – but many people refused to accept that. Most people, in fact. He said, 'You can live to a hundred for all I care, Morgan. Think for a moment. No one knows about me. When the police find the dead man in your lorry, who will they suspect of murder?'

Morgan mutely shook his head.

'You, of course. You were stopped, the policeman found you were carrying an illegal weapon and tried to arrest you. You shot him.'

'I did?'

'You'll deny it if they pick you up. You'll put the blame on some unknown hitcher. You'll describe his appearance in detail, but they'll barely listen because there'll be no trace of him. One phone call to your firm will tell them who you are, then they'll hunt you down. Now I come to think of it, you probably won't get a chance to deny anything. The police don't like cop killers – they give them short shrift. It's so easy for things to go wrong when you're arresting someone. A gun can go off by mistake, a warning shot can go astray, or perhaps someone will think you're going for your gun. In your place, Morgan, I really wouldn't try to fall into their hands. But *I* won't kill you.'

'No?' Morgan said incredulously.

Let Morgan keep the police busy for a while. If all went well, two days should be long enough.

'If I've got a dozen bullets in my body, someone else must have done it,' said Morgan. His tone was still dubious, but he seemed to be slowly catching on. 'Then I can't be the murderer!'

'Not the only one, at least.'

'But I *am* the only one! You don't exist at all. *I'm* the murderer. Just me!' Morgan glanced sideways at him. His eyes were shining. His face broke into a grin, then he laughed aloud. Relieved, liberated, probably happier than he had ever been. How good it could

137

be to be a murderer! At least if you clung to life.

'Keep your eyes on the road, Morgan!' It was almost laughable. Because the man could see a little future ahead of him, he promptly freaked out and risked it again.

'You can't kill me, because that would make you the murderer ... '

'I'll do it all the same before you kill us both.' He aimed the Kalashnikov at Morgan, who faced the front and pulled himself together. He steered the car more calmly now, carefully avoiding the larger stones, and changed down in places where long-ago rainy seasons had carved deep ruts into the road surface. When ordered to, he obediently turned off right.

The farm track was in such a wretched state, it was really passable only by a 4WD. Morgan drove as if they were travelling over raw eggs. He caressed the clutch, eased the car over obstructions wheel by wheel, and put his foot down only when they threatened to stall on a rise. At one point they had to get out and build a makeshift ramp out of loose stones, but the sump still fouled the edge of the rocks. Soon afterwards the right rear tyre burst, but changing it wasn't worth the effort. To judge by the map and the mileage, they were almost there anyway. They drove another few hundred metres on the rim. When they came to a largish rock, he made Morgan pull up, crawl beneath the car, and drain the sump. In the unlikely event that the man took it into his head to give himself up to the police, he wouldn't be able to do so in a hurry.

'Can I go now?' Morgan asked.

'Sit down,' he replied, pointing to the shady side of the rock. He sat down beside Morgan and said he would shoot him if he uttered another word. So they sat there side by side for hour after hour, watching the lizards scuttle past. A big, black and yellow spider suspended its web between the rock and a withered bush; shadows slowly crept across the stony ground.

Then dusk fell and the first few stars twinkled in the greyness.

He drew imaginary lines from one to another to see if they formed words, possibly a name, but when two many luminous dots appeared in the sky they muddled his self-invented network and he gave up. The Milky Way was glimmering in the darkness, and at some stage Morgan fell asleep beside him. He deposited 5000 rand on the spot where he had been sitting and weighed them down with a stone. Slinging the sports bag over his shoulder, he picked up the AK-47 and set off. He had no need to turn on his torch, the night was light enough. Any night was light enough for him.

❂

Donkerkop:

There was much speculation afterwards as to why the street lights in Sanderburgstrasse failed on the night of Lubowski's murder, of all times. There were people who based whole conspiracy theories on that fact. It couldn't have been a coincidence, they said, but it was. At all events, the others were just as surprised as I was. Ferdi Barnard swore – said it was a bloody nuisance. We could only hope that none of the neighbours minded the street being in darkness. The last thing we needed was a bunch of municipal electricians waltzing up.

So it was pitch dark when 8.30 p.m. came. I let the car coast slowly downhill. There was nobody around. I pulled up right outside Lubowski's gate. Donald Acheson got out, holding the Kalashnikov, and concealed himself in the bushes on the other side of the street. I backed ten metres, parked beside the verge, and turned off the lights and engine. I left the key in the ignition.

Acheson was now invisible. To give him a good target, I was to turn on my headlights as soon as Lubowski got out of his car and start the engine when the first shot was fired. Speed was essential after that. Drive forwards ten metres, stop to let Acheson get in, and then beat it fast!

'And make sure you don't overcook the first bend,' Barnard said over my shoulder.

'I have driven a car before,' I retorted irritably.

'If any of the neighbours stick their noses in, we open fire at once,' he said. 'All of us, is that clear, sonny?'

'Leave him alone,' said Maree.

'There'll be time for tears later,' Barnard added. I felt tempted to turn round and shoot the stupid idiot. The pistol they'd given me was on my lap.

And then I heard the sound of a car. In my rear-view mirror I saw two headlights and knew that Lubowski was coming even before I could tell what make the car was. Lubowski was normally driven home by his chauffeur, but van Zyl had informed us by walkie-talkie that he was on his own this time. I learned subsequently that his car had just been serviced. The garage had delivered it late that afternoon, and Lubowski had instructed his chauffeur to return the hire car. That saved the man's life, I'm convinced. When the car indicated left, turned into the entrance and stopped outside the gate, it was clearly identifiable as Lubowski's white BMW. The driver's door opened, a figure got out, and the door swung shut.

'Let there be light!' Maree muttered from the back seat. I turned on my headlights, and at that moment time stood still. For how long I don't know; thirty or forty seconds, maybe, but they might as well have been forty years or forty thousandths of a second. It's common knowledge that agonizing moments can expand into an eternity, but I'd never experienced this before. To me, what ensued was total inactivity. Nothing seemed to happen.

I heard the shots, the familiar sound of the starter and engine as I turned the ignition key, the shouts of the pair on the back seat, the barking of Lubowski's dogs – indeed, even the snapping of twigs as Acheson burst through the bushes beside the road. I saw nothing, though. That's to say, I saw certain situations perfectly well, but no motion. They were frozen tableaux like individual frames from a film running so fast that nothing could be discerned unless someone periodically pressed the pause button.

I saw Lubowski's dapper figure standing beside the gate, a briefcase in his left hand. He was bending forwards from the waist. Lubowski was a very tall man, almost two metres, so he had to stoop to speak into the intercom. But his head was turned in the direction of my headlights. His eyes were

*wide and unblinking, his expression conveyed that he knew what was about
to happen.*

*Except that for me, nothing happened. I didn't see the bullets from the
AK-47 hit him. The first time I saw him again he was frozen in a pirouette,
black hair flying out sideways, one knee already on the ground, the other leg
strangely twisted, and hovering vertically in the air above his hand, with its
widely splayed fingers, was the briefcase, seemingly exempt from the force
of gravity. That accursed briefcase used to hover before my eyes whenever a
subsequent nightmare jolted me awake.*

*The next picture I remember didn't show much. My headlight beams
were flooding the darkened street, and visible in them were Acheson's legs.
The upper part of his body was plunged in nocturnal darkness. He was
wearing jeans and boots, calf-length leather boots. Marlboro Man, I thought,
I don't know why. The soundtrack continued without a break, but my film
images were on pause. I continued to see Acheson's boots on the asphalt
when he had already wrenched the passenger door open and shouted, 'I got
him!'*

'Is he dead?' Barnard asked tensely.

'How should I know!' Acheson yelled.

'Someone must go over and give him the coup de grâce,' *Barnard
hissed.*

'Well, go on, youngster!' Maree urged me.

'Me?' I heard my voice ask.

'He's shitting himself,' Barnard sneered.

*'Anyone who isn't for us is against us,' Acheson said menacingly, and
the leather boots disappeared. Suddenly, I wasn't behind the wheel any
longer; I was standing outside in the darkness between the white BMW and
the gate with the intercom. Heaven alone knew how I'd got there. Two dogs
were barking behind the gate like mad things. I saw my hand in close-up. It
was holding a pistol, and the barrel was pointing downwards at the head of
black, curly hair on the asphalt.*

*He isn't moving, I thought. He's dead, you needn't shoot him, nobody
shoots a dead man! But I didn't know if he really was dead, and I still don't*

know to this day. Everything seemed to be frozen rigid, myself included. Even my finger on the trigger didn't move, but I heard a shot, so I must have squeezed it.

Then I was back in the car. As soon as I drove off, time and movement resumed without a break. I saw my right hand turning the wheel, my left changing gear. I accelerated and the car responded, eating up the road metre by metre. I turned off once, twice, and a few minutes later we got to Acheson's lodgings in Love Street. Staal Burger and Slang van Zyl were waiting outside. They wanted to have a beer and invited me in. I shook my head. I'd had enough. Of them, of myself, of the whole affair. Enough to last me the rest of my life.

Donald Acheson's parting words were: 'If we all keep our traps shut, no one will ever know who finally put Lubowski's lights out.'

'Good shot, anyway,' said Maree, patting me on the back.

'I guess you were right, Chappies. The youngster won't rat on us after all.' Barnard chuckled. 'Not now.'

I ought to have shot them all and turned myself in right away. I'd have been sentenced to life and served fifteen years. Okay, twenty. Then I'd have been a free man next year.

✵✵✵

The wind was blowing in the right direction, away from the farmhouse, and it was strong enough to prevent the bull terriers from picking up her scent. Clemencia had been afraid they were turned loose at night, but they were still chained up outside the front door, otherwise they would have chased jackals halfway across the Kalahari. Acheson's barricaded windows were lightproof. Only a thin sliver of light escaping from under the front door betrayed that someone was in the house.

The anti-terrorist fence had not been completed during the afternoon. There was still a gap about ten metres wide. Outside it was a wrecked car with no wheels. Angula had worked his way towards it. Clemencia couldn't see him, but she could picture him leaning motionless against the bodywork with his eyes shut, listening hard for the sound of stealthy footsteps, the muted breathing of a killer on the prowl.

The framework supporting the water tank was a little way off. Clemencia cautiously climbed the ladder beside one of the metal struts. Making her way out on to a wooden platform some five metres from the ground, she flipped her safety catch and put the pistol down beside her. The massive water tank overhead screened her from the moonlight. It wasn't an ideal place from which to intervene directly, but it did give her an unobstructed view across the double fence and over the roofs of the farm buildings. Crickets chirped in the night that lay, like a grey, motionless blanket, over the wastes of the Kalahari. The gloom was punctuated only by a campfire that flickered somewhere among the huts in which Acheson's workers lived with their families. Clemencia could hear sporadic snatches of conversation.

The killer was unlikely to come from that direction. Perhaps he wouldn't come at all. It was possible that he had discovered the police car they'd left down in the Nossob Valley. It was off the road, but they'd lacked both time and a suitable spot in which to camouflage it properly. Any normal man who knew that the police were waiting for him would abandon or at least postpone an attack on Acheson's fortress, but what did that mean? No normal man would be roaming Namibia with a Kalashnikov, intent on executing others. Even if they were former apartheid criminals.

Clemencia strove to picture the killer somewhere out there in the darkness. She imagined him squatting on his heels with his rifle butt on the ground, patiently watching the stars traverse the sky and awaiting his moment. Just as Angula and herself were waiting for him with their guns ready to hand. He probably wouldn't move until he thought Acheson was fast asleep. In his place, Clemencia wouldn't have made a move until three a.m., having spent at least an hour surveying the situation. He probably wouldn't budge before one.

The crickets' unending concert lent the night its monotonous rhythm. Coming from everywhere and nowhere at once, it seemed to be interwoven with the darkness. One might have believed that nothing at all could happen because everything had dissolved into that darkness – because every living creature was involuntarily resonating to that strange, omnipervasive song. Yet murder was continuously happening out there: the processes of eating and being eaten, hunting and being hunted.

Clemencia wondered how the killer proposed to gain access to the house unnoticed. There was no getting past the bull terriers. Through one of the barricaded windows? Across the roof and down the chimney? Had the killer devised a plan? He couldn't count on taking Acheson unawares like his previous victims. The almost completed double fence, the boarded-up windows, the guard dogs outside the door – all must have told him that he was expected. Even if he hadn't spotted the patrol car, he must at least be wondering whether the police had been informed and were laying a trap for him. No, as far as one could judge, he wouldn't dare to attack.

The campfire in the farmhands' quarters had dwindled to a faint red glow. Clemencia peered into the darkness. She didn't know why, but she felt sure that the killer would attempt it all the same. And that he would manage to bring Acheson to bay. Neither of them would hesitate for an instant. They would blaze away until one of them lay dead. The unknown killer had proved himself quite as ruthless as Acheson, yet there was a difference. *He* was different. His motive wasn't a lust for destruction but a wish to settle accounts with Lubowski's murderers. Once he had done this, he would probably bury the Kalashnikov and never harm a fly from then on. But what was the source of his savage determination and the unbridled hatred that recognized no solution but death? Clemencia now felt certain that they were rooted in something very personal.

She thought of the mother she barely remembered. All she knew of her was based on Miki Selma's and Miki Matilda's reminiscences.

Her father had never spoken of his wife, not even years afterwards. Had he seen or spoken with her before she died of her bullet wound? Would she herself ever recall being with her mother at the time? She didn't even know where her mother had been hit. In the head, in the back? When all this was over, she would …

She thought she heard a faint cough. Instantly, it revived her memory of the moments before Staal Burger's murder. The killer had uttered a cough as the sound of the shots died away. But hadn't it sounded different on the phone? Deeper? Or could that have been Angula? She peered at the dark shape of the wrecked car near the gap in the double fence. Not a movement, not a sound. The light beneath the front door had disappeared. The farmhouse and its outbuildings resembled black rocks with vignetted silhouettes. Clemencia picked up her pistol. The moon had set, the sky was thick with stars, the crickets continued to sing their unchanging song. Something was wrong.

Clemencia dared not move. She didn't smell danger, she could sense it like a cold breath wafting through the summer night, an irresistibly penetrating chill on the skin. She couldn't fight it off. The most she could do was grip her automatic although the butt felt unpleasantly greasy. What if she simply fired in the air? Would the killer take off or return fire?

She pictured his initial burst puncturing the tank overhead. Warmed by the heat of the day, the water would descend on her in a pleasant shower that washed away the dust and uncertainty and fear. The blood too, of course, if she'd been hit. She would watch the diluted red fluid dripping down and think of the mother she had never known, and wait for death to climb slowly up the ladder, put its hand on her shoulder, and say, 'It's time.'

But that was all nonsense. She didn't even know if the killer was really out there. Perhaps she hadn't heard a cough at all. Perhaps it was the grunt of an aardvark, the snort of a mule in the workers' quarters, or a growl from one of the bull terriers outside the house.

All she could now hear, at any rate, was the potent chirping of the crickets. She put her gun down on the boards in front of her and wiped her sweaty hands on her trousers.

There are sounds that leave you in doubt, either because they're too indistinct or because you have some reason not to recognize them for what they are. Something that sounds like a cough could be any number of things when you're staking out a lonely farmhouse in the Kalahari on a hot summer night. Other sounds are unmistakable. For instance that of a starter motor that whines and stutters, then catches. Someone floors the gas pedal, the engine roars into life, headlights blaze.

It was the *bakkie*, the pick-up laden with rolls of barbed wire, and it was less than twenty metres from her. That's to say, it had been there until a moment ago. Now it was on the move. It jounced along outside the two fences and swung left in a wide arc. The headlight beams swept the sandy, stony ground, briefly illuminating the wrecked car and the shadowy figure ducking down behind it, which had to be Angula. Then they picked up the entrance and turned into it. The driver made for the gap in the double fence, accelerated and turned on his headlights full beam. They floodlit the front of the farmhouse, revealing its sun-bleached walls, the green front door and the two dogs in front of it, which had sprung to their feet and were barking at the headlights with their heads to the fore.

Clemencia didn't reach for her pistol, nor did she climb down the ladder. Unable to move, she merely watched as the pick-up sped towards the bull terriers, engine roaring. She saw one of them cower away and the other leap forwards, teeth bared. Its chain glittered in the light and went taut. Then came a dull thud that reduced the animal to a contorted bundle of fur. Its pathetic whimpers were drowned by another, louder crash. Timber splintered, glass shattered. The rolls of barbed wire shot forwards under the impact, making a hideous noise as they scored the bodywork.

One headlight had gone out, but the other sufficed to show that the pick-up had smashed the front door in and was wedged in the opening at a slight angle. The bullbar was folded halfway back over the bonnet, the bodywork and near-side wing were grotesquely caved in. Now the second headlight went out too. A car door, evidently bent out of shape, was forced open and Angula called, 'Stop, don't move!'

As if roused by the sound of a human voice, Clemencia came to life at last. She stuffed the pistol into her waistband, climbed down the ladder and ran along the outside fence as fast as the darkness allowed. She darted past the gap to the wrecked car behind which Angula had taken up his position. Once she was in its lee she drew her gun, breathing fast and much too loudly. 'Angula?' she gasped.

No reply. He wasn't there. She peered over the bonnet at the farmhouse. The image of the pick-up wedged in the doorway had etched itself so deeply into her brain, she thought she could see it in every detail when all she could really see were dark shadows in the starlight. There was no apparent sign of movement. The house remained in darkness. God Almighty, there were two men inside whose only thought was to kill each other. Surely there must be some sign of life? And where the hell was Angula? Had he run off into the desert?

The night was fraught with the chirping of crickets. Clemencia couldn't have said whether it had continued unabated during the pandemonium moments earlier. Probably. Why should the crickets of the Kalahari be interested in whether a killer with a Kalashnikov was on the prowl? But she, being human and a policewoman, had to do something. First she would steal up to the *bakkie* unobserved, then she would see. Okay, move! She hesitated. You aren't scared, she told herself, you don't want to walk into a trap, that's all. It's only common sense to take another cautious look before you leave cover. There was nothing to be seen in front of the farmhouse but amorphous, motionless shadows.

Of course you're scared, she thought. You cling to life unlike those fools inside there, that's why. Better stay here like a good girl until they're through with one another. Better wait and see if one of them emerges and try to arrest him without running any unnecessary risks. It isn't a question of courage, Matti Jurmela had told her once, it's plain logical. If someone gives you the slip you've a chance of catching them another time. If you're dead, you haven't.

She instinctively ducked as the shots rang out. Four in quick succession, somewhere deep inside the house. Although muffled by the walls, they sounded crisp and dry. They certainly hadn't come from a Kalashnikov, sounded more like a handgun. Acheson? He had obviously not been taken by surprise. Another shot rang out, and another, all from the same weapon and all unanswered by the Kalashnikov. Clemencia half doubted whether the killer was inside the house at all. Perhaps Acheson was firing at incorporeal phantoms, enemies that existed only in his head, shades of his own past.

Someone uttered a sudden scream of unbridled agony, of mortal terror. It didn't come from inside the house, its source was definitely nearer. Clemencia glimpsed a wild tussle in progress near the pick-up, but she could make out nothing clearly. Throaty growls mingled with the shrill screams. That was when she recognized Angula's distorted voice. Darting out from behind the wrecked car, she ran towards the farmhouse. Another single shot rang out inside, this time answered by a short burst. The Kalashnikov. She took no notice, continued to run until she was only a few metres away. Angula had caught his leg on a roll of barbed wire and the surviving bull terrier had bitten his right hand. He was screaming and groaning and writhing and punching the dog's muzzle with his other hand, but the animal was hanging on like grim death. Its lips were drawn back and its teeth almost buried in Angula's flesh. Clemencia levelled her gun and steadied her aim with her left hand.

'Keep still, Angula!' she shouted. Angula tugged desperately at his hand and swung the animal around him in a semicircle without freeing himself. The bull terrier was now standing on its hind legs, so close up against him, they almost looked as if they were dancing together in an intimate embrace, a groaning, growling entanglement of limbs. Shooting the dog safely was impossible.

'Jesus, Angula!' she cried. Angula screamed something and clamped his left arm round the bull terrier. Bending over, he wound his arm around the animal's neck and squeezed with his hand buried in the fur on its neck. He was trying to throttle the brute.

'Goddammit!' she yelled. She jumped over the barbed wire, so close now that she could smell the sweat, the blood, the dog's effluvium. Its eyes glared up at her. It was still growling even though its jaws were firmly gripping Angula's hand, and even though his other arm must be cutting off its air supply. It had been trained to grip with its teeth and never let go. Clemencia planted the muzzle of the automatic between its eyes and adjusted the angle so as not to hit Angula if the bullet went right through. Angula gasped and panted, the dog continued to growl with the breath rasping in its throat. Clemencia shouted 'No!' and pulled the trigger. Once, twice.

The bull terrier reared up on its hind legs without a sound, without relaxing its grip. Then its limbs went limp and a final tremor ran through its fur. Its heavy body dangled from Angula's hand, teeth and jaws locked on it even in death. Clemencia had to prise them apart to release it. The palm and the ball of his thumb were a mass of bloody pulp, but there was no time to worry about that now. She went down on her knees to free his leg from the barbs while he stood there, mute and motionless. Issuing faintly from inside the house came a long, hollow bout of coughing. The killer.

'Come on, out of here!' Clemencia hissed. There was a ripping of cloth as she tore Angula's trousers free of the barbed wire. The dog's corpse flopped into the dust at last. The chain jingled as it fell.

'Come on!' she whispered.

Angula bent down in search of his pistol and picked it up awkwardly with his left hand. He pointed at the door. 'They're still in there,' he said.

'Exactly!' said Clemencia. She dragged him away from the house and through the gap in the fence until they were under cover. Angula sat down on the far side of the wrecked car with his back and head resting against the bodywork.

'My mistake,' he groaned. 'I thought he'd run over both the dogs. Then that one suddenly sprang out of the darkness and — '

'Did you see him?'

'It had me by the hand before I knew what was happening. I didn't have a chance to — '

'Did you see the killer?'

'The killer?' He stared at his mangled hand.

'Pull yourself together, man!'

'I didn't see any killer, just a shadowy figure that vaulted over the *bakkie*'s bonnet and disappeared into the house.'

'Tall or short? Fat or thin? Black or white?' Clemencia persisted.

'A ghost,' Angula said firmly, 'or he'd never have got past that bloody dog.'

'The dog's dead,' said Clemencia. It was highly unlikely that Acheson was still alive. Silence had reigned since that burst from the Kalashnikov. Even though she was otherwise engaged, she would have heard further gunfire. She kept her eyes on the farmhouse. All was dark, nothing was stirring.

'Can you tough it out?' she asked without looking at Angula.

'Acheson didn't have a chance,' he said, 'not against a ghost, but we ... '

'We what?'

Straightening up with an effort, Angula rested his left hand – the one holding the pistol – on the roof of the wrecked car. 'We'll gun him down as soon as he comes out.'

But he didn't come out, seemingly because he still had things to do inside. Perhaps he was looting Acheson's gun cabinet, or perhaps he was looking for something. Papers? Evidence relating to the Lubowski affair? Clemencia listened. They were too far away to hear a cough. They heard nothing until the Kalashnikov fired another burst. As the shots died away, Clemencia knew she'd been wrong: Acheson had still been alive. Until a moment ago. There could be only one explanation for the lull in the din of battle: the killer had had Acheson in his power since the end of the first exchange of shots. He must have disarmed or wounded him. Now he had executed him.

'He wanted to get some information out of Acheson,' Angula muttered. 'He was putting the squeeze on him, that's why he didn't kill him right away.'

He leant against the side of the wreck. The pistol in his left hand was trembling. He would fire at the first thing that moved, but he would miss. Clemencia would have to settle matters herself. She felt quite calm suddenly. While watching the door, she wondered if Acheson had talked. It might have occurred to him that the killer would take his life either way. On the other hand, if she herself had had to choose between certain death and an infinitesimal chance of evading it, she wouldn't have hesitated for long. She pictured the killer putting his questions to Acheson and saying, quite casually, 'The others wouldn't talk. That was their decision, Acheson, just as it's yours now. I'll give you five minutes. I won't ask you twice.'

Acheson had talked. The killer wouldn't even have promised to spare his life. In Clemencia's estimation, he hadn't done so. Although she'd never seen him, she felt she knew him quite well by now. Knowing how he acted was enough. He was a man who had no need to lie. He went his own uncompromising way, ruthless towards himself and others. He knew he would come to grief in the end and he didn't care. He had no future, only a mission in life, and it had yet to be fulfilled.

'Keep your eyes on the door,' Clemencia told Angula. Gun in hand, she stole along the outside of the double fence, going left. Almost exactly halfway round she saw a ladder leaning against the barbed wire. The boards over a window at the rear of the farmhouse had been prised off. She turned and gazed far out into the Kalahari. The sky was a tapestry of stars hanging down to the horizon.

✖✖✖

Ahead of them loomed the rocky escarpment on the western side of the Nossob Valley. They had gone cross-country, taking care to keep the Southern Cross on their left. They had climbed over cattle fences, made their way through *hakkie* bushes and trudged across the soft sand of the river bed. It had taken them an age to cover some two kilometres. He wouldn't have made it even this far on his own, but now he couldn't go any further.

The sports bag was slung over his shoulder like a rucksack. Coughing, he let it sink to the ground. The barrel of the Kalashnikov was protruding from one end. The wound in his thigh seemed to have stopped bleeding. At any rate, the tourniquet he'd improvised with his shirt was encrusted with congealed blood. His leg hurt like hell. If he'd had a knife he could have tried to extract the bullet.

'Don't make such a fuss,' his companion said in the darkness. 'It's only a harmless flesh wound.'

'The bullet's lodged in there,' he protested.

'It won't kill you,' said his companion.

'No?'

'No.'

'Well, you should know.'

His companion chuckled. He had appeared quite suddenly, up there beside the farmhouse. He had held the ladder for him when he clambered over the fence and he hadn't stirred from his side ever since. Whenever his knee gave way and he almost fell over, he had

152

urged him to stick it out. They still had things to do together, he said. The job wasn't finished yet.

'It's easy for you to talk,' he'd groaned.

'That's beside the point,' was the reply. 'Besides, I'm always with you.'

That was true. He had in fact been with him all the time. Outside the house in Ludwigsdorf, at Windhoek Airport, beside the burning car with the dead body in it, in the bus to South Africa, at Hluwluwe, inside the lorry when the doors were opened. He'd been a faithful companion from the start, but he hadn't talked to him until tonight. Now he said, 'It isn't safe here, you must climb the slope and go a little way into the veldt. Then you can sleep for an hour or two.'

He nodded. He had to climb the slope. If he crawled on all fours he wouldn't have to put so much weight on his injured leg. With the bag on his back he set off, scrambling uphill, slipping back, pressing on, feeling thorns prick his hands and red-hot needles transfix his thigh. Right at the top was some sand, soft sand. He rolled over on his side, coughing, and lay still. His companion bent over him. 'Come on, get up!'

'I can't,' he gasped.

'There's a farm track over there. You want someone to spot you when it gets light?'

'I've got to rest.'

'You'll have time enough for that later.'

He tried to sit up, pushing down hard with one hand, but fell back. His wound was still bleeding after all. Either that, or it had started again.

'There won't be any later,' he said.

'We still haven't reached that stage,' said his companion. His face was very close now. It didn't look the way one imagined. No empty eye sockets, no pallid, fleshless bones, no rows of grinning teeth where the lips had rotted away. The face resembled his own, as far as he could recall it. He and his companion could have been brothers, identical twins.

He shut his eyes. It was comforting not to be alone. He could count himself lucky to have a friend to watch over him, one whose cold hand froze all who approached. He could sleep easy, could even lose consciousness. Even if his companion had been lying and he was dying after all, he was doing so in the right company. Everything was fine.

He had restless dreams for all that. Dreams of a feverish dawn, of the colour red, of a glittering sun that shuttled to and fro overhead. He saw vultures circling and heard their ponderous wingbeats as they landed beside him. His tremulous hand waved them away. No, not yet. He couldn't feel his leg any more. Even his cough was better, but his companion had disappeared.

Then, when the sun was already reeling westwards, he surfaced again, probably because he had something important to do. A hand patted him gently on the cheek, a face bent over him. Grown old during the day, it had acquired deep-set eyes and leathery skin, and its mouth displayed more gaps than teeth. It looked more like a death's-head now.

'Is it time?' he asked.

Death replied in a language interspersed with clicks. Unable to understand it, he wondered what would happen if you failed to follow Death because you couldn't understand the order to accompany him. Would you live for ever? But Death knew what to do. It gripped him under the arms and knees, lifted him up, and toted him over to the farm track. Standing there was a two-wheeled, brightly painted cart with a donkey and a mule harnessed to it. Three grubby little children were seated on the box. Did *they* have to die too?

Death deposited him in the back of the cart and said something in its unintelligible language. The biggest of the children jumped down from the cart. Run, he thought, perhaps you'll escape with

154

your life! But the boy returned a moment later carrying his blue sports bag with the barrel of the Kalashnikov sticking out. Death clicked its tongue and the cart set off.

They lurched along through the heat. The children kept glancing at him surreptitiously. I need have no compunction now, he thought, not in Death's tumbril. Nothing mattered now. He gave the children a smile.

❈

'When's the stretcher coming?' Clemencia demanded. The policeman from Gobabis shrugged his shoulders. Donald Acheson's dead body was lying in his bedroom. His bare feet were protruding from beneath the blanket someone had draped over it. Heels uppermost, toes turned in. The blanket was grey and made of coarse, felted wool.

Between the body and the bed stood a waist-high chest of drawers which Acheson had obviously dragged into place for protection. As another precautionary measure he had positioned a large cheval mirror so that the bed was visible in it from the door. He had planned to shoot the killer from the side while he was firing at the mirror. The trick hadn't worked.

Acheson was dead, the bull terriers were dead, Angula was on his way to some doctor or other, the killer had disappeared without trace, and the whole of the Omaheke police force was hunting for a lorry driver named Morgan something, who was definitely the wrong man. It was a disaster. Clemencia stared at the soles of Acheson's feet, the calluses on the balls of his toes. If she'd arrested him yesterday, he would still be alive.

She could well have understood it if her boss had flown off the handle when she informed him on the phone of what had happened. She hadn't defended herself, merely noted in silence that Oshivelo proposed to contact the authorities in Gobabis in person and agree a future course of action. Clemencia was to return to Windhoek at

155

once and report to him, but she hadn't left right away. She couldn't. Not while Acheson's body was still lying there on the floorboards.

It was no use telling herself that she hadn't killed anyone – any human being, at least. She wondered how it had been for Acheson twenty years ago. Had he spared Anton Lubowski even a glance after gunning him down? Had he hesitated for one little moment? Had he felt a trace, if not of pity, at least of doubt?

She told herself that Acheson had been a murderous, racist swine. That he'd fallen prey to a crime made no difference because he'd brought it on himself. You reaped what you sowed, even if the seed took twenty years to ripen. Her sympathy for Acheson was limited, yet she couldn't come to terms with his death. She wanted to get away from this corpse beneath the grey blanket, but she couldn't.

Clemencia had seen more than one dead body. In Finland and Namibia, on the street and in the autopsy room. Men, women and children, shot and stabbed. It had never been a pleasant sight, but she'd always managed to preserve the detachment her job demanded. She couldn't understand why it should be different with Acheson, of all people. Was it that she'd been talking to him only yesterday? Or that she hadn't been able to prevent his murder? Or that she wasn't even certain she'd wanted to prevent it?

She eyed the bulges in the blanket. But for the feet, you might have fancied that a bundle of clothes was lying there. If you tried to cover them, the head would be exposed. The blanket wasn't designed to cover the whole of a corpse at full stretch. What if you bent him at the knees? She didn't move.

The policemen outside were looking for clues or supervising Acheson's workers, who were extracting the *bakkie* from the front door. There was no one in the bedroom except Clemencia and the dead man. No one visible, at least, but she felt she would bump into someone if she moved. It was as if death were still prancing around its victim. Death was more than present in this room; it seemed almost palpable. What if it reached for her?

'Hey!' she called in the direction of the door. 'Hey!'

She mustn't move, then nothing would happen to her.

'Hey!' she called again. She mustn't lose her nerve, not now. She hadn't slept all night, had witnessed a gun battle, shot a maddened bull terrier, applied a makeshift dressing to a mangled hand, found the body of an executed killer. No wonder she was in disarray.

One of the policemen came in. 'Yes, what is it?' he asked. He didn't seem to notice anything, moved quite naturally, and didn't – of course – bump into anyone.

'The body must be taken outside,' Clemencia told him. Her voice sounded strange.

'But the stretcher ... '

'Then carry it yourself!' she snapped.

The policeman said nothing.

'I have to examine the floor,' she explained, at a loss for anything else to say.

The man disappeared. She didn't move until he had returned with a colleague and carried the body out. Then she bent down. The bloodstains on the floorboards had already congealed. There was nothing to examine. She ran her hand over the wood. The body had gone but death was still there. She could sense it, smell it. It must have taken up residence in the room. She straightened up. At least she could move now, even though she groped her way along as if in utter darkness. She went outside.

She did, in fact, feel a little better as soon as she was out in the open. The sky was cloudlessly blue, the sun was shining. Leaving the scene to her colleagues from Gobabis, Clemencia asked if someone could drive her down to her car in the Nossob Valley. She noticed, when she was on the way back to Windhoek at last, that she still hadn't overcome her feeling of dread. Something dark and horrific was accompanying her in the car, clinging to her hands and forehead, chuckling maliciously when she mopped her brow. A residue of death had lodged inside her.

Shortly before Windhoek, she turned off right to the Avis Dam. Leaving the car in the car park, she set off along the top. The surface of the lake was lower than in previous dry seasons, so she had to climb down several metres to get to the water. It would certainly have done her good to jump in and swim, just swim, heedless of whether she reached the other side or succumbed to exhaustion and drowned, but she merely rolled up her trouser legs and dabbled her bare feet in the water. A white man was paddling his kayak far out. Little activity could be seen on the path round the lake. The joggers wouldn't turn up till evening, when the temperature was more tolerable. A few people were out walking their dogs. As far as she could tell, there wasn't a bull terrier among them.

She took out her mobile and read the latest text messages. Miki Matilda asked her to call back urgently. Miki Selma informed her that the minister had given an excellent sermon whose content she must convey to Clemencia as soon as possible. The other messages were from Claus Tiedtke. They read: 'Have you found anything out? Claus Tiedtke.' – 'I'd be much obliged if you kept me posted. Claus.' – 'Get in touch, damn it! Cl.' Clemencia deleted them all and turned off her mobile.

She had to get going, listen to Oshivelo reprimanding her, and get back to work. The dark shadow would disappear sooner or later. Acheson was dead, but it wasn't the end of the world. In front of her lay a calm, smooth expanse of water. The steep cliffs on the opposite shore were mirrored in the surface. At the flat, southern end, where the lake had retreated a long way, two Nile geese fluttered into the air, described a 180-degree arc, and landed again. In the sky, a handful of little white clouds were gliding leisurely westwards. Not a sign of anything that promised rain or relief. Clemencia blew an ant off her hand. All at once a bandy-legged dachshund material-ized beside her, gazing expectantly into her eyes. Then she heard someone behind her say, 'Well, did you come out here specially to give me back my 250 dollars?'

It was von Fleckenstein, who had put up Melvin's bail. That was all she needed. She tried to raise a smile but sensed that it was a failure.

'Very laudable of you,' he said.

'You'll get your money,' she replied. He nodded, then introduced his dachshund. Its name was Ludwig the Second, Luggi for short. She concentrated on the rhythmical movements of the kayaker across the lake.

'Anything wrong, inspector?' With a grunt, von Fleckenstein sat down beside her. The dachshund waddled off along the shore. 'There's something on your mind,' he added.

Clemencia's mind was her own business. She hadn't the faintest desire to unbosom herself to anyone, least of all a rather smarmy lawyer thirty years her senior. Nor was it she who answered. Something that defied her willpower said, 'You know who Donald Acheson was? He's dead. He was shot last night.'

'Did you … ?' von Fleckenstein asked.

'No,' she said. The kayaker had nearly reached the other side of the lake. He turned the craft and let it drift ashore. 'At least, not directly.'

'Heel, Luggi!' von Fleckenstein called to the dachshund. 'A puff adder bit him once,' he explained. 'We were near the car, so I was able to get him to a vet in time. Luckily.'

'Luckily indeed,' said Clemencia.

The dachshund came lolloping up, wagging its tail. Von Fleckenstein fondled the dog's furry head. 'Acheson shot Lubowski,' he said. 'Whoever killed him deserves a medal.'

Clemencia watched the kayaker get to his feet, retaining his balance with care.

Von Fleckenstein grunted. 'When a man like Acheson is ferried across the Jordan, it's a blessing for the entire country. An act of national defence, so to speak, and I've always been in favour of that, if only because it's a family tradition. Shall I tell you a story, inspector?'

'No,' she said.

'It's about an uncle on my mother's side,' he went on regardless. 'It must have been in the 'sixties – 1962, perhaps, or 1963. Anyway, he'd gone to the Skeleton Coast to find gold. To *look for* gold would be more accurate, or so you'd think, but it didn't apply in my uncle's case. He intended to find gold without looking for it. How? With the help of some home-made cartridges enriched with gold dust, which he planned to fire at appropriate veins in the rock. These were later to be shown to potential investors as evidence of worthwhile deposits.

'Don't call it fraud! His route to the Promised Land was arduous in the extreme. There's still nothing much on the Skeleton Coast north of Terrace Bay, and in those days there was nothing at all. No roads, no petrol pumps, no shops, no people, no water. Just a few desert elephants and any number of gemsbock you could eat your fill of if you were a reasonably good shot. My uncle didn't suffer from hunger, but it was a hard life all the same.

'Well, one evening after a long day's trek he was sitting on the beach, gazing out to sea with his rifle beside him just in case. The waves came rolling in with the sun sinking below the horizon beyond them. The likelihood that there was anyone within 200 kilometres of him, north or south, was wellnigh non-existent. So my uncle was all the more surprised when something grey – definitely not a sea creature of any kind – broke surface some 300 metres from the shore. He couldn't believe his eyes at first, but the further the thing emerged from the water, the less doubt there could be it was a submarine's conning tower! He screwed up his eyes. In spite of the unfavourable evening light, he clearly made out a red star on the side of the superstructure. It was a Soviet Navy submarine!

'I don't know, inspector, if you're familiar with the international situation in those days. The Cuban missile crisis was very recent. Everyone knew that nuclear war between the two superpowers had only been avoided by a whisker. Kennedy's naval blockade had induced Khrushchev to climb down at the last moment and withdraw his rockets from Cuba.

'But withdraw them to where? That was what my uncle asked himself that evening on the Skeleton Coast. Did the Russians intend to install themselves and their nuclear missiles in South West Africa? My uncle had little time for the Boers of the Union – he tolerated them as long as they let him swindle them – but he found the Communists more suspect still. If they came to power, it would be the end of staking claims for sale to the idiots who offered most for them.

'No, this incipient invasion must be firmly nipped in the bud! Kennedy and his marines were on the other side of the Atlantic, however, and the South African forces weren't much closer. My uncle would have taken several days to get to the nearest telephone. What could he do? He looked at the submarine. It was out beyond the breakers but definitely inside territorial waters. Though all on his own, he was a man with a gun and would do his best. So he cocked his rifle, aimed, and opened fire, reloaded and continued to blaze away. Eight shots, eight hits, all in the black. Or rather, in the red: in the centre of the Soviet star on the submarine's conning tower.

'"How do you know you didn't miss?" I asked my uncle later on. He admitted that the effect of a bullet on a submarine was harder to spot than the effect of a bullet on an oryx, but no one who could drill a gemsbock's shoulder blade at 300 metres was going to miss a stationary vessel. Besides, events proved him right. After the eighth shot, the submarine slowly submerged. The conning tower slid back beneath the surface, and moments later there was nothing to be seen, far and wide, but mirror-smooth sea. The other submarines in the invasion fleet, of whose existence my uncle was firmly convinced, had never surfaced at all. The Russians simply hadn't expected to encounter such stubborn resistance on such a remote and godforsaken coast.'

Von Fleckenstein stroked his dog's muzzle. The dachshund sneezed. Clemencia said, 'That's a cock-and-bull story if ever I heard one.'

He nodded mournfully. 'Few people believed my uncle either. He himself wished it hadn't happened, afterwards, because the tragic dénouement is still to come. In his excitement – which was only too understandable in someone who suddenly finds the fate of the free world resting on his shoulders – my uncle had reached into the wrong pocket and repelled the Russians with his doctored rounds instead of normal hunting ammunition. The red star on the submarine's conning tower was plastered with genuine gold dust, leaving him empty-handed. His basic investment had been wasted and the expedition was doomed to failure. My uncle would have made millions, sure as eggs, but he never recovered from this fiasco. I'm not complaining because he left our family nothing but debts when he died; I simply deplore the cruel irony of fate. Why should a man who unhesitatingly takes on a task of historic importance have to sacrifice his personal prosperity? Is that fair?'

Clemencia stared at von Fleckenstein. He tossed a pebble into the water and said, 'It's always fascinated me, the way the rings expand.'

'That wasn't about your uncle, was it?' said Clemencia. 'It was about Anton Lubowski. He paid with his life – unfairly so – for having taken a stand. Did you invent the whole story just to convey that? Did you mean that our killer has belatedly compensated for the injustice of fate? That I was right to let Acheson meet his end?'

Von Fleckenstein shook his head. 'It was only about my uncle, of course. He's largely forgotten outside our family – quite unfairly so, if you ask me. I could tell you some more stories —— '

'No thanks,' said Clemencia. It might well be that every tragedy was reflected in a comedy, but that wasn't true in this case. Even if the lawyer's story accorded with the facts, it wasn't comparable with the Lubowski affair, nor did it have anything in common with what she had done or neglected to do. It had been a well-meant attempt to help her, but it hadn't. The darkness of night didn't end when you lit a sparkler. As soon as the sparkler burnt out, it was darker than before.

Clemencia drove back to headquarters and returned the car. Robinson passed her on the stairs to the offices of the Serious Crime Unit. He swept past without a word. It seemed that Oshivelo hadn't deemed it necessary to speak to her before demolishing her in front of her team, so she could let him wait a bit longer. She went to see if Angula had reported back yet, but the only person in his office was van Wyk. He had his feet up on the desk and was gorging on potato crisps. The mountains of files that had filled the room were gone.

'Chief's orders,' said van Wyk. The files must be returned, Oshivelo had decreed. There was to be an end of all this chaos and time-wasting. They had to concentrate on essentials.

That sounded good, but what was essential? Essential to whom? Clemencia said nothing. Van Wyk folded up his half-empty bag of crisps, then changed his mind and offered her some. 'What news of Angula?' she asked.

Van Wyk shrugged his shoulders.

'And Robinson?'

'A successful interrogation at just the wrong moment.' Van Wyk grinned. With undisguised malicious glee, he announced that the Angolan Robinson had been grilling had actually confessed after a six-hour marathon in the interview room. He had done so at one that morning, or around the time the real killer had shot his latest victim 300 kilometres away. Robinson had first learned of this when Clemencia phoned in. Shortly afterwards, as luck or the devil would have it, the final report from ballistics had landed on his desk. This stated that the Angolan's Kalashnikov definitely wasn't the murder weapon. Robinson had blathered something about copycat killers and another weapon. In a desperate attempt to salvage the unsalvageable, he had questioned the Angolan yet again. Oshivelo had finally put an end to this palaver. A suspect no longer, the Angolan had been released and Robinson summoned to the chief's office. Their conversation didn't appear to have been too harmonious, van Wyk concluded.

The conversation facing Clemencia was bound to be little different. Should she take another few minutes to perfect her strategy? But there was no strategy she could devise that didn't amount to lame excuses. The fact was, someone had to take responsibility for the debacle, and who should it be but her? She left van Wyk to his crisps and knocked on the Deputy Commissioner's door. Oshivelo invited her to sit down. He himself remained standing beside the window.

'Very good, inspector,' he said. 'Congratulations on finding out Donkerkop's real name. We soon managed to trace Martinus Cloete's address, but the man has disappeared. There's a general alert out for him. It really looks as if Acheson was telling the truth. Martinus Cloete is our killer.'

'Or another potential victim,' said Clemencia. 'All that seems certain is that he was involved in Lubowski's murder.'

Oshivelo kept his back to her. He said, 'That's not your problem now, inspector. First you need time to get over that gunfight and so on. You've thoroughly earned a little break after such a stressful experience. So has Constable Angula. Policemen and policewomen aren't machines. I shall put it to the public in those terms, and I'm sure everyone will sympathize. I'm taking over the case myself. Go home and stay there until further notice.'

'Until further notice?'

Oshivelo was staring intently out of the window. Heaven alone knew what he saw out there. Sunlight, birds, passers-by, a case he could manipulate from now on? 'Any questions, inspector?' he asked.

Clemencia rose. 'Does this mean I'm officially suspended from duty?'

'You're recharging your batteries, that's all.'

She turned to go and had already reached the door when Oshivelo added, 'Oh yes, inspector, please turn your gun in. Just for our internal enquiry. We don't want it rumoured that you shot Acheson yourself.'

Clemencia exited without a word. As she was descending the stairs her mobile signalled a text message. It was Claus Tiedtke, asking if she was still alive. She texted back, 'Like to go out on the town tonight?'

'Nice to know you're still alive and kicking! When and where?'

'Where it's so loud, conversation is impossible,' she texted back.

❊❊❊

Ndangi Oshivelo, Deputy Commissioner of the Namibian police:

Lubowski was under surveillance, of course, like anyone else who occupied a responsible position, and those who kept him under surveillance were naturally under surveillance themselves. That's the way it goes when power is at stake. You have to know what's going on in your own camp or you're done for from the outset. If you're better informed about your enemies than they are about you, you're one step ahead of them. It's tempting but dangerous to go further. For instance, to create an impression from which your opponents are bound to draw the wrong conclusions. The South Africans gave a wonderful demonstration of this where the business of the cheques was concerned.

In 1989, Anton Lubowski was – among other things – SWAPO's deputy head of finance, in which capacity he carried out a large number of transactions on the Party's behalf. He was also entrusted with purchasing a large consignment of furniture for Party leaders returning from exile and our new Party offices. The South African firms capable of filling such an order were all owned by whites who were more or less closely associated with the apartheid regime. Lubowski was averse to doing business with them.

Opportunely enough, he had become acquainted via the French embassy with a French businessman resident in Windhoek. This Alain Guenon

165

was reputed to be a friend, not only of the Mitterand family but also of Winnie Mandela, and was thus, politically speaking, quite irreproachable. Guenon offered to help. He and his firm, Gijima Express, had the requisite contacts and could supply the furniture quickly and on favourable terms. He introduced Lubowski to his associate, Rob Colesky, who was to handle the transaction.

A purchase price of 2,000,000 rand was agreed and the contract was signed. The 100,000 rand remitted to Lubowski in three tranches corresponded to five per cent of the total price, and was thus the commission normal in such cases. One can argue over whether it was morally legitimate to accept the money personally. Lubowski had no qualms about it, anyway. In view of all he'd learned about his business partners, he could never have guessed that Gijima was merely a cover firm for South African military intelligence, and that acting as its agent was Colesky's main occupation.

What rendered the situation still more opaque was that each party was out for himself. The original aim of the operation seemed to have been to introduce bugged furniture into SWAPO offices and our leaders' private residences as a means of obtaining confidential information. For that, the transaction should have gone ahead in as above-board and unsuspicious a manner as possible. However, Guenon's and Colesky's personal intention was to make a packet by slapping more than eighty per cent on the purchase price and submitting part invoices to SWAPO twice over.

In September 1989 we finally spotted that there something fishy about the furniture deal – and 'we' definitely included Lubowski himself. He could perhaps be accused of being too trusting at first where Guenon was concerned, but no more than that. He had made no attempt to keep the payments secret or conceal his contacts, so the imputation that he deliberately betrayed us is absurd. No, he was simply taken for a ride. For all that, the matter could not be allowed to become public knowledge. Payments into Lubowski's account from the South African secret service would have cast an unfavourable light on him and the entire Party.

What has all this to do with Lubowski's murder? Nothing, absolutely nothing. On the South African side, it is clear that one hand didn't know

166

what the other was doing. The CCB and Acheson had their own agenda. This was to disrupt the SWAPO election campaign with acts of violence and prevent Sam Nujoma from returning to Namibia as planned. That the furniture deal coincided with this was quite fortuitous.

In retrospect, of course, no one believed this. Everything had to be bent so that each piece of the jigsaw fitted logically into the others. When the South African minister of defence, Magnus Malan, had his back to the wall, he made play with the bank transfers to Lubowski to prove that he, Malan, and his people had no reason to kill their own spy. The other side declared that the South Africans' aim from the outset had been to render Lubowski susceptible to blackmail, and, when he proved immune to it, that he had been killed and the responsibility palmed off on SWAPO.

What do the 100,000 rand in Lubowski's bank account prove? Nothing whatsoever. The more one endeavours to underpin one's version of the truth with facts, the more – curiously enough – it becomes a question of faith. One edifice of ideas stands opposed to another. Each is so solidly built that it seems indestructible, yet both cannot be valid. Perhaps neither of them is. Perhaps one should refrain from looking for underlying factors when there aren't any.

4

DREAMS

The morning turned out to be better than Clemencia had feared when she first woke up. She showered, and later they had breakfast together. That's to say, she just had some coffee. She didn't touch the muesli, fried eggs, toast and marmalade. Claus apologized for having no mealie porridge in the house. He'd never been able to stand the stuff, he said.

It didn't matter, Clemencia lied, she never had breakfast anyway. Then they talked about breakfast habits and their favourite meals. Clemencia said nothing of her bad dreams during the night. Acheson's corpse had played no part in them, strangely enough. Death had moved on and taken up its abode in the bull terrier's eyes with the muzzle of her pistol between them. Yellow, malevolent eyes expressive of only one regret: that an attack dog couldn't sink its fangs in more than one victim at a time.

'A little fruit, at least?' Claus asked. When she shook her head he chatted away and grinned at her. He had gathered without being told that he'd better not touch her. Nonetheless, she said she had to go. She firmly declined his offer of a lift to Katutura. Her relations were being difficult enough already, she said, and if a white man brought her home after two nights away …

'Who are you accountable to?' he asked.

'No one,' she replied. Only to myself, if anyone, she thought. 'All the same,' she said.

'I'll call you,' said Claus.

'Not today.'

'Text you?'

'Tomorrow.'

'Is there anything I ought to know?' he asked.

'No.'

For safety's sake, Clemencia turned off her mobile as soon as she was sitting in the taxi. She got to Frans Hoesenab Straat shortly after ten. As far as her family were concerned, Claus might just as well have driven her home and carried her in through the garden gate in his arms. It would have made no difference. In the front yard, Jessica and some neighbours' children were skipping around beneath the awning to the music blaring from the Mshasho Bar. Jessica danced up to Clemencia waggling her hips and giggling. 'Well,' she asked, 'what's he like?'

'Why aren't you at school?' Clemencia retorted.

'They've extended the holidays because there was something wrong with the enrolments, and ... Oh, I don't know. But do tell!'

'Mind your own business,' said Clemencia. Her father was sitting on the bench with his back against the wooden shack. He gave her a cursory nod and went on dozing, but she couldn't escape a remark from her brother.

'Respect, that's what you've got to insist on,' Melvin said. 'Especially because he's white. If he doesn't treat you with respect, he'll have me to deal with. Make that clear to him, Clemencia!'

Melvin turned away and went on tinkering with an old refrigerator which he had bought, stolen, found, or procured in some other way. Miki Selma clapped her hands above her head at the sight of Clemencia. They'd been so worried about her! And now, after nearly a week, there she was!

'It was only two days,' said Clemencia.

'The two longest days of my life!' Miki Selma cried. Her reproachful tone conveyed that Clemencia had personally put the times out of joint. 'I don't know what I'd have done if the minister hadn't reassured me. "It's quite normal when two young people have only just fallen in love," he said. "But Reverend," I said. "Just pray they haven't done anything foolish," he told me. Well, have you?'

'Help me, Selma, I must be going.' Miki Matilda scarcely deigned to glance at Clemencia. She was wearing several long dresses, one on top of another, and holding a rolled-up newspaper of the kind Herero women used to reinforce their traditional head-gear. She had a piece of material that matched her uppermost gown but couldn't tie it around the headdress by herself. No wonder, since Miki Matilda hadn't learnt to do this as a child. She was a Damara, not a Herero.

'It's because of Joseph Tjironda,' Miki Selma explained. 'He was a Herero.'

Miki Matilda brandished the newspaper in the air. 'I knew it was useless to treat him for pneumonia before the evil spell had been lifted. What am I saying, though! Useless isn't the word. They killed him, those qualified know-alls at the hospital with their tablets and transfusions, their beeping and humming contraptions. And I was well on the way – I almost had the spell under control. It could only have been a matter of hours before Tjironda — '

'And now?' Clemencia asked.

'Even I can't bring him back from the dead,' said Miki Matilda.

'The family want a traditional funeral before the church cere-mony,' said Miki Selma.

'Which is the least they can do after abandoning him to the mercy of the doctors!'

'Miki Matilda has to be there by ten,' said Miki Selma. The alarm clock on the chest of drawers said ten-twenty.

'Well,' said Miki Matilda, 'It isn't likely that Joseph Tjironda has any other plans for today.'

'They've engaged *you*?' Clemencia asked incredulously.

'Of course,' said Miki Matilda. 'My reputation has got around, even among the Hereros.'

Her secondary occupation was that of professional mourner.

Although Clemencia had never seen her at work, she'd been told that Miki Matilda was unsparing in her efforts. She tore her hair, beat her breast, wept and wailed and lamented to the point of exhaustion. She was so hoarse that all she could do for days afterwards was croak. This was a very agreeable state of affairs mainly because Miki Selma, far from exploiting the situation, maintained a sympathetic silence.

Clemencia thoroughly welcomed it when Miki Matilda contributed to the family's income in this way, but with certain reservations. Morally, at least, it seemed questionable that Miki Matilda did not draw a clear distinction between her two professions. Clemencia pointed out that accepting payment for mourning a person whose death she had failed to prevent in her capacity as a faith healer could give rise to wild speculation. People might, for instance, wonder if all her chicken's-liver hocus-pocus was simply a guarantee of further employment.

'It isn't hocus-pocus,' Miki Matilda hissed.

'It's the combination of the two,' said Clemencia. 'For instance, if I ran an undertaker's on the side – one that specialized in victims of violence ... '

'It would be very smart of you,' Miki Selma broke in. 'You'd always be a step ahead of the competition.'

' ... and if I shot a couple of suspects every week and profited from arranging their funerals, people would also think I might have — '

'After informing the families of the sad news,' Miki Selma pursued, 'you could offer them a complete package: coffin, floral tributes, paperwork – the lot.'

Miki Matilda elaborated on this theme. 'It's a great idea! What would one need to set up an undertaker's?'

'A few sample coffins, maybe. But Clemencia's savings would cover those.'

'We'd need a nice name, like ... '

171

'The Final Journey!'

'Nonsense, that sounds like some shady dive on the outskirts of town. It has to be something religious. How about "In God We Trust"?'

'Isn't that the name of a rival firm? I seem to have heard it somewhere ... '

'That's enough!' Clemencia shouted, but neither of them could understand why she was so worked up. Faith healers healed as best they could, the dead had to be mourned and buried, and the living had to wage a daily battle for survival. Life was like that. What was so complicated or reprehensible about it?

'Young lady,' said Miki Matilda, 'if you've got a problem with the world, it doesn't have to be the world's fault.'

There could even be a grain of truth in that, Clemencia told herself. Perhaps she ought to get Miki Matilda to teach her the professional mourner's trade. She might use the technique for her own purposes. It would be good just to yell, to rid her system of dread, darkness and death until she felt entirely empty – until she was once more capable of facing up to whatever each new day brought in its train ...

Miki Matilda was saying something. The Herero headdress, with its two hornlike excrescences, was now enthroned on her head.

'What?' said Clemencia.

'Can you lend me your mobile? I still haven't managed to buy myself some more airtime.'

Clemencia listened to Miki Matilda making extensive enquiries about the Tjironda relations who were present. Oh, so the aunts and cousins from Otjiwarongo had turned up too? The deceased couldn't have failed to be pleased, she said. Yes, Joseph was a good man with a great deal of family feeling. He definitely deserved a funeral with all the trimmings.

'The more dung, the bigger the family,' Miki Selma whispered. Clemencia didn't know the saying, but its meaning was clear. The more dung, the more cattle, and in view of such family wealth, even the most distant relations naturally expected to be subsidized. However, Miki Selma seemed to think that only blood aunts were entitled to batten on such members of the family as were employed by the police.

Meantime, Miki Matilda was phoning an assurance that she would be there any minute – in fact she was sitting in a taxi right now. Clemencia was already counting out the requisite small change for which her aunt would tap her at any moment. She naturally couldn't let Miki Matilda look a liar in front of the Tjirondas. Walking to the other side of Katutura in this heat and a heavy Herero headdress would have been too much to ask.

Miki Matilda took the taxi money as if it were due payment for returning the mobile phone. Then she swept out of the gate with head erect. Clemencia fled to her room before Miki Selma had a chance to pump her about last night. On the threshold she was assailed by a pungent smell. Rotting meat? Milk spilt a considerable time ago? She opened the window and went in search of its source as soon as she could breathe with relative ease. The origin of the stench was not hard to find, she had only to trace it to the flies swarming beneath her bed. She bent down.

Several little bones had been arranged in a circle, and the disgusting smell emanated from a cup in the middle, which was filled with some unidentifiable liquid. The bones, too, seemed to exert an irresistible attraction on the blowflies. Miki Matilda had probably marinaded them in the unappetizing brew. Propped against the cup were a little mirror in a pink plastic frame and a snapshot of Claus Tiedtke. A wooden rosary lying somewhat inconsequentially amid the bones betrayed that Miki Selma had also had a finger in the pie.

Clemencia straightened up, went out to the fruit stall in the street, hauled Miki Selma to her feet without a word, and marched her back to her room. Then she pointed beneath the bed. Miki

Selma's nostrils flared. Spreading her arms, she said, 'It may not have been the whole of the traditional recipe. You should really burn the bark or roots of some bush or other, but Matilda couldn't remember which. She hadn't done a love spell for ages, so we had to improvise a bit. It helped, though, didn't it?'

'Mikis, get rid of this muck at once!' Clemencia commanded.

'When a spell doesn't seem to work, Matilda says it's nearly always because you haven't given it enough time. I mean, you'd soon get used to the smell, and you could leave the window open at night until — '

'Get rid of it!' Clemencia snarled menacingly.

'Well, if you're sure ... ' Grumbling, Miki Selma went to fetch a dustpan and brush. She gingerly recovered the rosary, mirror and photo, then disposed of the cup. While sweeping up the rest, she told Clemencia that men shouldn't be trusted too readily. All men could behave themselves for a day or two when they wanted something out of a woman, but it took a while to discover which ones really had the makings of a husband. She wasn't trying to blight Clemencia's marriage plans, just warning her to be careful. And not to spurn the help of mature women with experience of life.

Claus Tiedtke's photo showed him smiling as pensively as if someone had just given him the low-down on Clemencia's family.

'Where did you get it?' asked Clemencia.

Miki Selma spread her arms again. 'Your intended gave it to me of his own free will, honest to God! "If she'd like it, of course she can have it." That's what he said.'

Clemencia shook head. 'How did you get in here, anyway?'

Miki Selma carried the laden dustpan outside. 'Ugh!' went Jessica and her girlfriends as she tipped it into the dustbin. Then she said, 'A friend of Melvin's helped us. A really smart youngster. You wouldn't believe how quickly he picked the lock.'

Melvin looked up from his refrigerator and grinned.

He wondered whether he was dead or alive. The absence of pain suggested that he was dead. The fact that he was coughing indicated the opposite. Perhaps he'd died and come to life again. Perhaps he was in the process of dying for the umpteenth time.

An arm inserted itself beneath his shoulders and lifted him. His head fell back. If he opened his eyes he would see what lay behind the darkness. The darkness wasn't really black; it was more like a thousand superimposed colours flashing in such a way that they almost neutralized one another. But only almost. The hectic flashes were driving him mad. He didn't want to see anything, anything at all, but he didn't know how to achieve this. He couldn't do more than shut his eyes, could he?

A hand supported his head and something metallic was applied to his lower lip. The rounded rim of a mug or a cup. He felt a few drops of liquid trickle down his chin from the corners of his mouth. He tried to open his mouth and apparently succeeded, because a little of the liquid moistened his parched tongue and gums. It tasted terribly bitter, but that was all right. How else should it taste? Sweet? He swallowed, coughed, waited for the mug to be put to his lips and swallowed again.

Slowly, the upper part of his body sank back. He wasn't sure if hands were supporting his head, just felt surprised that it didn't loll around in all directions. When he was flat on his back, the flashes of polychrome black reappeared before his eyes and he heard something that vaguely resembled birds twittering. He wondered where he'd heard it before. Then he realized that someone was addressing him in the click language. But it wasn't Death – not unless Death had borrowed the voice of an old woman.

He tried to say, apologetically, that he didn't understand bird language, but he couldn't utter a sound – couldn't even remember how you went about speaking. Besides, it wasn't true at all: he understood everything the voice was saying, even though not a single word was familiar to him. He heard stories of Creation, of the primeval time in which everything had been quite different. Hills roamed around and celestial bodies had yet to settle in their predetermined places. The Sun Man dwelt on earth with light concealed in his armpit. Only when he raised his arm did it become light, so people could go hunting. At the same time, it became so hot that they burned to death in agony. The stars did not appear in the sky until a girl lost her temper because her mother wouldn't give her any of the food she was cooking. She reached into the fire and hurled it all into the darkness. The roasted roots and the embers became stars, the ashes the Milky Way.

Animals were still human in those days, even though they already had their names. They spoke, danced and got married, and even the elephants ate meat when they could get it. Only when humans stole fire from the ostrich did animals become animals. Or – so others said – when Haitsi-Aibeb scattered them because they were celebrating his death.

He tried to nod. He thoroughly agreed that the first Creation had to be eliminated. On that point he was all in favour of Haitsi-Aibeb, or whoever. But the stories still weren't at an end. More and more of the old woman's bird-language sentences floated around him. They gyrated like guinea-fowl feathers in a warm breeze, drifted down and softly covered him up. He felt pleasantly warm, dozing beneath his coverlet of bird-language words, and grew weary.

Time stood still or went by, and whenever he awoke some more of the bitter drink was trickled between his lips. He gulped and choked and coughed and listened to the bird-language sounds that explained how humans and animals differed in the present age. An animal always remained what it was, whereas a human could turn into a jackal, a tortoise, an owl, or any of the other animals in the Kalahari. They liked to do this, too, so you could never be sure

176

when seeing a jackal whether it really was one, not a human who had assumed its form for some sinister reason. Those who overdid such metamorphoses would soon forget what they really were. And that, of course, made it difficult for them to slip back into their old skin.

He felt a sudden movement beside him, then something cool on his upper thigh. His eyes opened of their own volition, it seemed. Above him he saw an expanse of dried mud with criss-crossed branches protruding from it in places: the roof of a hut. He propped himself on his elbows. In the gloom he made out an old woman endlessly muttering to herself. She was squatting beside him on her heels and smearing the wound in his thigh with a herbal ointment. On the other side, the three children were watching in silence.

'What day is it?' he asked. The old woman shook her head. She covered the ointment on his thigh with an old rag and knotted it in place.

'How long have I been asleep?' he asked. He coughed, deep in his lungs. The old woman said something in bird-language. The boy on the other side twittered back, and the old woman responded briefly.

'*Nog nie lank genoeg nie,*' the boy translated into Afrikaans. Not long enough yet. The old woman's hand exerted gentle downward pressure on his chest. Her fingers reminded him a little of a bird's claws, but he didn't mind. He was now lying stretched out on his back again. Not long enough yet? He closed his eyes and allowed himself to be swathed in more stories in bird-language. There were many such stories, because every hill, bush and shower of rain had a story of its own that wanted to be told and contained the seeds of the next one. And so it would go on until the end of time, and even the end of time would have a story that was only waiting to be told during the next Creation.

He hoped to learn something of the jackal that tried to transform itself into a human, although this wasn't really possible, and he was eager to see if the jackal succeeded notwithstanding. But he waited in vain. It probably wasn't time yet, so he snuggled up in the twittered tale of Gatsing, the clever little girl who took refuge from a man-eater by climbing a tree. When the man-eater started to shake the tree, Gatsing called a vulture and told it to carry her home. The man-eater chased after her, fruitlessly lashing out at her shadow. Then he heard how Tsui-Goab acquired his name, 'Wounded Knee'. Gaunab overpowered him again and again, but his strength increased each time they fought. In the end he succeeded in killing evil Gaunab with a blow behind the ear. Before dying, Gaunab wounded him in the knee, which was why everyone called him Tsui-Goab and his real name was forgotten.

So story followed story. He heard more about Haitsi-Aibeb and other duplicitous demigods, about murderous predators and dauntless hunters, and at some stage he fell asleep and slept for hours or days. The old woman had gone when he awoke. Seated around him were the three children, the old man he'd mistaken for Death, and a younger woman who addressed him in Afrikaans.

'You're very sick.'

'No,' he said. The woman was probably the mother of the three children.

'They're looking for you,' she said. 'You killed a policeman. And another man, over there on the other side of the Nossob.'

'Yes,' he said. He remembered. The three children stared at him wide-eyed. They showed no fear. Children were afraid of all manner of things, but never of what was really dangerous.

'*Hoekom*? Why?' asked the woman.

He looked around the mud hut. His blue bag was lying near the entrance. The barrel of the Kalashnikov was sticking out.

'Why did you kill them?'

He coughed. He had slept for a long time, but not for long enough to be able to turn into something else. He said, 'I killed them because they wouldn't let my children live.'

178

He was sitting on a thin foam plastic mattress with a brown blanket on top of it. A blanket of the kind relief agencies distributed when the north of the country was half-flooded during the rainy season. He wasn't in the north, though, and there were no floods at present. Drought prevailed.

'Are you lying?' asked the woman.

'No,' he said.

✳

The hot, stuffy night was all-embracing, and the bull terrier's eyes shone like two outsize moons. They sucked in your gaze until you lost yourself in their cold light. It was useless to look for anything human in them. They were the eyes of an animal, after all. An attack dog, and it was dead. Clemencia was only imagining those pale yellow orbs. They were hovering above her in the darkness, so close that the bull terrier could have ripped her face to pieces with one quick bite. If it had really existed.

Dogs weren't Clemencia's thing. Once, when she was a child, they'd kept a stray mongrel for a few weeks. The animal was lame in one hind leg when they took it in. It had limped around, getting in everyone's way, and was run over in the street shortly afterwards. Clemencia would have liked to bury it in the back yard, but Miki Matilda said that was out of the question. Then the carcass had suddenly disappeared.

Clemencia didn't know how you trained dogs. Many breeds had an innate or inculcated instinct for killing, no doubt, but what she had detected in the eyes of Acheson's bull terrier was more than that. It was the product of careful training, after which the animal could not only be relied on to carry out its allotted task but became one with it. Nothing else mattered but biting, hanging on and destroying, even at the cost of its own destruction. Clemencia felt sure that the dog had known what would happen when she squeezed the trigger. It hadn't cared, it had no choice. To that extent, the merciless killing machine had also been a helpless victim. Was that why she couldn't forget the look in the bull terrier's eyes just before she fired?

She stared at the yellow orbs above her, less scared than before of their cold, cruel gaze, their suicidal certainty. Those eyes could see no chance of changing anything, were ignorant of any alternatives. Did that also apply to the unknown killer? Was what made him a perfect murderer the fact that he was a perfect victim imprisoned in obsessions, situations and relationships that were inescapable because of their all-determining and all-embracing nature?

Damn it, she thought. She didn't feel sympathy for him, surely? Not for a multiple murderer? It certainly wasn't her job to condone his actions. His motives must be of interest to her only insofar as they helped to catch and convict him. And not even that was true any more. She had been sent on leave. None of it had anything to do with her now. If only those big, yellow canine eyes wouldn't stare at her from every corner of the room!

It was stiflingly hot. She got up and went off to shower. Rhythmical thuds were emanating from the Mshasho Bar and a couple of drunks yelling in the street. The cold water felt good, but no sooner was she back on her bed than she started sweating as profusely as before. She turned on her mobile, deleted three text messages from Claus Tiedtke, and called Angula. Although it was nearly two a.m. he answered after the second ring. He couldn't sleep either, apparently.

'How's the hand?' she asked.

'All right.'

'Good, that's something at least.'

'Yes.'

'Angula?' She would have liked to know if the bull terrier's eyes were glowing above his bed too.

'Boss?'

'Donkerkop isn't the killer, or he wouldn't have run off. The killer isn't someone who murders, runs off and returns to his normal life. He doesn't have a normal life, I've grasped that now. His life is identical with his mission. If it had been Donkerkop who wanted to get rid of his accomplices in Lubowski's murder, Acheson's death would have completed the job. Donkerkop would have sat beside Acheson's body and waited for us. Or killed himself. The killer would have called it quits, because he's … '

Clemencia broke off. The killer was like an attack dog that has fulfilled its destiny, the moment it has lived for. There was nothing after that.

'Anyway,' she went on, 'he wouldn't have run off. But he did, and that means he isn't through yet. Someone who was there is still missing, namely Donkerkop. He's the last victim, so he can't be the killer. '

From outside in the street came the sound of a bottle smashing, then men's heated voices.

'Angula?'

'Boss?'

'What do you think?'

'Oshivelo had my files removed. All of them!'

'I know,' she said.

'Even if I got hold of them again,' said Angula, 'who could guarantee some vital piece of evidence wouldn't suddenly have gone missing?'

'No one.'

'Exactly.'

Outside the house a man shouted that he didn't care if Melvin's sister *did* work for the police. Let her show her face if she dared. Clemencia clamped the mobile harder to her ear and said, 'But your hand's better, isn't it?'

'My hand?' said Angula. 'I don't know. I guess so.'

'That's something at least.'

'Yes.'

'Well … ' she said.

'Goodnight, boss,' said Angula, and he hung up.

Laughter rang out in the street. It slowly receded, then silence fell. Even the music from the Mshasho Bar had ceased. In the darkness of Clemencia's room the bull terrier's eyes roamed wherever she looked. She wondered what the killer saw when he lay awake at night. Lifeless eyes, blood trickling? She sensed that he was tired, infinitely tired, and that he longed for the moment when he could lie down and rest.

It was light and terribly hot when she was roused by the protracted blaring of a car's horn. She managed to sneak into the shower unobserved and freshen up, but it didn't seem to do much good. When she emerged, Miki Selma clapped her hands above her head and loudly declared that Clemencia had never looked worse. Miki Matilda croaked in agreement: even Joseph Tjironda's corpse had looked perkier. The rest of her remarks tailed off into hoarse breathing. Clemencia's sister Constancia offered to plait her a nice hair extension and Miki Selma deplored her inability to make her some rooibos tea, which – as everyone knew – worked wonders in such cases, because the municipal authorities had chosen this morning, of all times, to turn off the electricity even though she wasn't *that* late paying the bill. It was scandalous, considering that the whole of Independence Avenue, from Katutura to Ausspannplatz, had been festooned with coloured bulbs throughout the Christmas period, consuming enough electricity – of that, she, Selma, felt quite sure – to permanently supply not only the rings of her electric stove but every light in the house from now until long after her – hopefully not imminent – death.

Miki Selma mentioned in passing that the municipal administration's inconsiderate power cut had also endangered the educational aims of the government's Vision 2030 programme. Timothy and Jessica really shouldn't miss their first day at school, but someone had to fetch wood so that food could at least be cooked on the barbecue in the yard. Where on earth had they got to? However, the radio was still working thanks to its batteries. Which reminded her: Clemencia's murderer – that was to say, not her murderer in the sense that he'd murdered her but the murderer she was after, this man Martinus Cloete – had been mentioned on the radio. On television too, probably, but that, alas, wasn't working. Anyone with knowledge of his whereabouts was to inform the police at once. Great care must be taken, because the man was armed and extremely dangerous. Did Clemencia know?

'Martinus Cloete?' said Clemencia. 'It wasn't him.'

'But if they said so on the radio ... '

'He's the wrong man,' said Clemencia. She fled to her room and called Tjikundu on his private mobile phone. He wasn't at headquarters, but at Martinus Cloete's service station on Mandume Ndemufayo Avenue. He was sitting in a little office with Cloete's secretary, rehearsing her in what she was to say if her boss called in. His colleagues outside in the forecourt, sweating under their bulletproof vests, were even worse off.

According to Tjikundu, Oshivelo had created the biggest commotion the Namibian police force had experienced since independence. Everyone who could hold a gun in one hand and Martinus Cloete's picture in the other had been mobilized. Dozens of roadblocks had been set up throughout the country, Windhoek's hotels were being combed and checks run on anyone who had ever been in contact with Cloete, from the paper boy to the customers of his service station. Oshivelo had said he wanted him dead or alive.

'He's the wrong man,' said Clemencia. She asked for Cloete's private address. Tjikundu merely laughed when she said the real killer would turn up there. If the man really existed, he said, he'd think twice about doing that.

'Why *would* he go there?' Tjikundu demanded. 'Cloete has gone to ground. Besides, the house is being closely watched.'

Tjikundu was right, but Clemencia knew that the killer would

183

turn up there all the same, or at least reconnoitre the place. He wasn't the type to rely on others or on hearsay. Was he biding his time? Would he try to discover where Donkerkop was hiding?

'What is it, Clemencia?' Miki Selma called from outside.

'Nothing,' Clemencia called back. She dialled Angula's number, but he didn't answer.

Miki Selma put her head round the door. 'Don't you have to go to work?'

'I've been suspended.'

'What?'

'Fired, or as good as.'

'Goodness me!' Miki Selma crossed herself and pulled the door to. Clemencia resolved to try Angula again later. She could use some back-up if she waited for the killer to turn up at Cloete's house. The policemen watching it wouldn't spot him; they didn't even believe in his existence and were focused solely on Cloete's return, which was pretty unlikely in any case. Instinctively, she felt for the holster on her hip, but it was in the armoury at headquarters. She left her room and locked the door behind her.

Some bits of wood were lying beside the barbecue, but no one had lit it. Her route to the yard was barred by the entire family: Miki Matilda, Miki Selma, Melvin, Constancia and her two children plus two cousins who had moved in temporarily while Clemencia was at Acheson's farm. Even her father had got up from his bench.

'What's all this?' she demanded.

'Where are you off to?' Miki Matilda demanded hoarsely.

'Out for a bit.'

'They've chucked you out?'

'You've no need to worry for the moment, I'm still being paid,' said Clemencia. 'I'm not allowed to work, but they haven't stopped my pay. Great, isn't it?'

'Did they chuck you out because they don't believe you know who the real murderer is?'

'I *don't* know who he is.'

'But you're on his track?'

Clemencia didn't reply. For some reason, she remembered how the bull terrier's eyes had glared at her last night.

'You're going after him,' said Constancia.

'All on your own,' said Miki Selma. 'But the man is dangerous. You can't, my dear!'

'Not without our help,' croaked Miki Matilda.

'The television isn't working anyway,' said Melvin. 'We might as well ... '

'You're crazy!' Clemencia shook her head.

Miki Selma crossed her arms. 'You aren't going on your own. No way!'

'Say something, Daddy,' Constancia urged. Miki Selma snorted. She occasionally intimated that a paterfamilias was there to look after his dependants. If he failed to do so, for whatever reason, she felt he had no right to speak.

Clemencia's father seldom did speak. He sat in silence on his shady bench or sometimes out in the street behind the vegetable stall, watching the world go by and greeting even his former friends with a nod, nothing more. How old and bent he had become, thought Clemencia. His cheeks were sunken and the flat cap he'd never removed for thirty years, except when going to bed, looked far too big for him. Now, when he opened his mouth, you could see the few crooked teeth he had left. He mumbled so softly, Clemencia could hardly make out what he was saying.

'When we became independent they promised us milk and honey. We were to be given land and work, the health service would be improved, the old would be able to live on their pensions and the young would receive the finest education. I never believed all that. Where was the money to come from? I believed in one thing only, because I hoped for it so much: that justice would prevail. That no more murderers would escape punishment in this country.'

185

He ceremoniously resumed his seat on the bench and pulled the peak of his cap over his eyes as if he had said all there was to say. Clemencia thought of her mother, of the wedding photos, of the grave in Katutura cemetery she hadn't visited for years. As soon as this business was over, she would ...

'We're a family, after all,' said Miki Selma.

'*Your* family,' croaked Miki Matilda.

Keeping a house under surveillance single-handed, all round the clock, was impossible, especially if you hoped to spot someone of unknown appearance – someone identifiable only by the fact that he was covertly trying to discover what was going on inside the house. Perhaps he would stake it out at a distance. Perhaps he would ring a neighbour's bell on some pretext. The essential thing was to register all that went on and be everywhere at once.

'Well?' said Clemencia.

'What do you want us to do?' asked Melvin.

'All right,' she said, 'but everyone must do exactly as I say.'

'Of course,' said Miki Selma, clearly offended by the idea that Clemencia might doubt that. Miki Matilda cleared her throat and nodded eagerly. Melvin grinned. The children bounced excitedly up and down until Constancia commanded them to go to school and not budge an inch from their grandfather's side thereafter. Clemencia explained what to look out for. If they noticed someone taking an interest in the house or its occupants, they were to do nothing but inform her at once. Had everyone understood that?

'All clear,' said Melvin.

'We aren't stupid, my dear,' said Miki Selma. Miki Matilda muttered something about a minor problem and pointed to her mobile. The others were also out of airtime, so Clemencia fished out thirty dollars and the children went off to buy some at the Mshasho Bar. Miki Selma wanted to see if their neighbour was there with his taxi. In an exceptional situation like this, she said, he could hardly refuse to drive her to the scene of the action free of charge. Melvin borrowed Clemencia's phone on the grounds that he had to organize something quickly. He wouldn't disclose its nature, but he faithfully swore that it was for the common good and not in the least bit illegal.

Clemencia's mobile went missing somehow. It wasn't until a quarter of an hour later that she discovered Miki Selma using it. She snatched the phone out of her hand. Miki Selma regretfully explained that their neighbour the cabby was out, but Clemencia needn't worry, alternative means of transport had already been arranged.

That was the least of Clemencia's worries. She started to regret what she'd agreed to in a weak moment. Where her family were concerned, opening a door only a crack was impossible. Before you knew it, the entire clan had barged in and made themselves at home. She wondered what Matti Jurmela and his Finnish colleagues would have said about her newly recruited surveillance team. Nothing, probably. They would simply have stood there with their mouths hanging open.

Miki Selma and Miki Matilda were debating whether to take broad-brimmed hats against the sun or umbrellas, which could if necessary be used for purposes of self-defence. Meantime, Melvin had disappeared, having left a message with Constancia to the effect that they should go on ahead without him; he would follow as soon as possible. Before Clemencia could ask any questions, someone honked his horn outside in the street. A car door slammed, and a moment later Claus Tiedtke's lanky figure appeared above the garden fence.

'We're nearly ready, Meneer,' Miki Selma called.

'Hello, Clemencia,' said Claus.

'Hello,' said Clemencia, 'what … ?'

'It's a matter of life and death, your aunt said.'

'Mikis!'

'It is, too,' Miki Selma said defensively. 'We're hunting a murderer, after all.'

'I had no idea … ' Clemencia's mobile rang. She let it ring and started again. 'I didn't choose this family of mine, I — '

'Your family isn't the problem,' said Claus.

'So who is?'

'You are,' he said. 'You could have called me.'

'Your phone's ringing!' Miki Selma interjected.

'I'm not deaf,' Clemencia snapped. Reluctantly, she pressed the key with the green telephone on it. Ex-judge Hendrik Fourie answered. Having heard the general alert on the radio and made a few enquiries, he felt extremely concerned. Was he wrong in surmising that certain police authorities did not want to capture Donkerkop alive? He knew he wasn't in Clemencia's good books, but he wanted her to use her influence. Surely they weren't going to …

'I don't have any influence,' Clemencia told him. That had never been truer than it was now.

'Someone *must* talk, and Donkerkop is the last person who can,' Fourie said.

'Meneer Fourie — '

'The Lubowski case will never be solved if you gun him down.'

'Meneer Fourie, kindly leave me in peace!' Clemencia hung up.

'No more dawdling,' Miki Selma called from outside, 'let's go!' She was just getting into Claus Tiedtke's Citi Golf.

※◈※

Judge Hendrik Fourie (ret.):

I didn't fully realize until much later why Lubowski's murder kept preying on my mind. In the first place, of course, it was a spectacular case involving politics, secret services and prominent individuals – one of interest to the international media. Any judge would have regarded it as more than just a routine matter. Professional ethics and personal indignation also came into it when I saw the way investigations were being thwarted on every side. I came

188

increasingly to look upon my inability to prevent this as a personal failure. It galled me deeply even in retirement, but it wasn't just about myself or my notion of justice. I realized that the events of 12 September 1989 concerned and still concern us all.

Those shots fired at Lubowski sparked a national change of mood. Night had fallen, and when the new day dawned it differed from the days that had preceded it. We had suddenly had our fill of decades of violence – all of us, SWAPO and the South Africans, racists and guerrilla fighters, whites fearful for their privileges and blacks jostling to get at the fleshpots. Very few people realized this right away. They scarcely noticed that they were agitating against each other with less conviction, and that a touch of indifference had crept into their condemnation of each other's dirty work, but in retrospect the sentiment that had settled over the country was unmistakable.

Why was this brought about by Anton Lubowski's murder, of all things? Why didn't it happen earlier, why not later? I don't know. Perhaps it was down to Lubowski's position. No matter whether one regarded him as 'SWAPO's white son' or a 'kaffir dandy', and no matter how unequivocal his political stance, he was an over-life-size figure with one foot in each camp. Perhaps his death created a gap in which blacks and whites could approach each other at last. That would make him – if you'll pardon the high-flown language – a victim slain on the altar of history.

However, all that matters in the case of such a blood sacrifice is whether it is graciously accepted and serves some purpose. It doesn't matter who actually slit the victim's throat – indeed, it's pernicious to name names, for the identification of a culprit with motives and interests of his own will destroy the secret of how such a sacrifice can rebound to the benefit of the community. A myth must take root in the dark; only then can its true power develop.

I don't believe that anyone realized this at the time, as I already said, and there were plenty of people who questioned the factors that underlay the killing and heaped one hypothesis on another. But I assert that, fundamentally, no one wanted to solve the Lubowski murder at all. It may even have

189

been necessary to dispense with its solution out of commitment to his sacri-
fice, so as to be able to focus on the future and the development of a unified
nation. It may at least have been necessary then.

Now that two decades have elapsed, however, the time has come to open
our eyes and look around. The mood of departure has disappeared without
trace, the early ideals have evaporated. A few blacks have grown wealthy
and a few corrupt, SWAPO wields power for its own benefit, doles out
jobs and takes advantage of the fact that the opposition would act no differ-
ently. A few whites grumble beneath their breath; others have adapted. They
give formerly disadvantaged employees seats on the board, donate occasional
boxes of crayons to AIDS orphans, and, in other respects, keep to themselves
exactly like the blacks. Is that what Lubowski died for?

Twenty years have gone by, and still no one wants to know what really
happened. The reasons for this have undergone a stealthy change, that's
all. People have settled into drab routine, into a rut unworthy of all the
struggles that raged in the past. They have no wish to be reminded that quite
different aspirations once prevailed, and that people were murdered for them.
Lubowski isn't buried under one-and-a-half metres of earth, but under the
guilty consciences of those who have outlived him. Because we don't want
to admit to ourselves that we've made nothing out of them, the dramas of
the past must remain unspoken. And so, Lubowski has been sacrificed twice
over. Not, this time, for a better future, but so that people can continue
to wallow in the dismal and rather dirty but otherwise not uncomfortable
morass in which they have somehow ended up. Insufferable, isn't it?

So what? some will say now. Lubowski doesn't care any more, dead is
dead. I take a rather different view. The dead can be murdered a second time,
but you can also try to prevent that.

※◈※

Perhaps he'd miscalculated. Perhaps he didn't, after all, have enough
time to finish the job. The wound in his thigh wasn't the problem,
but the other thing – the burning in his guts – had got worse.
The place where his internal organs must once have been was now

pure agony. Unbearable agony, and his coughing fits were almost choking him.

The other passengers had shrunk away from him as far as the crowded minibus allowed. He was hugging the blue sports bag to his trembling chest. He didn't know how he had withstood the drive to Windhoek. They must have been waved past the roadblock at Heja Lodge. He hadn't woken up with a start until he heard the manhunt appeal for information on the minibus's radio, but by then they were already past the development area on the outskirts of Windhoek. The bus was now turning into the car park of the Engen service station at the Sam Nujoma-Nelson Mandela Avenue intersection. He would get out here, even though he was well short of his objective.

He let two fellow passengers get out before him, then struggled to his feet. The sun beat down on him. He sensed that the bus driver was staring after him as he tottered through the shimmering inferno, but he couldn't help that. On the pavement, passers-by steered clear of him. When he spotted the sign of the Klein Windhoek Pharmacy across the street, he stepped out into the roadway. Brakes squealed and a voice swore loudly at him. He coughed, spat blood and doubled over, then staggered across the street without looking in either direction. Damn this burning sensation! He went into the pharmacy and gasped out a request for some pain-killers.

'You need a doctor!' the pharmacist exclaimed.

'In a moment,' he blurted out.

'No, at once! I'll call an ambulance.'

'I'll … I'll take a taxi, it's quicker,' he gasped. He put a hundred dollar note on the counter. 'First something strong. For the pain!'

The woman fetched a box of tablets, squeezed two out of the bubble pack and dissolved them in a glass of water. He drank them down and pocketed the box. Once outside, he swallowed another six tablets. The pain was eating him up, but he toiled on past an amusement arcade and across the intersection to the post office on Nelson Mandela Avenue. There were three public telephones outside the entrance. Leaning against the plexiglass hood of the first one, he removed the receiver and inserted a phone card. He knew the number by heart. He stared at the post office's brick wall and strove to concentrate. Someone picked up at the other end.

'It's me,' he said.

'Yes, everything's okay,' he said. The tablets would take effect in a minute.

'No,' he said, 'I'm fine.'

He listened. Beside the phone was a bus shelter. Two women were sitting there in the shade, but that meant nothing. He said, 'Good, will do.'

'No, no questions,' he said. Someone *in extremis* had no time to ask questions.

'Except … ' He hesitated. The pain was raging through his body. He emitted a harsh, staccato cough.

'It's not important,' he gasped, and tried to hang up. The receiver slipped off the cradle and dangled above the ground on its cord. When he bent down to retrieve it, coughing, he fell over. Lying at the foot of the phone booth, he reached for the sports bag and pulled it towards him. No one must steal that, he still needed it. The two women in the bus shelter looked over at him but remained seated.

At some stage he recovered sufficiently to struggle up and stagger to the intersection. He couldn't have said for sure whether the taxi at the lights had all four wheels on the ground, but he managed to wrench the passenger door open. The woman on the back seat hurriedly got out and disappeared. The taxi driver protested, but when asked how many people he thought he'd already shot he shut up and drove him to the industrial area north of town.

The sign said 'Chinatown'. The three blood-red Chinese characters beneath the word metamorphosed before his eyes into three writhing, viciously hissing poisonous serpents. He leant against one of the posts that supported the sign and fought off an urge to vomit. That was the tablets. They had no effect apart from that. Tightening his grip on the sports bag, he tottered past Asian food shops and cheap clothing stores. The shops at the far end of the long mall were more squalid, filled with plastic trash and cheap electronic goods. He made his way into one of these caverns. A young Chinese girl accosted him. He got her to take him to the proprietor and asked if there was a back room. The old Chinaman led him into a tiny, windowless cubby hole containing a bed. He sat down on it, fished out all the money he had left, stuffed 300 rand back into his pocket, and counted out the rest beside the bed. A good fifteen grand.

'First, some morphine,' he said. 'Enough to deaden all the pain in the world for three days.'

He doubted if his body would last that long, but it was better to be safe than sorry. He looked up. The old Chinaman's face betrayed no expression.

'Secondly, a uniform. The kind worn by Windhoek's municipal meter readers. And the ID to go with it.'

The cough shook him through and through. When he could speak again, he said, 'Thirdly, I stay here for a while.'

The Chinaman asked nothing, said nothing. He looked into his eyes, then at the money, then back again. It was unlikely he would go to the police, but a word of warning couldn't hurt.

'Death is my companion,' he said. The Chinaman gave an almost imperceptible nod as if it were the first sentence he'd understood. Then he turned and shuffled out.

There wasn't even a pillow on the bed. He used the sports bag instead and looked up at the naked bulb dangling from the ceiling. The pain was more bearable when he lay at full length. If someone had been there to tell him stories in bird-language, he might even have managed to fall asleep. Some two hours later the Chinese girl brought him the morphine. She said the uniform was harder to obtain and he must wait a while. He said he didn't have much time left. The girl inclined her head and tiptoed out backwards. He injected the morphine.

Then he lay down again and concentrated on the pain in his body. It came in waves. He could almost see one break, dissolve into spray and run up a flat, sandy shore while the next one broke further out and another beyond it was rearing its head. But the roar of the surf became fainter each time. The roar became a whisper, the whisper a ripple, and the sea spent itself and retreated, creating an ever broader expense of smooth, damp, pristine sand on which he was now trotting nimbly along. He looked round, saw a jackal's footprints, and trotted on. How he had effected this transformation he didn't know. Perhaps only those could do it who didn't know how it was done.

He spent the whole night roaming the world. He trotted across desert, climbed mountains, and entered a city that resembled Windhoek to a T, the only difference being that there were no humans there, only jackals, hyenas and any number of bats. He asked another jackal what had happened to all the humans and was told that they had killed one another. The last two had fired simultaneously and died almost as simultaneously. This didn't surprise him.

He sauntered down Independence Avenue and saw some red traffic lights turn green. The abandoned cars didn't move. The doors of some of them were open as though the occupants had fled in panic. Then the lights turned red again. Red, green, red, green, or was it steel-blue? Lying in front of the glass façade of the *Hungry Lion* fastfood restaurant, a Kalahari lion with a white mane turned its head lethargically. Spotted hyenas laughed their sinister laugh from the hill, from the neighbourhood of Christ Church and the Alte Feste. His fellow jackals trotted through the pedestrian precinct, skirting around benches and lamp posts and jumping up on rubbish bins to get at things to eat. He wondered how many of them were former humans who had metamorphosed before their kind became extinct.

194

Next morning the uniform and ID were lying at the foot of the bed. The 15,000 rand had gone. He got dressed. The faint mist in front of his eyes wouldn't be much of a handicap. He felt no pain but knew it made no difference; he didn't have much time left. Slinging the sports bag over his shoulder, he left the deserted shop and took a taxi to Windhoek West. He got out a few houses before his target, then walked to the garden gate and rang the bell. A woman's voice asked who he was over the intercom.

'Electricity and water,' he said curtly.

'But they were read only a few days ago,' the woman said.

'Internal check,' he said, and turned away to spit out the bloody mucus that had collected in his throat. A little while later, light footsteps approached the other side of the gate. He held the ID up to the window.

'One moment.' The woman who let him in was in her mid-twenties, tall, pretty and carefully made-up. The daughter of the house, perhaps. He stooped and unzipped his bag.

'The water meter's over there,' said the young woman.

He levelled the Kalashnikov at her and said, 'Keep quiet and nothing will happen to you.'

She stared at the gun muzzle and said, so faintly he could scarcely hear her, 'Please!'

'Lead the way,' he commanded. She nodded once, twice, almost eagerly, almost as if she wanted to avoid any embarrassment. Then she turned and he followed her into the house. A man was sitting at the breakfast table in his vest. He made no attempt to play the hero and raised his hands without being told to. There was a bowl of mealie porridge and a cup in front of him, and, on the other side, a glass of orange juice and a plate of sliced banana and pawpaw.

'Go on with your breakfast,' he said. With the AK-47 at the ready he sat down in an armchair some four metres away. He jerked the muzzle at the young woman. 'Your daughter?' he asked.

'We've been married four years,' she said.

'Children?'

She didn't reply.

'You're very pretty,' he said. 'Does your husband love you?'

The man slowly lowered his hands and said, 'You're asking for trouble.'

'Does he love you?'

'What do you mean by love?' she retorted.

He nodded, then turned to the man. 'You know what I want?'

The man shook his head. 'Money?'

Money? That was an amusing idea. He really couldn't help laughing. The laughter became a cough that shook his entire body, but he had the Kalashnikov to hang on to.

✖✖

Although Clemencia sensed from the outset that nothing would come of their surveillance, she had divided up her family and dropped them in the appropriate places in Claus Tiedtke's car. The women took over Martinus Cloete's service station. Miki Selma, shaded by her umbrella, sat right beside the Mandume Ndemufayo Avenue entrance to the yard at the rear. Miki Matilda and Constancia patrolled Tacoma and Acacia Streets so as to be in the right place if the killer approached from behind over walls and fences.

All three had camouflaged themselves as lottery sellers. The lottery tickets had been entrusted to them by a nephew of the late Joseph Tjironda in return for an assurance that seventy per cent of the prospective takings be handed over to him. The nephew normally plied his trade in the city centre – more specifically, outside the entrance to the head office of the First National Bank. Although doubtful of the profitability of the ladies' chosen catchment area, he quickly took to the idea of becoming an employer. He could now spend two days in idleness and leave others to take care of his livelihood.

196

Responsible for Martinus Cloete's private address were Melvin and his pals, who would, he asserted, be turning up any minute. Cloete's terrace house was situated in the middle of the Barcelona housing estate. The whole area was cut off from the surrounding wasteland by walls and electric fences and had its own security guards, who were now reinforced by Oshivelo's men. No home in Windhoek could be more secure. If at all, the killer would try to gain access by way of the electrically operated gate that formed the only entrance. The residents of the estate had their own remote controls for this gate. Visitors had to report to the guardhouse beside it and obtain permission to enter via the intercom.

Clemencia impressed upon Melvin that he must watch out for anyone admitted by the security personnel: messengers, delivery men, and all lone individuals. He was to make a note of their licence numbers and inform her at once. Melvin stationed himself on the other side of the road, far enough away not attract the attention of the security guards at the barrier.

Three hours later, when Clemencia went to check that all was well, Melvin wasn't there any more. Instead, five young workmen in day-glo high visibility vests were busy digging up the asphalt near the entrance to the Barcelona estate. She dialled Melvin's number. One of the workmen, who had been picturesquely leaning on his pickaxe, took out a mobile.

'Come over here at once!' she hissed into the phone. The workman looked around enquiringly, propped his pickaxe against the guardhouse, and, with studious nonchalance, strolled over to Clemencia's borrowed Citi Golf. She told him to get in and asked what the hell was going on.

'The municipality of Windhoek or the Roads Authority or someone is carrying out improvements to the infrastructure,' Melvin said proudly. 'For the benefit of all citizens. We regret any potential inconvenience.'

'You can't just dig up the road!'

'If anyone tries to get through that barrier, we'll overhear every word.'

'But — '

'We'd spot a thug with something to hide, I guarantee you. He'd only have to open his mouth.'

The killer Clemencia was after wasn't an ordinary criminal, he was something quite else, but Melvin wouldn't have understood that. He was experienced in his way – he knew Katutura and all the shady characters who hung around there. That was his world. He couldn't be blamed for knowing no other.

'The only thing is, what do we do tonight?' he asked. 'If we go on working, no one'll believe we're employed by the city. If we had some heavy equipment, one of us might be able to stay on as a watchman, so nothing got pinched, but … '

'Tonight?' Clemencia was surprised – almost a little touched – that her young brother should be taking his job so seriously. She said, 'He won't come after dark.'

'Are you sure?'

She was suddenly quite sure of one thing: day or night, the killer wouldn't come at all. He was quite prepared to run extreme risks, but only if something came of them. His chances here were nil, not only because the police had the whole place under observation, but because they'd questioned all Cloete's friends and neighbours and learned nothing. The killer possessed more effective means of bringing pressure to bear, admittedly, but they availed you little if you didn't know who to use them on. No, he would try to run Donkerkop to earth in some other way. But how? The surveillance operation Clemencia had launched with her family was very probably pointless, but she could hardly call them off now. She said, 'The killer needs information about Donkerkop's potential whereabouts. For that he'll have to question his friends and neighbours, but he can't go ringing their doorbell in the middle of the night.'

Melvin seemed disappointed not to be allowed to play the auxiliary policeman twenty-four hours a day. Clemencia said, 'What's important is that you're all back at your posts tomorrow.'

'Sure,' said Melvin, 'first thing!' He nodded and rejoined his cronies. The strip of road they'd torn up was about one metre wide and five long. They now proceeded to excavate it with their shovels. Their enthusiasm showed no signs of flagging.

Clemencia drove off to visit her second task force. Apart from the fact that the three women had sold four lottery tickets between them, nothing out of the ordinary had happened. Predictably enough, they had sighted no one suspicious. Clemencia persuaded them, too, to suspend operations overnight, then drove to the *Allgemeine Zeitung*'s offices in Omuramba Weg. Claus Tiedtke said she could naturally keep his car a while longer, but he wanted to know what was going on.

'Well, the killer will somehow try to — '

Tiedtke cut her short. He thought he knew what was wrong with her, he said. After the other night he'd thought – or, if not thought, at least hoped – that there was a little more between them than a willingness to lend each other cars.

'Perhaps we could talk about it some other time,' she said.

Entirely up to her, said Tiedtke. He would merely point out that he was a grown man. He could bear to hear the truth.

The truth was, Clemencia didn't know whether he meant anything to her. She didn't want to think about it now. In any case, it was far too soon to talk about 'the two of them', as if they were an item and had an amazing amount in common. All right, so she'd spent the night with him – a night when she hadn't wanted to be on her own – followed by a morning when she would sooner have been alone. Well, what of it? The truth was, the colour red made her think of blood, not roses, and she was currently closer to death than love. She wondered if she ought to tell him how the bull terrier's glowing eyes were awaiting her in the darkness, but before she could make up her mind, Claus Tiedtke took his leave of her. He had to get back to work, he said. She had his phone number, after all. Clemencia drove off. Perhaps it was better this way.

The rest of the family came home some time after her. Although neither of the surveillance teams had any tangible results to show, their mood was so exuberant that no one noticed how silent she was. She soon retired to her room and locked herself in. There was still no electricity, and the candle she lit wasn't bright enough to expel the bull terrier's eyes from the shadowy corners of the room. She could bear it as long as people were still chattering and laughing outside; as long as Miki Selma was expatiating on the pros and cons of a lottery seller's existence and Miki Matilda's raucous cackles filled the air. But when all she could hear was the music from the Mshasho Bar, whose muffled beat reminded her sometimes of an attack dog's growls and sometimes of a burst from a Kalashnikov, all thought of sleep was impossible.

Images kept flickering past her: a dead man's feet protruding from under a blanket, the sudden glare of a *bakkie*'s undipped headlights, an iron chain tautening as a bull terrier bounded forwards, a hanged convict, an ex-judge slicing smoked venison, a security firm's burnt-out vehicle, cartridge cases in a constable's hand, a screaming teenager rocking to and fro on a sofa, a little girl in SWAPO colours following a coffin out of a church, heavily armed South African soldiers advancing through the streets of Katutura, rolls of barbed wire, and a bull terrier's yellow glare that refused to fade even when the candle had gone out long ago.

At five a.m. she called Angula. He answered at once. 'Boss?'

'I only wanted — '

'My hand is fine.'

'Good, excellent.'

'I can hardly feel it.'

'You're better, that's the main thing.'

'Yes.'

'Angula?'

'What are you doing? Right now, I mean?'

'Me? Nothing.'

'Can't you sleep?'

'Yes, I sleep fine. It's just that ... I wake up sometimes. Because of the heat.'

'And then?'

'Boss?'

'What do you do when you wake up?'

'I think to myself, If you're awake you may as well get up and make a few notes.'

'The Lubowski affair? Are you still working on that?'

'Only on my own account.'

'How do you mean?'

'I'm simply writing down the way it was.'

'The way you think it may have been,' she amended.

'Yes, of course,' he said.

The room was hot and dark. Two yellow points of light were glowing above Clemencia's bed. She said, 'They say it's going to rain soon, maybe even tomorrow. Then it'll be cooler and easier to sleep.'

'Some real rain would be a good thing in general,' Angula said. 'For the countryside too.'

'Yes, for the countryside too.'

'Well,' he said, 'I think I'll put my head down for another couple of hours.'

'Goodnight,' she said.

'Goodnight.'

'Angula?' she said, but he'd already hung up. Anyway, she didn't know what she'd meant to ask him. Nor did she know why she'd called him in the first place. Perhaps because he had been with her at Acheson's farm and almost caught the killer with her. She groped her way across the room and found another candle to light. Should she also make some notes? Write down her own obsessions? A case could sometimes get on top of you, Matti Jurmela had admitted to her one long, Finnish winter's night. No, more than that: it could utterly consume you.

'And then?' she'd asked.

'Then you know you're really into the case,' Jurmela had replied with a laugh.

Perhaps she still wasn't sufficiently 'into' it. Perhaps she was making no progress because she was doing her utmost to avoid being consumed by it. Perhaps she needed to hurl herself into the monster's mouth. She proceeded to recapitulate the whole affair.

Once again, pictures took shape in her mind like a film unfolding, except that it showed the familiar plot quite differently. She saw a corpulent Boer watering some lemon trees before a burst of gunfire mowed him down. Another Boer emerged from airport arrivals and looked round. A match scraped against an abrasive strip, flew through a car's open window and sent its petrol-soaked upholstery up in flames. And so it went on. The parched, interminable landscape of southern Namibia glided past the window of a car. Clemencia replaced a telephone receiver on the cradle because a policewoman had asked for the truth. She surveyed the outer walls of Pretoria's central prison, in which a convict had been found hanged. She climbed into a lorry laden with furniture. A traffic cop collapsed on the asphalt, mortally wounded. His own fault, he shouldn't have flagged the lorry down. She turned on a *bakkie*'s headlights, floored the gas pedal, ran over a charging bull terrier, asked an Irish racist a question and failed to grasp that he had seriously hoped to save his life by answering it. The gunfire was nothing special any more. Then she was back in Windhoek. One left! Only one to go, but he'd disappeared. She hadn't the faintest idea where he was hiding and the whole of the Namibian police force was after him, but she was racking her brains for a way to get him first. Because she had to get him at all costs!

When dawn broke she blew out the candle. Through her little window she could see light fighting its way into the world from the east. It was having a hard time because clouds were gathering in the sky, low and dense. Rain clouds. The sky normally remained clear in the early mornings, even at the height of the rainy season. The clouds didn't gather until early afternoon and discharged their contents towards evening in violent thunderstorms. Normally, yes, but what did normally mean?

Clemencia didn't respond when Miki Selma knocked on the door and loudly stated that, although she would never let the municipal authorities get her down, a hot breakfast was once more temporarily precluded by lack of electricity. She heard Melvin set off and Miki Matilda announce that, instead of devoting herself to the unproductive selling of lottery tickets, she would try to predict the killer's future movements with the aid of a suitably prepared wooden doll. Clemencia decided that she wouldn't leave her room until she had figured out how to get hold of Donkerkop before the police did.

Constancia sent her children off to school, Miki Matilda indulged in some monotonous singing over the barbecue, and Miki Selma enquired through the closed door whether she should really squander the proceeds of the lottery tickets on a taxi when Clemencia's fiancé's car was parked outside the house. Clemencia made no progress with her attempts to put herself in Donkerkop's place. She had to accept that it was simply impossible to get at him. One person couldn't search an entire country. Only the combined police forces could do that, if at all, and even they had so far failed to find a trace of him. But at least they had a genuine chance. They would find the man sooner or later, and if they didn't shoot him in the course of arresting him, they would ...

The time by Clemencia's mobile phone was precisely 10.12 when she hit on the answer. It was so simple, it had to be right. The killer had no need to embark on a futile quest. The police would bring him his man. He need only wait there until they finally succeeded. They would guard Donkerkop closely, of course, but their vigilance would diminish once they had reached police headquarters and hustled him upstairs to the Serious Crime Unit's interview rooms. They might post sentries outside the entrance, but that wouldn't worry the killer because he had long been inside police headquarters. He was there on the premises already, having somehow sneaked in. He had to be, it was the only answer!

Clemencia drove to headquarters and parked the Citi Golf in one of the reserved spaces outside the entrance. She forced herself to climb the steps slowly, closely eyeing the uniformed policemen who passed her. The corridor on the second floor, the home of the Serious Crime Unit, appeared to be deserted. No workmen were replacing pipework or painting walls. She made for Oshivelo's office, determined to convince him. Suspended or not, she wouldn't let him send her packing. She would simply refuse to leave until he agreed to check every part of the building and everyone in it.

Clemencia knocked. The door was shut, the room empty. The only colleague she encountered was Robinson, who had made himself at home behind her desk. He probably lacked the imagination to conceive of how it would feel to supplant her as inspector, because he didn't seem embarrassed in the least. When she asked where the rest of the team were, he preened himself. In case Clemencia hadn't heard yet, he said, they'd launched a nation-wide manhunt for which every able-bodied man was required. Clemencia made a mental note to pay him back sometime for the way he emphasized the words 'able-bodied' and 'man'. At present she had other worries.

The operation was not only the biggest the country had ever seen, Robinson rattled on, but extremely ticklish as well. Why? Because influential circles had evidently gained the impression that the police meant to shoot Donkerkop out of hand before he could open his mouth. It was therefore essential to capture him alive. He, Robinson, thoroughly agreed with Oshivelo on that point. The relevant instructions had already been issued.

Robinson pointed to the big map of Namibia lying in front of him. He had just been doing some strategic planning but was going downstairs to the telephone exchange in a minute. As Clemencia must have gathered, he said, Oshivelo had asked him to coordinate the whole operation.

Because every able-bodied man was needed out in the field? It was on the tip of Clemencia's tongue to ask this, but all she said was, 'What's happened to the chief?'

'Sick,' Robinson replied. 'He called in earlier.'

Clemencia had no alternative but to tell him her theory. His response did not surprise her. 'In the first place, you're suspended. Secondly, there isn't any killer lying in wait for Donkerkop because Donkerkop himself is the killer. And thirdly, capturing him is my responsibility now.'

'But all I need is a few men and unrestricted access to — '

'Out of the question.'

'Robinson!' she said sharply. 'Maybe you're right and I'm out of the picture for good, but maybe not. I could still be your superior officer for another few decades. If so, there won't be anyone here who'd like to be in your shoes.'

Robinson smiled, but he seemed to be wondering whether it was really wise to adopt such a definite stance at this juncture.

'Well?' she said.

'I'd like to oblige you,' he said, 'but my instructions are absolutely clear. Arresting Donkerkop takes priority over everything else. Oshivelo's orders were quite explicit: every man must be assigned to the job.'

'Okay, let's call him.' Clemencia reached across the desk, picked up the phone and asked to be put through. She didn't hang up until the number had rung several times without result.

'He's sick,' said Robinson. He shrugged his shoulders. 'I'm really sorry, but … '

Idiot! thought Clemencia. She stormed out into the passage and called Angula. He seemed relatively uninterested in her explanations until he heard she wanted to conduct an unauthorized search of police headquarters; then he was eagerness itself. She promised to pick him up right away. First, however, she went to the armoury and retrieved her own and Angula's service automatics.

'Back in harness?' asked the officer on duty.

'It's the manhunt,' she said. 'They need every man. And every woman.'

'Of course.' The man pushed a list across the counter and she signed the requisite receipt for the weapons.

There was a parking ticket wedged under the Golf's windscreen wipers. Clemencia put it in the glove compartment and drove off to Katutura. She would simply press on regardless of the consequences. For some reason her thoughts turned to Oshivelo. If he left an idiot like Robinson in charge in a situation like this, he must be seriously ill.

✸❖✸

The pretty young woman sought his eyes above the muzzle of the Kalashnikov. 'You're ill,' she said.

He averted his gaze. The sky hung, grey and heavy, over the land. When the masses of water eventually fell to earth, no one would be able to understand how the clouds could have retained them for so long. He said, 'I'm not ill, I'm just dying.'

'No one dies for no reason,' said the young woman.

'There's always a reason for dying,' he replied.

✸❖✸

Angula's face twisted with pain as he cocked his automatic. Only two fingertips protruded from the thick bandaging that extended to his elbow.

'All right?' Clemencia asked. She would have to force the gate to the property herself. And then the front door. Angula had at least brought a crowbar, thank God.

'Are we really not getting any back-up?' he asked.

Clemencia indicated the Group 4 Securicor sign on the gate-post. 'If we're lucky, the alarm will be on.'

The security firm would be alerted as soon as she forced the front door. Its headquarters would receive a call and, because nobody answered, routinely send a car to investigate. Then, and then only, would they grasp that the matter was serious. The shooting would be over long before any substantial reinforcements arrived. But the alarm probably wasn't on. Not if there was someone in the house.

Clemencia inserted the crowbar. 'Shall we?'

'If you're wrong … ' said Angula.

'I'm not,' she said. Oshivelo had called in sick. He hadn't answered the phone, hadn't responded when she rang the bell, and – in complete contrast to his previous line – had given strict instructions that Donkerkop be captured alive.

'Okay, let's do it!' said Angula.

Clemencia levered away, straining at the crowbar and throwing her weight against it until the gate burst open with a splintering crash and the crowbar clattered to the paving stones. While she ducked behind the gatepost and drew her automatic, Angula darted through the gap. The alarm hadn't sounded. A pedestrian who had been approaching on the other side of the street promptly turned and broke into a run.

Clemencia counted up to ten. All remained quiet. She retrieved the crowbar and drew a deep breath. Gun at the ready, she slipped through the gate. Out of the corner of her eye she saw Angula on her left, crouching down behind a massive urn containing a small tree with shiny, dark-green leaves. A rubber plant, she thought, as if that mattered, then ran up the paved driveway to the garage and plastered her back against the door. The main house was to her right. Then came two metres of white roughcast wall and a range of windows inside which – if she remembered correctly – Oshivelo's kitchen-living room was situated. The front door was round the corner.

Angula raised his bandaged arm from behind the rubber tree. He looked like a drowning man waving for help but was probably just indicating that all was well. Clemencia jerked her head to the right and he made for the house at a crouching run. The two of them were now standing either side of the windows with their backs to the wall and their guns at the ready.

'We'll go in through here,' Clemencia whispered. She stuck the automatic in her waistband and edged along the wall with the crowbar in both hands while Angula covered her. The window pane shattered under the impact of her blow. Shards of glass clattered to the floor inside, then silence returned. Clemencia and Angula stared at each other, still hugging the wall. Why no reaction? Why didn't someone open fire? Why didn't they hear the rattle of a Kalashnikov?

'No one at home,' Angula said in a low voice. Had she been mistaken after all? Was Oshivelo simply taking a day off somewhere? She risked a look. There was no one to be seen in the kitchen. The door to the passage was shut.

'In we go,' Clemencia muttered. She knocked the rest of the glass out of the frame and squeezed through. Broken glass crunched underfoot. She covered the door while Angula struggled through. Breakfast things were still on the table. Two places. It wasn't hard to tell where Oshivelo and his wife had been sitting. Clemencia dipped her finger in the cup. The remains of the coffee were still lukewarm.

Angula growled something. He had already got to the door to the passage. When Clemencia was in position he depressed the handle and opened it. On the right was the front door, on the left the rest of the house. As Clemencia emerged into the passage she heard a stifled groan, as if someone were being throttled. She froze and held her breath. Angula nodded and tiptoed silently past her. The sound was coming from the first room on the right. The door was open a crack, and a thin strip of grey daylight was slanting across the passage. Angula darted to the other side of the door. Clemencia felt her way along the wall. The pistol grip felt moist. Angula's bandaged hand reached around the doorpost and gently pushed the door open. The strip of light on the floor widened.

'Police!' cried Clemencia. Her voice sounded unnatural.

'Hands on your head and come out of there – slowly!' she called. The only response was a muffled, effortful groan. She nodded to Angula, then indicated her gun, then jerked it in the direction of the room. Angula understood. He pointed his own pistol around the door without exposing more than his hand. Clemencia put her head round the doorpost on the other side. Situated at an angle beneath the window was a double bed, and on it, facing towards Clemencia with his eyes staring and a gag taped over his mouth, lay Oshivelo. His wrists and ankles had been lashed to opposite ends of the bedstead.

Clemencia didn't move. There was a wardrobe on her right and a blind spot behind the door. She said, 'Can you hear me, chief?'

Oshivelo nodded.

'Nod again if there's anyone in the room apart from you.'

Oshivelo shook his head vigorously.

'Anywhere else in the house?'

Another shake of the head. Clemencia sneaked round the doorpost with her gun aimed at the blind spot on her left. A bedroom chair, a home trainer, a mirror on the wall. She turned round. Angula was just opening the wardrobe doors. Nothing, the room was clear. Angula kept an eye on the passage while Clemencia removed Oshivelo's gag and set to work on the washing line that had been used to tie his wrists.

He drew a deep breath and said, 'He's gone.'

'How long ago?'

'An hour at most. And he took my wife with him as a hostage.'

Clemencia had seen Oshivelo's wife two or three times. A lovely young woman for whose sake he'd divorced his first wife after twenty-five years of marriage. It had been rumoured at headquarters she'd come second in a Miss Namibia Contest until someone – probably Robinson – had checked and discovered that she'd never taken part.

'We'll circulate the killer's description at once,' said Clemencia, 'and then — '

'No!' Oshivelo rubbed his wrists. 'The man is terminally ill, he's got nothing to lose. He'll pull the trigger at once if something doesn't go the way he wants.'

Clemencia had been right in principle. She had merely taken a little too long to grasp that it was less risky for the killer to put pressure on a senior police officer than to sneak into headquarters. An hour earlier, and she would have caught him here! She said, 'He wants Donkerkop. Alive. As soon as we've caught the man, you're supposed to hand him over to the killer, right?'

'Not entirely,' said Oshivelo. 'Donkerkop is to confess to the murder of Anton Lubowski, name everyone involved, and describe the surrounding circumstances. As soon as the killer hears his signed confession broadcast on NBC radio, he'll let my wife go unharmed.'

'So he says,' said Clemencia.

'Yes,' said Oshivelo.

'So what do we do now?' she asked. She had now untied his ankles. He put his feet on the carpet and flexed his ankles.

'What do we do?' Oshivelo gave a mirthless laugh. 'We capture Donkerkop, beat a confession out of him, and broadcast it on the radio. That's precisely what we'll do!'

'But chief, we can't just — '

'Damn right we can!'

'Your wife — ' Clemencia began.

'Exactly,' he cut in, 'she's my wife, and I want her back in one piece.'

From the door Angula asked, 'What else did the killer ask for?'

'Isn't that enough?' Oshivelo snapped.

'It's just that I'm wondering why he took *your* wife, of all people. There are plenty of other senior police officers.' Angula's spoke softly, but there was an edge to his voice. It might have been a shiny little scalpel slicing through flesh.

Oshivelo got to his feet. 'Go on, Angula.'

'Did he by any chance ask *you* to broadcast too, boss? You or some other member of SWAPO involved in the Lubowski affair? Couldn't *you* give a far better account of what happened?'

Oshivelo took a step towards Angula, but his circulation wasn't fully restored yet and his knees buckled. 'You freed me and I'm grateful,' he said, 'but now you're out of it for good, both of you! I don't want to see either of you again until this business is over. And if you dare to obstruct our enquiries, show your faces at headquarters or interfere in any way, I'll have you locked up. That I promise you on my wife's life.'

❊❊❊

Ndangi Oshivelo, Deputy Commissioner of the Namibian police:

Conspiracy theorists are successful because they content themselves with manufacturing a semblance of plausibility out of conjectures, coincidences, and individual aspects arbitrarily emphasized to suit themselves. You can sometimes attempt to refute such theories, but that only encourages their adherents to concoct new arguments. You will never get to the nub of the theory, because how can you prove that something non-existent doesn't exist? Verifying something that exists, on the other hand, is comparatively simple. If you want to prove to someone that there are jackals in the desert, you take them out into the Kalahari and catch one. But if you want to convince someone that disembodied spirits don't fly through the air out there, you don't have a hope. Although you can't see the spirits even if you look for years, couldn't they be invisible? Or appear to us in the guise of bats? Or some other such nonsense?

What do I mean by this? I consider it out of the question that anyone from SWAPO was privy to the plan to assassinate Lubowski, far less involved in it, but I cannot prove it. That is impossible. It isn't the task of the defendant in a criminal trial to convince the court of his innocence, and for good reason. No, his guilt must be proven.

Similarly, it isn't enough for self-important persons to whisper that Lubowski had rivals and enemies in his own camp. That may well be true. It may also be true that certain people coveted the government posts to which he would probably have been appointed after independence. Many were doubtless glad of Lubowski's inability to exert any more political influence on Sam Nujoma, whose return from exile was imminent. And one or two may secretly have sympathized with the slogan which some simple soul carried through Windhoek on a placard not long ago: 'Kill all whites!'

No one can prevail over conspiracy theories. It's no use exposing them, even when they're the most arrant nonsense – and we've had to listen to plenty of that! I can't prevent anyone from asking whether SWAPO knew about the imported team of killers and had got wind of the planned assassination. Or whether someone deliberately withheld the information until it was too late to remove Lubowski from the firing line. Or whether Acheson was not betrayed to the police until he'd done his job. Or whether anyone had reason to fear a trial on those grounds.

We weren't yet in power in 1989 and couldn't have influenced the investigation. I could repeat that a thousand times, but it would make no difference. As far as I'm concerned, anyone so minded is welcome to speculate on how Lubowski's killers learned that he would be alone in his car on the night in question. One may criticize subsequent political endeavours, question whether it was legally hopeless to request South Africa to extradite the CCB agents, and blithely cobble together one's own version of events. Personally, I refuse to do this. I would only take a view on all these matters if some relatively cogent evidence existed. But it doesn't, does it?

5

HEROES

The killer was terminally ill, Oshivelo had said. Could you tell that by looking at someone? Or had the killer said it himself, to emphasize his total lack of compunction? On the other hand, that would have been an admission of his physical weakness. Would you make such an admission if you wanted to put pressure on someone? Wouldn't Oshivelo have felt tempted to play for time and hope that the threat to his wife would dissipate by itself?

Far away to the west the clouds were broken enough to allow scraps of pale blue to show through in places, but towering into the sky above Windhoek were dense conglomerations of vapour that ranged in colour from grey to almost black. You fancied you could feel the electric charges pent-up inside them on your skin.

Angula grunted something. He had asked to be taken home, so Clemencia was now driving along Otjomuise Road with the Goreangab Dam on her left. The little water that remained in it was a motionless, matt grey expanse. The air inside the car was hot and stuffy, even with the windows open.

Clemencia didn't doubt that the killer really was terminally ill. It was so obvious, she wondered why she hadn't thought of it herself. The mixture of desperation, determination and utter ruthlessness he had displayed was perfectly in keeping with the *après moi le déluge* attitude of someone without a future.

This might also explain another puzzle in the series of murders: the twenty years that had elapsed since Lubowski's assassination. Possibly intent on revenge from the first, the killer might have feared the personal consequences of his actions. Now he didn't care any more. Life imprisonment isn't much of a deterrent when you know you've only got weeks to live at most, and that you'll probably be pronounced unfit to be incarcerated.

Doctors! thought Clemencia. Someone must have diagnosed the killer's condition. Someone must have credibly assured him that he would die soon. Did that present a chance of discovering who he was? Through doctors? But she couldn't possibly scour every medical practice in the country. She didn't even know what the killer was suffering from, only that it was serious, incurable, and very, very predictable. No doctor would announce such a finding just like that. He would try to cover himself by precluding any doubt with the aid of X-rays, CT scans, tissue sample analysis, blood values, electroencephalograms, or whatever. At any rate, with the aid of investigative techniques with which a normal practice was not equipped. A laboratory or ... a hospital! Yes, that had to be it. The killer might have gone to a hospital himself or been referred to one. Anyway, that was where he had been given the definitive diagnosis, and there weren't that many well-equipped hospitals in Windhoek.

'Katutura Hospital, Central, Rhino Park, Mediclinic, the Roman Catholic ... ' Clemencia muttered.

'I just want to go home,' said Angula. He was holding his bandaged arm with his left hand.

'I think,' she said, 'that we may find out who the killer is from a hospital.'

'Leave me out of it,' said Angula.

'There's a chance.'

Angula stared at his bandage. 'I'm not feeling too good.'

'Yes,' said Clemencia. 'I'm sorry, I only meant ... '

'I need to lie down.'

But he wouldn't, of course. He would take a pencil in his left hand and, in his spidery scrawl, write down accusation after accusation against Oshivelo and the SWAPO leadership, even though he knew perfectly well that nothing would come of them. Clemencia said, 'All right, Angula.'

'Really?'

'Really.'

Neither of them spoke during the few minutes it took to get to Angula's home. He got out of the car, turned to Clemencia and said, 'I know I'm right.'

'Get better, Angula,' she said, and drove off. She began with the Central Hospital.

From the car park she headed in the direction of the visitors' entrance, then paused. A little boy with a Superman cape and a plastic pistol was running across the scorched grass. Two curving ramps enclosed the forecourt like a pair of forceps. A white-gowned figure was standing near a side entrance, smoking hurriedly.

How could she find out which patients had recently been given only a few weeks to live? No such list existed, that was for sure, and the hospital administrators could probably produce one only by going through every single patient's medical history. They would scarcely do that. Alternatively, there were the doctors, of whom hundreds had to be employed here. Half of them would be off duty, however, and the rest would invoke professional confidentiality. Clemencia would never obtain a complete list. It would take ages, it was pointless.

She tried to imagine how the woman doctor – she could only visualize a woman doctor, not a man – had informed the killer of the results of his tests. Data, facts, medical terms, and – when the incomprehension on the patient's face became unmistakable, more explicit language: his condition had reached a stage at which treatments, far from holding out a hope of success, would impose an additional strain on his physique. However, an attempt could be made to alleviate his symptoms by means of medication and temporarily improve his quality of …

The killer had understood. 'How much longer?' he asked, and the doctor replied that one could never tell exactly …

'How much longer?' the killer insisted, jumping to his feet.

'A few months, perhaps.' After a moment's hesitation, she corrected herself. 'Well, weeks rather than months.'

And the killer? He didn't go to pieces. On the contrary, it was as if a huge weight had fallen from his shoulders and new strength were suddenly flowing through his body: the long lost energy he needed because he had only weeks to live and so much to do. As soon as he could, he had hurriedly got his things together. If that was how it had been, he certainly wouldn't have …

Clemencia looked at the entrance to the Central Hospital. No, she would tackle the problem differently. Not in the correct, Finnish manner, but more à la Miki Selma. She took out her mobile phone and got hospital's number from enquiries. Then she called it, posing as Claire Namases from the Ministry of Health, and asked to be put through to administration.

She explained that the ministry was holding an international conference that could mean generous funding for Namibia's hospitals. However, the UNESCO representatives had requested certain information which the minister did not have immediately available. He had undertaken to obtain it before the end of the day. This being so, would the hospital administration kindly compile a list of all patients who had left the premises without completing the official discharge formalities? Yes, exactly, the ones who had simply walked out. Complete with name, address, age, diagnosis, and so on. Would that be possible? By when? Well, straight away. They wouldn't have called if it hadn't been urgent. She would send an assistant to pick up the information in twenty minutes' time. Her name was Clemencia Garises – 'Please make a note of it!' – and the material was to be handed to her alone. Many thanks, much obliged.

The twenty minutes were up by the time Clemencia had telephoned the other Windhoek hospitals. No action had yet been taken by the Central's administrators, needless to say, but when

Clemencia threatened them with ministerial displeasure, a secretary actually sat down at her computer. It went quicker than expected. Half an hour later Clemencia was skimming the list on her way back to the car park. It comprised some seventy names. Most of the persons concerned had probably decamped to avoid having to settle their hospital bills.

She crossed off the women and children and two men over sixty-five, then the majority of patients whose diseases or injuries did not represent an irremediable danger to life and limb. That left a few diagnoses whose medical jargon Clemencia did not understand, one or two cancer patients, and, above all, men between the ages of twenty and fifty who had contracted HIV and were suffering from a whole range of secondary infections because their immune system had failed.

Another eighteen names that meant nothing to Clemencia. Another eighteen addresses that would have to be checked. Before she started on those, however, she wanted to check the cases from Katutura State Hospital as well. She considered it less likely that the killer would have visited one of the private hospitals. She might have got the wrong idea, but she simply didn't see a killer with nothing to lose as a wealthy man able to afford private treatment.

All went smoothly at Katutura Hospital too. Of the list she was given there, twenty-four names remained:

Ashipala, Manzambi
Autindi, Immanuel
Bobeje, Ebenezer
Damaseb, Dawid
Daurab, Amon
Elago, Lucas
Erastus ...

Stop! Elago, Lucas, Lewensvrede Farm, phone number ... Wasn't that Hendrik Fourie's farm? Wasn't that the phone number she'd already dialled more than once?

217

Elago, Lucas, male, born 23.01.1967, admitted on December 15th, disappeared without a discharge certificate on the 20th or 21st. In other words, barely two weeks before the first murder! Two weeks in which to procure a Kalashnikov, seek out victims, make plans, steal a vehicle and spray it to resemble a Group 4 Securicor car.

Elago, Lucas. Diagnosis: manifest AIDS, pulmonary tuberculosis with haematogenous dissemination to the lymph nodes. Recommended medication ...

Clemencia was standing beside the Citi Golf in front of Katutura State Hospital. The sky was so black, one could have believed that night had already fallen. To the north, in the direction of Brakwater, flashes of lightning looked momentarily like glittering, ramose trees ablaze beneath the clouds before they faded and died among the dark hills. She tried to count the seconds that intervened before the relevant claps of thunder rang out, but the flashes were so numerous she couldn't match them up.

Elago, Lucas!

The first raindrops were exploding on the windscreen as she drove off. They were fat, isolated drops. Reminded by their impact of rifle bullets striking home, she watched them plough thin, watery furrows through the film of dust on the glass.

✺❂✺

He was seated at the wheel with the blue bag beside him. He wouldn't be needing it any more. He wouldn't need anything any more. Just a place to die, but he'd better get there soon. He was already in danger of losing consciousness, he could feel it. His consciousness was trying to escape, to go somewhere. Somewhere away from his body, anyway. That would go on breathing for a while, its heart continuing to beat from force of habit until it realized there was no point. Then it would stop. It would be over. He coughed and spat blood.

It didn't really matter where you died. Any place would do. When bushmen sensed that their end was at hand, they stayed behind at the camp site while the others moved on. And there they died. That was of no concern to the members of their tribe, who were too busy ensuring their own survival. Those who had nothing more to contribute were best forgotten quickly, no matter what sacrifices they had made in the past. He himself was no bushman, though.

Thorn bushes scratched the car's bodywork with an ugly noise. He straightened up with a start and steered the vehicle back on to the sandy track. Not far to go now, maybe two kilometres. That he would manage! He had to cling to his consciousness by main force. He screwed up his eyes and opened them wide, the better to see through the veil in front of them. He noticed only now that the windscreen was beaded with drops of water. It had started to rain. He groped for the windscreen wiper control. He still couldn't see clearly even when he found it.

But his hearing was good. Almost as good as ever. Rain was beating a rhythmical tattoo on the bodywork. It ceased for a moment, then abruptly gave way to a rattle of drumfire. The wiper blades thrust a liquid curtain aside, labouring through the sudden masses of water, only to encounter another liquid curtain on the way back. The darkness that had fallen from one moment to the next was dispersed by a thunderbolt which exploded all round the car at once. Its instantaneous, ghostly glare lit up the thorn bushes, colourless, cowering creatures savagely whiplashed by the wind. The sky wasn't weeping, it was venting its fury upon the earth, and the thunder cracked like antelope bones between the teeth of a pride of lions, only more protractedly and far, far more loudly. It was the first thunderstorm of the rainy season and the last of his life.

He leant forwards and strove to make out which way the track was heading.

�֎

It had been raining bucketloads since Clemencia had driven away from the hospital. Although she had to drive slowly through town, she made it. The underpasses wouldn't flood until a little later, when the drains became choked with dust and refuse or were defeated by the sheer volume of water. She encountered no major problems heading south on the B1, either, except that she almost missed the exit because she spotted the sign too late.

Things became harder after that. It seemed as if the heat of previous months had baked the earth's crust into a solid, impermeable layer. The potholes in the dusty roadway quickly became long lakes through which the Citi Golf ploughed with difficulty. And it was still raining with undiminished violence. The headlight beams petered out amid the almost vertically descending streaks of rain. When she eventually turned off along the farm track, the terrain became hillier. Although miniature torrents were gurgling down the ruts, the water was at least draining away. She drove as fast as possible along the undulating track, well aware that a rainstorm like this could turn a dry gulch into a raging river within minutes. She negotiated the first few dips, but that was all. She braked to a halt just short of a watercourse a good five metres wide. It flowed across the track, sending a greedy wave curling along the bank, and vanished into the darkness on her left.

Damnation, this was impossible! She knew who the killer was, knew he would die before long, and even knew what of. Above all, she was almost certain she knew where he'd taken refuge, and now she couldn't get there. Because it was raining! Because she was half an hour too late. Because she'd driven Angula home so that he could fill sheets of paper with his futile jottings. Because Claus Tiedtke was the only white man in the country who owned a pathetic Citi Golf instead of a decent 4WD.

She got out her mobile. No reception, though she'd phoned

from the farm before. Perhaps it was the storm, or the dip in which she was stuck. The way back was bound to be equally impassable now. On her right loomed some dark rocks, on her left the ground fell away steeply for several metres. She couldn't even turn here. She backed the car a little way, engaged first gear, and put her foot down. Water flew into the air and one of the front wheels lurched over a rock, jolting her out of her seat. She clung to the steering wheel and floored the accelerator with her right foot, and then the car came to a standstill. It was immobilized, flooded, one metre – one miserable metre – short of the other side. Rain was drumming on the roof, water gurgling beneath the floorplates. The river would continue to rise, and soon the car would move once more. Sideways, towards the bank. She must get out while there was still time.

The water was barely knee-deep. She waded round to the front of the Golf, made the bank in two quick strides, and set off without a backward glance, keeping midway between the flooded ruts left by vehicles. Her shoes squelched at every step. She was soaked to the skin within seconds but did her best to protect her gun and her mobile. The rain eased off half an hour later, and by the time she reached the farm gate it was only spitting.

There was no little boy to open the gate for her this time, nor was anyone else in evidence, not even the dogs. The veranda was deserted and the farmhouse in darkness, but Oshivelo's Nissan was parked at an angle beneath the trees at the eastern end of the house. Although Clemencia hadn't asked Oshivelo, it was obvious that the killer had got him to hand over the keys before disappearing with his hostage. The killer who now possessed a name: Lucas Elago.

Drawing her automatic, Clemencia stole cautiously up to the Nissan and peered through the window. Empty. No, wait, there was a sports bag on the passenger seat. Buttons in the up position indicated that the car was unlocked. Someone had been in a hurry or felt very sure of himself. Clemencia quietly opened the passenger door, unzipped the bag and found a Kalashnikov on top. No, *the* Kalashnikov. She took it out and stashed it beneath the car, just in case.

Automatic in hand, she stealthily approached the farmhouse and made her way from window to window. Nothing. No one. Neither Lucas Elago nor Oshivelo's wife nor Hendrik Fourie. Former Judge Fourie and future prisoner in the dock, she thought, for he was somehow implicated beyond doubt. His professional connection with the Lubowski case, his trip to the prison in Pretoria, his more than suspicious behaviour there, the fact that the killer evidently lived on his farm – those were several coincidences too many. Elago must be an employee to whom Fourie had promised the earth if he would do a few things for him. But what use was the earth to a man who was doomed to die?

The workers' quarters. Seen from the driveway, they were situated at a respectful distance from the house and garden. A beaten track, now ankle-deep in water, led to the row of three flat-roofed shacks. A light was on in the nearest one. The first person Clemencia saw when she looked through the window was Hendrik Fourie. He was leaning against the wall with his arms crossed, tousled white hair clinging to his forehead.

On Fourie's left was a bed. The blanket covering it looked identical to the one that had been draped over Donald Acheson, except that what protruded from it was not a pair of feet but an emaciated face. The lips were thin and grey, the cheeks sunken, the eyes in their deep sockets closed. The man looked less like a killer than like death personified. The chair beside the bed was unoccupied. Fourie's housekeeper was squatting on the floor with her arms round her two children: the girl who had tried to ride on the dog's back, and the boy who had wanted to become a policeman ever since Clemencia had given him a ride in the patrol car; who couldn't understand how she had dared to arrest his *baas*, and whom she had lectured on everyone's equality before the law.

She holstered her automatic, opened the door and went in. The woman and the children didn't even turn their heads, but Fourie nodded as if he had long been expecting her and was glad she'd finally made it. She walked over to Fourie and stood beside him. Looking down at the tracks her sodden shoes had left on the concrete floor, she said softly, 'Lucas Elago ... ?'

'He got back today,' Fourie whispered. 'Two or three hours ago, perhaps.'

'Is he dead?'

Fourie shook his head. 'He comes to sometimes, then drifts off, then struggles back again. He isn't there yet, not quite.'

'We must get him to a hospital.'

'What's the point?' Fourie demanded. 'It would kill him anyway.'

'Meneer Fourie ... ' Clemencia broke off because the dying man on the bed had uttered a groan and flung his head sideways. The groan gave way to a cough that seemed to come straight from the underworld. A thin trickle of blood oozed from the corner of his mouth. The woman let go of her children, shuffled forwards on her knees and gingerly, almost tenderly, wiped away the blood with a cloth. Then she resumed the same crouching position as before. Clemencia sat down on the unoccupied chair and asked, 'Lucas Elago, where is Oshivelo's wife?'

The man's lips were fractionally parted. His breathing was rapid and shallow.

'The woman you kidnapped,' she persisted, 'where is she?'

Elago's eyes slowly opened. They were dark brown, the whites bloodshot. Clemencia felt sure he must know who she was. Not only because he'd heard her voice on the phone, but for other reasons as well: all the days and nights she'd spent on his trail, trying to foresee his movements and imagine what he was thinking and feeling. But his gaze betrayed nothing – no indication that he associated her with anything at all.

'What have you done with the woman?' Clemencia asked. She touched his shoulder. He mustn't die, not before he'd answered some questions. 'Please!' she added.

Lucas Elago wasn't dead yet. He even started to speak in a low, almost monotone voice, hurriedly blurting out the words and gasping for breath between times. It took him an age to say what he wanted. He had shot van Zyl. And Chappies Maree. He had put pressure on the wife of Barnard's cellmate. Then he had killed Staal Burger. And Acheson likewise. They were racists and murderers, all five of them. They had got what they deserved. He had only carried out the sentence passed on them by history. Why he, of all people? Because he had fought for freedom at the age of sixteen. He hadn't forgotten that, even though he'd wasted his life thereafter – ruined it, and not his life alone. When he learned he was dying, he'd seen a chance to make amends. And he had, for death was the truth and nothing else.

Clemencia jerked her thumb at the ex-judge behind her. '*He* put you up to it, didn't he?'

'No,' Elago groaned.

'How did you know about the Lubowski affair?' she demanded. 'About those CCB agents? Who told you where to find them? Who gave you the money for a Kalashnikov? For a trip to South Africa?'

'It was my decision,' Elago muttered. 'Mine alone.'

'Good God, man,' said Clemencia, 'there's no need to lie, not now!'

Even before Elago's eyes closed again, his gaze went blank and lost itself in distant memories, whether of the suffering he had undergone or the murders he had committed.

'Death is the truth,' Clemencia repeated, 'and the truth is, you're dying!'

Elago didn't react. Perhaps he was expiring at that moment. Perhaps he would come back once more.

'What the hell have you done with Oshivelo's wife?' Clemencia shouted.

'Leave him be,' said Fourie. 'You can see the state he's in.'

Yes, she could. And she could also see that he'd done his duty by Fourie. The killer had absolved him of responsibility for the five murders. Now he could die. 'You won't get away with it, Fourie,' Clemencia snarled. 'I'll nail you yet.'

'You already overreached yourself once,' Fourie said quietly.

She would examine his bank accounts and discover what sums he had placed at the killer's disposal. She would find witnesses to testify that the two men had long been in contact. She would confiscate Fourie's Lubowski archive and discover clues to the killer's mode of procedure, she would ... No, there was no need to delude herself. She would never unearth enough evidence to convict the former judge, or even to indict him. It had been the same with Donald Acheson. Even if she perjuriously claimed that Elago's dying words had identified Fourie as the instigator, it wouldn't be enough. It would be her testimony against that of the judge and his housekeeper. If she couldn't make it seem at least plausible that a dying man had committed murder on the orders of someone else, she didn't stand a chance.

She looked down at Elago's sunken face. He was still breathing feebly. In spite of all he had done, she found it hard to feel disgust. It was almost as if his death were effacing the sins he had committed during his lifetime. Death is the truth, Elago had gasped, and for a moment Clemencia considered turning round and putting her gun to Fourie's head. Truth or death! But not even that would be enough. Fourie would grin. He would know she couldn't pull the trigger.

Fourie's housekeeper and her children were sitting on the floor utterly motionless, like a group sculpture carved in stone. They did not look as if they were waiting for Elago's death or miraculous recovery or anything else. No hope or fear could be detected in their faces, just a stony submission to fate, and fate prescribed that they should sit on the floor, silent and motionless. One could have believed that time was standing still, but for the over-loud ticking of a clock in the corner of the room. An old-fashioned wall clock with curiously ornate numerals, it chimed resonantly every quarter of an hour.

That apart, nothing. Not a word, not a sound but Elago's spasmodic breathing, occasionally punctuated by a rattle in the throat or a cough that made Clemencia think the end had come. But it hadn't, not yet, so she wouldn't leave. She wouldn't budge an inch as long as it seemed possible that Elago might say something more. Or until it became certain that he would never speak again.

More rain came pattering down when the clock struck half past eleven. By one-fifteen it had stopped. Then it was back to the ticking of the clock and the hoarse breathing and the chime every quarter of an hour, and sometimes what sounded like a final death rattle. At two-forty Elago opened his eyes and slowly turned his head. His lips tried to mouth a word, but he no longer had the strength to utter a sound.

'Water,' said Clemencia. 'For God's sake give him some water!'

Elago grimaced, whether in pain or refusal it was hard to tell. He made another attempt to speak but failed. Looking at something beyond Clemencia, he jerked his chin twice.

'Nangolo, Taleni,' said Fourie, 'he wants you to go to him.'

The boy shook his head and clung more tightly to his mother. The girl had fallen asleep.

'Go on!' Fourie commanded.

The woman shook the girl awake and pushed both children towards the edge of the bed. Fourie followed. Reaching over their heads, he turned the blanket back. Then he took hold of Elago's right arm and placed his palm on the boy's head. The boy stared straight in front of him. There was nothing there, just an expanse of bare wall spattered with blood from swatted mosquitoes. Elago's face twitched again, possibly in the semblance of a smile.

'I promise you I'll care for the children as if I were their own father,' Fourie said. He now placed Elago's hand on top of the girl's head. 'I'll send them to the best schools and pay for their education – send them to university too, if they want. And when I die they'll inherit the farm.'

Elago's limp hand slid off the girl's head. Fourie caught hold of it and squeezed it twice in the conventional ritual greeting between blacks. And in farewell, thought Clemencia. 'I swear it by all that's holy!' Fourie added.

So that was the deal, Clemencia thought as the girl fled back into her mother's arms, and the boy continued to stand stiffly beside the bed, and Fourie laid Elago's arm at his side before he draped the blanket over him again. So that was the deal! The death of five racist murderers in return for two children's future. Elago hadn't been entirely untruthful. He really had wanted to make amends, except that what had motivated him wasn't revenge, politics or historical injustice, just two children who had scarcely known him. Perhaps it was all because he had fathered them but taken no interest in them until the moment he learned he was soon to die. Then, it seemed, they had suddenly become important to him.

Elago's head sagged sideways and his eyes closed. The clock ticked on. He had reached the end of the road, taken his leave of the world. What was keeping him? He would say nothing more, either false or true, and would probably not regain consciousness. Clemencia had no reason to go on sitting beside his bed. She ought to go in search of Oshivelo's wife. Perhaps there would be some clue to her whereabouts in the car. She eyed the moribund man in front of her, fancying that she could actually see the cheekbones glinting through the thin black skin. His lips had now lost all their colour, but still he continued to breathe, fast and spasmodically. Why didn't he simply stop breathing? He'd had enough. It was time.

Clemencia found the situation hard to endure, but she couldn't get up and go, couldn't tear her eyes away from Elago even though the sight of him caused her almost physical pain. Or was her feeling of discomfort gradually turning into anger? She was looking for a guilty party. This man's death would not atone for the murders he had committed. Everyone died. There was no merit in that. At most, it was a reason for her to sit there in silence.

For all that, Lucas Elago had been willing, for once in his life, to do the right thing. It was Fourie who had shamelessly exploited that for his own ends. Or rather, for what he had chosen to make his *raison d'être*: a final settlement of accounts with those responsible for a crime twenty years old. It was arbitrary, it was wrong, but not even Fourie could be accused of having acted from base or selfish motives.

But why hadn't Elago seen any other way of securing his children's future? What kind of society was it where a father thought he had to murder for the benefit of his offspring? For the most natural thing imaginable, nineteen years after freedom and equal rights had been fought for and won? What would Anton Lubowski have said about it if he were still alive?

The wall clock continued to strike every quarter, and Elago was still breathing, still slowly dying, when the grey light of dawn crept through the window. Glossy starlings twittered outside, a few rays of sunlight percolated the tattered clouds and lodged in the trees beside the farmhouse, and at 8.10 Clemencia's mobile phone rang. She went outside. It was Melvin. He and his pals had had to knock off early yesterday evening because of the cloudburst, but they'd covered the hole in the road properly, so they'd been able to go back to work at seven on the dot. It had paid off, too, because something had just happened – something Clemencia urgently needed to know.

'Has Donkerkop turned up?' she asked.

'No, but the police units who were watching the place have been withdrawn,' said Melvin. 'Every last one. We reckon the killer managed to trick his way in somehow.'

'No, it definitely wasn't the killer, because — '

'Leave it to us,' Melvin broke in. 'Got to hang up, my money's running out, but you can rely on us.'

'Listen, Melvin … ' Clemencia began, but he'd already severed the connection. She thought for a moment, then called Tjikundu.

'We've got Donkerkop,' said Tjikundu. 'That's to say, we've cornered him. He couldn't get away if he tried, but it looks as if he doesn't want to.'

'Where is he?'

'Heroes' Acre, at the foot of the big obelisk. He must have sneaked into the grounds during the night. Anyway, security didn't discover him till this morning. He's got some packages strapped to his body. Explosives, allegedly. He claims he's also mined the tombs of our national heroes.'

'What's he asking for?'

'Well,' said Tjikundu, 'I haven't really grasped that. He doesn't want to be shot. Does that seem logical to you, a guy threatening to blow himself up if anyone tries to shoot him?'

Clemencia heard the door behind her open. She told him she would call back and turned round. Mother and daughter emerged first, followed by the boy, who stooped to pick up some pebbles and tossed them one after another into the puddles created by the rainstorm during the night. The girl let go of her mother's hand and ran after the dog. She didn't call it by name, just shouted, 'Come here, dog!' The woman had dark shadows under her eyes. She said she was quickly going to make some breakfast. The children were welcome to play for a bit until it was ready. It was impossible to tell what she was thinking, if anything. Perhaps she was simply surprised that a new day had dawned.

Clemencia went back inside. Fourie was still standing beside the bed. Lucas Elago's hands were now lying on the blanket with the fingers interlaced. His grey lips were closed. He had stopped breathing. He was dead. If this was what the truth looked like, it was both banal and irrevocable. There was nothing left to say about it. About other things, certainly.

'The police have cornered Donkerkop,' Clemencia began.

'Good,' said Fourie.

'He's threatening to blow himself up, together with the whole of Heroes' Acre.'

Fourie made a dismissive gesture. 'He'll cling to life. He wouldn't have gone to ground otherwise.'

'He's been on the run for days,' said Clemencia. 'He's alone, confused, exhausted, and he thinks that a hitman and the whole of the Namibian police are intent on killing him. You can't tell how someone will react in such a situation.'

'Oh yes,' Fourie retorted. 'He'll confess to Lubowski's murder. Your boss Oshivelo will talk him into it.'

So Fourie was in the know! He knew precisely what Elago had demanded of Oshivelo. Elago could have told him, but why should he have, if the abduction of Oshivelo's wife had been exclusively his own idea? No, Fourie was also involved – in fact he'd probably concocted the plan himself. Clemencia realized that his concern from the first had not been vigilantism or the execution of Lubowski's putative murderers. All he had ever wanted was to extract a confession from them. If the suspects refused they were shot, and this automatically increased the pressure on the next man to whom Fourie dispatched his killer. Or whom, like Ferdi Barnard in prison, he had asked if he wanted to share the others' fate. They had stood firm, though. Maree, Barnard, Burger, Acheson – none of them had been willing to cooperate, and now they were dead. Only one remained, Donkerkop, and he mustn't die under any circumstances, or there would be no one left to tell what had happened on the night of 12 September 1989.

'No,' said Clemencia. 'Oshivelo won't talk Donkerkop into anything. Not when he hears that his wife's abductor can neither release nor kill her because he's dead himself, so how could his demands be met?'

'Lucas Elago could have had accomplices,' Fourie objected.

'Or an employer,' said Clemencia. A former judge, for example.

One named Hendrik Fourie.'

'Whatever.' Fourie shrugged his shoulders. 'Oshivelo won't dare risk his wife's life while she's nowhere to be found.'

Clemencia thought of Angula's theory. If Oshivelo really had something to hide, the danger was that he would order his men to blaze away as soon as it could be done without risk to his wife, even if the whole of Heroes' Acre were blown sky-high. Dead heroes' tombstones could be re-erected. That was no problem, just as long as the heroes themselves and their fate remained buried!

'Oshivelo will play for time,' said Clemencia, 'and mount a feverish search for his wife.'

'Best of luck,' said Fourie.

Was she wrong, or had she for the first time detected a trace of uncertainty in his voice? If Oshivelo's wife were found before Donkerkop talked, all of his efforts would have been in vain. The years of research, the five contract killings, the deal with the killer. Clemencia described a circle with her forefinger. 'One could start by searching these farm buildings, for example.'

'If you say so.'

'Let's think for a moment,' said Clemencia. 'Lucas Elago was already very weak when he abducted the woman. He knew his time was running out, or he wouldn't have come here to die with his family a few hours later. It's unlikely he drove halfway across Namibia to hide his hostage somewhere first. His inclination would have been to bring her here, but that might have implicated his family and – worse still – you, Meneer Fourie. He wanted to avoid that so as not to break his deal with you at the last moment, because you wouldn't subsidize his children unless he accepted sole respon-sibility for all the killings.'

'This is total nonsense. No sane person would ever — '

'What if Oshivelo's wife had seen you here? Of if it later trans-pired that you hadn't responded to her cries for help? Elago could have killed her, but you didn't want that – after all, the woman isn't a CCB agent or a murderer. So he must have dumped her somewhere between Windhoek and your farmhouse. Am I right?'

Fourie didn't answer. 'On the other hand,' she went on, 'it isn't so easy to hide a woman securely if you can't afford to trouble your only accomplice. At best, you'd find a suitable spot that's familiar to you. How long did Elago work on your farm? Long enough, probably, to know every corner of your 15,000 hectares? Every cattle station, every little hut in the mountains where a chained-up woman could cry for help for weeks with no one to hear her but jackals? Could there be a hut like that somewhere?'

'This is ludicrous,' said Fourie.

'Is there?' she insisted.

'No.'

'Fifteen thousand hectares are a lot of land,' Clemencia said, 'but not so much that it couldn't be searched reasonably quickly with the aid of a helicopter and a couple of hundred policemen.'

Fourie looked down at the dead man on the bed. He raised his right hand as if to cross himself but stopped short, then lowered it and turned to go. Clemencia followed him in the direction of the farmhouse. The soil around the lemon trees smelt damp. Beneath the bougainvilleas lay a carpet of petals spread there by the downpour. The clouds approaching from the east were white and looked innocuous. It was hard to believe they heralded another storm. Fourie said, 'Let's assume you found the woman … '

'Well?' It looked as if she'd been right. Oshivelo's wife was a prisoner somewhere on Fourie's land!

'Then your boss would have Donkerkop shot, wouldn't he?' Fourie went on. 'Another death, and Lubowski's murder would never be solved!'

'Perhaps, but I won't let an innocent woman starve to death in chains.'

Fourie came to a halt, picked up a fallen lemon and wiped the moist earth off its peel. He said, 'I've a suggestion for you: Let me talk to Donkerkop. Alone. Just for a minute or two.'

'Why should I?'

'I can imagine where Elago took the woman.'

'Then tell me, damn it!'

'Anton Lubowski was gunned down twenty years ago. Since then, nothing even remotely resembling justice has been — '

'If you know where Oshivelo's wife is and refuse to say, it's a criminal offence,' said Clemencia, although this was absurd. As if one more death mattered to someone who had already instigated five murders!

'We could be at Heroes' Acre in half an hour or so,' said Fourie. 'Ten minutes alone with Donkerkop, that's all I need, then you can go and get the woman. I'm asking you for less than an hour's grace. Do you know how many hours there are in twenty years?'

Clemencia had no idea what Fourie was planning. Did he intend to blow himself up in company with the last of Lubowski's assassins? Because he could see no alternative – because there was no further hope of shedding light on Lubowski's murder? Or did he genuinely believe he could persuade Donkerkop to confess? How? With what?

'I couldn't gain you access to Donkerkop even if I wanted to.'

'Let me worry about that.'

'Have you any idea what's going on at Heroes' Acre right now?'

'I've got some influential friends. Let me make a quick phone call.'

Without knowing quite why, Clemencia nodded. While Fourie was hurrying into the house, she went over to Oshivelo's car. Elago's young son was standing beside the driver's door with the Kalashnikov she'd hidden cradled in his scrawny arms. Barefoot and overtired, he was wearing a miserable, forlorn expression that reminded her of a photograph she'd seen of a child soldier in Uganda's notorious 'Lord's Resistance Army'.

'Please give me that,' she said as gently as she could. What was the boy's name again? What had Fourie called him? Nangolo?

'Give me the gun, Nangolo!' She took a step towards him.

'Is it my father's?' He hugged the gun to his chest.

She put out her hand. 'Your father doesn't need it any more, and you, you'll never need it.'

The boy said nothing. Clemencia grasped the barrel of the AK-47 and he didn't resist when she took it away from him. Without looking at her, he asked, 'Was my father a hero?'

Ndangi Oshivelo, Deputy Commissioner of the Namibian police:

To suggest that I meant to allow the situation at Heroes' Acre to escalate is wholly unfounded. In the first place, I'm a patriot and have proved as much over a period of decades. That being so, I would naturally have tried to prevent the destruction of a national monument and the death of innocent persons. Secondly, I'm not stupid. Although I couldn't precisely gauge Fourie's intentions at that juncture, I realized that he was playing with marked cards. And thirdly, I hadn't the slightest reason to want to eliminate Donkerkop — I mean, Meneer Cloete. On the contrary, I was extremely interested to hear any contribution he could make towards clearing up Anton Lubowski's murder. I had nothing to fear.

So why didn't I accede to Cloete's offer to negotiate? Why did I ultimately speak in favour of resolving the situation by force? Well, quite simply in order to coax Meneer Fourie out of his shell. I wanted to see how he would react if the reins escaped from his grasp. Whether I was right is a question each can decide for himself. Had I not been, I strongly doubt if we would be where we are now. And that, in my view, is what everyone should concentrate on instead of indulging in wild speculation.

Oshivelo was sitting with an army officer beneath the awning of the Heroes' Acre Restaurant, a megaphone at his feet. Negotiations seemed to have been broken off. Oshivelo put his binoculars down when Clemencia addressed him. He remained quite calm, making absolutely no mention of the fact that she had been suspended and should not have shown her face in his presence. Instead, he turned to Fourie.

'I see, so you mean to persuade the man to give himself up?'

'Yes,' said Fourie.

Oshivelo nodded. Someone had intervened on Fourie's behalf, he said. The judge evidently had influential friends, so if he insisted … At his own risk, of course. The senior officer beside him also nodded, and that appeared to clinch matters. Oshivelo raised his binoculars again.

The central part of the memorial ran uphill like a stepped pyramid: sloping surfaces faced with slabs of black stone that almost resembled tinted glass, horizontal areas occupied by flower beds containing withered ground-cover plants. Tombs and memorial plaques were let into the three uppermost rows only; the rest of the space was unoccupied, awaiting further heroes. Above the tombs, covering some four-fifths of the top of the slope, was a sizeable flat expanse. The curving frieze that bounded it illustrated the Namibians' struggle for freedom, from the colonial era to independence, in a series of over-life-size half-reliefs. In front of this was a black plinth with an obelisk mounted on it, and in front of that the monumental statue of a freedom fighter in gleaming bronze. That his features resembled those of a youthful Sam Nujoma, the country's first president, could not be seen at this distance, but the stick grenade in his raised right hand and, if you looked closely, the slung Kalashnikov plus short bayonet were both clearly visible.

Seated at the foot of the statue was a man, presumably Martinus Cloete, aka Donkerkop, the last of Lubowski's putative murderers. With his back resting against the stylized rock from which one of the freedom fighter's legs was sprouting, he looked tiny and somehow pathetic. Clemencia screwed up her eyes. He had something strapped to his body, but not even someone with a pair of binoculars could have told whether the explosives were genuine or fake.

Be that as it may, the security forces were keeping a respectful distance. Armed with rifles, soldiers in camouflage suits were lying in the bush veldt beyond the paved walkways. It was clear that the Namibian Defence Force was in charge and had tried to make the Donkerkop problem a matter of national defence. Uniformed policemen were only to be found among the men guarding the foot of the hill.

Fourie was just threading his way through the vehicles that served them as cover. He crossed the parade ground and headed for the eternal flame. Surrounding it on metal stands were a few withered wreaths. Although doubtless placed there with the opposite intention, they now demonstrated the transient nature of remembrance and renown. Reaching the foot of the steps, Fourie paused. He took a white handkerchief from his trouser pocket and waved it above his head. The man at the top of the hill did not react. Slowly, step by step, Fourie proceeded to climb.

Clemencia had remained silent until now, so as to allow him the conversation he had requested. If he came back — if he came back alive — the handcuffs would click around his wrists whether or not he'd fulfilled his part of the bargain and revealed the whereabouts of Oshivelo's wife. Then would be the time for her to disclose his involvement in the crimes. For the moment, she confined herself to telling her boss the incontrovertible facts. She briefly described her discovery of Oshivelo's car and the killer's death on Fourie's farm. No, she said, there was no definite trace of his wife. As soon as this business was over, Oshivelo said grimly, he would deal with the matter. He had laid his binoculars aside, probably in order to be able to watch Fourie and Donkerkop at the same time.

Halfway up the central flight of steps, Fourie came to a halt. The man at the foot of the statue leant forwards and called something to him. The wind carried his words away. They were as unintelligible as Fourie's reply, but they seemed to be satisfactory, because he didn't demur when Fourie set off up the next few steps. The policemen who had established a makeshift incident room inside the restaurant came crowding out on to the terrace. Tjikundu was among them, as was the loathsome Robinson. Meanwhile, activity had broken out among the soldiers stationed down in the car park on the left. Heavy machine guns were being unloaded from an NDF truck that looked as if it was a left-over from the East German army.

Unaware of this, Fourie continued to climb towards the statue with the outsize stick grenade in its right hand. His handkerchief fluttered in the wind as if he meant to surrender, but that impression was misleading. A frail, elderly white man had sought to impose, by violent means, a truth which everyone else would rather have left in historical obscurity. He would not be able to win his war, but he wouldn't surrender either, of that Clemencia felt certain. He would fight to the last breath.

Fourie had now reached the upper platform and was walking towards the sloping expanse of black tiles on which, in big, ornate lettering were the words: 'Glory to the Fallen Heroes and Heroines of the Motherland Namibia!'. For whatever reason – that inscription, or the bombastic architecture of Heroes' Acre as a whole, or Fourie's fluttering white handkerchief, or the soldiers now hauling one of the machine guns up the hill out of Donkerkop's range of vision, or just the white clouds drifting steadily over the obelisk – Clemencia was suddenly reminded of the Namibian national anthem: 'Namibia, land of the brave, freedom fight we have won, glory to their bravery whose blood waters our freedom … '

She felt like singing the words softly to herself, but it really wouldn't have done, not now. Not in the presence of those two

237

white men talking together at this moment. One of them was responsible for the death of someone whose blood had watered freedom, the other felt himself to be an implacable god of justice. They might always have lived here, but the land of the brave wasn't *their* land. It simply couldn't be, not after all the promises and hopes of 1990, because the pair of them were murderous, not brave. There was an immense difference between those attributes, even though you had to look hard to detect it. The important thing was to kill, not only for the right side but at the right time. And now was certainly not the right time.

Clemencia wondered what constituted bravery today. That you put up with the status quo or rebelled against it? That you crossed swords with the all-powerful government party like Angula or put your children's welfare before all else like Lucas Elago? That you muddled your way through life like Miki Selma and the rest of her family?

'Any moment now,' said Robinson. He drew Clemencia's attention to some soldiers who had just reached the look-out point above the obelisk and were hurriedly manhandling their machine gun into position.

'Not without my consent!' Oshivelo said sharply. 'That was the agreement.'

The army officer gave a thin smile. 'Not unless an immediate threat leaves us no choice … '

Oshivelo snorted. 'And what constitutes an immediate threat?'

'We have to be prepared,' said the officer.

Clemencia caught sight of a sign in the restaurant's car park: *Don't feed the baboons!* There weren't any baboons around. They would have been unwise to show their faces now in any case.

'He's coming back,' said Robinson. It was true. Fourie had negotiated for no longer than ten minutes, just as he had promised. While he was descending the steps, Donkerkop looked round and immediately spotted the machine gun that had just been installed above him. He raised his middle finger and pointed to the package strapped to his chest.

'We'll fill him full of holes before he can even blink,' said the army officer.

'An original idea,' Oshivelo said scornfully, 'but perhaps we should wait and hear what Fourie has to say.'

And Fourie did have something to say. For some reason, Donkerkop was convinced that the police were bent on killing him. If he had to die, he would take some of them with him and reduce Heroes' Acre to rubble, that he could guarantee. On the other hand, he would quite like to survive. That was why he had decided to tell all he knew about Lubowski's murder. Once that had been made public, there would be no further reason to silence him. There must be some journalists present, he said, so send them up to him.

'Oh, sure,' said Oshivelo. 'He'd like that.'

'Nobody goes near him until he surrenders the explosive,' the army officer interjected.

'He'll do that,' said Fourie, 'if you, Meneer Oshivelo, are also willing to grant an interview.'

Oshivelo raised his eyebrows. 'Me?'

'Yes, he wants you to tell the representatives of the press all *you* know about Lubowski's murder.'

'He's out of his mind,' said Oshivelo.

'In return he'll give himself up and tell you where to find your wife. Alive, what's more.'

'What?'

'*Still* alive, to use his exact words. But you mustn't take too long.'

'How would Donkerkop know where my wife is?' Oshivelo demanded.

'Yes, Meneer Fourie, won't you tell us that?' Clemencia put in.

'You must have misunderstood me, Miss Garises.' Fourie

smiled. 'I merely surmised that I could get it out of Donkerkop in the course of conversation. I didn't succeed, but believe me, he knows her whereabouts and he'll reveal it as soon as — '

'Then he must have been in league with the killer,' said Oshivelo.

'Exactly.' Fourie nodded. 'Lucas Elago confirmed that to me.'

'I thought so!' said Robinson.

'This is utter nonsense,' said Clemencia. Elago had carried out the abduction on his own and committed murder on Fourie's instructions. The two of them had had their personal motives and interests. They had made a secret but thoroughly understandable agreement. What part in it could Donkerkop have played? There was no room in it for him or any other third party. 'You can tell us anything you please, Meneer Fourie,' Clemencia went on. 'We weren't up there, after all. I think you've invented this story just to — '

'Send for those reporters!' said Fourie. 'Once they've gathered on the steps and everything's in readiness for the interviews, Donkerkop will remove the explosive and come down, you'll see!'

'If you're playing tricks, Meneer Fourie ... ' Oshivelo handed Robinson the megaphone he'd deposited beside his feet. 'Ask that man up there whether he knows where my wife is being held prisoner.'

Robinson cleared his throat and shouted in the direction of the freedom fighter's statue. A faint, disjointed echo came drifting back across the parade ground. Donkerkop cupped his hands round his mouth and called, 'Of course I know!'

Oshivelo nodded to Robinson, who yelled, 'Where is she?'

The answer was clearly audible despite the wind. 'Press conference first!'

'Do you believe me now?' asked Fourie.

'Meneer Cloete,' Robinson bellowed into the megaphone, 'we decide what happens around here. I can only advise you — '

'Enough!' said Oshivelo.

' — to tell us where — '

'That's enough, Robinson!' Oshivelo stroked his grey beard. He put the flat of his hand on the table top and massaged the knuckles. 'If he's really got my wife, why hasn't he come out with it before? It would have placed him in quite a different negotiating position.'

'The media representatives are waiting on the approach road,' said Fourie. 'Shouldn't one of you gentlemen see they're waved through?'

The army officer looked at Oshivelo, who shrugged his shoulders. 'I've nothing to say about the Lubowski case,' he said. 'What's more, I won't even tell the press I've nothing to say on the subject.'

The officer turned to Fourie. 'And Donkerkop really will dump the explosive before coming down to talk to the press?'

Fourie nodded.

'Good,' said Oshivelo. 'In that case, we can safely take him out on the steps.'

'Smuggle some marksmen in with the journalists, you mean?' asked Robinson.

'I mean the machine gun,' said Oshivelo.

'What about your wife?'

'Donkerkop knows nothing anyway.'

'You plan to shoot him?' Fourie demanded in a rather shaky voice. 'Just because you refuse to give a bloody interview?'

'Yes,' said the army officer, 'I don't quite understand that either.'

Two soldiers were squinting over the machine gun up in the look-out point. If Donkerkop went down the steps they would inevitably hit him in the back. One of the clouds drifting across the sky cast a shadow over the parade ground and the Namibian flag flapping in the wind at the far end. The army officer sat back in his chair and said, 'I think we should invite the press in.'

'You know my opinion,' said Oshivelo.

The officer gave orders for the guards manning the barrier to be informed. Then he said, 'And you'd better forget about the

241

machine gun, Meneer Oshivelo. With the best will in the world, I can't detect any immediate threat.'

Oshivelo spread his hands. 'The best of luck. But I'm not talking to the press.'

❊❊❊

Donkerkop:

Yes, I was present at Lubowski's murder. Yes, I shot him. At a range of fifty centimetres. I don't know if he was already dead. I've wondered that a thousand times over the years. I've tried a thousand times to remember if he was moving or breathing. But I don't know, and now it doesn't matter to me any more. Whether or not he was still alive, all that counts for me is that I pulled the trigger. That's why I'm guilty irrespective of who else had a hand in his death.

And do you know when I grasped that, Your Honour? While I was sitting beside that kitschy statue in Heroes' Acre. The white obelisk was looming over me, and when I looked up at it, it suddenly seemed to sway. I honestly thought it would topple over and smash itself and me, but it went on falling without getting any nearer. Then I realized it was just an illusion. An optical illusion occasioned by clouds scudding across the sky.

Look, I thought, turning the world upside down is as easy as that! A few drifting clouds are enough to throw everything out of kilter, a fleeting movement lasting not much longer than the time it takes to flex your forefinger and kill a man. What had seemed crucial – whether or not the obelisk fell over – suddenly became quite unimportant. I knew at that moment that my nightmares could cease, that I didn't have to run away from myself for the rest of my life, that I needn't keep wading through my memories over and over again. Yes, I had pulled the trigger. Yes, I was guilty. And I was firmly resolved to tell everyone so.

A little later, Fourie came up the steps. He asked me if I was interested in surviving.

'Certainly,' I said, although 'surviving' wasn't the right word. I felt I'd been reborn. It didn't scare me that I would go to prison. I was looking

242

forward, with indescribable anticipation, to my first night of dreamless sleep.

'Stupidly,' said Fourie, 'the police are hell-bent on gunning you down. Only I can get you out of here alive, and I will if you publicly state that you shot Anton Lubowski. Would you do that?'

'No problem,' I said.

'The truth, the whole truth and nothing but the truth?'

'Of course,' I said. I don't know if Fourie believed I meant it. He had no choice, I suppose. At all events, he told me his plan. I was to demand a press conference. The police would agree provided I took off the explosive before I came down.

'Then they'll shoot me anyway!' I said.

No they wouldn't, he told me, because I wouldn't reveal where I'd hidden the senior police officer's wife until the press conference was over. This rather surprised me, because it was the first I'd heard of her abduction, but I naturally grasped that it was my chance. The police would hardly kill me if they genuinely believed I knew where the woman was.

'So where is she?' I asked.

'How would I know?' Fourie retorted. 'Simply say, in a mountain hut on Lewensrede Farm, fifty kilometres south of here. They must leave the farm track and turn off right after four or five kilometres. By the time they discover they're wrong you'll be in police custody, out of range of any itchy-fingered marksmen. They may grill you hard in the course of subsequent questioning, but they won't kill you as long as they believe you know the woman's whereabouts. You won't tell the truth until you're up in front of the magistrate: say the abduction story was just a form of life insurance because the police were out to kill you. Once that statement is in the court records, you'll be safe at last. The police won't dare harm a hair of your head.'

That made sense to me.

�֍֎֍

Although the route Donkerkop had described struck Clemencia as rather vague, it proved to be absolutely reliable on the ground. Precisely four-and-a-half kilometres beyond the turn-off to

243

Lewensrede Farm, just short of the spot where the Citi Golf had been immobilized by the flash flood, a little-used track branched off to the right. The only one far and wide, it led straight down into a valley, then wound uphill and ended in a basin with a tumble-down hut in the middle. The roof had half collapsed, the water tank beside it had cracked open. Jutting well above it was the tower of a long dismantled windmill pump, which was still standing.

The iron chain with which Oshivelo's wife had been shackled to the stake was several metres long. Just long enough to enable her to retreat into the hut, where some food and two jerrycans of water had been left. She was uninjured apart from one ankle, which she had skinned in a vain attempt to free herself from the chain. She was all right, she said, everything was fine. She had managed to shelter adequately from the storm. Last night had been bearable, and she'd guessed she wouldn't have to spend another out there. The only question she asked concerned her abductor. When told that he had died that morning, she merely nodded. Then she ran her fingers through her hair and complained, in an overly casual tone of voice, that she must look a sight. There couldn't have been a clearer indication that she had no wish to talk about the last twenty-four hours. As soon as some cutting gear arrived, Oshivelo took his wife home.

Clemencia used the time to question Donkerkop at headquarters. When she assured him that his voluntary disclosure of the kidnap victim's hiding place would have an extenuating effect on his sentence, Donkerkop was utterly astonished. He had killed Lubowski, yes, and he was quite willing to repeat, to the police and in court and anywhere else, what he had told the journalists at Heroes' Acre, but he'd had nothing to do with any kidnapping. Clemencia questioned him further. She was just starting again from scratch when Oshivelo joined her an hour later. Donkerkop adamantly maintained that Fourie had pulled a fast one on him. He claimed that the ex-judge had told him the route 'in confidence'.

None of Clemencia's colleagues believed him at first. It was strange, on the face of it, that Oshivelo's wife had been found on Fourie's property, but that was because Lucas Elago, the killer and Donkerkop's accomplice in the kidnapping, was familiar with the terrain. The description had proved to be correct, so one of the two, Fourie or Donkerkop, must at least have known of the abduction. It was one person's word against another. Or rather, the word of a retired but respectable servant of the law against that of a self-confessed assassin.

'Exactly,' said Clemencia. 'He confesses to murder but denies a lesser charge?'

Surprisingly, Oshivelo agreed with her. If one of the two was lying, he said, it was Fourie.

'And not only on this point,' said Clemencia, and she proceeded to expound her theory of the murderous deal between Fourie and Elago, pulling out all the stops. Never in her life had she tried so hard to convince someone of something. She demonstrated how obsessed Fourie was with the Lubowski case and recalled his visit to the prison in Pretoria. Only he could have told the killer that Ferdi Barnard, too, had refused to come clean and must therefore be killed. She described the relationship between Fourie and Elago and his children, who did not believe that the *baas* was a man like any other. She drew attention to Elago's diagnosis, his stay in the hospital and precipitate departure. She speculated on what could be inferred about the killer's emotional state. She explained why the time frame fitted so perfectly. She gave her colleagues an account of the night preceding Elago's death and questioned why a man who could hardly speak should have engaged, unasked, in a long and agonizing asseveration that he had acted alone. She cited Fourie's promise to look after the children and interpreted his looks and gestures. She inserted stone after stone in a mosaic which at least convinced the others that she wasn't completely out of her mind. Even Robinson said simply, 'Well, I don't know.'

'It sounds reasonable, the way you put it,' Tjikundu said cautiously.

'Pretty logical,' van Wyk chimed in.

Then silence fell. It was Oshivelo who uttered the four words Clemencia had been expecting. The ones her exposition had been unable to silence within herself. The four confounded words that quite clearly and baldly defined the position: 'It won't be enough.'

They had a theory and some leads, but no firm evidence that Fourie had ordered five murders and an abduction. They had no witness – nothing at all that would stand up in court.

'Perhaps he made a mistake,' said Tjikundu. 'Perhaps there's a written agreement that covers Elago after his death. It's conceivable Fourie might have forgotten his promise inside six months.'

'Perhaps,' said Clemencia, not that she believed it.

'Or we'll find Fourie's fingerprints on the chain the chief's wife was shackled to,' said van Wyk.

'We could put the squeeze on Elago's widow,' Tjikundu suggested.

'Meneer Fourie too, of course,' said van Wyk. 'At least for as long as his lawyer lets us.'

'Maybe Fourie won't get through to him at all.' Robinson grinned. 'His phone could get damaged when we arrest him.'

'We must go by the book,' Oshivelo insisted.

'But can we give it a try?' Clemencia looked at the clock. It was 9.11 p.m.

'We'll start tomorrow morning' said Oshivelo. 'You can have twenty-four hours. I won't be able to protect you for longer than that in view of Fourie's excellent connections. And stick to the rules, all of you!'

With Oshivelo's consent, Clemencia called Angula. She really needed him now, but he didn't answer. However, Oshivelo promised her twelve men from various departments, nine of whom reported to the Serious Crime Unit the next morning. They were to help to take Fourie's farm apart.

And they did. They began by searching the farmhouse from top to bottom. Then the two cars. Then came the outbuildings, tool sheds, workers' quarters, dog kennels and garbage bins, as well as every nook and cranny in the vegetable garden, rockery and citrus orchard that might provide a hiding place for anything at all. At three p.m. they were joined by the colleagues detailed to examine the mountain hut for clues. An hour later it started to rain and they tackled the farmhouse once more. Meanwhile, Robinson and Tjikundu pumped Elago's widow and the farmhands. They called headquarters every two hours, as arranged, to report on the progress of their investigations. Or rather, on their lack of progress, because nothing was found that would have taken them even one step further. At eight p.m. darkness fell, and at nine-thirty Robinson called in for the last time, to say that they were knocking off and sending the team home.

At that stage Clemencia had spent thirteen hours in the interview room. Van Wyk divided his time between leaning against the wall, pacing up and down behind Fourie's back, and leaving the room, only to come hurrying in soon afterwards and whisper something in Clemencia's ear. But nothing could shake the former judge's composure. If he wondered why von Fleckenstein still hadn't obtained his release, he didn't show it. He steadfastly denied having induced Elago to commit any crimes but was happy to talk about anything else. About the anomalies of the Lubowski case, about his professional career, his farm, his workers – anything at all. He was currently delivering a speech about generosity. Although he sometimes made donations to good causes, he said, he was not particularly public-spirited. If some tragedy occurred in his immediate vicinity, however, it affected him as deeply as it did the majority of his fellow citizens. Everyone knew, of course, that there were dozens of charitable projects in Katutura aimed at hundreds if not thousands of AIDS orphans, but it was a different matter when you were in personal contact with two children whom you saw every day. Especially two youngsters as promising as Nangolo and Taleni. Why should he bequeath his farm to some distant relations whose names he hardly knew?

'Right,' said Clemencia, 'let's go back to your visit to Ferdi Barnard. What happened, exactly?'

'What did you do after leaving the prison?' asked van Wyk.

'We want to reconstruct your every movement.'

'Whom did you meet, whom did you speak to?'

Fourie talked, Clemencia and van Wyk asked questions, Fourie answered them, and the night wore on. Van Wyk took a break between three and four-thirty, then Clemencia put her head down in the room next door. Although Tjikundu and Robinson took over at eight, Clemencia stayed on. The twenty-four hours were up, really, but she wanted to stick it out to the end. Fourie could hardly see out of his eyes. He kept pointing out, more and more often, that he had already said everything umpteen times. That was true, but they would have preferred some different answers. From nine-thirty onwards Fourie refused to give any information at all, and at ten-thirty Oshivelo summoned Clemencia from the interview room. The public prosecutor and the magistrate were sitting in his office, he told her. He couldn't stall them any longer. Clemencia nodded. By eleven Fourie was out, a free man. They had lost.

Fatigue pounced on Clemencia like a starving hyena. Or was it resignation? Five wholly unequivocal murders and no trial! Fourie would never stand in the dock because she couldn't prove anything against him. Lucas Elago wouldn't because he was dead. It was a total disaster.

'Nonsense,' said Tjikundu, 'we're national heroes!' He tossed three dailies on to her desk. *The Namibian's* headline read: 'The truth after 19 years'. The *Windhoek Observer*, in addition to a close-up of Donkerkop with the blurred architecture of Heroes' Acre in the background, carried the words: 'I shot Anton Lubowski.' And

Die Republikein proclaimed: '*Lubowski – uiteindelik moordenaar gevang*' – 'Lubowski – murderer arrested at last'.

Clemencia swallowed a mouthful of coffee. The insipid taste in her mouth persisted, though Tjikundu wasn't entirely wrong. At least a forgotten cold case had been successfully laid to rest – and not just any old case, but one that had shocked the whole nation in its day. Admittedly, Angula would only have shaken his head at the headlines and said they couldn't claim to have got at the truth until the background conspiracy was exposed. He would also have doubted whether Lubowski's murderer had finally been caught. Still, they did have Donkerkop, and he had confessed. As for the background conspiracy, that might yet emerge in court, because the case would definitely come to trial.

'Hm,' said Oshivelo, 'I'm afraid that's rather doubtful. I spent a lot of time with the public prosecutor yesterday and today, and the subject came up. The trouble is, Donkerkop credibly asserts that he doesn't know whether Lubowski was already dead when he shot him. If he wasn't, the charge would at most be desecration of a dead body, not murder. But that offence is subject to the statute of limitations. Unless the original autopsy report turns up and definitely states that — '

'The report was among those files,' Clemencia broke in. She had seen it with her own eyes.

Oshivelo shrugged. 'Be that as it may, it's gone missing.'

'I don't believe it!' said Tjikundu.

'Donkerkop won't be charged, you mean?' asked van Wyk.

'The public prosecutor will make a careful study of the legal position,' said Oshivelo.

Clemencia tried again to reach Angula on the phone. No answer. She resolved to go there herself, right away. Angula knew the Lubowski files by heart. He would know what the autopsy report had said. She requested permission to stand down, saying she wouldn't be able to think straight until she'd had a good sleep.

249

Oshivelo dismissed her with a gracious nod.

She snaffled the last available police car. The tank was nearly empty, but it would get her to Angula's. The front door was locked. She knocked and called and questioned an inquisitive neighbour who was leaning over the fence. The woman hadn't seen Angula for days and assumed he was away on police business. Clemencia wondered whether to force the door. Angula would understand – it was an emergency, after all. There wouldn't be a trial unless ...

There *would* be a trial! She got back in the car and drove to the nearest petrol station. The attendant calmly watched her count out the money in her purse, then put forty-eight Namibian dollars thirty-five cents' worth of petrol in her tank. That should be enough for the one-way trip. If necessary she would cover the last few kilometres to Fourie's farm on foot. She had done so once before.

✖❖✖

Judge Hendrik Fourie (ret.):

At first I thought it was a dirty trick. The police couldn't get over having failed and were now trying it on like this. Besides, their reasoning struck me as far-fetched, not to say utterly erroneous. I've been a lawyer all my life, after all, and have – with respect, Your Honour – conducted many more criminal trials than yourself. So I explained to Detective Inspector Garises that Donkerkop could be charged with conspiracy to murder and attempted murder, irrespective of whether Lubowski was already dead when he shot him. Attempted murder can be defined as the failure of an act intended to kill someone. All three elements – intention, act and failure – are undoubtedly present here. Or, to be absolutely explicit: the reason for the perpetrator's failure can also, in addition to the unwanted survival of the victim, be that the latter has previously died from causes unattributable to the perpetrator. That makes no difference to the fact of attempted murder.

I further explained that, although our penal code does not expressly exclude that crime from the statute of limitations, prevailing opinion holds

250

that exemption from the statute of limitations automatically covers attempted murder as well as murder.

'Prevailing opinion?' queried Miss Garises.

'One can't go back to Adam and Eve in every criminal trial,' I replied. 'Where interpretation is called for, landmark decisions and recognized commentaries are consulted. If a broad consensus has formed on the relevant question, one is guided by that.'

'And what if a public prosecutor or a judge thinks he reads something different into the letter of the law?' she asked.

That happens repeatedly, but not at such a point in time. A murder suspect has just been arrested and is willing to confess. You question him closely, assemble evidence and endeavour to record the facts as fully as possible. Although doubts may arise later on, no public prosecutor in the world thinks first of grounds for quashing an indictment. Not unless he doesn't want the case to come to trial at all!

That made me wonder. I remembered 1994, when the public prosecutor had also declined to prefer charges in the Lubowski affair. Would history repeat itself? I considered that impossible, as things stood, but hadn't I thought the same thing back then? Were the circumstances surrounding Lubowski's assassination to be legally unelucidated yet again? Because someone with a great deal of influence wanted to conceal them at all costs?

I couldn't permit that, not after all I'd done to help justice prevail at last – indeed, to enforce it with all the means at my disposal. I realized from the first that this would claim victims, but far more blood had been shed than I'd wanted or even imagined. I had van Zyl shot, but Maree wouldn't talk. I had Maree shot, but Staal Burger refused to draw the right conclusions and Barnard hadn't believed I could hunt him down, even in prison. When they were dead, Acheson still thought he had to play the tight-lipped hero. With the greatest difficulty I managed to save the life of Donkerkop – my last surviving witness and accused, without whom my plan would come to nothing – and persuade him to volunteer the confession his accomplices would have done better to make at an earlier stage. And was everything now to have been in vain?

251

I said none of this to Miss Garises when she confronted me that day, but she must have guessed what was going through my mind. At all events, she said, 'There is one possibility.'

She was right. There was, Your Honour, and that is why I'm standing here before you now. That is why you are sitting up there, presiding over a trial which will probably be more distasteful to many a subpoenaed witness than it is to the defendant. You should take that into account. You must be aware that two cases are being tried here simultaneously – cases in which the roles could not be more unequally distributed.

In one of these trials the public prosecutor claims to be prosecuting the instigator of the murder of five former CCB agents. In that trial I am the accused, and to that charge I plead guilty. Convict me, but bear in mind that I alone have rendered these proceedings possible. I do not beg for mercy or plead extenuating circumstances, but I do insist that the second trial be conducted with all due rigour: the trial of the case to which the present indictment devotes scarcely a word.

I have confessed solely to enable this second trial to take place. It is the trial I have always wanted but could not conduct while still on the bench; the trial this country needs far more urgently than it realizes; the trial that will make clear, once and for all, what really happened on 12 September 1989, who bore responsibility for it, and who, for whatever reasons, prevented justice from being done. It is the trial that must finally reveal the truth about Anton Lubowski's murder.

In that trial I represent the prosecution. I am taking on the task because no one else will, and I may go even further than that. I tell you this quite frankly: If you fail to do your judicial duty, I declare myself ready to do it for you. Although my judgement may have no penal consequences, it will be valid in the sight of history. So help me God!

6

GRAVES

Fourie did not confess at once when Clemencia drew his attention to the existence of another possibility, nor did she press him to do so. Unless he came clean of his own accord, there was nothing to be done in any case. Having begged a canful of petrol from him and driven home, she locked herself up in her room and slept for fourteen hours, only occasionally woken by Miki Matilda knocking on the door, the Mshasho Bar's loudspeakers, the bawling of sundry drunks, and the matutinal oaths of the taxi driver across the way, who refused to accept that his car wouldn't start even at the hundredth time of asking.

When Clemencia turned up at the offices of the Serious Crime Unit late that morning, Fourie had already been there for several hours and was dictating a detailed confession into van Wyk's computer. He smiled at the sight of her. He hadn't found it hard to make up his mind, he said, but he'd wanted to spend one more night at liberty. It would probably be his last ever, he added almost apologetically. He had come accompanied by von Fleckenstein, who was in a better mood than usual. The lawyer amiably reminded Clemencia that her brother – or her family, whichever – still owed him 250 dollars and nodded indulgently when she asked him to wait until she got her next month's pay. Then he chattered away as if he were infected by Fourie's determination to make a full confession.

'At last something other than a bail application! I've become so sick of playing down every little misdemeanour and thinking up stories likely to melt a magistrate's heart on behalf of every common criminal. Difficult childhood, social worker's favourable report, sole breadwinner of an extended family, weeping infants, momentary lapse – I could hardly bear to listen to myself. But this is the big time! Before long, people won't know whether I'm Fourie's defence counsel or leading for the prosecution. Anyone implicated in the Lubowski affair will be torn to shreds without mercy. Your boss Oshivelo had better wear a flak jacket!'

'Can we go on?' asked van Wyk. He promised to bring Clemencia the printout as soon as they were through.

Clemencia nodded although she doubted if she would find anything new in it. Perhaps the trial that took place in the next few weeks or months would show whether Fourie's calculations were correct, whether von Fleckenstein would succeed in dragging the instigators of Lubowski's murder into the light of day, and whether there *were* any instigators apart from the dead CCB agents. Perhaps, but perhaps not. Clemencia had done her job anyway; she couldn't do more. Those who insisted on all or nothing – those who pursued an objective regardless – lost their powers of perception and soon transgressed the bounds essential to human coexistence. Like Fourie. It could also happen to Angula unless someone restrained him and brought him down to earth.

Clemencia called his number. Somebody picked up after the fourth ring and a man's voice said, 'Yes?'

'Angula?' she said, but it wasn't Angula.

'Oh, it's you,' said Robinson. 'I'll be with you as soon as we're through here.'

Robinson? What was *he* doing at Angula's place?

A moment's silence. Then he said, 'You haven't heard?'

'What?'

'A neighbour called, said there was something wrong. The patrol notified us and we broke in.'

'What's the matter with him?'

'Dead,' Robinson said. 'Blood poisoning, apparently from those dog bites. The doctor's still here, he can tell you more. Like a word with him?'

'No,' she said. She shut her eyes, saw the bull terrier's yellow eyes in front of her. Even when they went glazed, its jaws continued to grip Angula's hand.

'The doctor says his life could have been saved if he'd had himself treated in time. He couldn't have failed to know what the matter was and must have been in great pain. The whole arm was discoloured and badly swollen.'

Clemencia thought of their nocturnal telephone calls. She'd asked how he was. Good, he'd replied, no problem, everything's fine. She had known he was lying but pretended to believe him because she hadn't felt like burdening herself with his problems. She'd thought she had enough of her own.

'Why the hell didn't he go to hospital?' Robinson demanded.

Angula had admitted that he wasn't feeling well after they freed Oshivelo. Clemencia had mistaken that for an excuse. She had thought he was deserting her because he wanted to go home and devote himself to his obsession with a SWAPO conspiracy. He had probably done so, but that didn't mean he wasn't feeling genuinely unwell. She ought to have realized that.

'Are you still there?' Robinson asked.

'Yes.'

'He's laid out on his bed now,' said Robinson. 'I'll stay here till the meat wagon finally turns up.'

'Yes.'

'Well ... ' said Robinson.

'Where did you find him?' she asked.

'He was sitting at the table, bent over. Looked as if he'd fallen asleep.'

'Bring me his notes!' she said. She would go through them with an open mind. If they were merely unsubstantiated imputations, she would destroy the lot. But I'll read them first, she thought, that

I promise you, Angula!

'What notes?' asked Robinson.

'There must be some notebooks or loose sheets lying around. A whole stack of handwritten notes!'

'There's nothing here,' he said.

'Impossible,' she retorted. When she intimated that someone might have made away with them, Robinson was indignant. He knew she couldn't stand him, he said, but he refused to swallow that insinuation. The four of them had gone in together, himself, Tjikundu and two uniformed constables. Nobody could have made away with anything without being seen, and anyway, why should they? What next? Was she going to accuse them of having killed Angula and bribed the doctor to fake the cause of death? Were they hoping the undertaker wouldn't notice the hole in his skull, or what?

'It's all right, Robinson,' she said, and hung up. She didn't know what to think any more. She had never seen Angula's notes. Perhaps they genuinely didn't exist. Perhaps he'd been pretending to her in the same way as he'd concealed his state of health. And she'd wanted to believe him so as not to have to ask what was really preying on his mind and robbing him of sleep. What did she know about Angula, other than the fact that he was now dead?

Everything seemed somehow to be slipping from her grasp. What she had regarded as certainties were dissolving. All that remained of people were shadows, just as all that remained of her memory of them was a feeling that important things had never been said and crucial questions never asked. She wouldn't have been surprised if mist had billowed up outside the window, above and below, left and right – a dense grey mist in which every word from the street sounded like a half-smothered cry. But it wasn't so. The sun was shining in a radiantly blue sky, the air was transparent as glass, the heat far less oppressive than it had been before the first storm. One could almost have believed it was a fine day.

Clemencia shut the window. The mobile phone was still in her hand. She dialled Miki Selma's number.

'Clemencia,' said Miki Selma, 'I'm at a very important choir meeting, so be quick.'

'I only wanted … '

'What?'

' … to have a talk.'

'My dear, it really isn't convenient right now. We've got to elect a new leader, and I think, like a lot of other people, that things can't go on this way. What crawls over the foot will end by crawling up the leg, as the saying goes. Except that not everyone sees it that way, and so … I'll explain another time. I'd call you back later, but — '

'I know, you're running out of money,' said Clemencia.

'Try again in two hours' time.' Her aunt rang off.

Miki Matilda was with a potential patient, so she was busy too, but she did hand her mobile to Clemencia's father. In obedience to a spontaneous whim, Clemencia said she was going to the cemetery to visit her mother's grave. 'Care to come with me?'

Her father didn't reply for several long, gloomy seconds. Then he said, 'No.'

He was an old, broken man. She didn't want to make a fuss, let alone sound reproachful, so she said, 'All right, of course. I was only asking.'

She decided to go all the same. First she would buy some flowers, as many red roses as she could buy for the money she would borrow from van Wyk, and then she would drive to Katutura cemetery. She would have preferred it if someone had come with her, that was all.

When she emerged from the florist's on the corner of Independence Avenue and Fidel Castro Street, having bought five roses, she called Claus Tiedtke. He was out on an assignment for his paper. Apparently, a team of municipal road workers had dug up the fossilized skeleton of an animal at the entrance to the Barcelona housing estate. It might be a primeval dinosaur, but nothing was known for certain. They were waiting for a South African expert who had seen some emailed photos of it and agreed to come without delay. The residents of the estate were cursing because they could only get out of the place on foot. He, Tiedtke, had already collected a few choice quotations from them. What was really surprising, however, was the painstaking way in which the bones had been unearthed. You didn't expect municipal workmen to care what was damaged by their equipment, whether water mains or archaeological treasures.

Clemencia didn't reveal that they were her brother Melvin and his cronies, nor did she tell him that his car was stuck in a river bed fifty kilometres from Windhoek. And she certainly didn't ask him to accompany her, although that was why she'd called him. They would talk another time, she said.

'This evening, maybe?'

'Yes, why not?'

It took her just under an hour to get to Katutura on foot. The cemetery gate was open. Old folk called the place Golgotha, but she didn't know if that was its official name. The area immediately inside the gate resembled an expanse of scree-covered wasteland. The size of a football pitch, it displayed no trees or bushes, just some little mounds of earth that might have been anthills if they hadn't been arranged in dead straight lines and situated so close to each other. And if each of them hadn't been marked with a stone. 751, 752, 753 … They were the graves of children: dead babies and infants devoid of any tombstones or names by which to remember them. There were many of them – far too many.

Clemencia turned left and made her way along the cemetery wall. The ground sloped gently downwards, a few stunted acacias made their appearance, and the numbers acquired four digits. More and more tombstones came into view, many of them cracked or canted over, others barely touched by wind, weather and oblivion.

Plastic wreaths were lying in front of two of them, but Clemencia could see no real flowers on any grave, still less any flowering plants. There was no water here. The land of the brave was harsh enough for the living. They couldn't be expected to assuage the thirst of the dead.

Clemencia eyed the five roses in her hand. The dark red of the flowers and the fresh green of their stems looked out of place, but never mind. Her mother's grave would be the only one adorned with flowers. It had to be somewhere here. 5821, 5822 ... As soon as she left the cemetery, one of the workmen would pick up the roses and take them home to his girlfriend, wife or mother. And she, in her turn, would try to sell them by the roadside for a few dollars to spend on maize flour. Well, why not? Clemencia simply wanted to lay the meagre little bunch on her mother's grave. That was enough.

6212, 6213 ... She couldn't remember the number of the grave, but it had to be in this south-west section of Golgotha. How long was it since she'd been here last? That grave on the left with the iron rail around it – hadn't she passed that before? She recalled a small grey tombstone with nothing but her mother's name on it – possibly her dates of birth and death as well, but even that she couldn't remember. 6554, 6555 ... The dead were far too numerous. Should she ask her father?

She bent down and shovelled away some of the dirt beneath a fallen tombstone with her hand. The soil was parched – not a sign of the recent rainfall. She tried to lift the stone in order to read the name on it, but it was too heavy. Her mother's had looked different in any case. Paler, smaller. 6808, 6809 ... No, she must have passed it. The grave had been more in the middle and she was already nearing the perimeter wall, which had been freshly painted red and yellow. Three boys were tightrope-walking along the top. They looked two or three years older than her nephew Timothy. Beyond the wall was a street lined with squat houses, possibly a trifle shabbier than those in Clemencia's neighbourhood but built of brick nonetheless. The corrugated-iron shanties began further out.

Clemencia called Miki Matilda and asked to speak to her father. 'Are you there?' he asked.

'I don't know the number of the grave,' she said.

'I ... I've never visited it, not once,' said her father. 'I just couldn't.'

6949 6950 ...

'After the funeral ... ' His voice tailed off.

'Don't worry, I'll find it.' Clemencia walked along the row of graves. 6961, 6962 ... It couldn't possibly have been this far along, she thought, I ought to turn back and have another look among the five thousands. Just one more row.

6968. She came to a halt. The grave in front of her wasn't her mother's, but her mother might have liked it. It was strewn with pale pebbles held in place by a dark-grey granite surround. Hewn from the same material, the tombstone bore the following inscription in white lettering: 'Anton Lubowski, 3 February 1952–12 September 1989. We are proud of you. Your parents, brothers and sisters and children.'

Lying overturned on the pebbles was a rusty tin can. In other respects the grave looked good. Neat, plain, and more durable than the hummocks of soil that protruded from the ground like ugly excrescences capable of being flattened by the first violent rainy season. It wouldn't be this grave's fault if its occupant could find no peace. It was the grave Clemencia would have wanted for him, that was all. Truth and falsehood, heroism and betrayal, justice and presumption – any such thoughts refused to come to mind. The dead were too numerous, she reflected.

She righted the tin can and shifted it to and fro, then removed it from the expanse of pebbles altogether. Inquisitively, the three boys had climbed down off the wall and were sidling nearer. She tried putting the roses in the tin, but it was too wide and too shallow.

The flowers sagged sideways and hung their heads. They looked pathetic.

'What are you doing?' asked one of the boys.

She laid the roses down on the pale pebbles and fanned them out a little. That made a better impression.

'Is your husband buried there?' asked the boy.

'No.' She shook her head. 'This is Anton Lubowski's grave.'

He scratched his forearm. The skin was grazed and looked inflamed. 'Who was Anton Lubowski?' he asked.

POSTSCRIPT

Ever since I first heard of Anton Lubowski, his personality and murder have exerted an abiding fascination on me. Although I never imagined that I would be able to solve the case after twenty years, I did not expect to fail so signally. The more research I carried out, the more obscure and contradictory the facts and underlying circumstances became. It was a while before I recognized this as an opportunity. Then I proceeded to recount what *could* have resulted from an actual case which I, at least, found impossible to elucidate. *The Hour of the Jackal* is, therefore, a novel. It does not claim to portray historical truth, but aims to tell a story that embodies a truth of its own. It cannot, of course, replace a judicial reappraisal of what happened, but were it to help replace Anton Lubowski's murder on the agenda and ensure that justice is done after all, nothing could please me more.

I realize that this novel will open old wounds and draw fire from many of those involved in or affected by the actual events, whatever their role in them. That is why I think it important to state that the dramatis personae are purely products of my imagination, even if acts are attributed to them which actually occurred. The fact remains that Donald Acheson, Chappies Maree, Slang van Zyl, Staal Burger and Ferdi Barnard really were CCB agents who, among others, were cited in the preliminary hearing of 1994 as being responsible for the murder of Anton Lubowski.

Donald Acheson fled to the Republic of South Africa after his release in 1990 and was deported to London in 1991. He has not been heard of since.

In 1998 Ferdi Barnard was sentenced to life imprisonment for, among other crimes, the murder of the anti-apartheid activist David Webster. He is now in Pretoria's Central Prison.

In 2001 Slang van Zyl, Staal Burger and Chappies Maree sought an amnesty from the South African Truth and Reconciliation Commission for crimes committed while they were members of the CCB. Although this was largely denied them, they now live undisturbed in South Africa, Burger being a sugar-cane farmer in KwaZulu-Natal and van Zyl a private detective who successfully solves cases the police have failed to crack. The latter and Chappies Maree are fond of suing authors whom they represent as dangerous criminals.

Whether any members of SWAPO have anything to reproach themselves with in respect of the Lubowski case is as uncertain in reality as it appears in my novel.

Anyone who takes exception to my novelistic account of what might have happened is free to resort to litigation. That might result in a trial which finally shed light on the affair and would doubtless be – to quote one of my characters – 'more distasteful' to many people than it would be to the defendant.

❊❊❊

Not everyone to whom I am indebted has wished to be mentioned by name, so I shall confine myself to summarily thanking the many people who assisted me with information of most diverse nature. They will know who they are. Without them this book would never have come into being.

GLOSSARY

Afrikaans   Daughter language of Dutch spoken by the Boers of South Africa and still a widespread lingua franca in Namibia.

Avis Dam   Situated east of Windhoek, this also serves as a local recreation area.

Baas (Afrikaans)   Traditional form of address used by black servants to their white employers. The origin of 'boss'.

Bakkie   General purpose vehicle with an open load space. Pick-up.

Civil Cooperation Bureau (CCB)   Nominally independent but with close ties to the South African military, this secret organization existed from 1986 to 1990. Its principal task was to combat anti-apartheid activists by violent means.

Damara   Namibian ethnic group of negroid origin but linguistically and culturally regarded as belonging to the Khoisan group.

Haitsi-Aibeb   God of the Khoisan peoples. Noted for his artful behaviour and his capacity for reincarnation.

Harms Commission   Set up in 1990 by President F. W. de Klerk of South Africa and chaired by Judge Louis Harms, it investigated the activities of police murder squads.

Herero   Namibian ethnic group belonging to the Bantu language group.

Heroes' Acre National monument dedicated to the heroes of the Namibian fight for independence. Situated a few kilometres south of Windhoek.

Kaokoveld Dry and inaccessible region in north-west Namibia, some 50,000 square kilometres in extent.

Katutura Township established in 1959. The black residents of Windhoek were compulsorily resettled there as part of the racial segregation policy.

Khoisan languages Spoken by the Damara, Nama and San, they employ various click consonants.

Koevoet In existence from 1978 to 1989, this South African para-military police unit fought SWAPO rebels with the aid of native trackers.

Kwaito Musical genre similar to hip-hop. This originated in southern Africa during the 1990s. The name probably derives from *kwaai* (Afrikaans for 'angry', also 'cool'), and *to* for township.

Meneer (Afrikaans) Mr.

Mevrou (Afrikaans) Mrs.

Miki Term for 'aunt' when applied to the sister of one's father or the wife of one's mother's brother. In direct speech 'Mikis' is used without the first name.

Mshasho (Ovibambo) Handgun. Also the name of a well-known Namibian music label specializing in kwaito music.

Naartjie (Afrikaans, pronounced 'naarkie') South African variety of mandarin orange.

Nama Namibian ethnic group belonging to the Khoisan language family.

265

NG Kerk (Afrikaans)   Nederduits Gereformeerde Kerk. Reformed church of Calvinist complexion. Widespread in South Africa and Namibia.

Ovambo   Numerically by far the largest ethnic group in Namibia. Its language, Oshivambo, belongs to the Bantu language family.

Potjie (Afrikaans, pronounced 'poikie')   Three-legged cast-iron pot in which food is cooked over embers or an open fire.

Rand   South African unit of currency convertible into the Namibian dollar at par.

San   Also known as bushmen. The aborigines of Namibia, they belong to the Khoisan group.

SWAPO   The South West African People's Organization, originally a liberation movement founded in 1960 by Sam Nujoma and others. It conducted an armed struggle against the South African occupiers from 1966 onwards and now constitutes the political party which, by virtue of its absolute majority, has governed Namibia from the country's declaration of independence in 1990 until the present day.

Tombo beer   Home-brewed millet beer.

Truth and Reconciliation Commission   This was set up in South Africa in 1995 to investigate abuses of human rights during the apartheid era, rehabilitate victims, and – under certain circumstances – grant an amnesty to those perpetrators who are willing to cooperate.

Tsotsi   Term for a gangster in the townships of southern Africa. It probably derives from *tsotsa,* a Sesotho word meaning 'to dress flashily'.

UN Resolution 435 UN Security Council resolution dated 29 September 1978, which advocated the creation of an independent Namibia and called on South Africa to withdraw from the territory.

Vision 2030 Long-term programme launched by the SWAPO government in June 2004, its aim being to secure Namibia the living standard of an industrialized nation.

Wanaheda Township adjacent to Katutura. Its name is made up of the initial letters of four ethnic groups: (O)Wambo, Nama, Herero, and Damara.

Xhosa South African people belonging to the Bantu language family.